The Kirilov Star

The Kirilov Star

MARY NICHOLS

First published in Great Britain in 2011 by
Allison & Busby Limited
13 Charlotte Mews
London W1T 4EJ
www.allisonandbusby.com

A CIP catalogue record for this book is available from
the British Library.

10 9 8 7 6 5 4 3 2 1

13-ISBN 978-0-7490-0992-2

Typeset in 11/15.5 pt Sabon by
Allison & Busby Ltd.

Paper used in this publication is from sustainably managed sources.
All of the wood used is procured from legal sources and is fully traceable.
The producing mill uses schemes such as ISO 14001
to monitor environmental impact.

Printed and bound in the UK by
CPI Antony Rowe, Chippenham, Wiltshire

*To my family for their support
through thick and thin.*

OUT OF RUSSIA

1920 – 1930

Chapter One

November 1920

Countess Anna Yurievna Kirillova was weeping. Mikhail, her beloved husband of thirteen years, was sending her away and she could not bear it. She was weeping so copiously she could not see to thread her needle. She wept for a comfortable life that had been swept away, for her husband and her children, for the state of her once-elegant home, for a future which terrified her, for Russia. A petite woman in her mid-thirties, she had a fragile beauty which her husband was afraid would never stand up to the harshness of the new regime; she was an innocent, passing from the care of her father to the care of her husband and, until the Revolution, she had never known want or fear, had never had to lift a finger, not even to dress herself. Now there was nothing but fear.

'Let us stay here, Misha,' she begged for the hundredth time. 'We will be all right here. No one will trouble us, surely? We have already given up our home in St Petersburg, isn't that enough?' She had forgotten, or refused to acknowledge, that the city was now called Petrograd.

They had left it in the dead of night in the spring of 1918 when it became obvious that the old regime was gone for ever, that soldiers and sailors sent to put down the uprising had joined the revolutionaries. The tsar, on his way back from military headquarters supposedly to take charge of the situation, had been stopped and arrested. There had been pandemonium: people being shot for no reason except speaking up against the violence, others leaving the city on carts packed with personal belongings and being stopped and made to go back. Even more were looting, mostly furniture which could be chopped up for firewood.

Mikhail, fearing worse was to come, had brought his little family to their *dacha* near the small town of Petrovsk, in the foothills of Ukraine. He remembered as a child taking trips from there to the Black Sea to picnic and swim and enjoy the warm weather with his parents and siblings, of pony rides and walks in the woods, of swimming in the lake, of hunting and fishing, of picking grapes from the vines on the sunny slopes, of eating figs straight from the tree. If anyone gave a thought to the future, it did not filter down to the boy he was.

After he had married in 1907, he had brought his wife to spend the summer at the *dacha* with his widowed mother each year, and when Andrei was born the baby had become part of the annual exodus along with his nursemaids, Mikhail's valet and Anna's maid. The Great War, which had engulfed almost the whole civilised world, had put a stop to that; Mikhail had joined the army and there were no more trips to Ukraine. Andrei had vague recollections of the carefree holidays, but Lydia, born in 1916, had never been. When the time came to leave Petrograd, Anna had talked to the children of their villa and estate, painted a rosy picture of what it was like, and so the children, at least, had been happy to leave slushy Petrograd behind, unaware of the true reason for their flight.

In the old days they had travelled in luxury, with their own compartments and sleeping quarters on the train, and a mountain of luggage Mikhail's mother swore they could not possibly do without, but the journey from Petrograd in 1918 had been accomplished in a packed freight train with only the luggage they could carry between them. Their travelling companions had been a strange mixture: wealthy kulaks in fur coats, stockbrokers in suits and suede shoes, shopkeepers with nothing left to sell, former servants, army deserters, priests deprived of their status, peasants in tunics and felt boots, all living together in the close confines of what appeared to be a cattle truck.

The train had stopped frequently and people would jump down and wander up and down the line, anxiously asking, 'Why have we stopped?' and they would try to buy food and water before being hustled back on board and the train jerked into motion again. There had been a very long wait in Kiev where everyone was on tenterhooks while papers were scrutinised and some passengers taken off under guard, for what misdemeanour no one knew. More people had crammed on the train, and after another twenty-four hours of hanging about, during which they dared not leave their places, except one at a time to answer the call of nature, they had set off again.

By the time they had arrived at the house some thirty-six hours later, they were all exhausted, bruised and very hungry, having eaten what little food they had brought with them early on in their journey, expecting to be able to buy more; but all Mikhail had been able to obtain was half a loaf of stale bread and a lump of goat's cheese.

Kirilhor was a large white villa, the hub of an extensive estate, and had once been opulent. Servants had cared for it, had scrubbed the floors, beaten the heavy Persian rugs, polished the furniture and cooked delicious meals, but now it was run-down and faded, the paint was scuffed, the windows and much of the beautiful furniture had been broken. The four-poster beds, the elegant wardrobes and chests, the red plush sofas and armchairs, the grand piano, the pictures and ornaments, had nearly all been burnt or looted. Outside, the garden was rank and overgrown, its surrounding parkland had been seized by the peasants and shared out between them. The trees had been felled and sawn up for firewood, and crops were growing where once stately poplar, lime and oak had grown. A carriage and a droshky still stood in the coach house, presumably because the peasants had found no use for it. But without horses both were useless. Mikhail was glad his parents had not lived to see it.

It was not what the children had been led to expect because Mama had been describing it in summer, not in the winter when the trees were bare and the lake frozen. And the house was dirty – certainly not the little palace they had expected, with warm fires in every room. And where were the servants? Of the twenty or thirty servants who had served them before the war, there was only Antonina Stepanova Ratsina, the children's nurse and governess, whom they had brought with them, Ivan Ivanovich, a giant of a man with a head of thick black hair and a beard to match, and his plump wife, Sima. They were there to welcome them and had killed a chicken to make a dinner, though it soon became apparent that food was no easier to come by here than it had been in Petrograd, where long queues formed every day for what little bread there was.

Two days later, Mikhail had left them to rejoin his regiment. With Ivan's help, Anna had cultivated the patch of earth closest to the house to feed them, knowing that, according to the new laws filtering down to them from the capital, it was no longer theirs to cultivate. Anything they did not eat was the property of the state and had to be handed over, but as the area was in the hands of the counter-revolutionaries, there was no one to enforce the laws and they bartered their surplus for other things they needed, as everyone else was doing. Ivan had managed to buy a skinny horse for them so that he could take Andrei to school in the droshky. Lydia was not yet old enough to go.

It was far from the comfortable life Anna had been used to, but she had proved herself more resourceful and resilient than her husband had expected and they had established a kind of rhythm at one with the seasons. A colonel in the army, he had come home when he could, but in the last eighteen months he had only been back twice and then only for a few days at a time. It made the subsequent partings even more difficult. He had considered staying with his family, but he could not bring himself to desert as many others were doing. He wanted his wife just as she wanted him and those few days together were heartbreakingly poignant, but, loyal to the last, he had returned to duty.

Now even that had to end. The Constituent Assembly, formed after the Revolution under the Provisional Government, had been overthrown and there was civil war, the Red Army against the White, a war without frontiers,

13

where friend opposed friend, brother took up arms against brother, servant fought master and the enemy was unseen and yet everywhere. The Reds were determined to put an end to aristocratic privilege and power, and the Whites were equally determined to hold on to it. And in the middle of it all were the Greens who belonged to neither side and took advantage of whatever situation prevailed. It was chaotic and, what was more, dangerously anarchical. Mikhail felt they had jumped from the cooking pot into the flames of the fire.

'The fighting is getting closer all the time,' he told Anna. He was a tall man, with strong dark features and a handsome beard. Too agitated to stand still, he paced the room, window to door and back again, only just avoiding crashing into the table at which his wife sat sewing by the light of a feeble lamp. Oil was running low, so he dare not give her more light. They had chosen to use a room at the back of the house which looked out on the forest and not the road to the town and they had drawn the heavy curtains, so that no chink of light escaped to reveal their presence. 'And if the Reds find us . . .' He stopped, unwilling to put it into words, but she knew what he meant. He was a distant relative of the Romanovs and he was afraid they would share the fate of Tsar Nicholas. Officially he was being held for his own safety, but the rumours were flying that he had been executed by the Bolsheviks without even a trial, though how you could justify trying a ruler ordained by God, Anna had no idea.

'I am not risking it happening to you and the children,' he said, glancing down at the floor where two pairs of legs stuck out from beneath the cloth-covered table, one clad in knickerbockers, the other lace-frilled pantalettes. Andrei and Lydia were whispering together, playing some secret game whose rules only they understood.

'But why would they harm us?' his wife asked. 'We have done no wrong, broken no law, unless you count stealing the garden which always used to belong to us, and who else wants it? And you have served Russia faithfully as a soldier all through the war and since.'

'I served Russia but I also served the tsar, Annushka,' he said patiently, trying with a calm voice to make her understand and not frighten her any more than she was frightened already. 'According to the Bolsheviks, the two are not compatible.'

She wouldn't mind if he were coming too; she could face anything with him at her side, but no, he must take up arms for the White Army – as if they had a chance of winning! Why, even Pyotr Wrangel, who now commanded the White Army, was advising people to leave the country while they could. 'Misha,' she implored, jabbing the thread at the eye of the needle and missing. 'If we must go, then come with us. One man cannot make a difference, surely? In the general confusion you will not even be missed.'

'That would be desertion, Annushka. I cannot dishonour the name of Kirilov with such a shameful act. I begged leave to help you to escape, but that is all it is, a few days' leave.'

Anna made one more attempt to thread her needle and then tears overwhelmed her again. He took it from her and bent over the lamp to thread it for her, returned it to her, then sat down and picked up one of the pieces of jewellery from the velvet-lined casket on the table and began systematically to break the gems out of their silver and gold settings with wire-cutters.

'Do you really need to do that?' she asked, choking back another sob. Mikhail was adamant and tears were not moving him. 'It must be decimating their value.'

'Darling, pieces like this have no value in the new scheme of things, except for barter, and at the moment they are worth more as currency than the new paper money. Or even roubles. You will have to part with them one at a time for travel documents and food. And you will need to sell what is left to keep you going in England until I can join you.'

She sighed, picked up a ruby and sewed it carefully into a pair of stays she held on her lap. It was followed by another and then an emerald and a diamond. 'I shall be weighed down with it.' She attempted a laugh which tore at his heart.

'Put some in the children's clothes too. Lydia, sweetheart, go and fetch your best petticoat, the silk one with the lace flounces round the hem. And bring Andrei's best tunic too.'

Lydia scrambled out from under the table, followed by her brother. The ribbons had come out of her hair and Andrei's socks were wrinkled at the ankle. Both stood and watched their parents for a moment or two, then Lydia asked, 'Why are you breaking that necklace, Papa? Don't you like it anymore?'

'No, I don't think I do,' he said, taking a pair of pliers to a priceless antique, one that had been in the Kirilov family for generations. 'But we must hide the pieces from thieves, so Mama is sewing them into your clothes.'

'Why? Are we going on a journey?' Andrei asked, as Lydia disappeared on her errand, taking a stub of candle her father had lit for her.

'Yes, a very long journey,' his father told him. 'Over the sea to England.'

'England!' the boy exclaimed. 'I saw that in my atlas. It's the other side of the world. Why are we going there?' He was so like his father, especially his dark, intelligent eyes; looking at him made Anna's heart ache and she wanted to weep again.

'To be safe,' she told her son. 'Until this dreadful fighting is over and we can come back home.'

'I want to fight like Papa. I can shoot, you know I can. Didn't I bring down a hare the other day?'

'Yes you did, son,' his father told him. 'And a jolly good meal it made too, but shooting hares is not the same as shooting people and I pray to God you never have to do it.'

'You do.'

'I am a man and a soldier, that is different. It is not something I want to do.' He turned as Tonya, carrying the petticoat and tunic, came into the room with Lydia. She had been a roly-poly of a woman, almost as broad as she was high, though since the war the fat had melted off her and left folds of superfluous skin. 'Ah, Tonya, I am glad you are here,' he said. 'I will tell you our plans and if you have any suggestions to make I will listen.'

The countess, a little calmer now, continued to sew jewels into their clothes as he told of their plans. 'I am going to take the countess and the children to Yalta, where they will go on a ship across to Constantinople and from there to England,' he told her, smiling a little at her gasp of shock. 'You may go with them or not, as you please. I shall not insist.'

'But Your Excellency,' she said, addressing him in the old

17

way, forgetting she should not use that form of address now and she should have said Mikhail Mikhailovich. 'Where else would I be but with my babes? And the countess needs me.'

'Oh, thank you, Tonya,' Anna put in. 'I do not think I could bear it without you.'

'But how will we get away?' the servant asked. 'Someone is sure to see us and tell the *militsiia*.'

'We must leave separately and go in different directions. The countess and I will take the carriage to pay a visit to my cousin, Grigori Stefanovich. He is Chairman of the Workers' Committee of the Petrovsk Soviet and a visit to him will not be thought out of the ordinary. You will take the children in the droshky, as if you were taking Andrei to school, but you will not leave him there but go to Simferopol. We will meet you there and go to Yalta together.' He had considered sending them by train, but the trains, mostly made up of freight trucks, were packed with refugees, coming from further north, and they would never manage to get on one, even if they could obtain the necessary papers allowing them to travel.

'My parents live near Simferopol,' Tonya put in. 'You remember, Stepan and Marya Ratsin? They came on a visit. Years ago it was, before the war. We can take the children to them to wait for you.'

'Thank you, Tonya, if you are sure they will welcome them. It will only be for a few hours until the countess and I arrive.'

'Of course they will welcome them. The Reds haven't reached that far, have they?'

'No, Crimea is in White hands at the moment.' He shrugged his broad shoulders. 'Though for how long, I cannot say.'

'Then the sooner we set off the better.'

'Tomorrow,' he said.

'Where will we get the extra horses?' Andrei demanded suddenly. 'We've only got old Tasha and she's a bag of bones.'

Mikhail smiled at his son, though it was more than a little forced. 'I have arranged to borrow one from the stationmaster.'

'You surely do not mean one of those great railway horses that help shunt the trucks?'

'Yes, there is nothing else to be had and I had to bribe Iosif Liberov with your mother's white fur coat even for that. Ivan will return the animal when you are safely away.' Then to Anna, who had been stitching busily the whole time, keeping her fingers on the move, trying not to think about what he was saying, 'Have you nearly done, Annushka?'

'There's just this big diamond left. You haven't taken it out of its setting.' She held up the jewel which was set in filigree silver in the shape of a star. The diamond in its centre was very big and glittered in the light from the lamp. Graded rubies, dark as blood, were set down the centre of each arm, the corners of which held a smaller diamond.

'It won't budge. We'll have to leave it like that. Can you put it in Lydia's petticoat?'

'I'll try.' She picked up her needle and the garment that Tonya had brought and set about concealing the star among its flounces. 'She had better wear the petticoat; it will be found in our luggage if that is searched.'

'We cannot take luggage, my love; remember we are only supposed to be going out for the day. We can put a couple of carpet bags under the seat of each carriage, but no more. Wear all you can; you will need it anyway, the weather is bitter.'

'Mama, why are you doing that?' Lydia asked, watching her mother poke the gem into a false pocket she had made in the seam between the body of the garment and the flounce.

'We have to hide it, sweetheart. It is very valuable and bad men might try and take it from us if they know we have it. It is called the Kirilov Star. Did you know that?'

'No, I didn't. I can't remember seeing it before.'

'I don't suppose you have. I haven't worn it for a long time. Occasions for displaying such opulence have long gone. I do not know if they will ever come back. But you must take great care of it and show it to no one.'

'I won't.'

Mikhail sat down and drew his daughter onto his knee. 'You are my diamond, little one, the star of the Kirilovs and you must always remember that. Be good for Papa and help Andrei to look after your mother.'

Lydia rubbed her cheek against his tunic. He had discarded his wonderful scarlet and blue uniform with its gold braid for a plain tunic and wide leather belt, such as the better class of peasants wore. It was rough but strangely comforting. 'Aren't you coming with us, Papa?'

'Not right away. I shall join you later.' He kissed the top of her head and lifted her off his knee. 'Now off you go with Tonya and get ready for bed. You too, Andrei. We must all be up early in the morning.'

Anna kissed her daughter and hugged her son and it was not until they and their governess had disappeared that she burst into tears again. 'What is to become of us, Misha? Will we be parted for ever?'

'No, of course not.' He knelt beside her chair and took her hands in his own. 'You must not think like that, my dearest one. As soon as I can, I will join you. It will only be a few weeks, if that. No one among the Whites believes the war can be won, or that anything can return to what it was. Things have gone too far. When General Wrangel leaves, so will I, I promise you.' He bent forward and kissed her tear-wet cheek. 'Now, dry your eyes and come to bed. Tomorrow everything will look more rosy and you will be able to look forward to your new life. You must do it for the children's sake, let them see what a great adventure it is going to be.'

She gave him a watery smile. 'I shall try.'

But the next day could certainly not be described as rosy because it was snowing. Fat white flakes drifted down, swirling a little on the wind before settling on trees and rooftops and lastly on the lane that ran past the house. There was talk of postponing their journey but, according to Ivan, it would get worse before it got better, and if they were to go at all, they should go before it became too deep for the droshky. And what was more, he had heard gunfire in the night. It was still some distance away, but it heralded trouble. He had told his own family to take food and warm clothing into the cellar and shelter there if the fighting came to Petrovsk.

He was standing beside the carriage to which their old horse was harnessed, while the white flakes landed on their shoulders and decorated their fur hats. The vehicle was an ancient one with a soft retracting hood which Ivan had pulled up and which was already dotted with snowflakes. Before the war it had been used when the family came down for holidays, but had been laid up until they had arrived as

21

refugees in 1918. Since then they hardly dared take it out for fear of being accused of private ownership. If the Reds came, it would certainly be taken from them.

'You are right, of course,' Mikhail told Ivan, stamping his boot-clad feet. 'And I would not ask you to leave your family if I could manage without you, so the sooner we go, the sooner you will be back with them.'

'Yes, Your Ex—' He stopped suddenly, realising he should not have addressed the count in the old way. 'Yes, Mikhail Mikhailovich,' he corrected himself. 'When do you wish me to leave?'

'You must pretend to be taking Andrei to school and you have to take Lydia too because her mama and papa are out and there is no one to take care of her at home. The countess – I mean Anna Yurievna – and I are going now. We shall have to spend some time with Grigori Stefanovich and not appear to be in a hurry to leave, but he will give us safe conduct to travel. We can make use of that and will meet you at Tonya's home tomorrow evening. Tonya has assured me her father, Stepan Gregorovich, will welcome the children. I have given her enough money for you to stop at a hotel on the way.'

'Then I'll fetch the horse from the station and harness it up.' He wandered away, muttering that he didn't know what the world was coming to, with everything upside down and the wrong way round and he could see no good coming from any of it. He was certainly no better off under the new regime, and with the count and countess gone, how was he going to earn a living and feed his family?

The count turned and went back into the house.

Andrei and Lydia were sitting at the kitchen table eating *kasha*, a gruel made of buckwheat; Tonya was trying to stuff more of Lydia's clothes into one of the bags and Anna was trying to decide whether she had room to take the icon from her bedroom. No one was talking. Anna looked up as he entered, brushing snow from his shoulders and sleeves. 'Well?'

'Ivan Ivanovich thinks we should press on before the snow becomes too thick and I agree with him. Are you ready?'

'Yes.' She knew it was not the snow he was concerned about so much as the approaching Red Army. She put the icon down. It was bulky and would take up more room in her bag than it deserved; after all, she could pray just as easily without it. She pulled on fur-lined boots, a coat made of the best sable and a hat to match. On top of that she put a thick shawl which she intended to discard for her visit to Grigori. 'I am wearing so many petticoats I feel like a dumpling,' she complained.

'You look beautiful,' he said, bending to kiss the tip of her nose. 'Now, does Tonya have her instructions?'

'I don't know. I forgot whether I told her to lock the bedroom door when they stop at the hotel tonight. You never know . . .'

'Countess, you have told me a hundred times,' Tonya put in. 'And you have told me what to order for supper and what to say to my parents and not to let Andrei out of my sight for a minute. As if I would! And Lydia is to wear all her petticoats and her warmest dress and the seal fur coat you made for her out of your old one . . .'

'I am sorry I am such a fusspot,' Anna said. 'Of course you know all that. And we shall be together again tomorrow night, so I do not know what I am worrying about. Come, children, sit with us a moment and then we must go.' They all sat quietly as was the custom before undertaking a journey, but there was no time for lengthy contemplation of what lay before them and it was better not to think of it. Seconds later, she flung her arms about Andrei and hugged him so tight he squirmed to be free. 'Be good for Tonya and Ivan and look after your sister, won't you?'

'Course I will. I'm twelve, nearly a man.'

'So you are, and I am proud of you.' She reached for Lydia. 'Kiss me goodbye, little one, and then I must go. Papa is waiting.' She had managed to remain dry-eyed, but now the tears started to flow again. It felt as if she were saying goodbye to her children for ever, when it was not her children she might never see again, but her husband. Mikhail was going to see them all onto the boat at Yalta and then there would be real goodbyes. She must not think of that. She had two days to persuade him to travel with them; he had never refused her anything before and she could not believe that he would continue to hold out against her pleas. She brightened and kissed Lydia. 'Until tomorrow, my darling. Be good.' Then she drew on her gloves and picked up her muff and followed her husband out to where the carriage waited with the old horse in the shafts.

Tonya, Lydia and Andrei went to the door and watched as the count helped the countess into the carriage and tucked the rug about her before climbing onto the driving seat and flicking the reins over the rump of the old horse. It pricked up its ears and, with a jingle of harness, obeyed the command, 'Forward!' They stayed at the door watching and waving until the vehicle was out of sight, while the snow swirled about them and landed on the doormat.

Lydia was loath to move. She did not understand what

was happening, but seeing her mother cry had worried her. Mama was a grown-up and never cried. There was more to this trip than either of her parents had admitted. Why all the secrecy and the jewels sewn into their clothes and Mama and Papa going off separately? Papa had said they would be together again tomorrow, but something inside her, a huge dark lump in her breast, stopped her from breathing properly and frightened her.

'Come back inside, Lidushka,' Tonya said, taking her hand. 'They have gone. You can't see them anymore.' It sounded like a prophesy.

'Now, my cherubs,' she went on, drawing the children back indoors. 'We must get ready to go too. Go and make sure you have everything, while I pack some food to take with us. We shall have a picnic, eh?'

'In a snowstorm!' Andrei laughed, as he scampered up the stairs. He accepted what his father said without question and was treating the whole thing as a great adventure.

'Do you think we shall ever come back here again?' Lydia asked him as they reached the landing.

'Course we will, one day. This is our home. It has belonged to the Kirilovs for hundreds of years. One day it will be mine because I am the heir.'

Lydia looked about her at the carpets and curtains and her bed with its thick hangings to keep out the draughts, though now they were moth-eaten. She felt less sure than Andrei. Everything was changing, like summer suddenly ending and the snow starting, except that the snow would one day melt and spring would come again. But something in her bones, in her soul, told her that this was different and that the springs and summers to come would be nothing like those that had gone before, and it made her anxious.

'Hurry up!' Tonya called from the bottom of the stairs. 'Ivan Ivanovich is back and the droshky is at the door.'

Ivan had said goodbye to Sima and his children and now he was anxious to be off. They picked up the bags Tonya had packed for them and hurried down to the kitchen where Ivan was stamping the snow off his boots on the doormat. He took their bags from them and herded them out to the vehicle. The sight of it with a huge black carthorse in the shafts made Andrei giggle. 'Do you think you can make it gallop?' he asked Ivan.

'Let us hope we do not have to,' he said curtly, while he stowed the bags inside, lifted Lydia up and deposited her on the long fore and aft seat with her legs on either side, before turning to help Tonya up behind her.

'I'm going to sit behind you, Ivan Ivanovich,' Andrei said, moving the shotgun that lay on the seat and putting it on the floor at his feet.

'Do you think I should have fastened the shutters?' Tonya asked, looking back at the house.

'No, we do not want to let everyone know we are fleeing, do we?' Ivan said. 'Leave everything looking normal.'

'Normal!' She gave a cracked laugh as the big horse began to pull. It was used to shunting heavy engines and the droshky was feather-light by comparison. 'How can you say normal? I don't know what that means anymore. All this hole-and-corner stuff. You'd think we were criminals . . .'

'In the eyes of the Soviet, we are.'

They reached the end of the drive and turned south towards Petrovsk. It was only one straggling muddy street, lined with crooked wooden houses, which had thatched roofs and painted decorations around the doors and windows. The local Party headquarters on the square was built of brick, and so was the library and the school which was on the far side of the town. The railway station was only a rough wooden building but it also housed the telegraph and post office. There were a few people about, all known to them, and they called out a greeting as they passed. 'Good day to you, Ivan Ivanovich,' they said, laughing at the plodding horse. 'What have you got there? A sledgehammer to crack a nut?'

'Andrei Mikhailovich must be taken to school,' he called back. 'And Mikhail Mikhailovich needed the carriage to visit Grigori Stefanovich on business.'

'What's wrong with their legs?'

'Nothing. It is snowing, or had you not noticed?'

'Pshaw, they should walk like the rest of us.'

Ivan did not answer but urged the horse to go faster to take them past the hecklers, but it was used to its own steady pace and ignored him. At the school, he drew up. 'Am I to go in?' Andrei asked.

'No, but we will pretend you have. Get out and run round to the back, then cross the field. I will be waiting the other side.'

'I never heard such nonsense,' Tonya said. 'For goodness' sake, can't we take the children where we like without all this fuss?'

'No, we can't. It's the count's orders. Off you go, Andrei, and don't stop to speak to anyone.'

Andrei believed every word his father had said and had no doubt they would meet at Tonya's parents' house and was unworried. 'I'm going with him,' the governess said, as he jumped down. 'I gave my word I would not let him out of my sight. If I'm stopped I shall say I have a message from Anna Yurievna for the teacher.'

Lydia was frightened and clung to Tonya's hand. 'You go on with Ivan Ivanovich,' Tonya said, gently disengaging herself. 'I shall only be a minute.'

She hurried after Andrei and Ivan moved on. He didn't like it, he didn't like any of it. If it were not for his long service to the count's family and the fact that the countess had always been good to his wife and children, he would have nothing to do with it. The Reds were getting closer all the time, and if they overran the area, he did not want to be labelled a Tsarist or a White, or any other name used to denote an enemy of the state.

The road wound round the field and passed through a small copse of birch trees. One or two shrivelled leaves still clung to the branches, but most made a grey-brown carpet on a land rapidly turning white. Once hidden from the town Ivan pulled up and before long Tonya and Andrei appeared. They clambered aboard and they were quickly on their way again.

They could hear the rumble of guns in the distance and away to their left a plume of smoke rose above a slight hill. The fighting was coming nearer, might already have reached Grigori Stefanovich's village which was only about eight *versts* distant from Petrovsk. He looked at Tonya and inclined his head in the direction of the smoke. 'Whose house do you think that is?'

'I don't know and we had better not wait to find out. You know the count's orders as well as I do. Tickle that horse into a trot, for goodness' sake.'

He did his best and the horse lumbered on, dragging the droshky after it as if it were trying to free itself from a troublesome fly. The country hereabouts had once produced good grain, wheat, barley and oats, but the war against Germany had put an end to farming; the men had all been away fighting and the women who were left could not work the fields in the same way. When the war ended, the occupying Germans had left and their own men drifted back, but then came the Revolution and everything was confused and no one knew what they were supposed to be doing. Today, the rolling fields were covered in snow, and though the outline of the road was still just visible, a few more hours of bad weather and that, too, would disappear under a blanket of white.

'We should have harnessed the troika,' Tonya told Ivan.

'How could you, with only one horse?' Troikas, as a rule, were pulled by three horses but they could be harnessed with only two. 'Anyway, we are going south. If the snow turns to rain what good would a sleigh be?'

'Perhaps Papa and Mama will catch us up,' Andrei said. 'They will surely be going faster than this.'

'Perhaps.'

'When are we going to have our picnic?'

'Not yet,' Tonya said. 'Later we will find a shelter.'

'There is a wood ahead of us,' Andrei pointed out. 'There might be a woodman's hut.'

The road took them among the trees which, burdened by fresh snow, made the way dark as night. Most of the trees were conifers, but there were a few leafless deciduous trees. The last few berries which clung to them – orange rowanberries, wine-coloured elderberries, clusters of viburnum, some whitish, some purple – were being attacked by finches. Except for the creaking of the droshky the softly falling snow deadened all sound. Lydia shivered. 'I don't like it,' she said. 'It's like being shut in the cellar. I don't want to stop here to have our picnic, even if we do find a hut.'

'Be quiet and listen!' Ivan said.

Lydia stopped speaking as the sound of galloping horses came to them from among the trees. Ivan did not wait to see who rode them, but whipped up their own animal into a lumbering gallop. The droshky swayed from side to side and they hung on grimly. Half a dozen horsemen burst from the trees onto the road behind them and one shouted for them to halt. Ivan ignored them. Tonya sat forward with her arms about Lydia, as gunshots spattered round them. 'You had better stop, Ivan Ivanovich,' she cried. 'Before they kill us all.'

His answer was to go faster. The horsemen, who seemed to think chasing them was a great joke, continued to fire at the ground around them, laughing and shouting and not bothering to catch them up, which they could easily have done. Before anyone could stop him, Andrei had grabbed the shotgun and stood up in the swaying carriage to return the fire. It was the worst thing he could have done. The chase stopped being a joke, and although Tonya reached up and tried to pull the boy down, it was too late; they were subjected to a hail of bullets, this time not aimed to miss.

Andrei and Tonya both fell backwards and landed awkwardly on Lydia who screamed and kept on screaming, as Andrei's blood spattered onto her face; she could even taste it on her lips. So much blood, sticky and black in the darkness of the forest, soaking her coat. Andrei did not speak, was incapable of speech. Tonya was groaning. Was some of the blood hers? Ivan looked back once and then urged the horses on, but the horsemen galloped up and surrounded them, forcing them to stop.

'Why didn't you stop when we shouted?' one of them asked, riding close to the carriage and peering inside. 'Who was it fired at us?'

'The boy,' Ivan said. 'He did not understand. He is only a child. He thought he was defending his sister.'

'Is he dead?'

'I do not know.'

'Get down and look, for God's sake, and stop that child screaming. You'll have the whole army down on our heads.' Which army he did not specify.

'She is frightened.' Ivan clambered down awkwardly, knowing that the men's guns were trained on him. He reached across and pulled Tonya off Lydia. Unable to sit up, the nurse slid to the floor. 'Be quiet, little one,' he told Lydia. 'You will only make the men angry if you scream.'

Her screams became frightened sobs, which she tried valiantly to hold back, but the sight of Andrei laying across her lap with his head thrown back and his eyes wide and staring was enough to set her off again. Her coat had fallen open and the blood was staining her white dress, soaking through to the petticoat, the petticoat containing the Kirilov diamond. She remembered her mother saying bad men might try and take it from her and she supposed that was who they were. Ivan lifted Andrei out and held him out in his arms, as if to show him to the horsemen, none of whom had dismounted. 'He is dead.' Ivan's voice was toneless.

'And the other? Who is she?'

He was about to say their governess when he realised that admitting the children had a governess was not a good idea; it branded them as aristocrats. 'A friend of the family. They were going to stay with her in Perekop while their parents went to Kiev. They have been summoned to appear at some enquiry or other. I don't know the details.' The sight of Andrei, brave, foolish Andrei, had brought him near to tears himself and he could only mutter these untruths. 'Let me take them on, comrades. We are no danger to you. We have nothing you want. The boy did not mean any harm and he didn't hit anyone.'

The leader at last dismounted and came to look at Andrei, who was most certainly dead of a head wound. It had been a superb shot considering the smallness of the target and the fact that the droshky was travelling in a far from straight line; more of an accident than deliberate, if he were honest. 'You should have stopped him.'

'I couldn't. I was driving. Tonya Ratsina tried to stop him and she is badly wounded. Let us go, comrade. The little girl is terrified, can't you see?'

Lydia was no longer sobbing. She was staring with wide unblinking eyes at Ivan, who held her brother's body across his hands as if in supplication. Andrei's head lolled down one side, his legs down the other, unnaturally arched. She had always thought when people died they shut their eyes but Andrei's were wide open. Could he see her still? The man leant forward and closed the dead eyes with one hand and turned towards her. She opened her mouth to scream, but he quickly put his hand over her mouth. 'Silence, child! Your noise will not bring him back. I want to see the woman.' He reached down into the vehicle and lifted Tonya's chin. 'No beauty by any standards.' He let it fall, then picked up the picnic basket from the floor and flicked open the lid. 'Food, comrades,' he said, flinging chicken legs at them. They caught them deftly and began eating, obviously very hungry.

'Take it,' Ivan said. 'Take it, with pleasure. And the

pancakes. And the cold tea. Take it all. Just let us go.'

'We might. But who are you? Give us a name.'

'Ivan Karlov, cousin to Grigori Stefanovich, the Chairman of the Workers' Committee of the Petrovsk Soviet.' It was said without hesitation; he had had a few minutes to realise telling his own name would not help and could lead to his wife and children. He hoped using Grigori's name might influence the men for the good.

Tonya started to groan and cry out with the pain of her wound and both men turned to look at her. 'She needs help,' Ivan said.

'It's my view she is beyond help, but we do not make war on children. If the boy had not fired, you would be well on your way by now.'

'Why did you want to stop us?'

The man laughed. 'Our horses are spent, we thought we would requisition yours, but now we have seen that great carthorse, we have changed our minds. An unfortunate occurrence, comrade, but not our fault.' He reached into the carriage and picked up Tonya's purse. 'We will have this instead. Now, on your way.'

Ivan did not need telling twice. He laid Andrei on the floor the other side of Tonya and covered them both with rugs, then picked Lydia up and set her up in front of him, wrapping a fur round both their legs. It was done without speaking, without looking back at the horsemen, though he knew they were still watching him.

Chapter Two

Lydia did not scream, or even cry; neither did she speak. Her whole mind was numb, unable to absorb what had happened. The fur that wrapped her was warm, but she shivered uncontrollably. Not even when they left the forest behind, and came out onto open countryside again, did she come out of her lethargic state. It was better that way, Ivan decided; he could not cope with sobs and screams. The sun, rising over the snowy fields, bathed them in a rose-white glow, hiding the barrenness of the ground beneath them. They crossed a river and entered a small village, where Ivan stopped to ask if there was a doctor in the vicinity.

'No, comrade, no doctor,' the man returned. 'There's a midwife.'

'What would I want with a midwife? It's death not new life I'm concerned with.'

The man peered into the carriage. 'What happened?'

'We were attacked by Reds or bandits, hard to tell which these days.'

'Reds? Here?' He crossed himself fervently. 'Has the war come to Ukraine?'

'It is not far behind me.'

Tonya suddenly gave a huge sigh and then there was a gurgling in her throat, and an eerie silence replaced her rasping struggle for breath. There was a finality about it that was indisputable. The man looked into the carriage. 'It's a priest and a gravedigger you need, comrade,' he said, 'not a doctor.'

'Then direct me to the priest.'

The man gave him directions, though he did not need them; the church dome was clearly to be seen at the far end of the street. 'The child?' the man queried. 'Is she wounded?'

'No, shocked that's all. And can you wonder at it?'

'No.'

Lydia did not speak while the arrangements for a double funeral went on around her. She did not hear, much less respond, to the sympathetic enquiries of the women of the village and shook her head dumbly when they offered her food. One of the older women tried to take off her bloodstained dress and petticoat, but she resisted silently and fiercely, with a surprising show of strength, and the woman gave up and went to fetch Ivan who was busy helping to dig the graves.

He came to Lydia and squatted down beside her. 'Let the *babushka* have the dress, little one. She will wash it for you. You have another in your bag, don't you?' When she nodded, he fetched the bag and handed it to the old lady. 'Change the dress. Leave the petticoat on. She needs its warmth.'

Lydia did not utter a sound as this was accomplished,

nor later when she stood by the open graves and earth was scattered on the coffins of her brother and their governess. She watched with vacant eyes as the gravediggers began filling in the dark hole, hearing, but not hearing, the clump of the clods of cold earth as they landed on the wood. Ivan paid for the funeral with one of the jewels taken from Andrei's tunic, the rest he put in his pocket, then he picked Lydia up and took her back to the droshky which the villagers had scrubbed out. The bloodstains were muted, not so glaringly fresh, but the smell had defied all attempts to eradicate it. She fought silently against returning to it, kicking and struggling in his arms.

'Little one, we have to go on,' he said. 'I must take you to Simferopol. Your mama and papa will be there. You want to see them again, don't you?'

She nodded, her eyes full of tears, but she clung to him, hiding her face in his shoulder. He climbed onto his own seat, set her between his knees again and, encircling her with his arms, picked up the reins. 'Try to sleep, little one,' he murmured.

He was not an articulate man, did not know what to say to comfort her, and he did not try. Instead he sang an old Ukrainian lullaby, softly, liltingly, while the snow turned to rain and drummed on the vehicle, washing away the last of the blood. Exhausted by everything that had happened, she put her head back against his rough tunic, while the horse plodded forward.

They travelled in silence; Lydia sat leaning against his chest, her little brain so numb it had ceased to function. Perhaps it was just as well, he thought; he was finding it hard enough to come to terms with what had happened himself. He had been fond of Andrei; the boy had been intelligent and lively and had not adopted the imperiousness of some aristocrats, believing themselves superior beings. That was down to the count, who was a man he could respect and trust. A man he had failed.

What would he say when he learnt of this terrible tragedy? His son and heir butchered by Reds or bandits, it did not make any difference which it had been. He would blame him and he would be right. It should never have happened. He should not have left a loaded shotgun where the boy could reach it. Now what was he to do? The count had given instructions for them to stay at a hotel, but how could he do that? A man and a little girl, not even a relation. It wouldn't be right. He could not leave her in a room alone, not in the state she was in, and sharing a room was out of the question. Besides, they were well behind schedule, so he had better keep going all night. The count and countess would be there before him and be anxious about them.

The sun came up as they made their way down out of the hills and now it held more warmth. The snow had disappeared. The fields became fields again and the roads more clearly defined. Villages came and went. He bought food at one place, but Lydia would not eat; his efforts to make her speak failed miserably and he fell to talking to himself.

They arrived at Perekop in the early afternoon and by then the heat in the sun was fierce, making him sweat in his thick clothes. He stopped at a café which had tables under an awning, hitched up the horse and lifted Lydia down. She stood silently while he bought food and drink and took it to one of the tables in the shade. 'Eat,' he commanded. But she refused to open her mouth. It worried him. She had been twenty-four hours without food or drink of any kind and that surely was not good. After half an hour they set off again and arrived at Simferopol in the evening. The air had a salty tang and was redolent with the scent of rosemary and pine, but he hardly noticed it. He was dog-weary and worried. He had met the Ratsins only once when they had visited Tonya and he was unsure of his reception. He had to tell them of their daughter's death and then ask them to look after Lydia until the count arrived, if he had not already done so.

Finding the house was not easy, and then it turned out to be little more than a hovel on the edge of a village a couple of *versts* from the town, a log-built *izba,* with a dirt floor and a stove in one corner. There was a table in the middle of the room with a couple of benches. The beds were on the stove.

Lydia had never been in such a place before, but she was so numb she hardly took it in. Tonya's parents welcomed her with hugs and kisses and brought out the bread and salt to bid them welcome. They had not seen the count and countess, they said. Ivan wondered whether to keep their daughter's death from them, but that would be cowardly, and so he told them what had happened in his gruff, straightforward way.

They wept, of course they did, and when the weeping stopped, they began to question him. What had happened, who were the horsemen, why were the count and countess visiting them? Were the Reds coming? He answered as best he could, anxious to be on his way back. If those horsemen had been Reds, forerunners of the army, then they would soon be at Petrovsk, and he had left his wife and children there. He had obeyed his instructions in so far as he had brought Lydia Mikhailovna to Simferopol, now his duty was to his family.

He looked across the room, where Lydia sat silent and blank-faced. Poor little mite. 'May I leave the little one with you, Stepan Gregorovich?' he asked. 'The count and countess will be here soon, God willing. I am surprised they are not here ahead of us, but no doubt the weather in the hills delayed them. I have to return.'

The couple were alarmed at the prospect and would have liked to refuse; if the Reds were getting close, harbouring an aristocrat would cost them their lives. On the other hand, the money the big man was offering was more than they had ever seen at one time before and would enable them to move into better accommodation. And it was only for a few hours. They agreed and, having shared a meal of boiled mullet and fish soup with them, Ivan set off back to Petrovsk, leaving behind a child so traumatised, she was barely alive.

'I don't know how to entertain a countess,' Marya Ratsina said between sobs for her dead daughter. 'What would a countess expect? Where can I get food good enough for them?' She looked at the money Ivan had given her. It was made up of gold and silver coins, not Kerensky's paper money. Spending it would invite questions and they had to think of a good reason for having it. 'Should I go and buy some food? And plates. You cannot expect them to eat out of wooden bowls.' She went over to Lydia and peered into her face. 'You, girl, what shall I do to make your mother and father welcome?'

She received no reply and set about cleaning the house with frantic haste, taking the rugs outside and banging them against the outhouse wall, choking on the dust. She swept the floors, cleaned the one little window, stoked up the stove, shook out the blankets and squashed a few bugs, none of which made much difference. The place was still a hovel.

'For God's sake, woman, leave off fussing,' Stepan told her, filling his clay pipe with strong-smelling tobacco. 'They will probably not even come through the door, they are only coming to fetch the child.'

'What's the matter with her? Why does she not speak? I offered her soup and bread but she took neither. I shall be glad when they come and take her away, she is giving me the shivers, sitting there so still and staring. What is she staring at? Is she ill? Oh, I hope she is not going to be ill. I have no idea what to do . . .'

'Do nothing. Get on with your usual chores. Feed the chickens, milk the goat, and be thankful we still have them. If the Reds come, they will have them off us in a twinkling.'

'And if they find her here . . .' She jerked her head towards the corner where Lydia sat on a small stool. 'We will be arrested and probably shot for harbouring her. Do you think they really are coming? It must be very bad in the north. I saw hundreds passing by when I went to the market this morning. They have bought up all the supplies, inflating the prices so I couldn't afford a thing.' She sat down, suddenly deflated like a pricked balloon.

They waited the rest of the day. Stepan went on with his chores and Marya would sit for a while, trying to persuade Lydia to talk, and then would jump up and go out into the road to peer towards the mainland, hoping to see the Kirilov carriage. It did not come. They put the child to bed on the floor. She refused to allow them to undress her, struggling silently, and when it looked as though they might succeed, she opened her mouth and screamed so loud and long they gave up and let her sleep as she was, which she did from sheer exhaustion.

The next morning Stepan went into Simferopol to see what was happening for himself. The town was milling with strangers, soldiers in tattered uniforms, civilians riding in an assortment of vehicles or making for the railway station on foot. Some were in furs, having come from the colder climate of the north, and they had servants with them. Others were less well clad and carried their own cases. They all looked desperate. There was a larger police presence than usual, looking at people's papers, afraid Red soldiers might have infiltrated themselves among the refugees. The grand square in front of the railway station was packed with people, as was the station itself when Stepan managed to push his way through to it.

'Your Excellency,' he said, addressing a gentleman in an astrakhan coat and a shiny top hat, who was directing porters loading his luggage onto a trolley, while his wife, in a sable coat, and a boy in warm knickerbockers and belted wool jacket, stood watching. 'Why is everyone leaving? Are the Reds coming?'

'I fear it is inevitable,' the man said. 'If you have any reason to fear them, then I suggest you make your escape.'

'No, I have no reason to fear them. I am a poor peasant, I have nothing but a few chickens and a goat. They can come, it won't bother me, except that I have a child in my care, the little daughter of Count Kirilov. She was supposed to meet her parents at my house and they were going on to Yalta, but they have not come. I don't know what has happened to them, but what am I to do with her?'

'Can't you keep her?'

'No. She is a little aristocrat, dressed like one too. What would I do with one like that? She isn't used to work . . .'

'I should think not!'

'Her brother and nurse were shot dead in front of her eyes.'

'Oh, the poor thing,' the lady said.

'The nurse was my daughter and my wife is grieving for her. Even if she were not, she would not know how to look after the child. Can you take her? When her parents come I can tell them you have her. She will be better with you.'

They looked at each other doubtfully, while he waited, cap in hand, looking from one to the other hopefully. 'She is so sad, the little one,' he added. 'She has lost everything . . .'

'Where is she now?'

'At my place, less than two *versts* away. If you do not take her I shall have to take her to the orphanage.'

'No, don't do that,' the man said, his voice sharp. 'Fetch her here.'

Stepan darted off before the man could change his mind.

'Pyotr, what are you thinking of?' his wife asked him. 'We have problems enough getting ourselves away without taking on someone else's child.'

'But we cannot abandon her. If she is the daughter of Count Kirilov . . .'

'*If*,' she reiterated.

'We shall soon find out. I am sure the count would do the same for us if it were Alexei left alone. Just think about that for a moment, will you? All alone and no one to take care of him. We can take her as far as Yalta and can make enquiries there for Count Kirilov. If he hasn't turned up, the authorities will know what to do.'

She looked at her sturdy young son and gave in. 'I hope she does not make us miss our train.'

'It is not due for another hour and we shall be lucky if it leaves on time. Let's see if we can find something to eat in the station canteen.'

They had just finished their smoked fish, cucumber and pickled mushrooms when Stepan reappeared with Lydia sitting sideways on a donkey he had borrowed. Her weight was balanced on the other side with her bag of clothes. He had persuaded her to come on the promise of seeing her papa and mama soon. He crossed the square and pulled up outside the station, lifted her down, and taking her hand, led her through the crowds, searching out the gentleman, wishing he had enquired his name, so that he could ask for him. Lydia, her hand in his, stared about her, looking for her father and mother. And Andrei. He had not died, he had not shed his life's blood all over her dress. That had been a nightmare and was not real.

'There he is,' Stepan said, pointing.

It was not her papa but another man, and her heart sank. Of course, Stepan Ratsin would not know her papa, would he? She pulled against his hand, still unable to utter a word to tell him he was mistaken. Words choked her. She was dragged unwillingly towards the man. He had a woman with him and a boy, a boy a little older than Andrei who was looking at her with curiosity.

The man bent down towards her. He had grey eyes

and a blond beard, a kind face. 'Are you Count Kirilov's daughter?' he asked.

She nodded, her features brightening just a little at the mention of her papa.

'What is your name?'

She tried, she really tried, to say her name but all that came out of her mouth was a croak.

'She is still in shock,' Stepan said, shifting from foot to foot. 'Her name is Lydia Mikhailovna Kirillova.'

'How do you know that? Does she have papers?'

Stepan told the man everything Ivan had told him, about the count being a colonel in the White Army and sending the children off separately so as not to attract attention, how they were all supposed to meet at his *izba*, and about the attack in the woods – he choked a little over this. 'As for papers,' he said. 'Maybe they are in her bag.' He handed it to the man, who opened it to discover the bloodstained dress. 'Good God!'

'Sorry, Your Excellency.' If it took all the bowing and scraping and 'your excellencies' in the world, he would do it. He took the bag from the man and delved into it but there were no papers. 'I expect the count has them.'

Pyotr closed the bag and looked at his wife. 'No matter who she is, we can't leave her, can we?'

'No, I suppose not,' she said, putting out her gloved hand to touch Lydia's cheek. 'Poor little mite. My heart bleeds for her.'

Stepan bent to Lydia. 'You go with the gentleman. He will take you to your papa and mama.' He looked up at the man. 'What shall I tell the count if he comes? Who shall I say has her?'

'Baron Simenov. We are going to Yalta. If he has not

caught up with us by then, we will take her to the consul. Tell him that.'

Stepan touched his forelock and was gone, mounting the donkey and trotting it out of the town. What else could he have done? he asked himself. She would be all right with the baron. He was a kindly man and you could see the baroness was very taken with the child. Yes, she would be all right. And he crossed himself.

The trains were all crammed to suffocation, but the baron found a place for them all by dint of bribing the stationmaster and giving the porter a huge tea present. Lydia, believing she was being taken to her parents, went without demur.

'My name is Alexei Petrovich Simenov,' the boy told Lydia, when the luggage had all been stowed in the luggage van and they had taken their seats. 'What are you called?'

'Lydia.' It was so long since she had uttered anything but a terrified scream, the words came out in a whisper.

'How old are you?'

Her brain was working so slowly it was several seconds before she answered. 'Four.'

'A baby, then.'

'I am not a baby.' This was louder and angry.

'I am thirteen, nearly fourteen. When I am old enough I am going to join the army and fight against the Reds.'

'Hush,' his mother murmured, laying a gloved hand upon his sleeve. 'We will not talk of the war.' She turned to Lydia. 'When did you last see your mama and papa, child?'

Lydia could not remember. It seemed an age since they had hugged her mother goodbye and driven away in the carriage, longer still since Papa had sat her on his knee and called her the star of the Kirilovs. What had Ivan Ivanovich done with Andrei? Had he taken him to Papa and Mama? Why had he left her behind? A silent tear rolled down each cheek.

'She is crying,' Alexei said.

'I expect she misses her parents,' his mother told him, handing Lydia a clean white handkerchief.

'Where are they?' the boy asked.

'I do not know. I wish I did.' The baroness sighed. She turned to Lydia again. 'What did your papa say to you when you last saw him? Can you remember?'

Lydia shook her head, the unused handkerchief screwed up in her hand.

'It is no good quizzing the child,' the baron put in. 'She is too young and too confused to understand what is happening to her. Leave her be.'

'Then I sincerely hope Count Kirilov turns up in Yalta. I do not know what we shall do with her if he does not. She is such a strange child . . .'

'Katya, I think if you had been through what she has been through you might seem a little strange,' he said. 'She will come out of it, eventually.'

'What happened to you?' Alexei demanded of Lydia. 'Did the Reds get you?'

'Sasha!' his mother remonstrated. 'Do not be unkind. Lydia has lost her brother and her nurse and is all alone. We must take pity on her. Think what it would be like if you found yourself in a strange place without Papa or me.'

All this was said in Lydia's hearing, just as if she were deaf. She was numb with shock and misery but not deaf. 'Mama,' she said on a plaintive note. 'Where is my mama?'

'When we leave the train, she will perhaps be waiting at the station for you,' the baroness said. 'We do not know her, so you will have to look out for her and point her out to us. You can do that, can't you?'

Lydia brightened slightly at the prospect. Papa had said he would be there and see them onto a ship. And perhaps Andrei and Tonya would come back to her. But deep inside her she knew that was not possible. She had seen them in their narrow boxes lowered into holes in the ground and the earth piled on top of them. People did not come back from that.

The train took them to Sebastopol, the end of the line, and it was necessary from there to find other transport to Yalta. Pyotr herded his family, including Lydia, off the train. Some of the passengers hoped to embark on ships from there, but those who had chosen to go to Yalta were obliged to wait in line for a hire carriage. Their drivers, if no one else, were pleased that the tsar's father had refused to allow the railway line to go to Yalta on the grounds that the noise and smoke would spoil the idyll of their seaside holidays.

Yalta was a fashionable resort for Russia's aristocracy. Here they had built palaces and villas along the coastline and bigger estates in the hills, with vine-covered terraces sloping down to the rocky shore, and here they spent their summers in idleness, riding ponies, having picnics, swimming in the warm sea. Even now, with more and more people crowding into the town and British ships standing offshore, they were not all convinced they needed to leave.

Pyotr settled them in at an already overcrowded hotel, left his wife and her French maid unpacking and took Lydia with him to make enquiries about Count Kirilov, though how anyone could find him in this crush he was not at all sure. He set off to find a British Consulate official.

Sir Edward Stoneleigh's temporary office overlooked the harbour. He was standing at the window looking out on a seething mass of humanity, all hoping to be evacuated. Some had run along the pier in the hope of being first to board any vessel taking off refugees. There were abandoned motor cars everywhere, some with doors left open and engines still running. There was nothing worse than a mob in a panic, he told himself, unless it was an aristocratic mob, unused to discipline and orderliness. Edward could see British ships standing by to take people off, but so far the order had not come for them to come into the harbour and begin loading.

He had his own orders to see as many off as he could and then leave himself. How many could be safely taken he was not sure, and if they could not all go, what order of priority was he to use? There were more ships on the way and he hoped all who wanted to leave could be accommodated.

He turned away from the window as his clerk announced Baron Simenov. Another aristocrat claiming kinship with the tsar, he supposed, and hoping for preferential treatment. He smiled and went forward to offer his hand. 'What can I do for you, Baron?'

Pyotr shook the hand. 'A place on board one of your ships for myself, my wife and son would be greatly appreciated, Sir Edward.'

'There is a protocol . . .'

'I am aware of that, Sir Edward, and I would not ask to go out of turn, but I can furnish you with telling evidence that I have been of use to the British government in an intelligence capacity, for which the Bolsheviks would dearly love to shoot me.' It was said with a hint of dry humour which Edward liked.

'Then we shall have to see what we can arrange.'

'That is not the only reason for my visit, Sir Edward; I have another problem. I have been asked to look after a little girl, supposedly the daughter of Count Kirilov, though I have no way of verifying that. She appears to be all alone in the world and I am at a loss to know what to do with her.'

'There are dozens of children in Yalta who have become detached from their parents. Husbands have lost wives, wives their children. I have no idea how it will all be sorted out. What is so special about this child?'

Pyotr told him succinctly all he had learnt from Stepan Ratsin, which was little enough. 'Her parents were supposed to meet her and her brother in Simferopol, but they never turned up. I could not leave her with that uncouth peasant, and so I brought her to Yalta. According to the servant who took her to the peasant, that was where the family was heading.'

'Has she means of identification?'

'None at all. But she is dressed like a little aristocrat. Except for the bloodstains – her brother's and her nurse's, who were shot in front of her, so I was told.'

'What does she say?'

'Nothing. She has not uttered a word, except to croak her name and age. She seems to be in shock. Hardly to be wondered at, is it?'

'No.'

'I was hoping you might have news of the count, or some message as to what was to be done with her. I can hardly carry her off to England when her poor parents might be searching for her. And what would I do with her when I got there?'

'I see,' Edward murmured. 'Where is she now?'

'Outside in the vestibule. I have taken a room in a hotel for my wife and son. They are charging the earth for rooms and I was lucky to obtain one for all of us, but we cannot accommodate the little girl. She is, not to put too fine a point on it, somewhat smelly. You can see how we are fixed?'

Sir Edward did see. 'You had better bring her in. I'll see what I can find out.'

'Thank you. And you will remember a place for us on one of the British ships?'

'I will remember.'

They shook hands again and Pyotr fetched Lydia, his step lighter than when he arrived. Katya had always been a soft-hearted woman, but the last few months had hardened her and, like everyone else, she looked to her own safety and that of her darling son first. They had no idea who Lydia Mikhailovna was. She could be an impostor or a member of the Romanov family and, until they were safely in England, Katya would do nothing to risk being arrested; the penalties would be dire. He could hardly blame her. She would be glad the child could be handed over with a clear conscience.

Lydia was ushered into the office, more terrified and bewildered than ever. The man who had brought her here, promising to find her father, disappeared and she was left facing another man, who was still not Papa. He had a light moustache but no beard, his brown hair was parted in the middle and had a slight wave to it. His blue eyes regarded her kindly. He squatted down beside her so that he was on her level. 'Well, Lidushka, we shall have to see what we can do to help you.' It was said in perfect Russian, with hardly a trace of an accent. 'Are you hungry?'

Lydia was not sure if she was hungry or not, but decided it was polite to nod that she was.

'Good.' He rang a bell on his desk. 'First things first, eh?' Then to his secretary, Richard Sandford, who had arrived in answer to his summons, 'Richard, ask Madame Molinskaya to come here, will you? And then see if you can find out what has happened to Count and Countess Kirilov. The count, according to the information I have been given, is a colonel under General Wrangel. Or he was. He may have decided to call it a day. That would account for him saying he would meet his family in Simferopol. He may, of course, have assumed his daughter perished along with her brother and the nurse, so we need to reassure him on that score and tell him we have her safe.'

'It won't be easy, Sir Edward. Everything is a complete shambles. We have tenuous communications with the White command but that is becoming more and more difficult as their posts are overrun.'

'Do your best.' Edward bent again to Lydia. 'How old are you, sweetheart?'

'Four.'

'Four, eh? Then you are a big girl, aren't you? Perhaps you know where you live. Do you know the name of the place?'

'Kirilhor,' she said.

'Where is that?' Richard asked, but that was more than she could tell him.

'See what you can discover,' Edward told him.

He disappeared and a few moments later a fat, motherly Russian woman arrived and Lydia was given into her care. 'Get those clothes off her and give her a bath,' Sir Edward murmured, handing her Lydia's bag of clothes. 'Then feed her and put her to bed. After that . . .' He shrugged, having no clear idea of what he would do.

'Come, *golubchick*,' she said, taking Lydia by the hand and leading her from the room. 'We shall soon have you feeling more comfortable.'

'Mama.' It was a refrain Lydia was to repeat over and over like a mantra. 'Where is my mama?'

'Sir Edward will find out for you. You know who Sir Edward is, don't you?'

Lydia shook her head.

'He is the English gentleman we have just left. He is a baronet in England and what they call a diplomat. He is a very important man and very busy, so we must not trouble him if we can help it. I will look after you until we find your mama and papa. Now, you are going to be a good girl, aren't you? A good girl for your papa and Sir Edward.' As she spoke she led the child through the house to her own quarters above the kitchen. They consisted of a sitting room, a bedroom and a bathroom. She rang a bell and when this was answered by a maid asked her to prepare food for their guest. Then she ran a bath.

It was then the struggle began. Lydia did not want to be undressed. She was afraid the Star of Kirilov would be found and it was her bounden duty to hang onto it; Mama had told her not to let anyone see it. But Madame Molinskaya was hard to resist. She spoke softly, saying there was nothing to fear, everyone was her friend, and all the time she was unbuttoning, untying, stroking the little one's face, reassuring her. It was when she managed to remove the bloodstained petticoat and threw it on the bathroom floor and heard the heavy thud she realised something was hidden in it.

She picked it up again to examine it. 'Ah, my little one, what have we here?' The secret pocket was found and the Star extracted, while Lydia, filled with a sense of her failure, cried salty, silent tears. 'I see it all now. This is meant to pay your way. Now, why would anyone do that unless they knew you were going to be all alone? We shall see what Sir Edward says, but for now, I shall put it here.' She laid the jewel on a table against the wall. 'It will be quite safe while you have your bath and some supper, and then we will take it to Sir Edward. Now, into that warm water with you. There is some nice-smelling soap here.' She sniffed it and held it to Lydia's nose. 'Violets. You like it, don't you?'

Lydia nodded and was lifted into the bath. It was heavenly to be soaped with the luxury soap, something she had not seen since leaving Petrograd. Her matted hair was shampooed, and when that was done, she was lifted out and dried with a big fluffy white towel. This was more like it used to be, before they went to Kirilhor. Down in the bottom of her smelly bag was a nightdress which had escaped the staining. It was slipped over her head.

'Now you are civilised again,' Madame Molinskaya said, picking up a hairbrush from the table and, standing Lydia between her knees, beginning to brush the hair dry. It fell about her face in little corkscrew curls. 'My, you are a pretty little thing.' She was just finishing when a maid came to say food was on the table.

Lydia began to feel a little better. This lady was kind, a little like Tonya who had always looked after her and taken her to her mama after she had been bathed and made ready for bed. She would restore her to Mama and Papa. She followed the motherly woman into the adjoining room where the table was set for two. They sat down together and ate *pirozhki* and cabbage followed by a sweet pancake, smothered in honey. Lydia had not eaten at all for three days, had not felt hungry, but now she was ready to make up for it and ate with a hearty appetite, washing it down with creamy goat's milk, which pleased Madame.

By the time the meal was finished the traumatised little girl was drooping with tiredness. Madame Molinskaya picked her up and took her into the adjoining room and put her to bed in a little camp bed in her own room which had been made ready while they ate. 'Sleep, little one,' she murmured, stroking her cheek. 'We shall see what tomorrow brings.' Then she retrieved the Star and went to see Sir Edward.

'It's mayhem down there,' Captain Henry Conway said, jerking his head in the direction of the harbour where thousands of refugees were trying to cram themselves on the British ships which had come into the harbour. He had come up to the residence to discuss the situation with Sir Edward, who was an old friend from their student days. 'I'm supposed to take off the troops but how can I leave civilians behind, especially those with children? I'll make room for as many as I can, but I need some guidance on priorities.'

'That has been worrying me too,' Edward said, pouring a glass of cognac for each of them. 'Best take first come, first served and hope more transport will arrive in the next few days and we can get everyone away who wants to go. Wrangel is doing his best to hold the peninsula but I fear the cause is lost.' He paused to sip his drink. 'There is someone who needs to go as a priority. Baron Simenov has been working for British intelligence and, besides being wanted by the Reds, has important information to pass on. He has his wife and son with him. Shall I tell him you can take them?'

'Yes. Tell him to come to the ship and ask for me. We are planning to sail tonight. What about you? When are you leaving?'

'When my job is done. I still have work to do here. I'll see you in London perhaps.'

The captain finished his drink, shook hands and left. Edward sent for Richard Sandford. 'Any news of the Kirilovs?'

'I have located Kirilhor, Sir Edward. It is a *dacha* in the Petrovsk district of Ukraine. It was overrun by the Reds two days ago. It was more difficult contacting General Wrangel, but I got through by telephone to one of his staff who told me Colonel Kirilov was given leave to evacuate his family and was then to return to duty. He has not returned.'

'He could have deserted but in that case he would have been with his children, surely?'

'The officer said the colonel would be loyal to the last and they are assuming he has met his end.'

'He had his wife with him.'

'Then they might both have perished.'

Edward was inclined to agree. 'According to Baron Simenov, the servant who brought the child to the peasant was adamant the count meant to meet them there and bring them to Yalta. I have had no application from anyone called Kirilov to be evacuated.'

'Then the little girl is the only survivor.'

'It seems that way.'

'What are you going to do about her?'

'I do not know. Madame Molinskaya is looking after her. I had to send out for a whole wardrobe of clothes for her. Almost everything she had was covered in blood. Poor thing, she is still in shock and unable to tell us anything, except her name and that she is four years old.'

'An orphanage?' Richard queried.

'I am reluctant to do that. She is undoubtedly an aristocrat, so how can I condemn her to being one of thousands of orphans who will find themselves being looked after by the Bolsheviks when they come? They will ill-treat her, especially if they think she has any connection with the Romanovs.'

'Do you think she has?'

'I don't know, but she has some valuable jewels with her, which look as though they might be traceable. I can try and do that once we get back to England.'

Richard smiled. 'So, you are going to take her back with you?'

'I can't leave her here, can I? I'll see if I can engage one of the other passengers as a nurse for her.'

The evacuation, carried out in a strong wind and rough seas, lasted three days, during which the British ships took the remnants of the White Army who had made their own way to Yalta, and as many of the refugees as they could accommodate, including the Simenovs. Two days later, when nothing more could be done, Sir Edward left with Lydia, whom he had listed as his daughter in order to justify taking her with him.

He was glad he had done that when they arrived in Constantinople and everyone's papers were examined. Lydia, having none, would not have been allowed to continue otherwise. From there they went to Malta, where they stayed a week, while the refugees' papers were processed and some of them were taken off the ship, then they sailed for England.

Edward had engaged a young English girl to look after Lydia. Claudia was twenty-one and had been governess to a Russian family who had declined to join the rush to leave, but, in straitened circumstances, had not been able to continue employing her. She spoke a little Russian and he thought Lydia would like that, though the child gave no indication of it one way or another. She submitted silently to being helped to dress and undress, of having her hair brushed, of being shepherded from one place to another in a kind of daze. It was late November when they arrived in Portsmouth.

They went to London by train and stayed at Sir Edward's Mayfair apartment for the first night, and the next morning he left Lydia and Claudia while he went to the Foreign Office to make his report. What was going to happen to all the Russian refugees they did not know. Some had relatives in Britain where they knew they would be welcome, and some had already made up their minds to go on to America, but those left to fend for themselves would have to be helped to find accommodation and a means of earning a living, which was something many of them had never had to do before. They felt it demeaned them, but as few had brought enough money and jewels out of Russia to keep them in idleness for the rest of their lives, they had perforce to adjust their standards.

Edward said nothing to his superiors about Lydia. He had a feeling his actions would be frowned upon, and he did not know how to explain that the child's plight had touched a chord in his heart and that her very silence seemed to be a reproof. He could not do much to help hundreds, but he could do something for this little one. She was still not talking and now they were in England it would be doubly difficult for her. A strange country, a strange language, strange people and the loss of her family all had to be dealt with. He hoped and prayed Margaret would understand when he took the child home.

Chapter Three

1920

Upstone Hall was a country mansion in the village of Upstone in north-west Norfolk, surrounded by farming country. In the last few years Sir Edward had not often been in residence, having diplomatic postings abroad. Before the war his wife had always gone with him. They had no children, which was a source of great sorrow to them both, but she had enjoyed the social life in the different embassies to which he had been attached. But when war came he had been posted to Russia and she ceased to accompany him. He had returned home briefly at the end of hostilities, but because of his fluency in the language, he had been sent back to Russia specifically to help the refugees. It was frightening what was happening to that country and he wanted her to be safe, so once again he had left her at home. She lived at Upstone, managed the house, did good works in the village, raised money for the relief of refugees, visited friends and relatives and wrote long letters to him. He had written to tell her about

Lydia but there had been no time to receive a reply before they set sail.

Sitting in the first-class compartment of the train taking them to Norfolk he turned his head to look at the child. She was pale and drawn, as she had been ever since he had taken charge of her. Her face betrayed no emotion, either of misery or pleasure. She hardly spoke except to say 'please' and 'thank you' when offered food. He sometimes felt impatient with her, but then reminded himself of what she had been through and was filled with compassion. They changed trains at Ely and half an hour later drew up at the small wayside station at Upstone where they were met by Groves with the pony and trap.

He was home to a peaceful countryside, recovering from the war to end all wars and the dreadful flu epidemic that followed it. Many of the young men were gone, never to return, but those that were left, along with their womenfolk, were picking up the pieces and trying to get on with their lives. Times were hard enough in Britain, what with shortages and strikes; what was happening in Russia was so remote, so far away, they hardly gave it a thought. He smiled at Lydia. 'Nearly home,' he said in Russian.

'Mama?' she queried. 'Will Mama be there?'

'No, little one. I am afraid we do not know where she is. I promise I will do my best to try and find her for you, and in the meantime, you will live with us.'

He saw one large tear spill over her lashes and roll down her cheek, the only indication she gave that she had understood him. He put his arm about her shoulders and drew her to his side. 'We will look after you,' he murmured, bending to kiss the top of her head. 'I promise you that.'

They turned into the drive where the pony, as if sensing

it was nearly home, broke into a trot, and then they were drawing up beside the house and the door was flung open and Margaret ran down the steps to throw herself into his arms almost before he could get down. 'You are back. Oh, thank the Lord! I could not believe you were really on your way until I got your telegram. Welcome home!' She took his arm to drag him into the house, ignoring Claudia and Lydia who still sat in the trap, looking bewildered.

'Hold hard!' he said, laughing. 'I am not alone, you know.'

She turned to look at the occupants of the trap. 'Oh, I forgot you were bringing someone back with you. I'll send Mrs Selby out to them. I want you all to myself.'

'Later,' he said, turning to lift Lydia out and set her on her feet. 'This is Lydia Mikhailovna Kirillova. She is going to stay with us while I try to locate her family.' He turned to the child. 'Lydia, this is my wife, Lady Stoneleigh. Give her a little curtsy and say how do you do.'

Lydia, whose mama would have deplored bad manners on her part, obeyed, though she could not manage a smile.

Claudia was presented next and made her obeisance and then they all went indoors where Mrs Selby, the housekeeper, was sent for and the girls were delivered into her hands. She was a thin woman, dressed in dark blue with a white frilly cap on her grey hair. At her belt was a huge bunch of keys.

She conducted them to the top floor of the three-storey house, to some rooms she called the 'nursery suite'. They consisted of two adjoining bedrooms and a bathroom, adequately but not luxuriously furnished. Their bags, which had been filled with their meagre belongings, had arrived ahead of them and stood on the floor at the foot of one of the beds in the room they were to share. Lydia looked about her. This was like the nursery suite in St Petersburg. She remembered that every afternoon she and Andrei would be taken by Tonya downstairs to Mama's boudoir and they would talk about what they had been doing, the lessons they had learnt, the pictures they had drawn, the walks they had taken. Sometimes Papa would be there and they played games together. It did not happen when they moved to Kirilhor because, although there were many, many rooms, they had been desecrated first by the occupying Germans and then by vandals, and they had been obliged to live in one small section of the house. And Papa was more often away than at home.

'I have had no orders about where you are to have your meals,' Mrs Selby said, after she had shown them the schoolroom, where a bright fire burnt. 'For now you had better come down and fetch them up here. Supper will be ready at six. I will leave you to unpack.'

As soon as she had gone, Claudia took Lydia back to the bedroom and began opening drawers and cupboards and inspecting the washing facilities, talking all the time in her broken Russian, but when that became inadequate, she lapsed into English. 'We shall soon be comfortable,' she said. 'Sir Edward is obviously very wealthy. Look at the size of this house, a palace, it is. Lots of servants I shouldn't wonder, and horses and carriages. Maybe a motor car.' She was unpacking the trunk and putting things away, watched by a silent Lydia. 'We shall do all right here, but you will have to learn English. Are you hungry?'

Lydia caught the gist of the last sentence and nodded. She felt strange, as if someone had picked her up from Kirilhor and transported her on a cloud to this place. She could not remember how she got here. The time was a blank, a nightmare from which she was only now awakening.

'Will you be all right here while I go and fetch our supper?' Claudia asked her in Russian. She did not wait for a reply, but left her. Lydia went to the window and looked out. Way below her was a yard and men with horses. The trap in which they had arrived was now without its pony and was tipped up on its shafts. A black and white dog lay outside a kennel. Beyond that was a park whose trees still had a few russet and yellow leaves, but were mostly bare. The ground beneath them was green. Everywhere was green. When they had left Kirilhor it had been white. What had happened in between? She had lost Mama and Papa and Tonya and Andrei, but how? Why was she here? A tear gathered in her eye and rolled down her cheek unheeded.

'Edward, what am I supposed to do with her?' Margaret asked as they sat over their dinner. Cook had taken especial care over the meal in honour of his homecoming. There was vegetable soup, roast beef, roast potatoes, cabbage, cauliflower, carrots, Yorkshire pudding and rich gravy, and that was to be followed by apple pie and cream, a typically English meal and one she knew he would appreciate after being away so long. 'She is such a strange little thing. Does she speak any English at all?'

'I can't say, since she has hardly said a word either in English or Russian, but I doubt it.'

'Then how am I to communicate with her?'

'Claudia speaks a little Russian, she will translate until Lydia can learn English.'

'Learn English! How long do you expect her to stay with us?'

'Until I find out what happened to her parents. Baron Simenov is returning to Russia on government business and I asked him to find out what he could.'

'Baron Simenov,' she repeated. 'Isn't he the one who found the child in the first place?'

'He was one of the hands through which she was passed.'

'Why didn't he keep her, then? He's Russian. It would have been better for her.'

He sighed, trying to conceal his impatience. 'Darling, I explained why he did not. He thought I would find the count and his wife before I left. And he was taking his wife and son to a new home in England, knowing he would almost certainly be asked to return to Russia. He did not know until we reached England that I had not been able to trace the count or his wife.'

'Are you sure you were right to bring her out of Russia?'

'What else was I to do? Leave her to the Bolsheviks? She is an aristocrat, perhaps even a Romanov, and I am told her father is a White Army colonel. The Reds would have no compunction about doing away with her.'

'How did you manage to bring her out with you? Did no one ask questions?'

'I said she was my daughter.'

'Your daughter!' Margaret had stopped eating and was staring at him in consternation. 'But everyone in the diplomatic corps knows we have no children.'

He smiled crookedly. 'It was assumed she was the result of a Russian liaison . . .'

'Edward, how could you!'

'It was easier not to disabuse the authorities of that

idea. They would have refused to take her on board.'

'Why is she so important to you? Are you sure you have told me everything?'

'Darling, of course I have. If you had been there, seen the chaos, seen the state she was in, covered in blood and numb with shock, you would have done the same as I did.'

'There are homes for displaced children.'

'I know. I could not shunt her into one of those. We have this great house, ample funds and no children. I thought, hoped, you would welcome her.' He reached out and put a hand over hers where it lay on the table next to his. 'Give her a chance, darling. I am sure you will come to love her.'

'Do you? Love her, I mean.' It sounded like an accusation.

'I do not know her well enough yet,' he said carefully, alerted by her tone. 'But she touched a chord in me when I first saw her and I could not bring myself to abandon her.'

'Some might say you abducted her. Her parents might, even now, be searching desperately for her.'

'I know, but it was the only way to keep her safe. The situation in Russia is truly dreadful. If the Kirilovs are related in any way to the late tsar, they may have shared his fate.'

'What makes you think they might be related?'

'Only what I have been told and that big jewel Lydia had sewn into her petticoat. I have shown it to other Russian émigrés and they recognised it as part of the Kirilov collection. One of them gave me a photograph of the late dowager Countess Kirillova wearing it on the front of a tiara at a court function. I am told it is called the Kirilov Star.'

'It could have been stolen, along with her clothes, and

put on her to deceive the authorities – deceive you, too. She hasn't been able to tell you about it, has she?'

'No, but perhaps she will when she feels more comfortable with us.'

A maid came to clear away the dishes and bring in the apple pie and the subject of Lydia was dropped, quite deliberately by Margaret, who went on to talk about village matters. She was resigned to giving the strange little Russian child a home, at least for the time being, but that did not mean she had to love her. In spite of her faith in her husband's fidelity, a tiny doubt began to take root and she found herself wondering if Lydia really was Edward's child, especially as he was so vague about who she was. She could not believe he knew as little as he said he did. You simply did not pick strange children up off the street and bring them home for no reason.

He could have fathered her during the war when he was on the ambassador's staff in Moscow and kept her existence a secret. It would have stayed a secret if it hadn't been for the Civil War and the exodus of refugees. Had the Kirilovs ever existed? And if they had, was Lydia their child? Why was she so sceptical? Could it be her own inability to give Edward a child, her failure, after three miscarriages suffered in the early years of their marriage, to be a complete wife, her failure to be a mother? He had wanted a child so desperately. Not as desperately as she had, though. It might have been why Edward had been so taken with Lydia. She was torn between believing there was no other motive than Christian charity and the dreadful fear that he had turned to someone else. If he had, then it was the height of cruelty to bring the child here to torment her.

* * *

68

Lydia and Claudia set out to explore after breakfast next morning, creeping from room to room and talking in whispers. The schoolroom had a desk and a table, cupboards and bookshelves and on the wall a huge map of the world, most of it coloured pink denoting the British Empire, Claudia told her. It was here Claudia was expected to give her lessons and to teach her English. A little further along the corridor were several servants' bedrooms. Down the next flight of stairs there were what seemed like dozens of bedrooms, though they did not dare open their doors, and two bathrooms. The front stairs, of carved oak, led down to a huge hall. There were two large reception rooms leading off it which could be opened up to make one vast room, several smaller sitting rooms, a large and a small room for dining, though the smaller was called the 'breakfast room', Claudia told her. At the back of the house there were rooms for washing dishes, a laundry room full of steam, a dairy where a maid was busy churning butter and a huge kitchen with a big black range and a long dresser and hooks everywhere.

Seeing Lydia the staff began talking to her, and though she could not understand a word, she thought they were making her welcome, for they smiled a lot and gave her a jam tart. 'She's a bonny wee thing, isn't she?' Cook said to Claudia. 'Does she speak any English at all?'

'No,' Claudia said. 'Fact is, she hardly opens her mouth.'

'I expect she's shy. She'll soon get used to us. What are you doing today?'

'I don't know. I thought we would go for a walk and explore.'

'Yes, you do that. But don't go too far and get lost.' She

opened the back door for them and they found themselves in a courtyard. 'Luncheon is at one,' she called after them.

They crossed the yard to the stables where the grooms were working and an almost identical conversation took place. Lydia was nervous of the black and white dog and hid behind Claudia. 'Bless you,' a man in a thick tweed jacket and jodhpurs said. 'Bessie won't hurt you. Soft as butter she is. Come and stroke her.' And he took Lydia's hand and put it on the dog's rough fur. The dog wagged its tail and licked her other hand, making her smile.

'That's the first time I ever saw her smile,' Claudia said.

'Ah, well, that's animals for you.'

They left the stables and walked through a garden and out of a gate into the park that surrounded the house. Here there were walks carved out of the grass and they followed one to a lake and stood looking across the water. A light breeze ruffled the water and set the reeds swaying to and fro and made the leaves of the water lilies bob up and down. Some ducks were swimming a little way out, but seeing them, paddled towards them quacking noisily, expecting titbits. 'We must bring some crusts next time we come,' Claudia said in English, and when Lydia looked enquiringly at her, repeated it in Russian, adding, 'Time to go home. Sir Edward and Lady Stoneleigh might be looking for us.'

Home. The word obviously meant something different to Claudia.

In the days that followed, Lydia's young brain shut out the awful death of her brother and their nurse except in horrendous nightmares. The loud ticking of the nursery clock was an unheard background to gunshots, galloping horses, sleet and snow, the dark, menacing forest and a vision of brave little Andrei, his life's blood spilling all over her white dress, wine-red and sticky. It was a terror so huge that it surrounded her like a stifling blanket which had somehow wrapped itself around her and covered her face in her sleep, so that she could hardly breathe. She would wake up screaming and be comforted by Claudia.

They kept to their own quarters, except when they went out for walks with Bessie trotting along with them and sniffing in the hedgerows, and they saw little of Lady Stoneleigh. Her ladyship was not cruel, but she was not especially kind to her. It was a kind of indifference, a standing apart, on the sidelines, as if she were watching a play from the wings and at the end of it the actors would take their bows and go home. Lydia could not put this into words, but sometimes she wondered if Lady Stoneleigh really liked having her.

Sir Edward was different. He would come up to the nursery suite almost every day and talk to her in Russian and sometimes he joined them on their walks. He understood her bewilderment at being without her family, in a strange country surrounded by strangers speaking a language she could not understand. He and Claudia were the only stable things in her life and it was through his gentle perseverance that she slowly came to accept her new life, but she was desperately lonely and homesick for Mama and Papa and had not given up the idea of being reunited with them.

It was something Margaret wished for too.

'Edward, have you made any progress at all about finding that child's parents?' she asked him one day, just before Christmas. They had finished dinner and were sitting in the drawing room. She was on the sofa with a piece of embroidery in her lap but was making no attempt to ply her needle. He was in an armchair reading a newspaper. He put it down.

'No, I'm afraid not. These things take time.'

'Surely people, especially landed gentry, do not just disappear into thin air.'

'They do in Russia at the moment,' he said grimly. 'The situation is chaotic and the stories coming out are horrendous. Both Reds and Whites are perpetrating unimaginable horrors. If the count and countess have survived, heaven knows where they are.'

'I believe there is a charitable society in London that takes care of displaced Russian children. It is run by a Russian lady married to an Englishman. You could take her there.'

'Why? Do you want to be rid of her?'

'Edward, she does not belong here.'

He was disappointed. He had hoped, by bringing her to Upstone Hall, he would be making a loving home for her, but it had not turned out like that. Lydia and Claudia were like ghosts in the house, occasionally seen flitting here and there, sometimes heard talking quietly in a mixture of Russian and English, but never real, never part of the household. And sometimes, in the middle of the night, he heard Lydia screaming. He would slip on a dressing gown and go up to stand outside the nursery door, listening to her sobbing and Claudia soothing her. Unable to do anything for her, he would go back to bed, feeling helpless, wishing Margaret could bring herself to be a mother to her.

'She is not a nuisance, is she?' he asked.

'No, she is very quiet – too quiet, I think. She would surely do better among her own kind.'

'Darling, it would be cruel to uproot her again so soon after bringing her here. Can't you imagine what the poor child has been through? Her nurse and brother were shot in front of her eyes. Her clothes were covered in their blood when she was brought to me. It will be a long time before she gets over that.'

'You are determined on keeping her here, aren't you?'

'What else would you have me do? I brought her here, accepted responsibility for her and that responsibility is ongoing.'

She gave up. He was not going to change his mind, which only went to confirm her worst fears.

The household was gearing itself up for Christmas, doing a lot of cooking, buying and making presents, discussing the decorations and the parties they meant to attend, and though they talked to Lydia about it, she understood very little. She knew it was a happy time when wishes were granted to good little girls. Her wish was that Mama and Papa would come, which would be the best present of all, but when she told Sir Edward, he took her between his knees and kissed her. 'The trouble is, my little one, I still do not know where they are.'

'Are they lost? Or hiding?'

'You think they may be hiding?' he asked, surprised that she had thought of it.

'We were hiding at Kirilhor. We had to be quiet all the time and stay in the kitchen and back parlour. When the bad men were coming, we had to leave. Papa said we would go on a big ship.'

It was the first time he had heard her speak of that time. 'And you did, didn't you?'

'Yes. Did they come on a big ship too?'

'No, I do not think so, my sweet. I have asked everyone I know. I think they were left behind in Russia. As soon as I hear anything I will tell you, I promise.'

She was miserable for a few days after that but brightened as Christmas Day drew nearer. There was a Christmas tree which she helped to decorate and parcels were put all round the bottom of it which were not to be opened until after Christmas dinner. This would be at one o'clock after everyone had been to church, including all the servants, except Cook and the kitchen maid left behind to make sure dinner was on the table on time.

Church, which they attended every Sunday, was the only time Sir Edward and Lady Stoneleigh took her anywhere together. Dressed in a warm woollen coat in a soft blue, with a tam-o'-shanter on her curls and her hands in a muff, she stood and sat and knelt between them and enjoyed the singing. On Christmas Day she was allowed to join Sir Edward and Lady Stoneleigh for dinner of roast goose and Christmas pudding. She was becoming used to English food and, like all small children, her appetite was good.

After that the presents were distributed from under the tree. Lydia received a jigsaw puzzle, some books, and a china doll from Sir Edward and Lady Stoneleigh. From Claudia she had a handkerchief with her name embroidered in the corner and from the kitchen staff a box of home-made sweets. Claudia had helped her to make a needlecase for Lady Stoneleigh and a bookmark for Sir Edward. 'How beautifully you have done it,' her ladyship said, and kissed her cheek. Sir Edward kissed her too, but it was Lady Stoneleigh's peck which surprised and pleased Lydia. It was the first time she had shown any sign of affection. Sir Edward noted it too and decided it was a good sign; his wife was at last coming to accept the child.

Winter gave way to spring. The daffodils appeared in the grass and the leaves reappeared on the trees. People stopped telling Lydia she would be reunited with her parents, stopped talking to her about Russia at all. The past became a kind of dream; Mama and Papa, Andrei and Tonya were people who came to her in her sleep and had no presence in her daytime life. The people in her waking hours were Claudia, of course, Sir Edward, whom she loved, Lady Stoneleigh, whom she saw only occasionally, and the servants. With so many servants about, she soon began to pick up a little English, but it was not the English of Sir Edward and his wife; it was Norfolk with a strong Russian accent which many people found difficult to understand. Edward, hearing it, decided something must be done about it and employed an English teacher.

Miss Graham was young and enthusiastic. She wore knitted jumper suits, long strings of beads and did her dark hair up in a bun. She spoke no Russian and Claudia was needed to translate at first, but Lydia was a bright child and learnt quickly. In her head she had decided that if she were good, if she did everything she was told and tried hard at her lessons, everyone would be pleased with her and then she would be reunited with her family all the sooner. It was a childish logic she told no one until one day when Sir Edward came to the schoolroom to sit in on one of her lessons. It made Miss Graham all flustered, but he smiled to set her at her ease. 'Go on,' he said. 'Pretend I am not here.'

The lesson went on and after it had finished he drew Lydia between his knees. 'Well done, sweetheart,' he said in English. 'I did not realise how clever you are. You have learnt remarkably quickly.'

Some of the words he used were unknown to her, but she realised he was pleased because he was smiling. 'Does that mean I can go home now?'

'Home?' he asked, puzzled. 'Do you mean to Russia?'

'Yes, to Mama and Papa. I want to go back to them.'

He sighed. 'The trouble is that the bad men are everywhere and it would not be safe. If I could find them, I would bring them here. You would like that, wouldn't you?'

She nodded, her eyes alight with hope, and he felt a cur for giving her hope when he feared there was none. He gave her a little pat on her bottom and sent her back to Miss Graham and Claudia and then he went downstairs to find his wife.

She had been out riding and was in her room changing out of her riding clothes. Her complexion was pink from the exercise and her eyes bright. 'Good, you are just in time to help me off with my boots,' she said, sitting in a chair and lifting one foot.

He knelt down and pulled the boot off, stroking her stockinged foot as he did so. 'Did you have a good ride?'

'Yes, I went through the park, along the towpath, across the common and back through the wood. What have you been doing?'

'I had a report to write for the Home Secretary.' The second boot joined the first on the floor. 'He is concerned about the numbers of Russian refugees coming into the country and how best we can accommodate them. Fifteen thousand at the last count.'

She smiled. 'No doubt you advocated taking them into private homes.'

'Some could be housed like that, it is true.'

'Like Lydia.' She was still not totally sure Edward had been telling the truth about Lydia, though she had to admit she was a fetching child and really no trouble.

'Yes. She has come on by leaps and bounds. Her English is quite good enough for her to be sent to school.'

'Boarding school?'

'No. She is too young and too vulnerable. It would undo all the good we have been able to do. I think the local village school would be best. She is an intelligent child and will enjoy school and meeting other young children. I will arrange for her to go after the summer vacation.'

'Have you had no news at all about her parents?'

'Afraid not. I fear they have not survived. We must do our best to bring her up as they would have wished.' He paused. 'I think she is old enough to leave the nursery behind and have a room of her own, don't you?' It was said tentatively because the move represented another step Margaret had to take towards accepting the child.

He was still kneeling at her feet, still stroking her foot, gently massaging the toes, something he knew made her squirm with pleasure. She leant forward and taking his face in her hands bent forward to kiss him. 'You know exactly how to get round me, don't you?' she said, laughing.

'Do I need to?'

'No. We'll do whatever you think is best.'

He stood up, took her hands and propelled her towards the bed.

'Edward, it's the middle of the day.'

'So what? I love you at any time of day, all day, every day.'

Lydia was temporarily forgotten.

* * *

Lydia was given a lovely bedroom on the second floor. Unlike the nursery, it had a thick patterned carpet, curtains with a pretty pattern of flowers and leaves, a bed with a cover which matched the curtains, a tall wardrobe in which to keep her clothes, a dressing table and a little desk. Its windows looked out over the stables on one side and the terrace at the back of the house on the other. She loved it. It had a dressing room adjoining it which was made into a bedroom for Claudia. She was not told the reason for this change and would not have understood if she had. Claudia said it meant she was here to stay.

In September Miss Graham left and Lydia went to school every day, escorted there by Claudia. The school had only one classroom divided by a curtain. The little children on one side were taught their letters by Miss Smith, the big ones on the other had lessons in English, arithmetic, geography and history given by the headmaster, Mr Connaught, who had a wooden leg. There was a pot-bellied stove in the middle of one wall, surrounded by a fireguard on which wet coats were hung when it rained, causing steam to rise from them. Shoes, boots and clogs stood drying off in sentinel rows around it.

Lydia, bewildered and afraid, even though Sir Edward had explained why it was necessary for her to attend school, joined the little ones. It was not an unmitigated success. The other children looked on her as some kind of freak, mimicked her accent and laughed and pointed at her gymslip and pristine white blouse, her black stockings and shiny black patent shoes, something few of them could afford. She did not complain. Putting up with everything she found strange was all part of her strategy to be good enough to be allowed to go home.

This hope died, or rather was killed outright, when Sir Edward received a letter from Baron Simenov.

'They are dead,' he told Margaret as he read it over breakfast after Lydia had gone off with Claudia to get ready for school.

Margaret looked up sharply. 'Who are dead?'

'The Kirilovs.' He finished reading. 'This is a letter from Baron Simenov. He is back in London. The cause of the White Army is lost.'

'What did he say about the Kirilovs?'

'The count and his wife were caught and questioned on the way through Red-held territory, and in the course of a search, some precious gems were found concealed on their persons. It is punishable by death to export jewels from the country and they paid that price. The story was told to the baron by Ivan Ivanovich, the servant who had taken Lydia to Simferopol. He returned to Kirilhor. It was the talk of the village apparently.'

'How barbaric! What are you going to say to Lydia?'

'I don't know. She has been so much better lately.'

'You cannot allow her to go on hoping if you are sure there is no hope.'

'No, you are right. She must be told.'

'She may not believe you. She might think you are trying to keep her from them.'

'So, what do you suggest?'

'Perhaps you could invite Baron Simenov and his wife to stay with us for a few days. He could tell her.'

'That would be a cowardly thing to do, Margaret,' he said. 'I will tell her myself, but not about the execution. An accident perhaps. And I will ask the Simenovs to visit. Pyotr might be able to tell me more than he has written in the letter.'

So the baron and baroness and young Alexei came to stay at Upstone Hall for a weekend and Lydia was allowed to join them.

It was two days since Sir Edward had told her that her papa and mama had died on their way to meet her and her brother in Simferopol. An accident, he had said, taking her on his lap to comfort her. 'They were happy because they were on their way to join you and your brother. Their horse bolted and the carriage turned over. It all happened very suddenly, but at least you know they did not abandon you. They would not want you to be sad for them.' She had hardly seemed aware of what he was saying, had stared straight ahead at a picture of a wood carpeted in bluebells on her bedroom wall, but it was nothing but a blur of blue and green. It was like losing Andrei and Tonya all over again. Why did she feel betrayed, as if they had all deliberately left her?

But the Simenovs were Russian, they were her link with her past, if only a tenuous one, and though she was shy with them at first, hearing them speak Russian and answering them in the same tongue was lovely. For the first time since coming to England she really came alive, smiling and chattering.

Alexei seemed to have shot up since she had last seen him on the fateful train journey to Yalta. He was dressed in a Norfolk jacket and long trousers and he had a stiff white collar on his shirt. His brown hair was slicked back from a centre parting and his dark intelligent eyes looked at her with something akin to pity, but she did not recognise it as such. 'I am learning Russian history and European languages,' he told Sir Edward and Lady Stoneleigh in confident English. 'Papa says it will be useful in years to come. When the Bolshevik regime collapses, I mean to go back to Russia.'

'Do you think it will collapse?' Sir Edward asked, humouring the boy.

'Oh, it is bound to. The Russian people will not tolerate it when they find it is not the paradise they have been led to believe.'

Edward smiled; the boy was obviously repeating something he had overheard. 'You think they have been misled?'

'Oh, without a doubt. It was a way to get them out of the war. They will come to their senses.'

'Let us hope so,' Lady Stoneleigh said. The baron's story of what he had learnt about the Kirilovs had finally convinced her that Edward had been telling the truth all along and she berated herself for ever doubting him. She felt happier than she had for months. 'The Communists are at the root of all the strikes we have been having. The thought of them taking over this country is terrifying.'

'It won't happen in England,' her husband told her. 'The English people are not so easily led by the nose.'

'Neither are the Russians,' Baron Simenov put in.

Lydia looked from one to the other in bewilderment. She had hardly understood a word, not because her vocabulary was poor, though that was part of it, but because what they were discussing was way above her head. 'Would you like to go for a walk?' she asked Alexei in Russian.

Alexei was not keen to be a baby-minder, but the look of appeal he gave his father was ignored.

'Yes, show the young man round,' Edward told Lydia, smiling at them both.

They slipped out of the house by the kitchen door,

after begging some stale crusts from the kitchen maid, and walked down to the lake. The ducks paddled towards them, expecting the titbits Lydia threw to them.

'This is a grand place,' Alexei said, watching the ducks squabbling over the bread. 'Do you like living here?'

'Yes, but I miss Papa and Mama and Andrei and Tonya.' Speaking their names made her gulp back tears.

'I am sorry about what happened to them,' he said, remembering what his father had told him when he asked him to be kind to the little girl. 'But try not to be sad.'

'I cannot help it.'

'No, I suppose not. But you are a great deal better off than a lot of Russian émigrés. They are finding life in England hard, not speaking English and needing to work. You have a good home here. Be thankful.'

That was something Claudia said to her every day but she wasn't quite sure what it meant. 'I wanted to see them again so much. Now I can't.'

'I understand. I would feel the same if I lost my parents.'

'Where do you live?'

'With my mother's cousins in Berkshire, but Papa is looking for a home for us in England. I go to an English boarding school.'

'Do you like it?'

'Oh, yes. It's great fun.'

'I don't like school. They laugh at me.'

'I'm sorry about that,' he said. 'But you must hold your head up and pretend you do not care. You are a little countess, remember that.'

'I will try.'

'You have to learn, you know, nothing is achieved

without learning. When I have finished my education, I intend to go back to Russia.'

'But Sir Edward said the bad men were everywhere.'

'You mean the Bolsheviks. They have to be overthrown.'

'What are Bolsheviks?'

'Communists. Reds. They believe everyone is equal and there should not be any tsar or counts or barons or anything like that. And no one must be rich or own property. They call each other "comrade" and won't have anyone addressed as "Excellency". They killed the tsar and all his family. That was why anyone with a title had to leave. Didn't you know that?'

'No.' She really did not understand but it was nice hearing him speak in Russian.

'Would you like to go back, one day, when the Reds are defeated?' he asked.

'Perhaps,' she said with a sigh, though if the baron was right, there was no one there to go back to. He had taken her on one side soon after they arrived and gently reiterated what Sir Edward had said. 'Sir Edward is a good man,' he had said. 'And I know he loves you and will look after you.' She loved Sir Edward without reservation and knew she must try and settle down in England now. If what they said was true, her old home was no more, Russia had changed, nothing would ever be the same, not the village or the *dacha* or the servants. Without Mama and Papa and Andrei, what was the point of going back? But it made her very sad.

'We have to grow up first,' Alexei said.

The crusts were all gone and the ducks, realising there were no more to be had, were swimming away. He took her hand and led her back to the house.

* * *

Growing up was sometimes hard, Lydia decided, as the years passed and she moved on from infant school to Upstone High School for Girls. Although she was an apt pupil and did well at her lessons, she always felt a little apart from her fellow pupils and students. It wasn't that she spoke with a Russian accent – that was soon eradicated – nor that she was unpopular, because she had many friends, though some of that might have been down to her privileged upbringing. No, it was her continuing feeling that she was Russian.

Finding himself having to field questions about her origins more and more often as she grew older and went about more, and thinking her statelessness might be a barrier in later life, Sir Edward decided to adopt her formerly and changed her name from Lydia Kirillova to Lydia Stoneleigh. He told her that he and Margaret were to be her new mama and papa. It was then he had confessed to bending the truth about her parents' deaths. 'They did not die in an accident,' he said, taking her hand and speaking softly. 'They were executed by the Bolsheviks. I didn't tell you before because you were upset enough about losing them without the added distress of the manner of their death. And I was not at all sure you would understand at that age. But you are entitled to know the truth. I hope you can forgive me.'

She was shocked and angry at first, not so much about her parents' death, which she had come to accept, but because he had taken away her birthright, her very Russian-ness, the person she believed herself to be, but what he had done was done out of love. She kissed his cheek. 'Of course, I forgive you.'

'I have been given this for you,' he said, handing her an old sepia photograph of a very aristocratic-looking lady in a long evening dress. She was wearing a heavy necklace and long earrings, and on her head a tiara, on the front of which sparkled the Kirilov Star. 'I believe the lady is your grandmother, the dowager Countess Kirillova.'

Lydia studied it carefully. She did not remember the lady, but she did remember the jewel. 'May I keep it?' she asked.

'Of course. It is yours. Would you like me to have it framed, then you can keep it in your bedroom?'

'Yes, please.' It was something tangible from her old life, something she could look at and touch to remind her of her roots.

Gradually Margaret's attitude towards the little waif changed, possibly because she knew she could never have a child of her own, and they became close. They went horse riding together and shopping for clothes. Margaret loved buying clothes and embraced all the latest fashions, and she loved dressing Lydia. They talked about her life at school, especially after she left the village school and went to the high school. They discussed what she would like to do when she grew up. The world, so Sir Edward said, was changing and women were no longer restricted in what they could do. She could be a doctor, a lawyer, a teacher, even stand for Parliament, if she so chose. Of course, she need not do anything; she could have a Season, be presented at court and wait for the right man to come along.

But she was still only fourteen and marriage was a long way from her mind. She was intent on going to college and studying the Russian language and Russian history. She needed to understand what had happened to her.

KOLYA

1937 – 1941

Chapter Four

'I want to talk to you about this,' her tutor said, tapping the essay Lydia had been asked to write about the causes of the Russian Revolution and why the Kerensky Government failed to halt the rise of the Bolsheviks in 1917, which led to the execution of the Romanovs and the Civil War. Lydia had spent an inordinate amount of time on it, drawing from stories she had heard from Sir Edward and Alexei, who frequently visited Upstone Hall, and her own very clouded memories of Kirilhor and the privations her family suffered there. Sir Edward's accounts were factual, couched in the words of a diplomat, but Alexei's were fiery and one-sided, which was hardly surprising since his father had returned to Russia once too often and been arrested and executed for spying after Stalin came to power in 1927. His mother had become frail because of it. 'We got out safely in 1920, why did he have to keep going back?' she had lamented on a visit to Upstone Hall.

The tutor was in his mid-thirties, a handsome man, a

good teacher. 'This is very interesting,' he said. 'How did you come to be so passionate about it? Have you ever been to Russia?'

'I was born there. My name was Lydia Mikhailovna Kirillova then. My father was Count Mikhail Kirilov. He and my mother were executed by the Bolsheviks. I have every reason to be passionate.'

'I'm sorry, I didn't know that. Is that why you decided to read Russian history?'

'Yes. I want to understand how it could have happened.'

'You will not understand if you only study one side of the argument. There is a lot to be said for Communism, you know.'

'I can't think what it can be. They take people's belongings without compensation and murder for no reason except fear of losing control. If they are so sure they are right, why do they have to execute people? My parents never did anyone any harm. In fact, they did a lot of good, employing people who would otherwise be out of work, making sure they were fed and housed and educating the children. When their assets were taken from them, they could no longer do that.'

'A lot of that is Western propaganda, you know. The freeing of the serfs did not change much; the rich still exploited the poor, which is neither fair nor just. The peasant is as much of a human being as the tsar and deserves better than that. Now the Communist state employs and feeds everyone.' He held up his hand to stop her interrupting. 'Oh, I know it is not the Utopia the purists want and there is a lot of putting right of old wrongs before that can happen, but it will come, you'll see.'

'And you think murder by the State is justified?' It was not only her parents' death in 1920 she was thinking of, but the arrests, trials and executions which had been taking place in Russia since Stalin came to power.

'In some cases, yes. We execute murderers and traitors in this country, don't we?'

'It's not the same. We do not kill innocent people.'

'In an ideal world no one would, but with so much evil to sweep away, there is bound to be a degree of injustice. It cannot be helped.'

She was becoming increasingly angry. 'My brother and nurse were killed by soldiers in front of my eyes. You call that sweeping away evil? It was horrible and senseless and I shall never forget it.'

'I am sorry for that, but do you know for sure who perpetrated the deed? They might have been bandits, there were a lot of those about. The Red Army was being blamed for everything, whether guilty or not. How much do you actually remember?'

'Very little, I was too shocked.'

'So you relied on what other people told you.'

'But I saw them die. Andrei fell across me, his blood was all over me.' She shuddered at the memory. 'It doesn't matter who did it.'

'If you want to separate what is true from what is false, you need to study both sides,' he said. 'I advise you to set aside your prejudice and be more even-handed, so that you can offer a reasoned and balanced treatise. You have exams coming up and I should not like you to fail.'

Lydia took the sheaf of papers and left the room, seething. It seemed she was not to have an opinion of her own. For two pins she would abandon the whole course.

After all, as a woman she was not going to be given a degree, even though her studies were on a par with the men's. They wouldn't have women in their colleges, and Girton had been built so far out of town, the ladies felt cut off from university life. A certificate to say she had done the study and passed the exams was all she could hope for. But she knew Papa would be disappointed if she walked out, so she had better grit her teeth and rewrite the essay. The result was a cold, dispassionate dissertation which made her feel a coward.

Lydia went home to Upstone Hall for the traditional Christmas, though it was both the same and somehow different. There was still much hardship after the severe depression earlier in the decade and the village did not seem to be the happy place it had once been. Or was it that now she was grown up, she saw things the child had missed? On the surface Sir Edward appeared to be his usual urbane self and Alexei, who joined them with his mother as usual, was charming and teasing – a kind of big brother, to whom she found it easy to confide – but underneath there seemed to be a heaviness about their conversation. The situation in Russia was worrying, though Lydia did not think it was that. It was as if Alexei had something on his mind he could not speak about, which had never happened before and puzzled her. When she asked him what was wrong he laughed and said, 'Nothing. What could possibly be wrong, here at Upstone?'

In early January, in wintry weather, she went back to college where the discussion centred around the abdication, which seemed to have stunned everyone. Opinion was divided. There were those who could not understand the king falling for a twice-divorced American fortune-hunter, who had threatened the very fabric of British life and tradition, and there were those of a romantic bent who applauded his decision to put love before duty. At least, Lydia thought with wry humour, no one was going to execute him as they had his kinsman, the tsar.

The coronation in May of George VI cheered everyone up. The new king did not have the charisma of his older brother but he had a strong sense of duty and a lovely family. Undeterred by the cold damp weather, crowds packed twenty-deep behind barriers in Trafalgar Square, to watch the glittering State Coach pass in procession. Many more listened to the broadcast on the wireless, an innovation which was a great success. A few who had television sets watched in their own homes, though the cameras were not allowed into the Abbey. Lydia, who had completed her final examinations, went up to London with some college friends to join the crowds. Her Russian roots were not forgotten, but she felt as British as anyone, cheering and waving a little Union Jack.

The following month she learnt that her hard work had paid off and she had been awarded what would have been considered a good degree if she had been a man, and she went home to Upstone with her certificate and no idea what she was going to do next.

Edward met her at Upstone station with the Bentley. He hugged her and then held her at arm's length. She was wearing a straight mid-calf-length skirt in deep blue, a silk blouse with ruffles down the front and two-tone shoes. On her chestnut-brown hair was a small pillbox hat set at an angle. It had a brooch pinned to the front of it. 'You look splendid,' he said. 'All grown-up. Not my little girl anymore.'

'I'll always be your little girl,' she said, as they walked out of the station arm in arm, with a porter bringing up the rear with her luggage on a trolley.

'Your mama has gone to one of her charity meetings but she will be back for tea,' he said, directing the stowing of the cases, the tennis racket and the box of books in the boot and on the back seat. Then he held the door open for her to settle in the passenger seat before walking round to get behind the wheel. He enjoyed driving and dispensed with the services of a chauffeur except when on official business. He was doing less and less of that now and was planning to retire in a year or two.

'What are you going to do with yourself now?' he asked as they pulled out of the station yard. 'Do you still want to be a translator? I could probably find you a niche somewhere.'

'I've been thinking about it, but I can't make up my mind.'

'There's plenty of time. A holiday first and your twenty-first birthday. Mama is planning a ball for you. A sort of come-out. That will be fun, don't you think?'

No one knew when her birthday actually was and so they had always celebrated it on the sixth of June. 'It's a lovely time of year for a birthday,' Margaret had said when she and Edward discussed it after she had been with them a few months and Margaret had come to accept her as part of the family. 'Long warm days when we can use the garden or go for a picnic.'

'It will be a lot of extra expense for you and Mama,' Lydia said, not really sure she wanted it. The country was only just coming out of the depression which had seen thousands out of work. Many still were. Poverty was everywhere and the twin evils, as she saw it, of Communism and Fascism were rife. And yet, she, who had seen horrors most British people could not even imagine, was cocooned from it by money and privilege. It made her feel guilty.

'But you are worth it, sweetheart. And I know Mama is really looking forward to it. She has already drawn up a guest list and put the preparations in hand.'

She chuckled. 'I must not disappoint Mama, must I?'

They both knew that Margaret was thoroughly spoilt and liked to have her own way, but as both loved her, they went along with whatever she wanted. It was a long time since she had objected to Lydia's presence in the house and she would probably have denied it if someone had reminded her.

The ball was the talking point of the village. Margaret was immersed in making the arrangements, hurrying about with lists. An orchestra was booked and the two largest reception rooms opened out for a ballroom and the carpets taken up. Since the war, they had had to manage with fewer servants, so temporary staff were called in to polish the floor, prepare the bedrooms for those guests who would be staying overnight, and to help with the catering. 'Mama, you will wear yourself to a frazzle,' Lydia said the day before the ball when everyone seemed to be at odds and the servants were falling over each others' feet. 'Do take a break. Let's go for a ride and blow the cobwebs away.'

Riding was Margaret's passion and the only thing likely to tear her away from the preparations. Lydia enjoyed it too and whenever she came home from Cambridge they would spend hours on horseback, roaming the Norfolk countryside she had come to love. It lacked the spectacular views of the Pennines, the Lakes and Scotland, but it had the Broads and the Fens, gently rolling countryside and wide, glorious skies. 'I loved Cambridge, but it is good to be home,' Lydia said, breathing deeply as they walked their horses towards the common.

'You really think of Upstone Hall as home now?' Margaret queried.

'Of course. I have done for a long time. Why did you ask?'

'I just wondered. When you first came to us you talked of nothing else but going home to Russia and I wondered if, now you are growing up, you might have started thinking about it again, especially as you have been studying it.'

'Sometimes I think about it, but it doesn't seem real anymore. It's like a dream. One day I might like to go on a visit, but that's a long way into the future.'

'It would not be safe. Papa is worried about what's happening in Germany too. He thinks Hitler is as bad as Stalin and there could be a war in Europe.'

'Oh, they talked a lot about it at Cambridge, especially among the men, who seemed to think it would be a great adventure. Do they never learn? War tears families apart.' She shuddered as a sudden glimpse of a droshky and bloodstained bodies clouded her vision. 'Let's not talk about it.' They had reached the edge of the common and she spurred her horse into a gallop. 'Come on, I'll race you to the oak tree.'

Margaret followed and the ugly memory was dissipated and they trotted back home refreshed and ready to tackle whatever problems cropped up.

On the day of the ball, a florist arrived in the morning to arrange the flowers, and after the last-minute instructions and a look round to see nothing had been forgotten, Margaret went to lie down before getting ready. Lydia went to her room too, but instead of lying down she sat at her window looking out on the park that surrounded the house. Every inch of it was known and loved. Here she was, at twenty-one, loved, cosseted and privileged. Others had not been so lucky. So why did she sometimes feel unsettled, as if there was something missing, something she ought to be searching for? Not her parents; they were long gone. Not Andrei and Tonya, whose deaths still haunted her dreams.

Was she twenty-one? The only evidence they had for that was her own declaration that she was four when she met Sir Edward in Yalta. How had she known that? Had she just turned four or was she nearer five? It felt strange not knowing when her birthday was. She supposed somewhere in Russia there was a record of it. Or had all the records been destroyed? She gave up musing and left her seat to go and run a bath. It was time to start getting ready.

Claudia, who had stayed on making herself useful in a dozen different ways for no other reason than she had nowhere else to go and Edward would not dismiss her, helped her dress. The gown, which had cost Edward a fortune, was of heavy cream silk embroidered with seed pearls. Without a distinguishable waist, it was cleverly cut to emphasise the slimness of her figure. Its back was very low and had a train which she could loop up on a catch at her wrist for dancing. Claudia helped her with her hair which was swept up in a chignon and fastened with two glittering combs, a present from Mama. She put a pearl necklace about her throat, slipped into her shoes and went down to the small parlour where Edward and Margaret waited.

Margaret was in a soft dove-grey crêpe dress and Edward in immaculate tie and tails. She entered the room demurely, smiling. 'Will I do?'

'Beautiful,' her father said, coming forward to take both her hands. 'Absolutely stunning – isn't that what the young bloods would say?'

She laughed. 'I'm very nervous.'

'No need to be, you will be the belle of the ball, as is only right and proper.' He turned from her to reach for a jewellery box from the mantelpiece. 'This is already yours,' he said. 'I have kept it safely for you, but now I have had it made so that you can wear it.' He opened the box and took out the Kirilov Star, adapted and hung on a silver chain so that she could wear it as a necklace. The central diamond sparkled in the light from the electric chandelier above her head and all the smaller diamonds in its points glistened like drops of water.

Another of her fleeting memories came to her of her mother sitting at a table in tears, sewing it into her petticoat, and her father taking her on his knee and gruffly telling her she was the star of the Kirilovs. She thrust the recollection from her and turned dutifully at Edward's command so that he could take the pearls from her throat and replace it with the necklace. 'There!' he said as she turned back to him. 'All yours now. Wear it with pride for what you were and what you have become.'

'It's lovely,' she said, fingering it. 'I didn't know you still had it.'

'I could never part with the Kirilov Star,' he said. 'Neither the jewel, nor the child.'

'Oh, Papa,' she said, throwing her arms about him. 'I do love you.' She turned to Margaret and embraced her too.

'You are so good to me. I sometimes wonder what I have done to deserve it.'

'Just been yourself,' Edward said, embarrassed. 'Go on being that. Now, I think we had better go into the hall to receive our guests.'

There were more than a hundred of them: distant relations of Sir Edward and Margaret, family friends from far and wide, Lydia's school friends and others she had met in Cambridge, people from the diplomatic corps, a few displaced Russians with whom Edward had kept in touch, the vicar and the doctor and Alexei, all dressed in their finest, come to wish her well, all bringing gifts. It was exciting and slightly out of this world, a dream from which she might wake and find herself . . . where? Back in a droshky in a snowy forest or crammed into a freight wagon with hundreds of others? Watching her weeping mother sew? It was strange how those visions kept coming back to her now, clearer than they had ever been. It was as if her traumatised body had shut them out at first, refused to acknowledge recollections that were too painful to bear, and only years later released them, as if saying, 'Yes, you are stronger now. Now you can face them. You should not forget. It is part of what you are.'

Edward partnered her for the first dance but after that Alexei claimed her. Since the death of his father in Russia, Edward had taken him under his wing, though he really did not need it. He had become a tall, handsome man, popular with everyone, though there was a serious side to his nature that perhaps only Lydia and Sir Edward understood. His mother had died the year Lydia went to Cambridge – of a broken heart, he had said. Since then he had become a naturalised British subject, taking the name of Alex Peters, easily able to pass himself off as an Englishman. He was completely self-assured.

Lydia was very fond of him, had been ever since she had taken him to feed the ducks and he had been kind to a lonely, frightened little girl. He was a presence in her life, not an especially frequent one, but a stable one, someone she knew instinctively she could lean on if need be. He was practical and down to earth, the only one who could curb her more exotic flights of fancy and cheer her up when she felt pulled down by her memories. He understood.

'You are looking ravishing,' he said, as they waltzed. 'I would hardly know the little waif I met in Simferopol.'

She laughed. 'The waif is still there, underneath.'

'You would never know it. All this . . .' He moved his head to indicate the room, the dancers, the orchestra, the heady scent of hothouse flowers. 'All this for a little waif.'

'I do realise how privileged I am,' she said. 'Others were not half so fortunate. I should like to do something to help them. Surely there is a way of tracing their relatives and perhaps bringing some of their assets out of Russia?'

'That was what my father was trying to do and he paid for it with his life.'

'I'm sorry, I should not have reminded you.'

They were silent for a minute or two and concentrated on their dancing, each thinking of the past – unhappy, disjointed, another time, another world. And then he suddenly shook himself as if shaking off a cloak. 'Are your studies all finished now?'

'Yes. I have the equivalent of a degree, but I can't call it a degree. It's not fair, is it? I bet I worked just as hard as you did to get your BA.'

'I've no doubt you did.' He whirled her round. 'But times are changing. Your day will come.'

'I want to be useful, so I am thinking of taking work as a translator. Do you think I should?'

'My dear Lidushka, it's no good asking me. You must go where your heart leads you.'

Prophetic words, she decided later.

'I don't have to make my mind up just yet. We are going to Paris for a holiday in a couple of weeks.'

'And is there a young man waiting in the wings?'

'Oh, lots of them,' she said lightly, oblivious of the intensity of his question.

'But no one special?'

'No one special. I've been too busy getting an education. What about you? Anyone special?'

'No,' he said quietly. 'I, too, have been busy carving out a career for myself in the diplomatic service.'

'Have you ever thought about going back to Russia?' she asked, as the dance came to an end and they left the floor.

'That, my dear little Countess, would be the height of folly. The Russia we knew has gone for ever.'

He did not tell her that he had been back because he had been sworn to secrecy. Nor did he tell her that the regime under Stalin was worse than it had been after the Civil War, that almost everyone, particularly the intelligentsia, waited for the knock on the door in the middle of the night when they were hauled off to prison and sentenced to death or years in a labour camp for being an 'enemy of the people' or not being 'sufficiently vigilant', for which little proof was needed. A simple denunciation was enough. Out of loyalty to the Party, or greed, or jealousy, neighbour was denouncing neighbour, sons and daughters were denouncing fathers, wives their husbands. It had become a cult of fear. It was an omission he would come bitterly to regret.

He delivered her back to Edward and Margaret and others came to ask her to dance and he did not see her again until they went into supper, when Edward asked him to join them.

'Lydia tells me she is thinking of becoming a translator,' he said to Edward, as they enjoyed a lavish meal.

'It is one of her ideas,' Edward said, smiling. 'I don't think she knows what she wants.'

'She doesn't have to do anything,' Margaret put in. 'She can stay here with us until she marries. I am sure that won't be long.'

Lydia laughed. 'I'm not ready for marriage yet, I want to live a little first. Besides, I haven't met anyone I want to marry.'

Alex was not sure whether to be pleased or sorry about that. The little waif he had befriended was long gone and been replaced by a lovely woman, spoilt and yet not spoilt, whom he loved. The trouble was she was not aware of it and he would not tell her. He had nothing much to offer her. The money his mother had managed to bring out of Russia had soon been used up, and like so many others, he had been obliged to work for a living. He owed his present job at the Foreign Office to Sir Edward. He was thankful they paid him well and in time he would be in a position to marry, but the job he was doing could be dangerous and it would not be fair to Lydia to ask her to share his life. Besides, she must be allowed to make up her own mind about the man she married and he was perfectly aware she looked on him as a kind of older brother.

He escorted her back to the ballroom after supper and

claimed another dance before relinquishing her to others: lively, confident young men who knew their place in the world. He watched her treating them with smiling courtesy, listening to their compliments with her head cocked on one side, intent on what they were saying. By the end of the evening more than one was sighing after her.

When the last waltz was over, everyone, except those who had come some distance and were staying the night, made preparations to leave. Lydia stood beside Edward and Margaret, wishing them goodnight and thanking them for their gifts. Then she looked round for Alex, but he was nowhere to be seen. She said goodnight to everyone else and made her way to her bedroom. The evening had gone off without a hitch and she was tired and happy and a little tipsy on champagne. But it was too bad of Alex to disappear like that; she would have liked to mull it all over with him and talk to him about his gift of Tolstoy's *War and Peace* in the original Russian. She wondered if it was a message to her not to forget her roots.

She went with her parents to Paris for the last two weeks in June, taking the train to Dover and then the ferry to Calais, where Edward hired a car and drove them to Paris and the Hôtel St-Germain-des-Prés on the Rue Bonaparte. It was warm and sunny and their days were filled with sightseeing, visiting museums and exhibitions, and going to concerts and the theatre. And when they weren't doing that she and Margaret shopped for clothes at the best couturiers, until both were exhausted and Lydia began to wonder how they would get everything into their trunks for the return journey.

Paris was home to a great many Russian émigrés who tended to congregate in the area of the 15th arrondissement. Most of them were educated, former aristocrats, bourgeoisie, skilled workers, poets and writers, but few were wealthy enough to support themselves without work and had been obliged to take menial jobs in order to survive. But they maintained their own culture. They had their magazines, publishers, theatre companies, dance troupes, schools and churches. When Margaret was resting in the afternoons, Lydia would wander about those streets, listening to Russian being spoken and daydreaming of finding her parents there, safe and well. She even approached groups of women and asked if they had heard anything of a Count Kirilov or his wife, to which the answer was always a shake of the head and a muttered 'sorry'.

One day, after a particularly long walk, she found a small park and sat down on a bench to rest. One shoe was hurting her foot and she kicked it off, rubbing her toes up and down her other calf. She did not notice the small dog until it had her shoe in its mouth and run off with it. She shouted and began limping after it, but could not catch it.

A young man noticed her predicament, caught the dog and retrieved her shoe which he presented to her with a half-mocking bow and a broad smile.

'Thank you,' she said, hobbling back to the bench to slip it on again. 'I did not fancy walking back to my hotel in stockinged feet.'

He was blond and blue-eyed with rather appealing boyish features, probably older than he looked. 'No, your stocking would be in ribbons and so would your foot. Such a pretty foot too.' He sat beside her, fetched a cigarette packet from his pocket and offered her one. She shook her head. He lit one for himself and sat back to smoke it. 'Whew, it's hot today,' he said.

'Yes, but I don't mind it.' She was wearing a lilac silk dress, loosely tied on her hips with a sash. A large brimmed straw hat shielded her face.

'On holiday, are you?'

'Yes, are you?'

'No, I live here.'

'But you are Russian.' Although they had been speaking in French, she had recognised his accent.

'What makes you say that?'

'Your accent.'

He laughed. 'Since the Bolsheviks took away my family's citizenship and France decided to recognise the Soviet Union, I am stateless. But yes, you could say I was Russian. What about you? In the same boat, are you?'

'No, I was adopted by an Englishman and his wife, so I am English now.'

'But you were Russian once?'

'Yes. My father was Count Mikhail Kirilov.'

He whistled. 'Wow. A count. What's your name now?'

'Lydia Stoneleigh. My father is Sir Edward Stoneleigh.'

He held out his hand. 'How do you do, Lydia Stoneleigh. I am Nikolay Nikolayevich Andropov.'

She turned to take his hand. 'How do you do, Monsieur Andropov.'

'Oh, please, let us have it the Russian way. Nikolay Nikolayevich, if you please. Or Kolya, if you like.'

'How long have you been in France?'

'Since the end of the Civil War. My father was in the White Army and was killed by the Reds.'

'My father was in the army too. He and my mother

were killed by the Bolsheviks. My brother and nurse were murdered. I was the only one who survived. I came out with Sir Edward in 1920.'

He smiled. 'You could not have been very old.'

'I was four.'

'Do you remember anything of it?'

So she told him all she could remember.

'How interesting,' he said when she finished. 'Our lives have run almost parallel, though I am two years older than you are.'

'Yet you have retained your accent.'

'That is because I have lived among exiled Russians all my life and we continue to speak Russian. I should think you have forgotten it.'

'No, I kept it up and studied Russian and Russian history at college. I am thinking of becoming a translator.'

'They are ten a penny in Paris. So many Russians who need to earn a living are doing that as an easy option. It is better than waiting at table in some sleazy restaurant, or cleaning floors, or portering on the railways.'

'Is that what you do? Translating, I mean.'

'No. I am a poet.'

'And do you make money at it?'

He laughed in an embarrassed way. 'I get by.'

'I must be going back. Mama will be wondering where I have got to.' She stood up and held out her hand. 'Goodbye, Nikolay Nikolayevich. It was nice to have met you.'

He stood up beside her, slightly taller than she was. 'I'll walk you back to your hotel. We can talk some more as we go.'

She knew she ought to discourage him, but she wanted to learn more about the Russians who had been forced to leave their mother country and how they had survived. She had always known she had been lucky, but as he talked, slipping into Russian, she realised just how lucky. Some of her countrymen had been destitute when they arrived in the West, and because there were so many of them, they were not welcomed. The native Parisians, as many English people had been, were suspicious of them, believing there were Bolshevik spies among them. He was still talking when they reached the hotel.

She turned to shake hands with him again. He took it and squeezed her fingers with a gentle pressure that shocked and excited her. 'Do you go to the park often?' he asked.

'Sometimes in the afternoon when my mother is having a nap. She is not strong. Papa is a diplomat and is combining our holiday with meetings at the embassy.'

'Then go again tomorrow. I will be there.'

It was after their third meeting that she plucked up courage to tell her parents about him. They were horrified. 'But darling, you don't know a thing about him,' Margaret said. 'He could be anyone. You do not know he is telling the truth. He might be a Bolshevik spy.'

'But he isn't,' she said. 'His father was killed just as mine was. And I could not refuse to speak to him when he had rescued my shoe, could I?'

'I think we had better meet him,' Edward said. 'Bring him back to tea tomorrow.'

And so Kolya came to tea. He behaved impeccably, answered all Edward's questions openly and without hesitation, and at the end of the visit bowed stiffly to them all and asked if he might take Lydia to the ballet the next evening.

'I think we will all go,' Edward said, unwilling to let her go unchaperoned.

It was only after he had left and Lydia had gone up to her room to change for dinner that Edward told his wife he was not at all happy about this turn of events. 'I must check up on him,' he said. 'I have no idea how he makes a living but I am prepared to bet it isn't writing poetry.'

'You cannot fault his manners,' she said.

'Manners can be learnt and I have no doubt he is clever enough to realise what we would expect of any young man making friends with our daughter. She would be quite a trophy for him, wouldn't she?'

'She is going to meet young men, Edward, you cannot stop that. And she is very sensible.'

'I hope so. I had hoped Alex . . .'

She laughed. 'Oh, Edward, you cannot make something happen if it is not destined.'

'No, I know.'

In the event it was Edward who paid for the tickets for the ballet and the supper afterwards. Kolya, in white tie and tails, behaved with just the right amount of diffidence and assurance. Lydia, who had wanted to impress him, wore her cream silk with the train taken off, and the Kirilov Star. She did not notice him staring at it, nor the stiffness in Edward's conversation. At the end of the evening, they delivered him back to his lodgings in La Ruche, a collection of small apartments and studios arranged round an octagonal wine hall where many Russian émigrés made their home. She only saw him once more before they returned to England.

'I wish you were staying longer,' he said when they met

108

in a small bistro near his home. 'I am only just beginning to get to know you.'

'I know. I am sorry too, but all good things must come to an end. Papa has to work and I have to find a job.'

'You have to work? Surely not. Sir Edward is loaded. I should think those rocks you had round your neck last night would keep you in comfort for years.'

'I could never sell that. It is a Kirilov heirloom.'

'Oh. Sir Edward didn't give it to you, then?'

'No, I brought it out of Russia sewn in my petticoat. We all had jewels sewn into our clothes. That was the reason my parents were executed, because they were trying to get assets out of the country, or so I was told.'

He did not comment, but kissed her, firmly and expertly, setting up a quivering in her body that she had never experienced before. She had been kissed by boyfriends in an experimental way while at Cambridge, but had never reacted like that. It was frightening and exciting at the same time. 'Will you write to me?' he asked. 'I don't want this to be goodbye.'

'Yes, if you like.'

They returned home next day and a couple of weeks later Edward secured a post for Lydia as a translator at the Foreign Office. She was at the very bottom of the hierarchy and nothing she was given to translate was in any way secret, simply translating articles in *Pravda*, the Soviet newspaper, and others like it. Edward warned her not to speak about her work, however mundane it seemed to be.

She lived at their Balfour Place apartment just off Mount Street, looking after herself. The housekeeper had left and Edward had not thought it necessary to hire another; he rarely came to London since he had retired. When not at work, she enjoyed a busy social life. At Cambridge she had joined several groups and societies and had made many friends, some whose heads were filled with ideological nonsense, but they were good fun and she had kept in touch with them, meeting those who had gravitated to the capital for visits to the theatre or the ballet, or simply for coffee in one of the cafés. She enjoyed the cut and thrust of their debate.

There was plenty to debate about: the progress of the Spanish Civil War; Japan's attack on China; the visit of the Duke and Duchess of Windsor to Germany, where they were made welcome by Hitler. It did not go down well with the British public at a time when everyone was worrying about a war with Germany. Lydia worried about that because she knew Alex was in Germany.

He did not join them at Upstone Hall that Christmas, but sent her a huge card and a lovely multicoloured evening shawl in a soft gauze. She missed him, as did Edward and Margaret, who had come to look on him as one of the family. They went to church, sang carols, exchanged presents, ate and drank too much. The day after Boxing Day Lydia returned to London and her job.

She had hardly got in the door and taken off her coat when the doorbell rang. She went to answer it to find Kolya standing on the landing with a suitcase at his feet. 'Kolya, what on earth are you doing here?' she asked in surprise.

'That's a fine greeting, when I have thrown caution to the winds to come and see you,' he said, pretending to be aggrieved. 'Aren't you pleased to see me?'

'Of course I am. But why didn't you let me know you were coming?'

'It was a sudden decision, one of those spur-of-the-moment things.' He picked up his case and followed her into the apartment where he stood looking round him. 'Wow! This beats La Ruche into a cocked hat. Is it yours?'

'My father's.'

'Is he here now?'

'No, he's at Upstone Hall. He's retired so he doesn't come to town so often now.'

He seemed to relax visibly, put his case down and took off his overcoat, shaking off a few flakes of snow on the carpet. She took it from him to hang it up. 'Sheer luxury,' he said. 'You don't know how lucky you are.'

She had never taken much notice of the flat but now she saw it with his eyes. The thick carpets, heavy curtains, fine furniture and beautiful ornaments screamed wealth. 'On the contrary, I do know,' she said. 'Have you eaten?'

'I had a sandwich at Dover. Terrible crossing it was. And then to find you not at home was the last straw. The janitor said you were expected back this evening, so I've been sitting in the café round the corner waiting for you to put in an appearance.'

'Serves you right for not letting me know.' She led the way into the kitchen. 'I'll see what I can rustle up.'

'No servants?'

'Not here. There is no need. I am perfectly capable of producing a simple meal. Or we could go out to eat.'

'No, let's stay in.'

So she made them omelettes and opened a bottle of wine and they sat over it talking into the small hours, when it became too late for him to find a hotel. She made a bed up for him in the spare room. Whether that was what he had in mind, she did not allow herself to conjecture.

* * *

111

Kolya had made no arrangements about where he was going to stay, something she realised was typical of him. He seemed not to consider what the morrow might bring and took it for granted she would continue to house him. It was part of his charm and she was charmed. She had no idea what he did when she was at work, nor how he supported himself. Sometimes he was in funds and would take her out for a meal and a show and buy her costly presents, at other times he professed to be broke and borrowed off her. She supposed it was all to do with selling his poetry and, as money had never been an issue in her life, she did not mind it.

He had a great sense of fun and laughed a lot and swore he loved her to distraction, though she would not allow him to do anything more than kiss her. Even that was enough to set her pulse racing. She had been brought up to believe sex was for after you were married and had always held off any too amorous advances by the young men she knew. It had not been difficult because none had roused her to anything like passion. Her feelings for Kolya were different and entirely new to her and she was not sure how to deal with them. She wondered if she might be falling in love with him. She certainly said nothing to her parents and Kolya always managed to be absent on the few occasions when Sir Edward paid a visit. Her friends, to whom she introduced him, assumed they were living together. She had a feeling that it might end up that way, or he would tire of her continual refusal to let him make love to her and take himself off. Would she overcome her scruples to keep him or let him go? As the question had not yet arisen she let it lie.

The Civil War still raged in Spain and many of her friends

were discussing joining the mercenaries, but Kolya, who had become part of the group, was against going himself. 'Their cause is not our cause,' he said, referring to himself and Lydia. 'Our cause is in Russia.'

Stalin's purge of those who opposed him in a great wave of show trials was reported in the papers Lydia translated. They were accused of being members of counter-revolutionary groups, or of acts designed to overthrow, undermine or weaken the authority of the workers' and peasants' soviets. She was shocked by the numbers, but as they had all confessed, she had no way of knowing how guilty they really were. She discussed it with Kolya, one warm evening in June when they were sitting on the balcony listening to a concert on the wireless. Below them the hum of traffic and the distant barking of a dog served as a backdrop.

'Whether they are guilty or not is neither here nor there,' he said. 'It's Stalin's way of eliminating opposition. People who were once in favour are now not to be tolerated.'

'Does it mean that those who executed my parents are themselves being executed?'

'Possibly, but how can you be sure they were executed?' he countered. 'Have you ever been given proof?'

'No, but Papa asked a Russian friend to make enquiries and he had access to information other people didn't and he told us they had been shot.'

'He might have been misinformed.'

She had never thought of that. 'But if my parents had not died, they would have tried to trace me.'

'How do you know they did not? They might be alive and believing you dead. Have you ever considered that?'

'No.' She was shocked. 'Do you think it's possible?'

'The situation in 1920 was so confused it easily could be. After all, there are still stories going round that some of the tsar's family survived, and if them, why not yours? They might have been sent to prison and not executed, and in that case they might have served their term and been released.'

She was thoughtful. Was that the reason for the slight uneasiness with her life? Was that why she had a feeling of incompleteness, as if she ought to be doing something, a kind of sin of omission? Was Kolya putting into words something that had been simmering in the back of her mind for years? 'How can I find out for sure? Would the Russian authorities tell me?'

'I doubt it. And if the count and countess are living incognito somewhere, they would not thank you for drawing attention to them, would they?'

'I suppose not.'

'So where would they go, if they were free?'

'I don't know. Probably Kirilhor. It was the last place we were all together, but it was such a long time ago and they would have been told what happened to me and Andrei.'

'Not necessarily. Ivan Ivanovich might not have made it back to Kirilhor and he was the only one in Russia who knew you had escaped.'

'I never thought of that.'

'Had it ever occurred to you, sweetheart, that Sir Edward might have lied to you, taken advantage of the situation to get him a child, knowing his wife could never have one?'

'No, of course not,' she said hotly. 'If they'd wanted to adopt a child, they could have had an English child through a proper adoption society. Why take a little Russian waif who was so shocked she could not speak?'

'All the better. She wouldn't have kicked up a fuss when he took her, especially if he told her he was taking her to be reunited with her parents.'

'Kolya, that is a shocking thing to say.' She was indignant, but she did remember everyone at the time – Ivan Ivanovich, Tonya's father, Alex's father and Sir Edward – saying just that. 'Papa is an honourable man, he would never do such a thing.'

'Papa! Papa!' he mocked. 'You have truly been indoctrinated, haven't you? Sir Edward is not your father. Alive or dead, your father is in Russia and the only way to find out what happened to him is to go to Russia yourself.'

She laughed a little shakily because he was undermining all she had grown up to believe and it was an uncomfortable feeling. 'They'd never let me in. I am, or was, Lydia Kirillova, the daughter of a count.' It was the first time she had thought of herself in that way for years, not since becoming Lydia Stoneleigh. Perhaps she had been too complacent about it. Perhaps she should have remembered that more often.

'I don't see why not. You've got a British name and a British passport, haven't you?'

'You *are* joking,' she said, laughing.

'Perhaps, perhaps not. We could go as tourists. It might be fun.'

'We?'

'I couldn't let you go alone and I wouldn't mind seeing what the Bolsheviks have done to poor Mother Russia. So, what do you say?'

'Kolya, it's impossible. Tourists are escorted everywhere and have to have their itinerary vetted. It would be the sights of Moscow and Leningrad and then only what they want you to see.'

'I know, but we could give our minders the slip and take a train to Kirilhor, couldn't we?'

She stared at him. 'You mean it, don't you?'

'Yes.'

'But you'd no more be allowed into the country with your background than I would.'

'I wouldn't have that background, would I? I can invent something else. I could be a Party faithful. Some of my Paris friends have gone back and they tell me they've had no problems. If they invited us to stay we wouldn't have to stick with the tour.'

She did not ask how he had made contact with them. He could have been meeting people in London. 'How did they travel?'

'I've no idea.'

'Oh, you're impossible,' she said, throwing a cushion at him.

Darkness had fallen and the evening was turning chilly. They went back inside and made cocoa before going to their separate beds. Nothing more was said about returning to Russia, but Lydia could not sleep for reliving the conversation in her mind. Russia. Kirilhor. Mama and Papa. Beautiful Mama, handsome Papa, both of whom had loved her and tried to protect her. Could they possibly be alive? Would they be grieving for a child they thought they had lost? Had Sir Edward done all he could to find out the truth? Had she been lied to? The questions went round and round in her head, unanswered, unanswerable.

Chapter Five

Three weeks later, when she arrived home from work, she was greeted by a jubilant Kolya. 'I've got them,' he said, waving a sheaf of papers at her and grinning broadly. 'An invitation from my friend to visit and entry permits to go to Russia. It's all here.'

'You're never going?' She kicked off her shoes and went into the kitchen in stockinged feet to put a kettle on to make tea.

He followed her. 'Yes. That's what you want, isn't it?'

'Me?'

'Yes, you're coming with me.'

'Don't be silly, Kolya. My father wouldn't hear of me going.'

'Then don't tell him. You can write to him after we've left.'

'I couldn't do that.'

'Why not? The only way to find out if he has deceived you is to go to Russia and see for yourself.' He put the

117

papers on the table and went up to her to take her shoulders in his hands and look earnestly into her face, his blue eyes alight with excitement, unable to comprehend that, for her, going to Russia was something so momentous she found the concept difficult to grasp. And yet something was pulling at her heart strings, something she found hard to deny. 'You do want to go, don't you?'

'Yes, but . . .'

'Oh, don't let us have buts,' he said. 'I thought you'd be pleased.'

'I would be under normal circumstances, but to go secretly . . .'

'We aren't going secretly. Haven't I just said? It's all open and above board. Besides, sweetheart, I don't want to go without you. I need you.'

'How can I go?' The kettle whistled. She warmed the pot, put two teaspoons of tea leaves in it and poured the boiling water onto them. 'I have no papers and I wouldn't be given any.'

He grinned. 'You have got papers. I have them here, for Lydia Stoneleigh, to accompany me.'

She stared at him. 'How could you, Kolya? How could you assume—?'

'I assumed nothing but I knew you would dither and dither if I asked you first, so I decided to present you with a fait accompli.'

'But we aren't married and it wouldn't be right . . .'

'No, but we could be.'

She gave a brittle laugh. 'Nikolay Andropov, is that a proposal?'

'Yes.' He gave her shoulders a little shake. 'Lidushka, you know I adore you, don't you? I want to make you happy. I want to help you put the past to rest so that we can go forward together. We cannot do that if you are dragging ghosts behind you.'

Ghosts. Was that what was troubling her? She began to waver. His enthusiasm was infectious. Obstacles, in his book, were there to be swept away. If you wanted something badly enough it was attainable. How badly did she want to explore her roots? 'But it would mean leaving my life here behind me.'

'Not for good. We will come back. Please, Lydia, darling, sweetheart, love of my life, say you will.'

In the face of such an onslaught, how could she hold out? 'When?'

'You will? Oh, happy, happy me!' He pulled her into his arms and smothered her with kisses. He would have gone further than just kissing and began fiddling with the buttons on her blouse, but she pulled away. 'Hold on!' she said, laughing. 'It hasn't happened yet.'

Reluctantly he desisted. 'Sorry. I'll be good until we're married, but it will have to be quick. I want to go next week.'

'Kolya, I can't arrange things that quickly, you know that. I have to tell my parents and Mama will want to do everything properly.'

'You don't have to tell them. You are twenty-two and they are not your real parents. I thought the whole idea of going to Russia was to find the couple who gave you birth.' He laughed suddenly. 'Let's get married in Moscow.'

He had a mesmeric quality about him she found impossible to deny, perhaps because what he was offering was something she had subconsciously wanted for years. Not marriage, she had hardly given that a thought, but the opportunity to go to Russia and find out the truth. Did she want to marry him? He was fun and made her limbs ache when he was kissing her and it was with the greatest difficulty she had managed to hold him off, not only because he was so ardent, but because of her own weakness where he was concerned. And he must love her, if he could be so patient with her. 'All right,' she said.

He hugged her. 'All you have to do is pack. I must go and book seats on the train.' And he was gone, leaving her with a pot full of tea, wondering what on earth she had done.

By the time they arrived in Moscow, in squally, chilly rain, after more than a week on a succession of trains through Germany and Poland, she was so tired and bemused all she wanted to do was sleep. Her study of pictures and maps did not prepare her for the dreariness of the place, notwithstanding that many of the buildings were new and the new arterial roads extraordinarily wide. Everywhere there were signs of change: roadworks, old buildings being pulled down, new ones built. She saw ragged children, *babushkas* in patterned cotton dresses and shapeless cardigans with the elbows out, butchers standing beside their trucks hacking meat from carcasses with bloody axes, fashionably dressed women and men in smart suits. She could not help noticing the huge contrast between the rich and the poor; neither seemed to notice the existence of the other.

Kolya took her to the Savoy Hotel, which was nothing like the Savoy in London. The accommodation was poor and the food worse. 'Never mind,' he said. 'We'll only be here a couple of days, just long enough to get married and for me to meet my friend. Then we'll make tracks for Crimea.'

'Aren't I going to meet him?'

'No, better not.' He went to the door and looked along the corridor and, apparently satisfied, returned to her. 'You have to be careful,' he said in a low voice. 'Even the walls have ears.'

'Kolya, what's going on?' She was whispering now. 'What's this friend of yours done?'

'He's a kulak and Stalin is afraid of the kulaks.'

'Why? They are only a superior kind of peasant with more money than most. I thought most of them were eliminated when the collective farms were set up.'

'Not all, some were simply dispossessed and sent to the labour camps and some of those have returned home. My friend belongs to a secret organisation preparing a kulak uprising. It's very powerful and growing rapidly.'

'I never heard of them.'

He laughed. 'They would hardly advertise their existence in *Pravda*, would they?'

'No, I suppose not. You don't belong to them, do you?'

He laughed. 'No. I am a loyal Party man, you saw my application to travel.'

She knew the information on that had been a fabrication. 'How long will you be gone?'

'Only an hour or two. You wait here for me.'

She wondered afterwards why she had not asked more questions, but then it would not have made any difference; the die was cast and there was no going back. Behind her she had left a letter to her parents, explaining why she felt she had to go, reaffirming her love for them and promising to write regularly. How had she come to be so unfeeling and ungrateful?

121

It filled her with remorse every time she thought about it and she wished she had discussed the huge step with them first. But they would only have tried to dissuade her and she hated arguments, especially with those she loved. She could have said something to Alex but he was out of the country, and in any case, he would be bound to side with Sir Edward.

If she had imagined getting married in Moscow would involve a religious ceremony, she should have known better. Most of the cathedrals and churches had either been destroyed or turned into warehouses, and getting married meant they both had to stand in line to book a time at the Civil Registration Bureau, known to the Russians as the Palace of Weddings. Having done that, they returned two days later for the ceremony, which could hardly be called a ceremony and all it did was confirm the legal status of their union. It was far from the wedding of her dreams; instead of a white wedding gown with a long train and a veil held by orange blossom, she was dressed in a light wool skirt and jumper and a raincoat. Instead of friends and family wishing her well there was only a dour registrar. Leaving the building hand in hand with her new husband, she didn't feel married at all, even though she had his ring on her finger. He was cock-a-hoop and bought caviar and cheap champagne which they took to their room.

'Well, Lydia Andropova,' he said, when she was more than half tipsy. 'Tonight is our wedding night and I have been a patient man, don't you think?'

'Yes,' she murmured, consumed with nerves.

'Then you will not mind if I make up for lost time.' And

with that he picked her up, deposited her on the bed and fell on her.

The next morning, sore and more than a little disillusioned, she followed him to the railway station and boarded a train for Crimea. Unlike the train in which she and her parents and brother had travelled in 1918, this one did have seats and it was possible to buy food from *babushkas* with baskets of fruit and bread whenever the train stopped at a wayside station. After they changed trains at Kiev, the countryside seemed to be one vast wheat field, the result of Stalin's collectivisation policy. This was Crimea, this was where her roots were, and as they rattled through the countryside, going further and further south, she began to wonder just what was ahead of her.

By the time she found herself standing beside Kolya at the station at Petrovsk, with their cases at their feet, she was a bundle of nerves. He didn't seem to notice. 'Well, here we are,' he said, picking up the cases and leading the way out of the station building into the street, where he hailed a battered Lada which was apparently a taxicab. The driver did not think it was any part of his duty to help with the luggage, so Kolya loaded it into the boot himself.

Lydia sat in the car looking about her while this was happening, trying to recognise the place. Everything seemed more run-down than her childish memory had painted it. There was a huge new apartment block next to the station, built to house the families sent from other parts of Russia to work the fields. The recent famine had decimated the local population. The church at the end of the street had lost its dome and the windows were boarded up. As they rattled along the main street, she caught sight of the school and that seemed not to have changed.

Kirilhor, when they reached it, shocked her. It looked derelict. The paint was peeling off and half the windows were broken. One end of the building seemed to be falling down. The garden which her mother had been at such pains to cultivate was overgrown. It didn't seem habitable.

But it was. As they drew to a stop, the door was opened and several small children ran out, screaming and chasing each other. They stopped and stared when they saw the car. Lydia got out, making them stare even harder. She smiled at them. 'Do you live here?'

They nodded shyly.

'Where is your mama?'

They pointed to the house. 'In the kitchen.'

'Will you fetch her, please?'

Giggling, they ran to obey.

'This is terrible,' Kolya said, curling his lip in disgust. 'I thought we were coming to a considerable *dacha*.'

'So it was. Once.'

A woman in a long black skirt and a white blouse emerged from the house, wiping her hands on her apron. 'What can I do for you, comrade?' she asked, speaking to Kolya.

'We are looking for anyone who knew Mikhail Mikhailovich Kirilov,' he said.

'Never heard of him.'

'It would be before the Revolution,' Lydia put in. 'He was my father.'

'Still can't help you. We've only been here eighteen months. You had better ask Grigori Stefanovich. He might know, he's lived here a long time.'

'Where can I find him?'

'He'll be back when he finishes work. Do you want to come in and wait for him?'

Lydia indicated she would and they were led through the house to the kitchen where three women were vying with each other for the use of the cooking stove. 'This is . . .' she started, then turned to Lydia. 'What's your name?'

'Lydia Andropova. This is my husband, Nikolay Nikolayevich Andropov.'

'And I am Sofia Borisovna.' She pointed to the other women in turn. 'That's Svetlana, Grigori Stefanovich's wife. That's Katya Ivanova Safanova, and over there, Olga Denisovna Nahmova. They work night shift in the tractor factory.' Lydia and Kolya greeted them and shook their hands.

'Sit down,' Olga said, fetching out bread and salt, the traditional courtesy offered to guests. 'Tell us all about yourselves.'

'We have come from England.' It was Kolya who answered because Lydia seemed suddenly tongue-tied. She was back in her childhood. Although it was dirtier and more dilapidated, the kitchen had not changed and it was easy to recall playing under the table with Andrei while her mother stitched jewels into their clothes, to feel again the frisson of fear she had felt then and not understood. It was the last place she had seen her mother and father and, in spite of the years between, she felt her eyes filling with tears. She brushed them away impatiently and tried to listen to what Kolya was saying to the women, whose mouths were agape at his story.

'Lydia was abducted by the Englishman,' he was saying. 'She was given no choice and it is only now, when she is old enough and married, that she has been able to come back to search for her parents.'

125

'You don't look as though you have suffered,' Olga said, looking Lydia up and down and reaching out to finger the material of her coat. 'You don't see coats like this hereabouts.'

'I have been well looked after,' Lydia said, shrinking from the woman's exploring fingers.

'That doesn't mean she hasn't suffered,' Kolya put in. 'The mental anguish has been unbearable.'

When they had eaten the bread and drunk a glass of tea, Svetlana offered to take them to meet Grigori. They rose and followed her through the house, along a corridor to a separate wing. This was a huge improvement on the rest of the house. All the best of the old furniture had been collected up and brought to furnish what was a comparatively well-ordered apartment.

'Please sit down,' Svetlana said. 'Grigori will be here soon. He's the head of the Petrovsk Land Department. How long is it since you lived here?'

'I was four when we left in 1920,' Lydia told her, perching herself on a sofa. Nikolay went over to the window and stood looking out at the tangled garden.

'That was a bad time, but there have been worse times since.'

'How long have you lived here?' Lydia asked her.

'Since 1922, the end of the Civil War, soon after I married Grigori. He got promotion and was sent here and we took over this house. Ah, here he is.' She looked up as the door opened and her husband came in. He was a big, broad man, dressed in a neat grey suit, though his shirt was collarless. 'Grigori, we have visitors from England. This is Nikolay Nikolayevich Andropov and his wife, Lydia.'

Lydia stood up and Nikolay turned from the window to

greet him. They shook hands. 'All the way from England, eh?' he said. 'You are a long way from home.'

'On the contrary,' Kolya said. 'We are home. My wife is the daughter of Mikhail Mikhailovich Kirilov. This was his *dacha*. She has come back to search for her parents.'

Grigori sank into a chair and stared up at them. He looked shocked and his ruddy face turned pale. 'The count's daughter,' he said, at last.

'Yes, did you know him?'

'He was my cousin. On my mother's side, you understand, but it is not a relationship I boast about.'

'No, you wouldn't,' Kolya said, with a wry smile. 'But do you know what happened to the count?'

'Why, in God's name, did you come back, Lydia Mikhailovna?' he said, angrily, ignoring Kolya's question. 'You are risking your life and ours as well.'

'Lydia is a good Communist, as I am,' Kolya said. 'We have nothing to fear.'

Grigori laughed, though there was no humour in it. 'The very fact that you have lived in the West is enough to condemn you – and us by association. Go back, Lydia Andropova, go back where you belong.'

'Not until I find out what happened to my parents,' she said.

'I told Pyotr Simenov what happened to them when he came asking questions. Did he not tell you? He said he would.'

'He said they had been executed for trying to take jewels out of the country.'

'So they were, and for being counter-revolutionaries. They were shot by a firing squad.'

'Do you know how they came to be arrested? When?

127

Where were they at the time? Are you sure they were shot and not just imprisoned? Was there a trial? Did no one defend them?'

'Questions, questions, questions,' he said irritably. 'What difference does it make?'

'I need to know for my peace of mind. I should like to see their graves and say a prayer for them.'

'Prayers!' he mocked. 'There is no religion in Russia now.'

'Perhaps not officially. I expect people still say their prayers privately. And that is beside the point. Will you help us?'

'The count and countess were denounced and arrested by the Cheka. They were tried by the People's Court and found guilty. The death sentence was carried out the next day.' It was said flatly, as if he were bored with it all.

'Who denounced them?'

He shrugged. 'It makes no difference. It was done.'

'Where were they buried?'

'Where they were executed in the Cherkassy Forest. I doubt the grave is marked.'

'But you do know where it is?'

'Roughly. I couldn't be exact. If you think I'll take you there, you are mistaken, Lydia Andropova. I haven't the time for such sentiment. The harvest is about to begin and I am responsible for meeting the grain quotas, so I shall be very busy. I suggest you go back where you came from.'

'We'd like to stay awhile,' Kolya put in. 'You can put us up for a few days, can't you? My wife has been looking forward to this visit for years. You'd not deny her that, would you?'

Both Grigori and his wife looked at Lydia. There were

tears running down her face. She did not seem aware of them. Kolya took his handkerchief and wiped them away. 'Don't cry, sweetheart. Grigori Stefanovich will let us stay a few days, I'm sure.' He looked at Grigori. 'Can I have a word with you in private?'

The big man shrugged. 'Very well. We'll go next door.'

Kolya followed him from the room, leaving Lydia and Svetlana facing each other. 'Tell me what life is like in England,' Svetlana said.

Lydia smiled wanly and obeyed. England seemed a world away and unreachable, and already she regretted leaving it. She wondered what her father would make of the letter she had sent him. He would be heartbroken and Mama angry. She had been wicked to come away in that hole-and-corner way, after all they had done for her. Now, when it was too late, she realised she should never have listened to Kolya. Alex's father had been right and her parents were dead.

'After the bandits shot my brother, I was all alone in the world. My brother and nurse were dead and my parents had disappeared. I was only four and so shocked I could not speak. I was taken to England by an English diplomat who adopted me. He has been very good to me . . .' She choked on the words. 'I was brought up like an English child: school, university, a job . . .'

'What job did you do?'

'Translating Russian into English.'

'You speak Russian with an accent.'

'Do I?' she queried. 'I suppose it's because I have not needed to speak it at home.'

'But you say this is home,' Svetlana pointed out.

'It was, but everything has changed. I don't recognise the Russia I knew.'

'That is not surprising, is it? You were no more than a baby when you left. And life is different now.'

'I know, but some memories are very vivid. They come to me in a series of unconnected pictures. What I wanted to try and do was put them together and make sense of them. Do you think anyone in the village would remember me?'

'Some of the old *babushkas* might, those who didn't die in the famine. It killed a lot of people.'

'But the fields are full of grain.'

'That is needed to fulfil our quota; we are allowed very little of it, though Grigori is luckier than most because of his position, and those who work in the tractor factory are kept fed.' It was said flatly, in a manner of acceptance.

'Oh.' She had read about the Ukrainian people going hungry, but the Russian papers were very cagey about how extensive the famine had been. 'I have money to buy food, we won't be a burden on you. As soon as Kolya has arranged for us to go to Cherkassy, we will leave.'

The men came back. Kolya was smiling broadly. 'We can have a room in the attic which is not occupied,' he said. 'We'll have to find some furniture, but there might be something useful in the part of the house that's uninhabitable.'

'How did the house come to be like that?' Lydia asked.

'It was done in the Civil War,' Grigori said. 'There was fierce fighting hereabouts. Come, let me show you the room.'

They followed him through the house. Every room they passed seemed to be occupied, though the occupants were absent, presumably at their work. 'How many people live here?' Lydia asked as they climbed the stairs. There was no carpet on the treads as there once had been.

'Twenty families in all,' Grigori told them. 'Some are

allocated one room, some with big families have two. It is big enough to house more if need be. If we are sent extra workers for the harvest, they will have to be housed. In that case you will have to move out.'

'I know,' she said. 'I thank you.'

The room was one at the top of the house which had once been the bedroom of a servant. It had a small iron bedstead without a mattress, and a cupboard. There was room for little else but they scavenged a small table and two chairs from an empty room and bought a mattress, bedlinen, a few pans and some crockery from the *Insnab*, a shop stocking foreign goods for which Grigori, because of his privileged position, had coupons to use.

'I don't know what we're doing here,' Lydia said to Kolya after they had arranged everything and were sitting on the two chairs which had once been part of a set of Queen Anne dining chairs. 'We have achieved nothing. I want to go home.'

'Home?' he queried. 'This is home now.'

'Kolya, you can't mean that,' she said, looking at him in dismay. He was smoking a cigarette he had rolled himself from makhorka, a rough, strong-smelling tobacco, and appeared completely unruffled. 'We only came to find out what happened to my parents and we've done that. We could go to Cherkassy to try and find their graves and then go home.'

'I have no intention of going back to England,' he said. 'I've work to do here.'

'Work? What work?'

'Never you mind.'

'You mean you are involved with the kulak uprising?'

He tapped his nose. 'Shsh. Walls have ears.'

'Kolya, that's madness, you'll be arrested and shot. Give it up, take me home. I cannot go alone. I'd never get past all the checks.'

'Then you had better resign yourself to staying here until I choose to move.' His voice had a hard edge to it she had never noticed before. He was suddenly not the fun-loving, affectionate Kolya he had been and she realised, with a great jolt that sent her heart into her shoes, that she had made a terrible mistake marrying him. He did not care for her; all his loving words were so much hot air to get her to come with him, though why he needed her she did not know.

'When will that be?'

'When I am given orders to go elsewhere.'

Why didn't she believe him? Why did she think he had been lying to her all along? As a member of a subversive organisation, he was in constant danger, but he was far too complacent. Either he was a fool or there was something else going on, and she did not think he was a fool. 'Kolya, just what are you up to?' she asked. 'What did you tell Grigori Stefanovich? He changed his mind about letting us stay after you spoke to him.'

'None of your business.'

'But I am your wife. Surely I should know.'

'Better you don't.' He stubbed out his cigarette in a saucer. 'Go and see to some food for us. I'm starving.'

She took some of the potatoes, cucumber, mushrooms and sauerkraut they had bought and made her way down to the kitchen. The other women had gone and the kitchen was empty. Thankful for that, she set about cooking.

She was in the middle of it when the outside door opened and a huge man with a shock of white hair and a white beard came in carrying a pile of logs. He dropped them in a basket beside the hearth and turned towards her. 'You're new here.'

She smiled, a little wanly because she had been crying. 'Yes and no. This used to be my home, years ago, before the Revolution.'

He stared. 'Lydia Mikhailovna. Is it you?'

'Yes.' She brightened to think someone knew her. 'Did you know me then?'

'Did I know you! Why I used to carry you on my shoulders. I took you to Simferopol that time . . .'

'Ivan Ivanovich!' His hair, which had been so black, was now white, and he was thinner than he used to be, but he was still the Ivan she had known, her saviour in the dark days of the Civil War. She ran to him and grasped both his hands. 'Oh, how good it is to see you. How are you? And Sima and the little ones?'

'All dead,' he said. 'They died in the famine. I earn my bread doing odd jobs and maintenance round the house. It's not the same, not the same at all.' And he shook his big head and sighed. 'What are you doing here? Did you go to England?'

'Yes. I am Lydia Andropova now.' She turned from him to take the pan off the stove and sat at the table to tell him all that had happened to her.

'You should not have come,' he said when she finished. 'If the authorities get to hear of it, you will be arrested.'

'My husband has proper papers for us. Did you know my parents were arrested and executed?'

'Yes. I'm sorry. It was on the day I took you to Simferopol. They were on their way to join you as arranged. They never knew about Andrei and Tonya.'

'I'm glad of that. I was told they were denounced. Do you know who could have done that?'

'I didn't,' he said sharply. 'I would never have betrayed them.'

'Of course not. Who else knew?'

'Grigori Stefanovich. They went to visit him that day. They hoped he would give them travel documents.'

She was shocked. 'You think it might be him? Why would he do such a thing? He is family.'

'People betray their grandmothers nowadays. One boy betrayed his own father and was subsequently murdered by his grandfather for doing it. The boy is revered as a hero and the grandfather paid with his life.'

'But what motive would Grigori have for doing that?'

'He knew about the jewels sewn in their clothes.' He gave a bark of a laugh. 'I'll wager only one or two ever reached the authorities.' He stopped suddenly. 'Do not trust him, Lidushka. Do not trust anyone. Get out of here, it's not safe.'

'I can't. My husband won't leave.'

'Then I pity you.' The sound of footsteps came to them and he hurriedly turned to leave. 'I live in the woodman's hut in the forest,' he murmured. 'Come to me if you are in trouble. I will do what I can to help, but it will be little enough.' And he was gone.

She returned to her cooking, as Kolya came into the room. 'I wondered where you'd got to. You've been a long time.'

She was about to tell him about meeting Ivan but changed her mind. If he could be secretive, so could she. 'I'm not used to this stove. It's ready now. Do you want to eat it down here or up in our room?'

'Down here. Then I have some business with Grigori Stefanovich.'

'I think I'll write to my parents and tell them what's happened.'

'If you must,' he said. 'But be careful what you say. Everything is censored nowadays. I'll see that it's posted.'

They ate in silence and then he went off to find Grigori and she returned to their room to write her letter. She was dreadfully sorry about the way she had left, she wrote, and begged their forgiveness. She did not know how to describe Kirilhor without finding fault with the regime, but put as bright a view on it as she could. She hoped soon to come home. When it was done she took it downstairs, looking for Kolya.

She found him in the coach house talking earnestly to Grigori. 'I think you're mad,' Grigori was saying. 'You're on a wild goose chase. If I were you—' He saw Lydia and stopped speaking suddenly. 'What can I do for you, Lydia Mikhailovna?' he said, making Kolya, who had his back to her, swivel round to face her.

'I was looking for Kolya. He said he would send this letter for me.'

'Better let me have it,' Grigori said, holding out his hand. 'I can send it from my office in the town. That usually goes safely.'

She put it into his hand and thanked him. 'I think I'll go for a walk.'

'Not a good idea,' Grigori said. 'If you are seen, questions might be asked. You would almost certainly be arrested.'

'Whatever for? I've done nothing wrong.'

'As the daughter of an aristocrat who was found guilty of subversive activity, you would be considered guilty by association.'

'But I was only four years old the last time I was in

Russia. At least, I thought I was four, I've never been sure.'

'1920,' he said. 'Yes, you were four that April.'

'April?'

'Yes. You were born on Easter Day. I remember your father telling me. Very auspicious, so the old *babushkas* would have us believe. I can't remember the actual date and Russia was still using the old calendar then.' He gave a grunt of a laugh. 'Thirteen days out, but what does it matter? What's more important is you being here now. I'm risking my own skin harbouring you, so you stay out of sight.'

The matter of the date of her birthday could wait. 'I can't stay indoors all the time, and besides, I've changed my name since I was last here. Kolya is safe enough, isn't he?'

'We can't even be sure of that.'

She turned to Kolya. 'What have you done? What are you up to? We should never have come. I wish I hadn't listened to you. I want to go home to England.'

'All in good time,' he said complacently.

'I'll go alone.' It was said out of bravado.

'How do you propose to do that? You are married to me and I've got your passport, papers and money in my safe keeping and that is where it stays.'

'If you must go out, keep to the forest,' Grigori said. 'And get some different clothes. You are too conspicuous in that finery.'

It wasn't finery; back in England the clothes she wore would be considered very ordinary. She turned and went back to her attic room in despair. She longed for Sir Edward and Margaret, who loved her, her comfortable apartment, her work and her friends. When her letter arrived would

Papa realise she wanted to come home and manage to do something to rescue her? Perhaps he would wash his hands of her and who could blame him? If she didn't hear from him, she would have to find her own way back. She wished she had not trusted Kolya with her savings because she would need those when the time came. If all else failed she would have to sell the Kirilov Star.

Afraid Kolya would take the Star from her, she took it to Ivan Ivanovich and asked him to hide it for her. 'It will be safe with me,' he told her, his old eyes lighting up at seeing her. 'I'll bury it where no one will find it.'

'Thank you. I know I can trust you.'

He seemed a little uncomfortable at that and blurted out, 'I took the rubies Andrei had in his clothes. I was going to keep them for the count when he came back, but he never did and when my little ones were starving . . .' His voice faded. 'I only got a few roubles for them in Cherkassy and dare not demand more for fear of investigation. I beg your forgiveness.'

'Of course I forgive you,' she said softly. 'I do not blame you.'

'It was a terrible time in Ukraine,' he said, his dark eyes glistening with tears. He wiped them away with the back of his hand. 'The army took all the grain to feed themselves and the industrial workers in the factories. Those who tried keeping anything back were shot. We were left with nothing and lived on berries and whatever we could scavenge in the forest. The villagers left in droves to find work in the city and died on the pavements there. When there was no one to bring in the harvest, Grigori Stefanovich took over Kirilhor and filled it with strangers.'

She laid a hand on his arm. 'I am so very sorry, Ivan

Ivanovich. I wish I could help you. Kolya has taken all my money and only allows me enough kopeks to buy food.' Grigori had relented about letting her go into town because she had sold her clothes and was now wearing a thin cotton skirt and blouse and had covered her hair with a scarf, so that she looked the same as all the other women. 'But you go no further than Petrovsk,' he had warned.

'I manage,' Ivan said. 'But you must go as soon as you can. I don't trust that lot up at Kirilhor.'

'I will if I can but it won't be easy without money or papers. I might have to sell the Star.'

Knowing she had an ally, she returned to Kirilhor feeling a little more cheerful, prepared to put up with a life she had brought upon herself, enduring Kolya's taunts, always hungry, always watchful, always listening for the knock on the door in the middle of the night. The rumblings about war in Europe were growing louder and she would have to move soon, but it would take some planning and she would say nothing to Kolya because he would stop her. She told Kolya she had lost the star. The chain had broken and it had slipped from her neck without her realising it. He was furious and demanded to know why she had been wearing it.

'I thought it was the best way to keep it safe,' she said. 'I wouldn't have brought it to Russia at all, but if you remember, you said I might need it to prove my identity when or if I met my parents. I should have known Baron Simenov was telling the truth and they were dead. I don't know why I let you persuade me . . .'

'Because you were not sure, were you? There was always that niggling doubt. Admit it.'

'I think it was more a need for confirmation.'

'Well, now you've got it. But that's beside the point. We were talking about the Star. Where were you when you last knew you had it?'

'Walking in the forest and the garden.'

'Then we had better go and look for it.'

The search went on for days, and when it could not be found, Kolya came to the conclusion someone had found it and was hanging onto it. It made him suspicious of everyone in the house and he instigated searches of all their belongings to no avail. The Star was lost. It did not improve Kolya's temper. She had never seen him so angry.

Finding she was pregnant was the last straw.

It was good to be back in England, Alex thought, as a taxi took him to his London home. He was hardly in it these days. He was being employed as a sort of roving commissioner by the Foreign Office, intelligence gathering, which made him a sort of spy. It was not a label he liked, but he had been assured his work was necessary, and as he obviously spoke and read Russian, was fluent in German and had passable French, who better to do the work? Sir Edward knew what he did, but no one else did. His friends thought he was away on trade missions, which was the official reason for his absences abroad.

He had spent the last year in Germany, watching Hitler becoming ever more powerful and dictatorial, and some of the time in Russia trying to get at the truth of the purges taking place there. The NKVD, under the leadership of the ruthless Nikolai Yezhov, was waging war against so-called traitors in the Party, torturing them into confessing ridiculous crimes and betraying their friends. It had become a kind of frenzy which depleted the Comintern staff so that nothing could be done, no decision made, nor plans put forward. And it decimated the ranks of the officers in the army, from generals downwards. If there was war, they would never be able to wage it successfully. And he did not think war could be avoided in spite of the work done by Neville Chamberlain to appease Hitler and his declaration of 'peace in our time'. It was a breathing space, no more.

He let himself in the house and dropped his case on the floor to pick up the pile of post from the table in the hall, put there by Mrs Hurst, who came in to keep an eye on the place when he was away. He rifled through the envelopes quickly to pick out what was important. There was a letter from Sir Edward, whom he had not seen since Lydia's twenty-first birthday party. He put the rest down and wandered into the kitchen to put the kettle on. While it boiled he slit open the letter and began to read.

I don't know where you are but I assume you will come home at some time and find this, Sir Edward had written. *Lydia has run off to Russia with Nikolay Andropov. I am at my wits' end and Margaret is distraught. Ring me, if you can.*

He looked at the date on the letter and realised with horror it had been written three months before. He switched off the kettle and picked up the telephone.

'Good of you to come,' Sir Edward said, leading the way into the drawing room of Balfour Place where they had arranged to meet. 'Sit down, my boy. Have you eaten?'

'Yes, thank you.' He sat down and watched as Edward poured brandy into two large glasses. 'Tell me what happened. Who is Nikolay Andropov?'

'A young Russian she met in Paris when we were on

140

holiday last year.' He handed Alex a glass and went to a bureau to extract Lydia's letter, which he gave to him to read. 'As you can see from that, she had some strange idea that her parents were not dead after all and might not know she is alive too.'

'My father was convinced they had died. Didn't she believe him?'

'I always thought she did, but apparently not. I am sure Andropov put the idea into her head, but what his motive was, I've no idea.'

'Why would she believe him rather than us?'

'I don't know. He can be very charming and I suppose she was bowled over by him.'

'She says she is going to marry him.' Alex read on, hiding his dismay under a calm exterior, something he had learnt to do over the years. No one knew exactly what he was thinking. 'Do you think she has?'

'I have no way of knowing. I didn't know she was still seeing him or I would have taken steps to put a stop to it.'

'If she was determined, it would have been difficult to stop,' Alex said. 'She is twenty-two, after all.'

'I could have bought him off.'

'Perhaps. Do you think he is genuinely fond of her?'

'I don't know.'

'If it were me, no amount of money would make me give her up.'

'But it is not you. I wish to God it were. I had hoped—' He stopped suddenly and gulped a mouthful of brandy.

'We cannot choose our children's life partners, Sir Edward.' It was said evenly, though his heart was racing. Lydia, his love, was in Russia, where all foreigners were viewed with suspicion and her background would be

141

'enough to condemn her. It was a terrifying thought. But he must not let Sir Edward see his disquiet; the poor man was worried enough as it was. 'What do you know about Andropov?'

'Nothing but what he told us. He escaped the Civil War with his mother after his father was killed fighting with the Whites. She subsequently died and he has been on his own, living in Paris ever since. Having similar backgrounds was bound to attract them towards each other. I didn't even know he had come to England. How could she be so secretive? You think you are doing your best for your children . . .' His voice tailed off.

'But you did. No child could have had a better father. She has grown into a lovely young woman and I am sure she loves you and appreciates all you and Lady Stoneleigh have done for her.' He paused, clinging onto hope. 'I suppose she really did go?'

'I think she must have. Her letter was written months ago. I have written to her at Kirilhor over and over again, but have had no reply. Maybe she's gone somewhere else; she wouldn't have ignored my letters, would she?'

'No, of course not. Maybe they have been kept from her.'

'That's what terrifies me. I contacted the Foreign Office, but there's nothing they can do if she went of her own free will. I've also been in touch with Lord Chilston at the British Embassy in Moscow, but he can't do much. The embassy staff are not free to travel about as much as they were and diplomatic relations are difficult.' He smiled a little stiffly. 'But you know all that. I even tried the headquarters of the British Communist Party, but they were not very helpful.'

'I'll go back,' Alex said. 'I've got to report to the Foreign

Office first to be debriefed after my last trip, and it would be a good idea to have an official reason for being in Russia again so that I have proper entry papers. That might take a little time to arrange, but I'll go the minute I can.'

'It's a lot to ask. Too much perhaps. I'd go myself, but Margaret is sick with worry and to have two of us in Russia would be too much for her to cope with.'

'I know. You mustn't think of it. Leave it to me.'

'Bless you.' He held up the decanter, but Alex declined a second glass. He needed a clear head. 'Margaret will be relieved to know you are going,' Edward went on. 'But if you should meet her before you go, don't say too much to her about the difficulties and dangers.'

The difficulties and dangers would be considerable, Alex knew, especially as he risked arrest on the grounds that he was his father's son and the Bolsheviks had a tendency to assume guilt by association. But nothing on earth would prevent him from going. Lydia had always been his especial concern, ever since his mother had told him to be kind to her on the train to Yalta. He had watched her grow from a frightened toddler who had lost the power of speech, through childhood to womanhood, and had loved her all the way. He had not recognised it as love to begin with, it was simply a feeling he ought to protect her and he still felt that, but now it was more than that, the feeling had blossomed, as she had blossomed, into something far deeper and more complex. He found himself wondering how she would have reacted if she had known that. Would it have prevented her from going off with Andropov? He had never met the man but already he disliked him intensely.

'When you find her,' Edward went on. 'Tell her how much she is loved and missed and persuade her to come home. I want her here, even if it means recognising Andropov as a son-in-law, much as I should dislike it.'

Sir Edward would not dislike it any more than he would, Alex decided, but for different reasons. But it would not stop him trying to rescue her from her own folly.

Chapter Six

7th April 1939

'Push, for goodness' sake,' Olga said. 'It'll never be born if you don't do something to help yourself.'

Lydia grunted through the pain and tried to do as she was told. It was Good Friday, a day of suffering and mourning in the Christian calendar, but she did not think anyone in Russia commemorated the fact, unless it was secretly. She should have been eagerly looking forward to the birth of her child, buying baby clothes, shawls, nappies, a cot and a pram, deciding on names. But it hadn't been like that. The moment she realised a baby was on the way, she knew her hope of returning to England in the foreseeable future had faded to nothing. She didn't want this child. She had hated the lump growing inside her all through the months of pregnancy. The bump was a symbol of her folly and there was no going back, no undoing what had been done. She felt trapped.

To make matters worse, the love she thought Kolya had for her had turned out to be nothing more than a delusion.

His political loyalties seemed to change with the wind and she never knew what he really thought or believed; he never confided in her and more recently hardly troubled to talk to her at all. The day, soon after they arrived, she had overheard him discussing her with Grigori had been a real shock and very frightening. She had come upon them in the coach house pulling the old carriage apart. Battered and broken it had stood gathering dust and woodworm ever since that fateful day when her parents had sent her to Yalta. Someone must have returned it; she supposed it had been Grigori. It was of no use to anyone; its wheels and shafts had already been plundered for firewood. She wondered what they were looking for and had stood in the shadows watching. They evidently had not seen her.

'Do you think I haven't looked there before?' Grigori said, watching Kolya throw the cushions off the seats. They had been nibbled by mice and the stuffing was bursting out of them. He pulled them apart, throwing the wadding behind him and coughing on the dust that flew out. 'There's nothing there, I tell you,' Grigori went on. 'Everything they had on them when they were arrested was confiscated. There was only a tiny diamond and one small ruby.'

'You can't persuade me that was all they had. They'd have hidden the rest somewhere and they wouldn't have given the most valuable pieces to the children. The Kirilov Star was only the tip of the iceberg. There's more hidden here somewhere. What about the droshky?'

'The same. It's all been searched. More than once. Every inch of the house too. If there had been any valuables left here during the Civil War, they'd have been found years ago.'

'Not necessarily,' Kolya said. 'Bits of the Romanov

jewels are still turning up in odd places: down wells, in chimneys, buried in gardens. I believe it's the same with the Kirilov treasures.'

So Kolya was on a treasure hunt. It was then she realised with a dreadful shock that he had been using her to come and look for wealth. He had no feelings for her at all, nor any loyalty except to himself. He had no interest in kulak uprisings or the Communist Party. It was all a sham. Everything about him was a sham. The realisation had made her feel sick, more sick than her pregnancy ever had.

'I'm not happy about you being here,' Grigori had gone on. 'You've been searching for days now and found nothing. I thought you knew where to look. Doesn't that wife of yours know what happened to it?'

'No, she was too young to remember.'

'You could try jogging her memory. And if that doesn't work, the best thing you can do is get rid of her. Having her here is putting us all in danger, you included.'

Lydia had put her hand to her mouth to stop herself crying out and betraying her presence. Were they considering murdering her? No, not even Kolya would stoop so low. But if they did, no one would ever know. They could bury her body in the forest and she would sink into oblivion, unmourned, not even by Sir Edward who had answered none of her letters. But who could blame him? She must be a dreadful disappointment to him and she was filled with shame.

'I'll try and get something out of her,' Kolya had said. 'If that doesn't work, you can denounce her to the NKVD, but not until after I'm safely away.'

Lydia had crept silently away and gone back to her attic

room where she sat on the bed, shaking with fright. She really was on her own.

The following day had been the beginning of day after day of interrogation by Kolya. It began slowly, with loving words and gentle hints, but when she told him she didn't remember, he had pressed her more forcefully, and when that hadn't worked, with shouts and threats. She had decided it might be better to pretend to remember odd little things, places the jewels might have been hidden. He would rush off searching wherever she had suggested: cupboards, drawers, nooks and crannies in the old house, outbuildings, troughs, water butts, up in the attics among the accumulated rubbish, but when he found nothing, he came back and the questions started again. She became good at acting a part, forgetting and then accidentally letting something slip, a faint memory which might be a clue. She felt relatively safe while he still thought there was something to be found, but sooner or later, he would give up and then she would be in mortal danger.

When she told him she was pregnant he had laughed, but it was not a happy laugh. She had no idea where he was now; she had been left to the ministrations of Olga because they dare not call in a doctor or a midwife for fear of being arrested. A surge of pain filled her body and she pushed for all she was worth, anxious to rid herself of this lump which had caused her so much grief.

'It's coming,' Olga cried triumphantly. 'I can see the head. One more push and you will have your baby.'

It took more than one, but suddenly it slid out into Olga's waiting hands. Lydia sank back in exhaustion and shut her eyes, but the wail of an infant made her open them again. Olga was wiping mucous from the baby's face. 'It's a boy,' she said, wrapping him in a towel and putting him into Lydia's arms. 'Here, hold him while I see to the afterbirth.'

Lydia wasn't sure she wanted to look at him, but his thin wailing touched a chord she could not deny and she found herself gazing down at a little screwed-up face, bright pink and squalling, as if he had not wanted to come into this contentious world and wished he had never left the dark warmth of her womb. This was her son whom they had decided, after much debate, to call Yuri. Suddenly, it did not matter who had fathered him, he was hers, hers to love, to cherish and protect. Her hate fled as she held him to her breast, helping him to find the nipple. The sharp pain of it as he pulled was exquisite pleasure and she wept with love and tenderness.

Olga took him away to wash him and dress him in the garments they had managed to buy from the *Isnab*. Lydia watched, wanting to do it herself, but feeling too weak. She didn't like the way Olga took charge of him, crooning to him and talking softly to him as she wrapped him in the shawl she had knitted from the pulled-out wool of old jumpers she had bought in the market. Grigori allowed her to shop in Petrovsk now she was dressed in the same way as all the other women. But she had been warned not to talk about herself. This was not considered strange; people simply did not speak freely about themselves for fear of saying something which might be construed by their listeners as subversive, something for which they could be denounced, arrested and imprisoned.

'My little Yurochka,' Olga murmured. 'Your papa is going to be so proud of you. Another little one to grow up to be a good little Communist, eh, *golubchick*?'

Lydia was about to protest at that, but decided against

it. It would cause dissent, something she had been careful to avoid over the months of her pregnancy, and it did not matter, considering she would take him out of Russia at the first opportunity. She decided that if she pretended to settle down, to be content, they would allow her more freedom and Kolya would give her more money. Food and fuel and the everyday things they needed were so exorbitantly expensive, she had been able to save very little from what he had given her. It would be a great wrench but she would have to sell the Kirilov Star. It could not be done in Petrovsk, which was too small a community, but in Kiev there would be places where things like that were bought and sold, so her first step must be to save enough for the train fare to Kiev. And she must steal her passport and papers from Kolya. But first she would have to regain her strength and make sure Yuri was healthy, and not, by a single word or deed, let anyone know what she was planning.

Her love for her son grew day by day and her dearest wish was to get him safely to England. If she were no longer welcome at Balfour Place or Upstone Hall, she would have to find some way of supporting herself and him. She did not like the way Olga tried to take over looking after him, changing his nappy and tickling him to make him chuckle. And Kolya encouraged her, laughing when Lydia protested. 'You should be glad Olga is so fond of the child. She could denounce us both if she chose. And it helps you, doesn't it? You are hopeless when it comes to managing.' This was said because she always told him she was no good at bargaining and had to pay more for goods than she really had, in order to squirrel a few kopeks away. Even so, saving enough to leave was taking longer than she had hoped. Her milk soon dried up and she had to buy milk for Yuri, which meant walking some distance to a collective farm, standing in line for hours and then paying through the nose for it.

The day Kolya found her little hoard in a purse in her underwear drawer was the most miserable of her life and she was left drowning in despair, quite apart from the humiliation of the slap he gave her which left a red mark on her cheek. 'What do you think you were going to do with it?' he demanded, throwing the contents of the purse across the bed in fury.

'I saved it for emergencies,' she said, praying he would believe her and let her keep it. 'I don't like being without any money at all.'

He laughed. 'No, I don't suppose you do. You've never had to go without a thing. Rich, bourgeoise, cosseted all your life, now it's time to learn what it's like to be poor.'

He didn't give it back, but put it in his pocket, deaf to her entreaties that Yuri's milk cost so much. And from then on, he kept her even more short of money and gave Olga the task of buying Yuri's milk. Lydia became a kind of drudge for the rest of the household, and though she silently raged against it, she decided submissiveness was the only way she would be given the freedom she needed to move about.

In order to have time with her son, she would carry him into the forest when Olga was at work at the factory, and walk about where it was cool, a welcome relief from the heat of the sun. 'I'll have us out of here, my darling, but we have to be patient,' she murmured over and over again.

Sometimes she would go and sit with Ivan in his crude hut and make plans for her escape. But Ivan, who knew the way the Soviet system worked, advised caution. If she were arrested, they would take her son from her, and she would be sent to a prison camp in Siberia for years, that is if they didn't decide to execute her. 'They don't need much of an excuse to do that,' he said.

'Do you think there'll be a war?' she asked. There had been talk among the residents of Kirilhor and reports in the newspapers Grigori brought into the house. Hitler was spreading his tentacles. German troops had occupied Sudetenland, Bohemia and Moravia, which became German protectorates, and marched into Austria, which had been declared part of the Reich. Slovakia, too, had been put under German protection. Countries and principalities all over Europe were making non-aggression pacts in the hope of averting disaster. The USSR had proposed a defensive alliance with Britain which would make them strange allies, but might help those Britons living and working in Russia. Lydia hoped so.

Ivan shrugged. 'Who knows? It might be wise to go while you can, but be careful. Tell no one. I wish I could help you, but I have nothing, no money, no land, no family . . .'

'Come with me, then.'

'No. This is my home, I have no other, but it is different for you. You stopped belonging here in 1920.' He sighed. 'How long ago that was, and yet how close in our memories.'

'Yes, I shall never forget,' she said, standing up to go back to the house. 'I think I must steal the money. It is the only way.'

She was in for another shock when she returned home and climbed the stairs to her room. Kolya and Olga were in bed together, both as naked as the day they were born. She gave a strangled cry and fled downstairs and out of the house, wanting to run, anywhere away from that haunted place. She looked wildly about her, uncertain which way to go, and ran into the old stables. It had been years since there had been horses there, but the place still smelt of the animals and there were a few wisps of straw and hay about and odd bits of harness. Here she crouched in a corner, hugging her child to her and weeping all over his colourful shawl.

Kolya found her there and, pulling her to her feet, dragged her back to the kitchen. Here Olga took Yuri from her and set about giving him the milky gruel he was being weaned on. Lydia's fury was so great it dried her tears and she set about pummelling Kolya with her fists. 'I knew you were a liar,' she shouted between thumps. 'But I never realised you were also an adulterer. I hate you! I hate you!'

He laughed, grabbing her hands and holding them to her sides. 'Good, because I can't say I have any use for your affection. Terrible disappointment you've turned out to be.'

'Because I lost the Star and cannot tell you the hiding place of the jewels! Well, I'm sorry about that, but you should ask Grigori Stefanovich what happened to them. I bet he knows. Give me back my money and my papers and let me go home.' She was calmer now; the storm had passed and left her cold. Very cold.

'You can go wherever you like,' he said, 'but if you think I'm going to help you, you are mistaken. I've got plans of my own.'

'To go back to England?'

'No, to Minsk. Olga has been given a job in a munitions factory. I'm going with her.'

She slumped into a chair and stared up at him. 'You are going to abandon me without any means of support?'

'You can work, can't you?'

'But what about Yuri?'

'What about him?'

'How can I work when I have to look after him?'

'I'm sure you'll manage. When we go, I'll leave your passport and enough money to get you to Odessa. You can throw yourself on the mercy of the British consul there, though if war is declared, he isn't likely to have much time for a runaway.'

'When are you going?'

He shrugged. 'When Olga's travel papers come through.'

Wearily she rose and went to take her things from their room. She would not sleep there again. She took her belongings to the old part of the house where the windows were missing and the plaster was falling off the ceilings and walls, where rats and mice scurried, huge spiders built their webs and where the birds nested in the remains of the chimneys. There were even weeds growing up between the tiles on the floor. She made several trips, piling her belongings in a corner, went back for Yuri's crib and then poked about for something to use as a mattress for herself. A sack and some straw was all she could find.

When she had added that to the rest, she went back to the kitchen to fetch Yuri. Kolya and Olga had gone and so had the baby. She searched frantically for them in the house, running into every room that hadn't been locked by its occupants. She rushed outside and ran into all the outbuildings but there was no sign of them. They were having a game with her and it made her angry. Returning indoors, she met Svetlana who had just come back from shopping. 'Have you seen Kolya and Olga?' she asked her.

'Yes, I met them in Petrovsk, going to catch a train they said. Olga's got promotion to a factory in Minsk.'

'Did they have Yuri with them?'

'Yes. I thought it was strange but they said you had given him to them—'

Lydia heard no more; she had fallen to the ground in a faint.

When she recovered she was lying on the tiled floor and Svetlana was squatting beside her, fanning her with a newspaper. 'You gave me a fright.'

It was a moment or two before Lydia's brain cleared and she remembered. She sat up. 'How long ago since you saw them? What time does the train go? Was Yuri crying?'

'He wasn't crying, why should he? He knows Olga Denisovna as well as he knows you. And the train has gone. I heard its whistle as I was walking home.'

Lydia struggled to her feet. 'I must go after them. What time is the next train?'

'There isn't another until tomorrow, not one that goes to Kiev and connects with a train going north.'

'No. Oh no. It can't be. It can't be.' She sank to the floor again, but Svetlana hauled her up and, putting her arm about her, led her to the kitchen where she sat her down at the table and put a kettle on the stove. 'A glass of tea, isn't that the English cure-all?'

'It won't cure this, will it?' She put her arms about herself and rocked to and fro. 'Yuri, Yuri, my baby. They have stolen him. Why? Why?'

'I should think because Olga cannot have children of her own.' Svetlana busied herself brewing tea, while Lydia watched, her mind on a train steaming north. 'She was married once, you know, but when her husband found she

155

could not have children, he divorced her. It has been her shame ever since.'

'I didn't know that, but it's no excuse for taking Yuri from me. He is all I have, my whole life. I have to go after them and get him back.' She stood up and began pacing the room. Was this her punishment for not wanting him? But she hadn't known then what it was like to be a mother, had she? Now she would willingly have died for him.

'It won't be easy. Even if you catch them up, Yuri is Kolya's son and he won't give him up.'

'Do you think I'm going to stand by and do nothing? What sort of mother would that make me? I'm going after them. Kolya promised to leave me my passport and a little money.' She ran from the room and up the stairs to the room she had shared with Kolya. Lying on the crumpled bed was an envelope. She snatched it up. It held her passport and a few roubles but no travel permit. She didn't want to stay in that room a moment longer than necessary and returned to the kitchen. Svetlana put a glass of tea on the table in front of her. 'Sit down and drink that. I put some vodka in it. When Grigori comes home, we'll ask him what he can do to help.'

She was still shaking with a mixture of fear and fury when Grigori came in about eight o'clock. The summer had been hot and dry and the wheat harvest was better than it had been the year before, and it looked as though they might meet their quota with a little to spare. He was dusty and tired and had little advice to offer. It was not in his power to arrange travel documents, he said, but he did know the name of the factory to which Olga had been posted. 'You won't get anywhere near it,' he added.

'I've got to try. I can't let them get away with kidnapping my son.'

'He is Nikolay Nikolayevich's son too, you know. He will claim him, and as he is a good Party man and you are who you are, they will give him custody.'

She hadn't thought of that. 'I don't care. I'll get on the train and hope for the best. Perhaps in Kiev I can obtain the necessary permits.'

'I'll give you the name of the man to ask for.' He was evidently as anxious to be rid of her as she was to go.

'Thank you.'

The train left at five-thirty the next morning. Afraid she would oversleep and miss it, she packed a few belongings in a bag and went to Ivan's *izba* where she told him of the latest developments and asked him to fetch the Star; she would need every penny she could raise on it. He was shocked but not surprised by what had happened, but refrained from saying 'I told you so'. 'Stay here tonight,' he said. 'I'll make sure you wake in time to catch the train.'

But she would not, because if it was discovered he had helped her, he would be in trouble himself and it was best he went on with his quiet life and let her go. They embraced, both of them in tears, and then she left him and walked to the station to spend the night in the waiting room.

It was midday when Alex left the train at Petrovsk and made his way out of the station. The situation in Europe and the demands of the Foreign Office meant that he had taken far longer than he had hoped to get there. He had been sent to the embassy in Moscow first to act as an interpreter during the negotiations between Britain and the Soviet Union, but even while the talks were going on, he heard rumours that the Soviets were negotiating a non-aggression pact with Germany. He had been ordered to find out all he could and orders like that could not, should not, be disobeyed. He had put on a Red Army uniform and spent some time infiltrating the military command which was extraordinarily disorganised, but all he had learnt was rumour and counter-rumour, while he grew more and more frustrated and impatient to be going to Kirilhor. When at last he was able to ascertain the truth, that even while negotiating with Britain, the Soviets had signed a pact with Germany, he was free to go to Ukraine. Praying that Lydia was still at Kirilhor, he boarded a train, sporting an untidy beard and wearing a Red Army major's uniform, to all intents and purposes Alexei Petrovich Simenov going on leave.

There was a plain brick building calling itself a hotel and he booked in there and had a meal before venturing out onto the street and asking the way to Kirilhor. His uniform was enough to ensure cooperation and deter questions about why he wanted to know, though he was conscious of the curiosity of those he asked. He smiled; no doubt there would be gossip, but as long as his disguise held, he was safe, although he was wary of walking directly up to the *dacha* in case Lydia saw him and gave the game away. He had to find some way of seeing her alone. He turned off the road and onto a path through the forest which he guessed would bring him out to the back of the house.

What if she was happy as she was? What if his arrival was unwelcome? He could not forcibly take her away if she did not want to come. His head was full of questions and it was not until the sound of an axe striking wood impinged on his consciousness that he took note of where he was. There was a crude hut in a clearing and a big man with a shock of pure white hair was chopping firewood. He stopped to look at Alex as he approached. 'Good day, Comrade Major,' he said.

'Good day, to you. Am I going in the right direction for Kirilhor?'

'Yes, this path will take you there.'

'How many people are living there now?'

Ivan shrugged. 'Several families. I cannot tell how many.' He paused. 'Do I know you, Major? Have we met?'

'I don't think so. I have never been here before.'

'Strange. I never forget a face. But it was a long time ago.' He shook his white head as if to clear it. 'It must have been someone who looks like you.'

'Possibly. Tell me your name.' Alex could see the man was reluctant and added, 'You have nothing to fear.'

'Ivan Ivanovich. It is a very common name, Major.'

'Yes, but perhaps not in connection with Kirilhor. I believe you met my father, Baron Pyotr Simenov. He was here in 1921, making enquiries about the Kirilovs. Do you remember?'

'Yes, now I remember. He asked about the count and countess and the little girl.'

'Lydia Mikhailovna,' Alex said. 'Have you seen her recently?'

'No. I thought she went to England.'

Alex had, over the years since working in intelligence, learnt to tell when someone was lying and the big man's mumbled reply and inability to look him in the face were evidence enough. He smiled. 'I believe you have seen her, Ivan Ivanovich. I wish her no harm, quite the contrary. I have come from England to take her home, if she wants to come. She is very dear to me and has been ever since I met her the day after you left her in Simferopol.'

Only the son of the baron could know that. Ivan's wariness disappeared. 'You are too late,' he said. 'She left to go to Kiev on the early train this morning. Oh, if only you had been a day sooner. I fear she will be in trouble with the authorities . . .'

'Why? Is she not with her husband?'

'That vile worm!' Ivan spat in the sawdust at his feet. 'He left her for Olga Denisovna and took the baby with him. She was going after them, but she had money only to take her as far as Kiev.'

'Baby?' He hadn't thought of her having a child and it caused him a few pangs of jealousy, before he took hold of himself. Lydia had married the man; so what did he expect?

'Yes, she had a child, a boy called Yuri. They, that is Nikolay Andropov and his mistress, took the child. Poor Lydia was distraught. She was determined to go after them.'

'When is the next train?'

'Later this afternoon.' He stuck the axe in the next log. 'Come inside, Major. I can offer you tea and a little bread, while you wait. I don't advise you to go to Kirilhor.'

'Thank you.' Alex followed him into the dismal little hovel. Both had to duck their heads under the lintel. Alex watched as Ivan set about poking more wood into the *burzhuika* and putting a kettle on it. 'Tell me all you know,' he said. And Ivan did.

Alex was appalled at what Lydia had had to endure and vowed not to leave Russia until he found her. One side of him rejoiced to think that there was no love lost between her and Kolya, that the marriage had been a failure. But there was a baby to consider. Getting Lydia out with her child would not be easy. He would have to call in every favour he had ever done. And how could he square it with his work as an intelligence agent, for which he was paid by the British government?

'Where was she hoping to go after Kiev?' he asked.

'Minsk. That was where the woman, Olga Nahmova, was going. I'm afraid my little Lidushka is walking into trouble.'

'Not if I can help it,' Alex said grimly. 'You do not need to mention I have been here.'

Ivan laughed. 'I am not likely to do that. I have never set eyes on you.'

Alex found her standing in line at the railway station in Kiev, waiting to buy a ticket. She had a small case at her feet. Her clothes were shabby, her hair unkempt and she was so thin she was hardly recognisable as the lovely girl he knew. Her face was pale and drawn and her eyes bleak with misery. She had not seen him and he wondered if she would recognise him with his beard and uniform. He walked up behind her and bent to put his mouth to her ear. 'Lidushka,' he whispered. 'I am here. You are not alone.'

She whipped round with a cry of such joy it lit her face, and threw herself into his arms. 'Alex! Alex! Oh, thank God! Thank God!' And then she burst into tears.

He held her close, for a few moments, feeling the boniness of her and cursing himself for not arriving sooner.

'Come,' he said, wiping her eyes with his handkerchief. 'We must find somewhere to talk.'

'But I have to go to Minsk.'

'I know. I'll take you.'

'I thought I was hearing things, that it was a ghost saying my name. Oh, how did you get here? How did you know where to find me? Kolya's gone off with Olga Denisovna and they've got Yuri. I have to find them . . .'

'We will.' He took her to a hotel and ordered food for them both. And while she ate, he questioned her about her life since coming to Russia. She was so glad to see him and so bewildered, she could hardly speak coherently, but he managed to follow her. 'I had to sell the Kirilov Star, to pay the train fare,' she said. 'The man who bought it said it was not of the highest quality and would only give me a few roubles. I daren't argue with him . . .'

'He lied,' he said. 'Show me the place.'

As soon as she had finished eating and drinking her fill, she took him to the jeweller's where she had sold the Star. He left her outside while he went in and demanded its return, telling the man he would be in trouble for buying stolen goods if he refused to hand it over. He offered more than Lydia had been given as compensation and returned to her with it in his pocket. 'Now, back to the station,' he said, taking her arm.

'Are you coming with me?'

'Sweetheart, you need me, and while you need me, I shall be at your disposal.'

'It's all my fault and I shouldn't involve you.'

'It is my privilege. There is no need to apologise.'

She was still desperately worried about Yuri, but with Alex at her side, she became more cheerful. And now she had time to notice what he was wearing. 'Alex, what are you doing in that uniform? Are you in the Red Army?'

'No, of course not.' He spoke very quietly so only she

could hear, though everyone passing them seemed intent on their own business. 'But it saves me having to answer a lot of awkward questions and it opens doors.'

'You could be in dreadful trouble if anyone finds out.'

'They won't. Don't worry.'

He was right about opening doors. They went to the head of the queue and in no time had tickets to take them to Moscow. 'You are my prisoner,' he told her as they boarded the train. 'I am taking you to Moscow to be interrogated for not having the right papers, so do not look too happy to be with me.'

'I can't help it,' she said, not questioning why they should go to Moscow instead of directly to Minsk. 'I am happy. No, not happy, because we still have to find Yuri, but as happy as I could be under the circumstances. Oh, you don't know the relief it is to have someone to talk to, someone who isn't going to swear at me and slap me. And all because he thought there were more jewels to be found. I am sure Grigori had whatever were left, though he pretended to search for them as well.'

'I am surprised he did not take the Star from you.'

'He wanted to but I said I'd lost it. I gave it to Ivan Ivanovich to look after.'

'Why did you take it out of England?'

'I thought I might need it to prove my identity if I met my parents. What a fool I was. Do you think Papa will ever forgive me?'

'Of course he will. It was he who asked me to find you and bring you back. He said he wanted you home, no matter what.'

'I wrote to him several times, but he never answered.'

'He wrote to you at Kirilhor.'

'I never received a single letter. They must have kept them from me. Oh, how I wish I had never come here. It was wicked of me.'

'You are not wicked, sweetheart. Led astray.' He paused. 'What are you going to do about your husband, when we find him?'

'Divorce him. I want nothing more to do with him. I only want my son.'

He was immeasurably relieved. 'Then let us see if we can find him,' he said, ushering her onto the crowded train and sitting beside her, whispering in her ear. 'Remember to play your part. You are my prisoner.'

As the train began to move and pick up speed, the events of the last few days and her lack of sleep, together with her implicit faith in Alex, combined to send her to sleep. He smiled as her head nodded and then settled on his shoulder. Let her sleep. They were not out of the woods yet and he must be careful, very, very careful. And when they did catch up with that devil, Nikolay Andropov, he still had to decide how to wrest the baby from him. Money would be the answer; it seemed to be what had been driving the man all along.

In Moscow he booked them into the Metropol Hotel and then left her to rest while he went to see about their onward journey. 'Try and be patient,' he said before he went. 'I'll be back before you know it. Don't, on any account, leave this room.'

How could she be patient when her child was missing? She was desperately anxious to continue and having to stop was frustrating, but she knew Alex was right when he said they must keep within the Soviet rules and regulations as far as possible. Resting was out of the question, and as soon

164

as she was alone, she began pacing the small room, back and forth, back and forth, thinking of Yuri, wondering if he was being well treated and Olga had been able to obtain baby food for him, praying he would know her when he saw her. Would they give him up without an argument? Or would she have to fight for him? Thank God for Alex.

She stood looking out of the window onto the busy street. Cars, lorries, military vehicles, horses and carts went up and down. Young women in light cotton dresses hurried along with shopping baskets on their arms, a *babushka* with a scarf tied over her head was endeavouring to sell small items from a tray she had round her neck. There were soldiers in breeches, businessmen in light tussore suits, peasants in belted tunics, students and children. She wondered if any of them were as lost, bewildered and miserable as she was.

Alex was gone a long time. By the time she heard the special knock on the door they had arranged, she was in a fever of anxiety. 'Thank God!' she said, pulling him into the room. 'I was beginning to think something had happened to you.'

'I had a lot of calls to make and a lot of queueing. I went to the embassy and told Lord Chilston your child had been kidnapped. He was all sympathy and promised to do what he could with the Russian authorities, though he is due to return to London soon and I don't know who his replacement will be.'

'I can't wait for diplomatic wheels to grind, Alex, I must find Yuri before they spirit him away somewhere where I can't reach him. You did tell him that, didn't you?'

He smiled. 'Yes, of course. Now, we will have something to eat and a good night's sleep and go on tomorrow.'

'No, Alex, no. I want to go now.' She grabbed his arms and looked into his face, seeing the lines of worry and concern for the first time and realising how much she was putting on him. 'I'm sorry, I've no right to ask you to help me. I brought this trouble on myself and ought to resolve it myself. I'll go on alone.'

'No, Lidushka. You will not even get out of Moscow alone, so don't try it. You need me and my uniform and my papers, and Olga and Andropov won't disappear.' He took her hands from his arms and held on to them. 'Olga is going to take up a job she has been directed to. It is more than her life's worth not to go, so we shall find her. Rushing off into the night will not make any difference. And you need to eat and rest, you are nearly dead on your feet.'

Reluctantly she admitted he was right and they went out to find a restaurant where she picked at her food with no appetite. Nor did she have much conversation; her head was too full of Yuri. He took her back to her room. 'Stay with me,' she said.

'Are you sure?'

'Yes. I don't want to be alone.'

He watched her undress and get into bed, then he slipped off his own clothes and got in beside her, putting his arms about her and drawing her towards him. He wanted very much to make love to her and he did not think she would object, but he desisted. Now was not the time and place. He kissed her forehead. 'Sleep tight, my darling,' he murmured. Whether she heard him or not, he did not know; safe in his arms, she had fallen asleep.

When Lydia woke, the place beside her was empty and the only evidence that Alex had ever been there was a dent in the pillow. She sat up in alarm. Where was he? Had he left her? Even as her heart began to race in panic, he appeared in his underclothes with a towel about his neck. 'There's a bathroom along the corridor,' he said. 'The water is only lukewarm, but better than nothing.'

The sun was streaming in the window. It was going to be another scorching day, not the sort of day to be travelling on crowded trains. She rose and kissed his cheek. 'A lukewarm bath sounds like the height of luxury to me. I shan't be long.'

'While you dress, I'll go down and order breakfast.'

It arrived while she was towelling her hair and they sat down to eat. She had not unpacked the night before and it was the work of a moment to put her toilet things into her bag and declare herself ready to go on.

He picked up their cases and she followed him from the room.

The train, which was full of noisy troops, rattled through the countryside; hills, forests, small towns flashed past and all the time Lydia was praying. 'Please let him be there, please let me get him back.' It became a litany in time with the rhythm of the wheels. And then, just short of their destination, the train came to a sudden stop which jolted everyone out of their seats. Alex stood up and put his head out of the door. 'The line is blocked up ahead,' he said. 'Stay here. I'm going to see what's going on.'

He jumped down onto the track and made his way up the line, together with the colonel in command of the troops. 'It looks like an explosion,' he said, as they walked. 'Do you think the war has started?'

'I don't know,' Alex said. 'But I heard that Germany and Russia have signed a non-aggression pact.'

'So they have, to divide Poland between them. We're off to the front. I'm surprised you didn't know that, Major.'

'I did, of course,' Alex said. 'But we are some way from the border and they surely won't start an offensive until all the troops are in position.'

They had reached the site of the explosion which was centred on the station itself and had taken place a few hours before. 'A bomb was left in the luggage room,' a railway official told them. 'The station building is a wreck but we have to concentrate on clearing the line. We could do with some help from your men.'

'I'll arrange it,' the colonel said and returned to the train.

'Were there any casualties?' Alex asked the railwayman.

'Some. Ten dead. They are laid out in the station yard. The wounded have been taken to hospital in Minsk. Twenty of those, women and children too, all waiting for trains.'

'Who did it?'

The man shrugged. 'Who knows? Probably a Jew. There are plenty of those in Minsk who don't like the idea of Russia making friends with Hitler.'

The troops arrived and began helping to clear the line of rubble. The rails beneath it were only slightly damaged, Alex noted. Once the line was clear they would be able to continue their journey. He wandered off to inspect the damage to the station, which was considerable, and from there went out to the station yard. Why he decided to look at the bodies, he did not know. He lifted the tarpaulin that covered their faces. Some had terrible injuries but others were unmarked. There was even a baby, lying beside its mother. He was about to replace the covering when Lydia joined him. 'I wondered where you'd got to. Oh—' She put her hand to her mouth and stared at the dead man lying almost at her feet. 'Oh, my God, it's Kolya.'

'Are you sure?'

'Of course I'm sure.' She rushed up and down the line of bodies, bending over each. Alex held his breath as she reached the woman and the baby, but she passed them with barely a glance. 'They're not here! Olga and Yuri are not here!' She looked wildly about her. 'Are there any more?'

Alex counted them. 'No more dead. The wounded have been taken to hospital in Minsk.'

'How soon can we go on?'

'As soon as the line is cleared.'

'Is there any other way? A bus or something?'

'Nothing that will be any quicker.' He put his arms about her to try and calm her. 'Don't despair, Lidushka. He might not be hurt at all. If Olga was hurt, they would have sent him with her, wouldn't they? We shall find him.'

How could he understand her obsession with her child? He was not a mother. Nor even a father. She shook him off and ran out to see how quickly the line was being cleared, and paced backwards and forwards between the blocked section of line and the stationary train. He could do nothing but walk beside her, uttering banalities which he knew were no comfort at all.

It was nearly midnight when they were told to return to their seats and the train moved off very slowly over the damaged bit of track, before picking up speed. Lydia was so keyed up and anxious, Alex began to fear for her sanity. She had been through so much and, though he kept reassuring her, he knew there were still enormous obstacles to be overcome before she could be reunited with her baby. If it were not for the child, he could have had her safely out of the country and on her way back to England by now.

They arrived in Minsk just as dawn was lightening the sky behind them and then there was another long delay as everyone's papers were examined. Germany had invaded Poland, they were told, and Britain and France had declared war. It meant security was tighter than ever. Lydia was shaking with nerves as the queue in front of them diminished and they moved nearer the table where an official was examining papers and interrogating everyone.

'Leave it to me,' Alex whispered.

His own papers, though forged, were passed without comment. 'Lydia Andropova lost her papers in the explosion along the line,' he told the officer. 'Her husband was killed and her sister-in-law was wounded. They had her baby with them. I am taking her to the hospital to see them. She is out of her mind with worry. I beg you to let us pass. I will be responsible for her.'

The man pretended not to notice the roubles Alex had laid on the table almost under his hand and looked up at Lydia who was white-faced and shivering uncontrollably; obviously in great distress. He returned Alex's papers and waved them on.

They took a taxi to the main hospital where they were told to wait. Lydia sat beside Alex on the hard bench, holding tight to his hand, waiting in torment. The place was crowded. She could hear children crying in the distance and wondered if one of them might be Yuri. It was all she could do not to run along the corridor to trace the source of the crying. At last a big woman in a dark-blue uniform and a white cap came to them and Lydia sprang up to meet her.

'You were enquiring about Olga Denisovna Nahmova,' she said.

'Yes, can we see her?'

'It won't do any good; she is dying and not expected to recover consciousness.'

'The baby,' Lydia moaned, hanging onto Alex's arm to stop herself falling to the floor. 'What happened to the baby?'

'Taken to an orphanage.'

'Which one? Where?'

The woman shrugged. 'I've no idea. He wasn't hurt, though he was bawling loudly enough to wake the dead. Hungry, I expect. I couldn't feed him, so he was handed over to the authorities to deal with.'

Alex decided to intervene before Lydia said something rash and alienated the woman completely. 'Have you no idea where the baby might have been taken?'

'There are two orphanages in Minsk. He could be in either. I'll write the addresses down for you.'

But Yuri Nikolayevich Andropov wasn't at either of them. '*Ewo nyeto*,' they were told at each one. 'Not here.'

'Can I look at the children?' Lydia asked. 'He may have been admitted under a different name.'

The woman shrugged and conducted her to the nursery where dozens of small babies were lying in rows of cots. Some of them were asleep, some crying, all were painfully thin. The stench of urine-soaked nappies and stale milk caught in their throats. If Lydia had not been so absorbed in looking for Yuri among them, she would have been filled with pity for these little scraps of lost humanity. But Yuri was not among them.

'Why do you think he may have another name?' Alex asked, as they left.

'Because everyone would assume he belonged to Olga and she would not have told them any different, even supposing she was conscious enough to do so. Her name was Nahmova and that would be on her papers.'

She would not, could not, stop and insisted on walking about the city, a city obviously preparing for war, searching, searching, looking at every baby being carried or pushed in a pram, much to the annoyance of the child's mother. She was exhausted, but still she dragged herself along. When she could no longer put one foot in front of the other and night was drawing in, Alex took her to the best hotel he could find and sent for a doctor.

'She needs rest,' the man told Alex after he had examined her. 'I will give her something to make her sleep. As for the child, I suggest you try the children's allocation centre. It's on the edge of the forest just out of town. They decide what is to be done with parentless children.'

Alex thanked him and paid him, then went back to Lydia and sat by her bed until she slept. Then he lay down beside her and drew her towards him, nestling her back into his stomach.

He lay awake for hours, listening to her breathing, heard the little cries she made occasionally in her sleep and soothed her with murmured words of love, hoping her subconscious absorbed them. Tomorrow they would try the allocation centre, but even if Yuri were there, how could they convince the authorities that Lydia was his mother? It would almost certainly have been assumed Olga was. He was too tired himself to plan that far ahead. It was almost dawn when he drifted off to sleep.

Chapter Seven

The allocation centre knew nothing of a baby survivor of the station explosion under any name. Undeterred, Lydia continued scouring every orphanage within miles, every charitable home for lost and parentless children and all in vain. Yuri had vanished. Her misery, frustration and anger filled her to such an extent she could think of nothing else. She cried a lot, snapped at Alex when he tried to talk reasonably to her, was sorry for it afterwards and wept on his shoulder. He was unfailingly patient with her. Dear, faithful Alex, who loved her. He demonstrated it in everything he did for her, holding her in her tantrums and her bouts of despair, gently persuading her to eat, suggesting new avenues of search which all turned out to be abortive, making sure she kept clear of the NKVD and fielding enquiries being made about her.

More and more troops arrived in Minsk as German troops swept over Poland. Britain issued an ultimatum to Germany to withdraw, which was ignored, resulting in a declaration of war. The Poles put up a spirited resistance but, assailed on all sides, they were forced to admit defeat and by early October Poland had been divided up between Germany and Russia. It put an end to Alex's plans to take Lydia and Yuri out of the country overland.

'I think we should go back to Moscow,' Alex said. 'I've contacts there. If Yuri has been evacuated east with all the other orphan children, there must be records somewhere. We would do better to look for him that way. It is better than this aimless searching we have been doing.'

She didn't want to go and it took all his persuasive powers, but what he said made sense and in the end she agreed.

He took her to the Metropol that first night back, but hotels cost money and he had used much of what he had brought with him in retrieving the Kirilov Star; if they were to spend more than a few days in the city, they needed something a little cheaper. He found them a tiny one-roomed apartment in a large building which had been converted into a *kommunalka*, a house for communal living looked after by a *dvornik*, a sort of doorman-cum-odd-job man, who watched everyone coming and going and reported irregularities to the police. Lydia was always polite when she could not avoid him, but most of the time kept out of his way.

Some of the rooms housed large families, or even two families, who were expected to make their beds wherever they could: under the stairs, in cupboards, on the living room floor. Because of Alex's rank which, luckily, no one questioned, they had a room to themselves and a proper bed, though they had to share the kitchen with nine other families, who each had their own small space containing a cooker and a few pots and pans. The bathroom was even worse; there was a pitted bath with a dirty tidemark round the middle which could not be cleaned, though Lydia tried, a basin and a lavatory pan which stank. The water was rarely hot enough for a proper bath. The whole building reeked of boiled cabbage and drying laundry.

In those squalid surroundings, she and Alex made love for the first time. Nothing that had gone before was anything like the soaring emotions he aroused in her. She was at once uninhibited and shy, giving way to the utmost sensual pleasure, exploring his body and making him groan with pleasure and then stopping for him to return the compliment, until she could stand it no more and begged him to enter her, now, at once. But it was not only the sex, it was the way they fitted together, like two spoons in a drawer, liking the same things – food, music, animals – laughing at the same jokes, decrying cruelty and injustice. She realised, with something of the surprise of discovering a long-lost treasure, that she loved Alex, not as a big brother, but as a woman loves a man, with her whole heart and soul. She wondered how she could have been so blind not to have realised it before.

'I love you, Sasha,' she said, snuggling up to him in the narrow, lumpy bed. Downstairs someone was playing a tune on a scratchy gramophone and someone else was knocking a nail into a wall. 'I think I always have.'

'And I love you too, sweetheart, and I don't think it, I know it. I always have and always will, however long or short my life.'

'Don't say that, Alex, please don't.'

'Say what? That I love you?'

'Not that, say that as often as you like, I love hearing

it. I meant about life being short. It frightens me.'

'Then we shall both have to live to a ripe old age.' It was said light-heartedly but both knew the precarious position they were in. If only they could find Yuri. If only he could be restored to her, she would be so happy and they could leave.

The search for him continued at a slower pace. She was resigned to the fact that it was going to take time and tried to be patient, writing long letters to Sir Edward and receiving some in reply, which made her feel more cheerful. Winter came and the snow hardened in the streets, bringing out the sleighs and sleds. People went about huddled in so many clothes it was sometimes difficult to recognise who was beneath the layers.

Alex was often involved with other matters which took him away from her for days at a time. He never said what he was doing but it was nothing to do with the search for Yuri or he would have told her about it. Something was going on, something dangerous; she could feel it in her bones. And worry for Alex's safety did battle with her overriding need to find her baby.

She could not bear to be left alone in the apartment and would spend her time trudging about the city in her felt boots. Her previous stays had been so short she had seen nothing of it, but now, especially on days when Alex left her, she saw the city as it really was. It was a mixture of old and new, the ornate and the downright shabby, wide boulevards and narrow alleys, huge characterless apartment blocks like the one in which she and Alex lived, churches and monasteries which were being used for a number of purposes unconnected with religion. Then there was Red Square and the Kremlin with its great red walls which housed the government offices; palaces and churches whose domes had once been crowned with golden crosses – now only one could be seen, atop the beautiful St Basil's Cathedral, somehow saved from destruction; the Arbat, once the abode of the wealthy, whose mansions had been converted to communal living; and street markets and GUM, the department store.

But sightseeing was not what was in her mind as she roamed the city, looking for children's hospitals and orphanages where she produced a snapshot of Yuri which elicited nothing more than a shake of the head and the familiar '*Ewo nyeto*'. In case of war, children were being evacuated to the east and she stood and watched the snaking lines of them, looking lost and bewildered, waiting to be taken away in trucks. But there was no Yuri, though she annoyed the children's caretakers by peering closely at the babies being carried by the older children.

When she wasn't doing that she was shopping, which meant queueing for hours on end for potatoes, bread, onions, lard and perhaps a few sausages; anything with which to make a meal. There was a great deal of panic buying and prices doubled day after day as supplies became scarcer. Sugar, flour, tinned goods, dried peas, cooking oil and fuel all disappeared off the shelves as war seemed inevitable. It was all the talk in the queues, though there were still some who believed the non-aggression pact would hold. Russia, they said, was too big and too powerful to be attacked.

Alex did not like her wandering about on her own and was afraid she would be picked up for interrogation. Everyone was getting more and more jittery and looking for traitors everywhere. And women were being directed to help build defences. He didn't want that to happen to her. 'Darling, you must go back to England, it's not safe for you here,' he told her, when winter turned to spring, the snow disappeared and a little sunlight entered their room through the tiny window. 'I don't trust Hitler to honour the non-aggression pact. He's driven our forces out of France and is cock-a-hoop. Now he's free to turn his attention towards the east. He wants the whole of Poland, not half of it. Russia isn't going to stand for that and there'll be all-out war.'

'I can't go, Alex, you know I can't. There's Yuri . . .'

'I'm afraid you must. I cannot always be with you and I shan't have a moment's peace knowing you are here alone. I promise I will continue to search for Yuri. The minute I know anything I will let you know and find a way of bringing him to you.'

'You mean you aren't coming too?' She couldn't believe that he would calmly send her away.

'I can't. There is work for me to do here.'

'What work? Are you a spy?'

He smiled a little grimly. 'Don't ask, Lidushka, please. I'll arrange for someone I trust to escort you safely home.'

'But London has been all but destroyed by German bombs, it says so in the papers. I wouldn't be any safer there.'

'The papers exaggerate. Besides, London isn't Upstone. You should be safe enough there. As soon as I'm free to come, I'll follow.'

She wept and wept, which wrung his heart, but he would not give in. He almost dragged her, silent and numb with misery, to the British Embassy, an imposing building on the bank of the river overlooking the Kremlin, where he gave her into the care of Lieutenant Robert Conway, a naval attaché who was being recalled. Robert's father, Henry, had been a great friend of Sir Edward's and Lydia had met him once or twice in happier times. Tall, fair-haired and unfailingly cheerful, he was going home to active service.

Once the arrangements had been made, Robert left them alone to say goodbye. They stood facing each other, unable to put into words what the parting meant to them. Alex opened his arms and she flung herself into them. 'Alex, Alex, I can't bear it. Let me stay.'

He hugged her and kissed her. 'No, sweetheart, I can't. It is for your own good. I will come back to you, you see, and I might even have Yuri with me.'

Empty words, she knew, but she took comfort from them. The alternative, that she would never see him or her son again, just didn't bear thinking about. Gently he put her from him and left the room without looking back.

Lydia was so steeped in misery on that journey home, she remembered it as a series of unconnected images. Robert was always cheerful and kind, taking her elbow to guide her, encouraging her to eat when she thought food would choke her, talking to her gently when she needed conversation, remaining silent when she did not want to talk.

They travelled north to Murmansk where a Royal Navy ship was waiting to take on British citizens who wanted to leave: engineers and businessmen, families who had been resident in Russia for many years, some who had arrived after 1917, wanting to help build a perfect state. It hadn't happened and now their loyalties to the country of their birth had been revived.

The great distances between places in Russia made journeys tediously long, but every mile they travelled had been taking her a mile further from Alex, and as the train sped between Moscow and Novgorod, she wished it would slow down, or better still, stop and take her back. Novgorod was an ancient city whose cathedrals, churches and monasteries seemed to have escaped the Bolshevik destruction, but whether that was an illusion she did not know. They didn't stop long enough to find out.

One night there in a very indifferent hotel, and they were on their way again. Forests of oak, ash, birch and conifers hemmed them in and blotted out the landscape as they travelled north. Lydia found her eyelids growing heavy and succumbed to sleep, her head on Robert's shoulder. She stirred when they slowed down at Petrozavodsk where Robert left her to buy food and drink for them at the station. She ate it with little appetite.

By the time the train chugged to a halt in Murmansk she felt tired, dirty and sweaty. The port, once nothing more than a fishing village, was navigable throughout the winter owing to a quirk of the Gulf Stream, and so the last tsar had made it into a naval base for his Northern Fleet. They went straight from the railhead to the harbour and hurried on board just as the ship was sailing.

The weather was atrocious, with squally ice-cold rain and mountainous seas. Like many of the passengers she was sick and stayed in her bunk, but had recovered sufficiently to go on deck the day they were attacked in the North Sea by a lone German bomber. As its bombs landed unbelievably close, sending up huge columns of water, Lydia thought her last hour had come, but in her state of misery viewed the prospect with a kind of indifference. The ship's guns were firing all the time, causing a great din, but eventually the bomber veered off, leaving the ship's crew to assess the damage, which was thankfully slight, and they continued to Scotland where they berthed in Leith, cold and fearful and glad to be on dry land again.

Here they were questioned about who they were, why they were coming to Britain, and if they had relatives who would take them in. Lydia's connection with Sir Edward and the fact that she was escorted by Robert stood her in good stead and she was allowed to continue her journey, though others were detained. From Leith they went to Edinburgh and from there to London by train, and then on to Upstone Hall and she was home. Home at last. Without her son and without the man she loved.

A few days later she was summoned to the Foreign Office for debriefing. Because British officials living in Russia were chaperoned wherever they went and only saw what the Soviet government wanted them to see, they did not get the full picture and were not able to talk to the people. They relied on spies to inform them – spies like Alex, because she had realised that was what he had been doing in Russia besides looking after her and getting her out safely. What a terrible burden she had placed on him.

She was questioned long and hard about why she had gone to Russia in the first place and asked to describe in minute detail everything she had seen: army movements, guns, factories, what the people were thinking, wearing and eating. She did not think she had been able to tell them much, but they accepted what she said, perhaps because she was open about it and also on account of her being Sir Edward's daughter.

At the end of the interrogation, she was asked to sign the Official Secrets Act and offered the job of translating and summarising reports coming out of Russia. To do this she was required to enlist, which she did, becoming a lieutenant in the Auxiliary Territorial Service, the women's branch of the army, known as the ATS. After training she was posted to London and allowed to live at Balfour Place with her father. He had come out of retirement to work at the Foreign Office and stayed at Balfour Place during the week, going home to Upstone Hall at weekends.

It was a very different London from the one Lydia had left. Everything was blacked out after dark; not a chink of light was allowed to escape to guide the German bombers. Doors were protected by walls of sandbags and windows criss-crossed with brown paper tape. There were air-raid shelters everywhere and anti-aircraft gun emplacements in the parks. At first the Luftwaffe had gone for the aerodromes, hoping to win the war in the air, but when that failed they had turned on London. Sitting in the cellar of the apartment block with the other residents, eating sandwiches and drinking tea from flasks, Lydia could hear the drone of aircraft and the answering boom of the ack-ack guns, then the crump of an exploding bomb and the bells of fire engines. The people in the shelter reacted in different ways; some were silent, others tried singing and joking, some women calmly went on knitting.

On her way to work the morning after one of these raids, Lydia would see half-destroyed buildings, some still smoking, their contents crushed or scattered in the street, people walking about in a daze, tripping over coils of hosepipe, trying to avoid the broken glass, unable to believe their homes or businesses had gone. The casualties were frightening, but the buses and trains still ran, the theatres still opened, the shops continued to serve their customers, though their stock was much depleted. Food, coal and clothes were rationed. And yet the birds still sang in the plane trees and the ducks still swam in the Serpentine. Contrary to what she had read in Russia, London was far from destroyed.

It was a world away from Russia. And yet she maintained her contact with it through her work. Alex had been right; the Polish territory the Russians had gained in their pact with Germany was lost in a matter of weeks and, in June 1941, they moved over the border into Russia proper. Lydia's fears for Alex and her son increased a hundredfold and she prayed constantly both might be kept safe. She read every bit of news that came her way, official and unofficial. None of it was cheering. A policy of terror was being pursued by the German troops who considered the Russians, like the Jews, to be subhuman and killed them with extreme brutality, even stringing some of them up on gallows by the roadside. They were apparently making no provision for prisoners, who were left to fend for themselves without shelter, food or medicine. The situation was not helped by Stalin's scorched-earth policy; nothing was to be left that the Germans could use – guns, ammunition, food, fuel or shelter – which punished the local population as well as the enemy. Minsk, which had been extensively bombed in the early days of the campaign, was soon surrounded, trapping thousands of Soviet troops, some of whom melted into the surrounding forests and formed partisan bands to harass the conquerors.

'I can't help thinking of Yuri and wondering where he is,' she said to Sir Edward, one Sunday in July as they strolled in Hyde Park in the sunshine. Huge barrage balloons swayed lazily overhead, creating moving blobs of shadow on the grass, but the Luftwaffe no longer came over every night, being more concerned with the Eastern Front.

'I am sure all children will have been evacuated to the east long ago.'

'I hope so.'

He laid a hand on her arm. 'You mustn't torture yourself over it, Lydia. You did all you could and so did Alex. Have you heard from him?'

'No, not a word, not even through official channels. He was in Red Army uniform when I left him and I worry about him too.'

'Try not to. He knows what he's doing.'

But how could she not worry, especially when the German army seemed unstoppable, sweeping towards Moscow? The only way she could cope was by working, hoping that what she did might shorten the war and bring nearer their reunion. In her mind she coupled them together, Alex and Yuri, the two people she loved above all others.

She worried about Robert too. He was serving with the convoys taking war supplies to Russia and, apart from the weather and treacherous seas, they endured attack after attack from U-boats and German bombers, both during the voyage and in harbour at Murmansk while they were unloading. Whenever he came back from a voyage, he telephoned her to tell her he was safe. They wrote each other long letters, which had to be censored, so they were careful what they said, but the affection was obvious and that affection was gradually becoming more profound, but she did not try to analyse her feelings. It was enough that he cared.

They met as often as they could, sometimes going to a

show or a dance. On one occasion they went to the first night of Noel Coward's play, *Blithe Spirit*, at the Piccadilly Theatre. It was a comedy starring the indomitable Margaret Rutherford as Madame Arcati, a dotty medium who conjured up the spirit of a husband's first wife and caused mayhem with the second. There was not a single reference to the war and, for an hour or two, they forgot their troubles and laughed.

Taking her home to Balfour Place afterwards, Robert stopped in the hallway and kissed her. She was taken by surprise, but did not protest. She supposed she had been half expecting it and it was not unpleasant or even unwelcome. In fact it roused her far more than she would have expected. He stood back and surveyed her with his head on one side, smiling. 'What, no outrage?'

'No, Robert, no outrage.'

'But you're not really ready for it, are you?'

'For a kiss? Or something more?'

'You tell me.' He wasn't smiling now.

'A kiss yes, something more, no. I'm sorry, Rob. I still hope, you see . . .'

'I understand. But we can still be friends, can't we?'

'Of course. I should be very sad if we couldn't.'

'Good, because I am a patient man.'

She knew that already and she knew she would try his patience sorely in the weeks to come.

Minsk fell to the Germans a week later and they had their sights set on the ancient city of Smolensk, on their way to Moscow. According to reports Lydia read, a pall of yellow smoke, caused by burning villages and the dust stirred up by the tanks, hung over everything. A few photographs came in the diplomatic bag which illustrated poignantly what was happening to the populace. One was of two little children, one aged about three and one a little older, standing in the ruins of Smolensk, crying. Another was of some refugees, trudging along a road away from the fighting. In the foreground a shawl-clad woman carried a little boy about the same age as Yuri. She studied the child, wondering if it could be her son. It was difficult to conjure up his face, and in any case her memory was of a four-month-old baby, and though she tried, she did not seem able to add the two years in her mind's eye. Her eyes filled with tears and she couldn't see to work.

The nightly blitz on London, the industrial cities of the north and the major ports around the coast stopped while Hitler concentrated on bombing Leningrad into submission. The Royal Air Force, which had been England's saviour during the Blitz, was able to take a breather and bomb Germany to exact some retribution. But the convoys of vital shipping were still being lost to German U-boats in the Atlantic, the Mediterranean and the North Sea. And as another winter approached, the North Sea run became even more hazardous, with rough seas and sub-zero temperatures. Leningrad was under siege and Moscow threatened. All foreign embassies in Russia were being evacuated eastwards, which meant even less news reached the West, and rumours flourished until it was difficult to know what to believe.

But winter was Russia's ally, not the invaders'. The cold affected everything: tanks and trucks would not start, vehicles and guns were frozen in and could not be moved until the ice had been tackled with pickaxes. According to reports reaching London, the Germans had been so sure of their swift success they had not even supplied their troops with winter clothing. Comparisons were being made with Napoleon's march on Moscow a hundred and thirty years before; the winter had defeated him and it would defeat Hitler. At home in London, Lydia realised how lucky she had been and how much she owed to the absent Alex. He had been a constant presence in the background of her life all through her growing up, but it was only in Russia, when he had appeared just when she needed him most, that she realised how much she loved him, when it was almost too late. She longed for him to return to her.

Her daily scrutiny of all the reports arriving on her desk for his name became a ritual before she began translating, but it was never there. Surely if he were alive, he would have found some way of letting her know? She worked diligently, putting in long hours, using it as a kind of anaesthetic to numb the pain of being without her son and the man she loved.

It was Sir Edward who broke the news to her. She had arrived home a little before him and was in the kitchen preparing an evening meal for them both when he came in. He hung up his hat, coat and scarf and dropped his briefcase on the hall table as he always did. She heard the clunk of it and then his footsteps coming along the polished parquet floor towards the kitchen. 'You're just in time,' she said without looking round. 'I've made a casserole.'

'Later,' he said. 'There's something I have to tell you first. Come and sit down.'

She turned as he sank into a chair at the kitchen table, and noticed how tired and drawn he looked. He was working long hours and at his age it was taking its toll. She sat opposite him, the table between them. His hesitation was alarming her. 'Papa, what is it?'

He reached out and put his hands over hers on the table. 'It's Alex. He's . . .' He stumbled, then collected himself. 'I'm afraid he's dead.'

'Dead?' She stared at him. 'He can't be.' But even as she denied it, she realised she had been half expecting it, but refusing to acknowledge it, as if by even thinking of such a possibility she would bring it about. 'Are you sure?'

He nodded. 'He was in Minsk when it was overrun by the Germans. He had apparently been acting with immense courage during the battle, single-handedly disabling a gun which had been shelling a convent being used to house children orphaned by the war, but it cost him his life. The action was reported by a senior officer in the Red Army who had witnessed it and recommended Major Alexei Petrovich Simenov for a posthumous medal. And then it came to light there was no such person serving in the Red Army, and enquiries revealed who he really was. Unfortunately the government in London has had to deny he was anything to do with them and he was acting off his own bat.'

She hardly heard what he said. She was back in Russia, in that squalid room in Moscow, loving and being loved by Alex. An Alex who was no more. He had declared he would always love her however long or short his life. Had he known how short it would be? Had he said he would rejoin her and bring Yuri to her, simply to get her safely away? He had saved her life, but lost his own. She sat looking at her father's hands covering hers and could not take it in. 'I can't believe it. I don't want to believe it.'

'I know. I didn't want to believe it either. I looked on him as a son, especially after his parents died. I had hoped you and he might . . .' He stopped and took his handkerchief from his pocket, pretending to blow his nose. It was enough to set her off and she put her head into her arms on the table and wept, huge gulping sobs. He stood up and went round behind her and laid a hand on her shaking shoulders. He did not speak. There was nothing he could say that would in any way mitigate her misery. They stayed that way for a long time, not speaking, a little tableau that epitomised the war and all it was doing to ordinary men and women.

She lifted her head at last and sat up. 'I suppose I knew, in my heart of hearts, that it was the end when we said goodbye in Moscow. I have been living on hope, but now hope is gone, not only for Alex, but for Yuri too. There's no one left to look for him, you see, and it's been too long . . .'

'I know.' It was said quietly. It was the easiest thing in the world for people to disappear in Russia, especially children who were more often than not given new names when they arrived in the orphanages.

'But when the war is over, perhaps we can try again . . .' He did not know how to go on giving her more hope when it would be better for her to accept her loss.

She stood up, dry-eyed now, as if every single ounce of moisture had been sucked out of her, as if she were the withered shell of the person she had been. 'We had better have our dinner before it's all dried up.'

But neither could eat.

ROBERT

1941 – 1945

Chapter Eight

Theirs was not the only tragedy; it was being enacted all round them every day and, like everyone else, they pulled themselves together and got on with their lives, more than ever determined to defeat Hitler and all he stood for. Lydia stopped looking for Alex's name in the documents she had to translate, and slowly, as the weeks and months passed, she found she could look back in gratitude for what time they had had together and not yearn for what she could not have. Not that she could forget – that was impossible – but her time in Russia was becoming unreal; Yuri and Alex were ghosts who haunted her dreams but had no place in reality.

They celebrated Christmas Day 1941 at Upstone Hall, though 'celebrate' was perhaps the wrong word. Hong Kong surrendered to the Japanese on that day, and that was followed in February 1942 by the fall of Singapore. And still the Allied ships were being sunk. But the Russians were rallying and the RAF was hitting back and hitting hard.

'They're getting a taste of their own medicine,' Robert said when he had leave at the end of May 1942, which coincided with Lydia's own leave and they were spending it at Upstone Hall with Margaret. The night before there had been a huge raid on Cologne involving over a thousand bombers. They had heard wave after wave of them droning overhead as they lay sleepless in their beds.

The Hall had been gradually modernised over the years, but externally it was exactly the same as it had been in 1920 when Lydia had first arrived there, a bewildered, traumatised four-year-old, crying for her parents. The servant situation was very different; except for Mrs Selby, a daily woman and Claudia, they had all left for the armed services or more lucrative employment and it was impossible to recruit more, so Margaret lived in one wing and shut the rest of the house.

It was a peaceful island surrounded by noisy airfields. The Japanese had bombed the US fleet at Pearl Harbor the previous December, which had brought the Americans into the war, and they had arrived in large numbers and parked their flying fortresses on the airfields, filled the pubs, smoked fat cigars and flirted with the local girls – much to the chagrin of the local young men. They were generous to a fault, especially to the village children, whom they plied with what they called candy, and oranges. Some of the little ones had never seen oranges and were not quite sure what to do with them. The soldiers sliced them in half and showed the children how to suck the juice out of them.

None of this impinged on Lydia and Robert, who wanted to make the most of their leave, going for long walks in the countryside, taking picnics to local beauty spots and shopping in Norwich or Cambridge, using up their precious clothing coupons on utility clothes.

'What about you? Are things any easier for you?' she asked him. They were walking alongside the river, hand in hand.

'Oh, not so bad,' he said dismissively.

'I worry about you.'

'Do you?'

'Of course.'

'And I worry about you,' he said, raising the hand he held and kissing the back of it. 'I wish you could be here at Upstone Hall all the time. It's safer than London.'

'London is where my work is, just as the sea is where your work is and we have to do it. In any case, the Blitz has moved on from London. Nowhere is any safer than anywhere else these days.'

'No, I suppose not.' He paused, took a deep breath and then went on as if he had to summon up the courage to say what he had to say. 'Lydia, do you still think of him?' He paused. 'Alex, I mean.'

'Sometimes,' she answered slowly. 'It happens when I least expect it, but I have learnt to accept that he has gone, a victim of war, as so many other young men were, dragged into more danger than he should have been because of me and Yuri. Yuri will be three now, you know.' Counting the birthdays she had missed was still heartbreaking. She would not even consider that he, too, might have died, in spite of her nightmares.

'I know,' he said softly. 'I just wanted to know because there is something I want to ask you.'

'Oh.' She half-knew what was coming.

'I know I'm not Alex . . .'

'No, but that doesn't mean you are not a lovely man. I have been fortunate to have both of you.'

'That's what I wanted to ask. Will you have me? Marry me, I mean. You know how much I love you. You are everything to me and it will make me the happiest man alive if you would.'

She smiled. 'You haven't asked me if I love you.'

'Do you?'

'Yes, I think I do.'

His blue eyes lit up. 'Then you will marry me?'

'Yes.'

He stopped walking, twisted round and gathered her into his arms. 'Oh, my darling, you have no idea how happy that makes me. I promise I'll be good to you . . .'

'But Robert, you already are good to me.'

'It will be better.' He kissed her long and hard, and others on the towpath passed them with a smile. 'Oh, thank you, my darling, thank you.'

She laughed. 'I ought to thank you, for being so patient with me, for being my friend when I needed one most and putting up with my bouts of despair . . .'

'That's what love is all about,' he said. 'And it works both ways. Knowing you were waiting here for me helped me get through the worst. I had your picture in my pocket next to my heart, keeping me safe.'

She laughed. 'Oh, Robert, that's nothing but superstition.'

'So what, if it works?'

They turned, arms linked, and went back to tell Margaret their good news.

Margaret had initially been angry with Lydia over the way she had disappeared and left Edward desperately worried. 'You've put years on him, you ungrateful child,' she had said when Lydia reappeared. 'You have no idea what it's been like here, not knowing whether you were alive or dead. And Alex going after you. Heaven knows what will happen to him. I suppose you expect to walk back in here as if nothing has happened.'

It had made Lydia feel terribly guilty, and she would have left again, if Papa had not said Mama did not mean to sound so unforgiving, it was just her way of saying she was relieved and pleased to have her home again. Alex's death had brought them together again, and though she was often in London, they became almost as close as they had been before. Robert's visits were welcomed and encouraged and, with the news of their engagement, the last of the resentment disappeared. Robert's father, Henry, had been a lifelong friend of Sir Edward's and would surely have applauded their decision if he had still been alive.

They were married in St Mary's Church in Upstone six weeks later. It was an austerity wedding; few people were free to travel and many were in the forces and could not get leave. Robert was in uniform and Lydia wore Margaret's wedding dress, which fitted her surprisingly well. They had flowers from the garden, but rationing meant catering was a problem. But somehow Margaret coped and even managed a small cake.

Edward, who was giving her away, had questioned her closely on her reasons for wanting to marry Robert. 'He's a good man,' he had said. 'None better. But are you sure you're not marrying him out of gratitude? It wouldn't be fair on him if you were.'

'No, Papa. I really love him. Alex belongs in the past

and that has become a kind of dream. It's not real anymore. Today is real and Robert is real, and I must get on with a life that is real.'

'So long as you are sure.'

'I am sure.'

They had a short honeymoon in the Lake District and then it was back to their wartime jobs, long weeks apart, punctuated by leaves that were all too short and rarely coincided.

In 1943 the tide of war seemed to turn. The Russian army drove the Germans out of Stalingrad, the city which symbolised the Russian character in its determination not to surrender. It was a city in ruins where thousands upon thousands had died. And that was only the beginning. Russian troops were victorious all along the line and the Germans were retreating. The Battle of El Alamein had been the turning point in the West; Italy was invaded, surrendered and changed sides, and the Royal Air Force used bouncing bombs to destroy the Möhne and Eder dams in the Ruhr, causing massive flooding and destruction. In November Winston Churchill, President Roosevelt and Stalin met at Teheran to talk about the second front, something the Russians had long been lobbying for.

Lydia and Robert's marriage was a calm and peaceful oasis in the midst of noise and confusion, death and destruction. They had no marital home, having decided to leave looking for a house until after the war. Whenever they could get a few hours off together, they spent it either in London at Balfour Place or at Upstone Hall. It was here that Bobby was born in May 1943, ten months after they were married. His birth had not been planned but he was welcomed all the same. He was nothing like Yuri to look at, being more like Robert, after whom he was named. Robert was at sea, but as soon as he docked, he managed a forty-eight hour pass and came home to see his month-old son. He was ecstatic and kept going into the nursery to look at him, a wide grin on his face.

Margaret and Edward were equally pleased. 'Our first grandchild,' Margaret said, walking about with him in her arms to shush his crying. She seemed to have forgotten that Lydia was not her flesh and blood. And Claudia suddenly found she had a use after all. She had looked after Lydia as a child and now she could help look after Bobby, who was the apple of her eye, and she spoilt him dreadfully.

Lydia had left the ATS to have her baby and so she was no longer privy to secret intelligence and had to rely on news bulletins like the ordinary citizen. But even the ordinary citizen knew something was up the following spring. For a start, a ten-mile-wide strip of coastline from the Wash right round to Land's End was forbidden to visitors, and the concentration of troops, tanks, guns and aircraft could not be concealed. The second front was imminent. What was not known was when and where the landing might be and speculation was rife. The first Lydia and Margaret knew it was beginning was when they were woken in the night of the fifth of June by the droning of aeroplanes, hundreds and hundreds of them. They ran out onto the terrace in their nightclothes to stare up at the sky which was black with aircraft. And the following morning, the day on which Lydia had always celebrated her birthday – knowing it had really been in April had not changed that – they heard it confirmed on the wireless. As she opened utility cards of birthday wishes, she heard John Snagge's steady voice announce: 'D-Day has come. Early this morning the

Allies began an assault of the north-western face of Hitler's European fortress . . .'

They stood in the kitchen, hugging each other. 'What a birthday present!' Lydia said. 'I wonder where Robert is.'

Robert, she discovered two days later when he rang her, had been in the thick of it, taking troops across the English Channel, but unlike his passengers, he didn't have to stay. 'From where I was standing it looked like hell,' he told her. 'But it was magnificent.' He didn't add that he would be going backwards and forwards for many more days, taking reinforcements and equipment, but she had guessed it anyway. They were assembling a harbour of precast parts, so that ships could dock and unload their cargoes, and they were being ferried out under intensive fire; the Germans had no intention of giving up.

'Did you get my birthday present?'

He had sent her a silver brooch in the shape of an anchor, with their two names entwined in the rope around it. 'Yes, it's lovely. I'm wearing it now. I'll thank you properly when you come home.'

'I shall look forward to that. Don't know when it will be, though.'

'Never mind. Look after yourself.'

'And you. Love you lots.'

'Love you lots too.'

She put the telephone down and returned to Margaret, who was knitting thick socks for Robert in oiled wool. She was not a good knitter and the wool was hard on the hands; Lydia wondered if they would ever be finished. 'Robert is fine,' she said. 'Looking forward to coming home.'

'It won't be long now,' Margaret said. 'It will soon be over.'

It was over for Margaret just ten days later.

She had gone to London to see Edward who was busier than ever and had little time to spend at Upstone. Lydia, who had stayed behind at the Hall with Bobby, was unprepared for the distraught telephone call and could hardly make out who was speaking, his voice was so thick with distress.

'Papa, Papa, what are you saying?'

'She's dead, Lidushka. Your mama is dead.'

'Dead?' she echoed, hardly noticing that he had called her by the Russian diminutive of her name, something he had done when she was little. 'When? How?'

'A flying bomb. This morning on her way to meet me.'

Having no pilots, flying bombs had no specific targets and simply flew until they ran out of fuel and the engines stopped, then they whistled down, mainly on London and its environs. No one had known what they were at first and all manner of rumours abounded about crashed planes and pilots baling out and Allied shells falling short, but only that morning the BBC news had announced, 'The enemy has started using pilotless planes against this country.' It was only three days since the first one had arrived but already the damage and loss of life was huge. It stifled the optimism of the D-Day landings; Hitler wasn't done for yet. If only they had known about the new weapon before Margaret left, Lydia might have persuaded her not to go.

'I'm coming up.'

'You can't do anything.'

'I'm coming anyway. Claudia will look after Bobby.'

She caught the first available train and took a taxi to Balfour Place. She found Edward sitting at his desk, staring into the distance. He had flung off his jacket and was in his shirt sleeves. His tie had been loosened and the top button of his shirt was undone. He had obviously been raking his fingers through his hair and it stood up on end. In one hand he held the brooch Margaret had been wearing and the pin had dug into his palm, but he didn't seem aware of the blood. A cold cup of tea stood at his elbow. He hardly noticed Lydia's arrival.

'Papa,' she ventured.

He turned towards her, his grey eyes so bleak they made her shudder. She ran to him and knelt at his feet, taking the brooch from him and laying it on the desk before wiping the blood from his hand with her handkerchief. 'Oh, Papa, I don't know what to say.'

'We didn't even have time to say goodbye,' he said. 'It was so sudden. One minute she was there, coming along the road towards me, smiling and waving and then . . . and then . . . Oh God, it was terrible. A whistle, a bang and I was thrown in a heap in the road. It winded me and for a moment I couldn't get up, but when I did, I saw half the street had gone. Bodies everywhere. I ran looking for her. I kept hoping it hadn't been her I had seen, that it was a stranger coming towards me, someone who looked like her. But then I found her. She was unmarked, not a scratch on her. I thought she had been knocked out by the blast and tried to rouse her. A warden came along and stopped me, took my hands away from her. Then an ambulance came and took her away . . . Oh, Lidushka, how am I going to live without her?'

She had never seen him cry; he had always been so strong, so in control, the one to whom she turned in distress. When they heard Alex was dead it was she that had collapsed and could not function, while he, who must have been mourning himself, was her comfort and gave her the strength to continue. Now it was her turn to comfort him. She made more tea and made him drink it. She made sandwiches for them both and sat on the sofa beside him the whole night while he talked. He seemed to want to talk, on and on he went, hardly drawing breath. It was as if he was afraid to stop for fear of being overwhelmed.

He spoke of his love for Margaret and how beautiful she was, how he had courted her, how she had resisted at first but then agreed to marry him. He described their wedding day, how happy they had been and how disappointed they were when they found she could not have children, and his joy when Lydia had come into their lives. The pace slowed in the early hours of the morning and at dawn he slept from sheer exhaustion. She covered him with a blanket and left him to prepare breakfast. Only then did she weep herself, a paroxysm of tears which ran down her face as she boiled a kettle and made tea. She found some bread and some dried egg in the pantry. The only way dried egg could be successfully cooked was by scrambling it. By the time it was done and the bread toasted, her tears had dried on her face and she was ready to continue being the strong one.

They took Margaret's body home to Upstone Hall for burial. Most of the village turned up for the funeral, for she had been much loved. Life went on but Edward was bowed down with grief. He seemed to become old overnight, stooped and silver-haired. Lydia did her best to help him over it and sometimes she thought she had succeeded, and then he would say something about Margaret as if he had forgotten she was no longer with them, and when she gently pointed this out to him, he would say, 'But Lidushka, she is still with us. She will always be with us.' To which there was no answer.

And sometimes she wondered if it was the same with Alex. Even in death, was he still with her? Did he, in some way, watch over her as he had done in life? That did not mean she was unhappy with Robert; quite the contrary, their marriage was happier than she had any right to expect and she thanked God for it. It looked as though the war would soon be over and they could settle down in peace. After the turbulence that had gone before, it was all she asked.

ALEX

1945 – 1955

Chapter Nine

April 1945

The rumours were running round the camp like wildfire. Where they had come from, when no newspapers or radio were allowed to the prisoners and possessing either was punishable by death, Alex did not know. But the whispers passed from mouth to mouth, were whispered in the bleak shower rooms as they stood naked under a trickle of cold water, muttered on the seats of the rows of toilets, sung as a kind of ditty as they waited in line every morning during roll call. 'The Russians are coming. Didn't you hear the guns?'

He had certainly heard gunfire, no one could be unaware of it when they were in camp, which was only at night if they were on the day shift and during the day if they worked nights. The overcrowded huts shook and it felt as if they would tumble about their ears. When they were in the factory which had been built alongside the camp, they could hear nothing of the outside world. The windows and doors were tight shut and blacked out against air raids, and

207

the noise of the machinery drowned out every other sound, even their voices. The work was hard and unremitting and the shifts, which had begun as ten hours at a time, soon lengthened to eleven and then twelve as the need to supply the German army with weapons became more acute. Quotas had to be reached; the punishment for failure was a beating and a spell in the punishment block in total darkness on bread and water, and little enough of that. For many of the inmates, already on starvation rations, it meant almost certain death.

Alex had no illusions about what would happen to him if the Russians arrived. He would be executed, probably without the refinement of a trial. His alias as Major Alexei Petrovich Simenov would not save him. In fact, he doubted if any of the Russian prisoners would be sent back to their homes. He had learnt enough of Soviet ways to know they would almost all be accused of collaboration, simply for allowing themselves to be captured and made to work in German factories. If not put in front of a firing squad, they would be sent to prison camps in Siberia, from where few would ever return. As for what the Soviets did to spies, he dare not think of that. It would have been better to have died in that field outside Minsk. By all the laws of nature he should have died. According to Iosef Ilyievich who saw what happened, no one ought to have survived the barrage of gunfire that rained down on him.

He had been in the area, trying to keep his promise to Lydia to try and find Yuri. In spite of telling Lydia he thought all the babies must have been evacuated to safety, he had decided to resume the search back at the beginning and that meant returning to the hospital where Olga and Yuri had been taken. Someone who had not been on duty the day they visited might remember something others had missed. Sticking to his military disguise had been easier than he expected; officers were often sent from the high-ups in the Kremlin to find out what was really happening on the ground. Communications were chaotic, and provided he kept out of the way of officialdom, he felt reasonably safe, though always on his guard. At the hospital, he had been surprised to learn that Olga Denisovna Nahmova had not died but had been evacuated with hundreds of other badly injured patients to a Moscow hospital.

Remembering what Lydia had said about how Olga idolised Yuri, he felt sure the woman would not give him up and would set about looking for him as soon as she was discharged. If he found Olga, he might find Yuri. But the boy was a Russian citizen, he reminded himself; even if he found him, he would not be allowed to take him out of the country legally. He would cross that bridge when he came to it. It might be that all he would be able to tell Lydia was that her son was safe and well. Even this slight feeling of optimism was dashed when Minsk came under attack from the invading Germans with thousands of troops, tanks and big guns.

He had found himself watching a field gun firing on what had once been a convent but which had become a home for orphan children and, for all he knew, might contain Yuri. It had incensed him. Without thinking of the possible consequences he had taken a couple of hand grenades and crawled round to encircle the bunker from which the gun had been firing. He had managed to get below the gun's trajectory without being seen and approached it from the side, but hand grenades were puny weapons against the gun and so he had crept closer than it was safe for him to

209

do so. He was right on top of it when he pulled out the pin of the first grenade and flung it in the bunker. It did not disable the gun but it caused enough injury and confusion among the crew for him to toss the other down the barrel, a satisfyingly accurate lob. For what happened after that, he had only the word of Iosef, who had been hiding in a nearby ditch.

'There was a great explosion,' he said, when Alex recovered consciousness several days later. 'There were bits of gun, limbs and flesh flying everywhere. You were flung ten metres into the air like a rag doll. And then it all went quiet. I crept out to look. I did not expect to find you breathing, but you were. All the gun crew were dead. Such heroism could not be allowed to perish. I carried you home.'

Iosef was a peasant who lived with his aged mother in an *izba* a few *versts* outside Minsk. He was big and strong but lacking in wit and that had somehow saved him from conscription into the Red Army. How they lived Alex had no idea, being only half-conscious at the time and unable to walk on account of a broken leg, not to mention a lump the size of a chicken's egg on the back of his head. The Russians' scorched-earth policy meant that nothing was left for them to live on. When the Germans threatened to overrun the area, he had carried his mother and then Alex into the nearby forest where they met other Russians, civilians and troops who were determined not to fall into German hands. It was an area of mixed forests and swamps, often hidden in mist and fog, an ideal habitat for partisans. Iosef, who was not as simple as he appeared, told him they stole food, rifles and ammunition from the Germans. 'We are causing them no end of inconvenience,' he had said with a chuckle.

It was inevitable that they would be rounded up in the end. Many of the partisans had been shot on the spot; the injured were left to die by the roadside, while those who were able to walk had been herded like cattle along the road to Germany. They were given no food, no shelter and very little rest. Alex, hobbling painfully, had been supported by Iosef and another of their number. 'We saved you before, we are not going to let you die now,' he had said. His mother had died a few weeks before and he clung to keeping Alex alive as a sort of compensation. The fact that he had never been a soldier and could not truthfully be termed a prisoner of war was not taken into consideration; he was between fifteen and sixty-five and therefore of military age.

That first camp had been nothing but a field surrounded by barbed wire. There were no huts and they were left to try and make themselves what shelter they could with whatever materials came to hand: brushwood, old posts, bits of clothing and ragged blankets. As for food, that was so minimal it consisted of onion skins boiled in water and little else. The prisoners ate the grass until the field became a desert. They gnawed the bones of dead animals who had strayed into the camp and been killed; dogs, cats, rats, pigeons brought down with catapults, it didn't matter what they were as long as they had a little flesh on them. Fighting over scraps was rife, though the weakness of the combatants meant they were half-hearted affairs. When winter came they died in their thousands and were flung into mass graves. How he had survived Alex did not know.

The Germans needed workers to feed their great war machine and who better to supply them than their prisoners? Towards the end of 1942, they were taken to Sachsenhausen concentration camp. It was triangular in layout, with a three-metre-high perimeter wall within which was a path patrolled by guards and dogs and inside that an electric fence. Barrack huts lay beyond the roll-call area and these had tiered bunk beds, though they were so overcrowded, the beds were pushed together so that three and sometimes four shared beds intended for two. A factory had been built just outside the camp, in which the prisoners were expected to work for the German war effort. Refusing to work was not an option, but few would have done so because workers were fed – not generously, but enough to keep them working and alive. But for some it was too late. Friendships made were often broken by death.

Iosef had been singled out for the gas chamber almost as soon as they arrived. He was mentally deficient and therefore even more reviled than the ordinary Russians, who, as Slavs, were considered like the Jews to be *Untermensch*: subhuman. Alex, who could do nothing to save him, had mourned his passing.

Because he spoke excellent German, he was often asked to translate the official pronouncements of the camp commandant, and as few Germans knew any Russian, he was able to put whatever interpretation he liked on his words, warning his listeners of new edicts and suggesting ways that the sick could be saved from being carted off. If you were not well enough to work, you were not worth your rations.

Although skeletal, he did not quite become the numbed, unthinking automaton that many of them did and would often lie in his bunk listening to the quarrelsome words of his fellow prisoners and dream of better times. It was then he would conjure up a picture of Lydia in his mind's eye. His filthy unsanitary surroundings faded and he was in an orchard with apple blossom all around him and a blue sky above. The voices of those around him faded and he heard laughter. Lydia's laughter – light, carefree, mischievous.

Had she got safely back to England? Had she been given a hard time by the Foreign Office? Had she gone back to work? Was she in London or at Upstone Hall? Sometimes he liked to imagine her in a printed cotton frock, sitting on the swing Sir Edward had made for her in the garden at Upstone, with the sun shining on her hair and daffodils in the grass at her feet. Sometimes she would be in a lavish ball gown, dancing with him on the terrace to the music of a waltz, the Kirilov Star glittering at her throat. He had hated having to send her away without her child. Her misery over the loss of Yuri had torn his heart to shreds. He had done his best to be cheerful and optimistic for her sake, but as soon as he was alone, his despair had overtaken him and he had wept, knowing, as he handed her over to Robert Conway, that he would almost certainly lose her. Now, weakened and unsure if he was meant to survive, he tried only to think of the happier times and wish her well.

The rumours they were hearing reminded him of the previous year when they had told of the Western Allies' invasion of France. Not even their captors, who refused to admit defeat was possible, had been able to go on denying the truth for long and they had maintained the enemy would soon be driven back into the sea. How long would they take to come clean about this latest piece of news? Hearing the whispers, they instructed Alex to tell the prisoners that what they were hearing were German guns firing on Allied bombers and the flames they could see in the distance were planes that had been shot down and exploded. Some believed it, some didn't.

Your category as a prisoner influenced your reaction. Dressed in the rough striped uniform of a prisoner, each wore a patch which indicated their group: yellow for Jews, red for Communists, black for Gypsies and anti-social elements, green for common criminals, purple for Jehovah's Witnesses, who called themselves 'Bible Students', and pink for homosexuals. Alex's patch was red. It had afforded him some wry amusement in the beginning, but he knew it would be a death sentence if the Russians reached them first.

Now, four years after being taken captive, his thoughts were turning to freedom. But how to obtain it? How near were the Russians? How far away were the Western Allies? What plans had their captors made should they come under attack? Would they resist or retreat? What would they do with the prisoners? At the far end of the camp they had built a crematorium to dispose of the thousands who died, but no one was in any doubt that it also contained gas chambers where those who were too weak to work were disposed of. Would they all be herded in there? His questions were echoed by everyone else and no amount of shouting and beating could stop the prisoners talking.

Alex began to make plans to escape, which he told no one. It would have to be done on the march from the camp to the factory, the only time they went outside the gates. Being spring, they went in daylight, but when they returned at the end of the day's shift it was growing dark. He decided to make the attempt on the return journey at a particular spot where there was a hedge overhanging a ditch. If he could roll into that without being seen by the guards who accompanied them, he might not be missed until roll-call when the column arrived in the camp. It would give him a few minutes, no more, to get away. He began to hoard a little of his food each day.

His plans were thwarted because production in the factory suddenly stopped and they ceased to be taken out of the camp. It was a sure sign the Germans were expecting the worst. Lorries drove up and down the roads, taking the machinery and the German workers further west, and clouds of smoke in the factory yard indicated papers being burnt. No one told the prisoners what was to become of them. And their already starvation rations were cut.

The Jews had been rounded up some time before and driven away in trucks, no one knew where. Towards the end of April, the criminals, the Jehovah's Witnesses and the homosexuals were marched out escorted by guards. Alex learnt later that as soon as they were a few miles from the camp, their guards had returned to camp, leaving the prisoners to fend for themselves. How many of them survived, Alex never knew. It left only the political prisoners and the Russian POWs still in camp. This caused more than a little consternation. They were going to be handed over to the advancing Russians. A few saw it as a good thing, their belief in Bolshevism so firm they could not envisage anything but joy and a return to their homes and loved ones. Most, including Alex, were more realistic.

Those that were left were rounded up, lined up in batches and herded out of the gates like cattle. At first Alex thought they might be going west, away from the advancing Russians, and he was content to go along with that, but after a time it became apparent they were going north. What their captors had in mind he had no idea, but his mind was intent on reaching the Allies. They had not been going for long when the weaker among them began to drop like flies and were shot on the spot or left to die by the roadside. Could he fake collapse and be abandoned? But how could he be certain one of the guards would not put a bullet in him to make sure?

As they shuffled along incredibly slowly, they met civilians trudging along the road in the opposite direction, preferring to be taken by the Western Allies than the Russians. When, at midday, they were allowed to stop and rest by the wayside and eat the crust of bread with which they had been provided, he spoke to one of the women trudging southwards. '*Gnädige Frau*, what news is there?'

He had at first thought she was in her forties, but when she came closer to answer him, he realised she was at least ten years younger than that. She was thin as a rake and her hair, which had once been dark, was streaked with white. 'Are you German?' she asked.

'No. English.'

'*Ein Engländer!* How did you come to be with this lot?' She nodded at the column of men in their striped camp uniforms.

'I was attached to the Red Army when I was captured. They took me for a Russian. How far away are they?'

'The Reds? No more than a few kilometres. Where are they taking you?'

'I don't know, but I don't want to fall into the hands of the Russians.'

'Why not, if you are English?'

'I can't prove it and the Communists would arrest me for a spy. Can you help me?'

'Why should I?'

'No particular reason. On the grounds of common humanity, if you like. On the other hand I might be able to help you when the time comes.'

She stood looking at him with her head on one side, turning over his request. If the Germans lost the war, it would make sense for her to have helped an Englishman, a sort of insurance policy. Not that they would lose; the Führer had promised them they would drive the invaders out and be victorious. 'I wouldn't help a Russian,' she said. 'I'd spit on him. You are sure you're not Russian?'

He smiled crookedly, better not admit his origins. 'No, I am not Russian.'

'What do you want me to do?'

He looked round him. Their guards were sitting on the side of the road, eating bread and cheese and swilling it down with beer while their charges stood or squatted waiting for the signal to resume the march. 'Find me some civilian clothes. I'll get nowhere dressed like this. I can't pay you, not until after the war, but I will do it then.'

She didn't ask him how that was to be achieved. 'You want them brought to you?'

'No, I'll have to slip away, roll into a ditch or something.'

'They'll shoot you.'

He shrugged. 'It's a risk I'm prepared to take.'

The guards had finished their break and were rounding up their prisoners again. She thought for a moment. 'I'll claim you for my long-lost husband. What's your name?'

'Alex Peters, though I am known here as Alexei Petrovich.'

'My name is Else Weissmann. My husband's name was Erich.'

'Was?'

'He died outside Stalingrad in '42.'

'I'm sorry. That was a bad business.'

'Yes. Come, I haven't got time to waste.' She grabbed his hand and hauled him towards the sergeant of the guard. 'You have my husband here,' she told him belligerently. 'How did that come about? He is a good Wehrmacht soldier, not a Russian. They said he was missing on the Eastern Front and here he is, not two kilometres from home. I would not have known about it, if he had not called out to me. Let him come home.'

The sergeant looked Alex up and down. 'Is this true?'

'Of course.' He launched into a story of being taken prisoner by the Russians who were subsequently captured by the Germans and he had been herded along with them. His German was perfect and everyone knew the Russians couldn't speak anything but their own tortured language, so the guard laughed. 'What does it matter?' he said. 'What does it matter if you all walked off? I wouldn't have to stay if you did. Go on. Clear off.' He turned back to hustling the rest of the prisoners into line.

Alex made a show of embracing Else. 'Let's hurry before he changes his mind,' he said.

She took him back to an apartment in a block on the eastern outskirts of the nearby town of Prenzlau where she had been living. From her top floor living room they could see the smoke clearly, and even as he stood there while Else searched the wardrobe for clothes, he heard the whistle and then the bang of an exploding shell. The windows and doors rattled and some plaster came down from the ceiling onto his shoulders. He moved away from the window. 'They're getting closer,' he called out to her.

She appeared with a bundle of clothes and a pair of shoes in her arms. ' Try these.'

He was taller than her husband had been and definitely thinner; the trousers barely came to his ankles and had to be held up with a belt. But it was better than the prison uniform with its conspicuous patch. The shoes, although a mite tight, were better than the clogs he had been issued with for his march to the factory and back. While he was changing, another shell came over, nearer this time. 'They've got the factory,' she said, looking out of the window. 'Hurry up, we'll be next.'

They clattered down the stairs and out into the street, then dodged from building to building as more shells came over and more heaps of rubble appeared where once buildings had stood. 'I'm sorry,' he said, when they paused in a doorway to get their breath back. 'I have delayed you. You could have been far away by now.'

'Where do you want to go?' she asked.

He laughed. 'As far from here as I can get, preferably to the Western Front, wherever that might be.'

'Have you got any money?'

'No.'

'I have a little. You had better come with me. I could do with the company.'

And so he did. They escaped from the town which was rapidly becoming a ruin, plodding slowly along with hundreds of others, carrying whatever they could in the way of belongings. Some had donkey carts, some handcarts, some prams, some nothing at all. There were women and children and old men and, here and there, a soldier in a tattered uniform. Occasionally they were overtaken by camouflaged cars with officers sitting in them, their drivers

219

hooting to make the pedestrians get out of the way. This was an exodus. No one wanted to be left behind for the Russians to find. Occasionally they met convoys of military vehicles going in the opposite direction and they learnt from experience to scatter into the surrounding woods and fields when that happened because they were almost certain to be dive-bombed.

As they walked Else filled Alex in on her husband's details in case he should be asked: where he had been born, how old he was, where he had been educated, what job he had done in civilian life – he had been a bricklayer for the city corporation in Potsdam. Because Alex still limped from the effects of his broken leg which had not been properly set, the others on the road accepted that he had been invalided out of the army and he became used to being addressed as Erich.

Else herself was the daughter of a grocer. Her father had become more and more depressed by the rationing and the shortages and, having nothing to sell, had taken his own life. 'Hanged himself in the cellar,' she told him. 'When *Mutti* saw him hanging there with his mouth and eyes wide open, she had a heart attack and died in hospital a week later. I shut the shop up and took a job in the garment factory, making Wehrmacht uniforms. It was while working there I met Erich. He drove the lorry that came to collect the finished goods. We were married just before he was sent to the Eastern Front. We had no married life to speak of.' She spoke without inflexion, giving no indication of how these tragedies, coming one after the other, had hit her.

'I'm sorry,' he murmured. 'War is bestial, no matter whose side you are on.'

'What did you do before the war?'

'I was a diplomat.'

'Not a soldier?'

'No. I left England before the war started, or I might have been.' He paused. 'Do you know where the Allies are?'

'Not exactly.'

'But France has been liberated?'

'Yes, and the Netherlands. But we are not done yet. There is a secret weapon the Führer says will change the whole course of the war and give us victory.'

'And what is that?'

'A flying bomb. It is already devastating London. The population is in panic and the government gone into hiding.'

He smiled at her simple confidence in what she had been told but he did not believe Londoners were panicking. While in Russia at the beginning of the war, he had heard reports of the London Blitz and how everyone had coped, and he imagined Edward in his business suit, bowler hat and rolled umbrella going to work at the Foreign Office, just as if nothing had happened. Oh, how he hoped that was an accurate picture. Hitler's invasion of Russia had brought the nightly attacks on London to an end as the Soviets had never ceased to remind everyone when lobbying for a second front to relieve the pressure on them. Now they had it and Germany was being attacked on both sides. 'Then perhaps I am fortunate to be here,' he said mildly.

'How are you going to find the Allies?' she asked.

'I don't know. Catch a train, I suppose.'

She laughed, assuming he was joking.

'What about you?'

'I have an aunt and a cousin in Potsdam. I shall go there.'

'You are not going to come with me and surrender to the Allies, then?'

'No. I have no wish to be a prisoner.'

They stopped at night to try and find lodgings, but every hotel, house and barn was already crowded with refugees and the unlucky ones built fires beside the road to cook what they could and slept where they were. The trek continued. The weakest fell by the wayside and were abandoned. When baggage became too heavy that was also abandoned to lie beside rifles, anti-tank guns and ammunition boxes – all the detritus of war. There was no food and they resorted to begging at farmhouse doors. Sometimes they were welcomed, sometimes turned away, and Else's money was soon gone.

He had been half starved and was painfully thin, but forced labour had made him stronger than he looked. It was Else who faltered first. She had seemed so strong and determined, but all the walking took its toll. Her feet became covered in blisters which suppurated and became infectious, and as day followed day, their progress became slower and slower. He could not in conscience abandon her and helped her along as best he could, and thus they arrived at Neustrelitz, still too far east for Alex's peace of mind. He half dragged, half carried her to the railway station.

'Come to Potsdam with me; my relatives will give you food and clothes,' she said that night as they waited on the platform, hoping, along with hundreds of others, that a train would come. When it did, it was packed to suffocation and steamed straight through without stopping. Alex cursed, but cursing did no good, and Else had a fever which worried him. He left her to go in search of a doctor and found one at last, trying to tend the sickness and wounds of the thousands of refugees who had descended on the town. They were queueing two- and three-deep for hundreds of yards. Alex realised he would have to bring Else to the queue. He went back for her but she could not move. He left her again and found a pharmacy, where he was given salve for the blisters.

The salve helped a little but she still could not walk. She gave him her wedding ring and, with the money it fetched, he bought bread, a small lump of cheese and a tin of soup, which he took back to her. 'Don't leave me,' she begged, wolfing down the food. He watched, hungry himself but reluctant to take anything from her. Nor could he leave her.

Two days they rested there, while all the while the Red Army was coming closer. Something had to be done. He went into the countryside and found a farmer who had a horse and cart which he was loading, ready to flee himself. Alex, telling the story about being captured by the Red Army and then the Germans, which ensured him a sympathetic hearing, begged a lift for Else. Reluctantly the man agreed. Else was fetched and lifted onto the back of the cart behind a table, chairs, a bedstead and mattress, several bundles of clothes, a sack of potatoes and a cloth-wrapped loaf of bread. The farmer and his wife sat at the front and Alex walked alongside.

Progress was even slower than walking because of the number of refugees and the abandoned debris of war on the road, but at least Else was resting. They arrived in Fürstenberg late at night to discover the town was being evacuated en masse. The Russians, so they were told, were only a few kilometres away and the Americans were at Bad Kleinen. Alex would have liked to strike off in that direction, but Else was determined to go to Potsdam, convinced the Allies would be halted long before they reached there; leaving her would be a cowardly and ungrateful thing to do. There was a train going south the next morning and they managed to squeeze onto it.

They arrived in Berlin the next day after a night in a siding during an air raid. Alex had stayed in the city during his time as a diplomat and thought he knew his way about, but very little was recognisable among the ruins. They were confronted by whole streets which were nothing but rubble. Else, only able to hobble, was horrified and insisted they go to Potsdam at once. They caught a local train but that stopped short of Potsdam and everyone was told to leave it. 'The station has been blown up,' they were told. 'You'll have to walk the rest of the way.'

The lovely city of Potsdam, once the state capital, full of ancient palaces and churches, was also in ruins. Else, leaning heavily on his arm, guided him to the street where her relations lived, but it had been totally destroyed. She stood looking at the heap of bricks, stone, broken windows and smashed furniture with tears raining down her face. 'Now I have no one,' she wept. 'I am alone.' She turned and flung herself into his arms. 'You will stay with me, won't you? If the Americans come, you will stand up for me? Tell them I helped you.'

What could he do but agree? Without her and the clothes and money she had provided he would have died on the march, because the straggling line of prisoners would almost certainly have been taken by the advancing Russians. Someone had told him they had been destined to be put on board a ship which would have put to sea and been deliberately sunk. Either way, he would not have survived. He was not as sure as Else was that it would be the Americans who reached them first and his only hope of staying out of a Russian prison was to remain Erich Weissmann.

They lived like rats in the cellars of bombed houses, coming out now and again to try and find food, begging and scavenging. Money had no value, so they traded whatever they could find in the bombed buildings for food. By the time the Russians overran the city, they were living skeletons dressed in rags. But the anonymity was a blessing.

The conquerors were in jubilant mood, drunk much of the time, raping the women, which they said was no more than the Germans did to the Russian women. Else was afraid all the time and clung to Alex, who managed to keep the soldiers at bay with his ready command of Russian. They heard daily reports of the Battle for Berlin which was raging street by street and getting closer and closer to Hitler's headquarters in the Reichstadt. The day it was overrun was a black day for the inhabitants but one of jubilation for the Russians, who celebrated with noisy parties and drunken orgies. No one believed Germany could win the war and none was surprised when it ended with the news of the Führer's suicide, and very shortly afterwards, Germany's unconditional surrender.

'Now we can live in peace,' Else said, as she emerged from the cellar in which they had been living to see their conquerors celebrating. 'Now, perhaps they will go home and we can get on with our lives.'

Alex did not believe for a minute the Russians would go; it was their avowed intention to spread communism throughout the world and they set out to sovietise all the land they had overrun. Germany became a country divided between the Allies; Potsdam was in the Russian zone.

The civilian men were rounded up and put to work clearing the rubble so that life could return to some kind of normality, for which they received a small wage and minimal rations. Alex, known as Erich Weissmann, became one of the workers. England, Upstone Hall and Lydia seemed a far-off dream and it was best not to think about it. But sometimes, when life seemed more than usually drear, he could not help thinking of the life he had left behind and wondering if Lydia were safe and happy. He prayed that it was so, or all he had endured would have been in vain.

He sometimes looked longingly towards the west, wondering if he could escape, but Else was the stumbling block. He could not abandon her and she would not go with him. As far as she was concerned, she was home where she belonged and she had a man to take care of her and life was not so bad, especially when they found an apartment in a block of flats which had been repaired and made habitable. The *Hausfrau* in her came to the fore and she delighted in making a home for him. It was all she asked. She did not see his restlessness and would not have understood it if she had.

Unfortunately there were those in the city who had known the real Erich, and one day in autumn 1946 four armed policemen knocked at the door in the early hours of the morning and arrested him, taking no notice of Else who clung to him, weeping and protesting that he was Erich Weissmann to whom she had been married since 1941. He was taken to the town gaol, his only hope that they did not know his real name; only Else knew that.

Several nights and days of interrogation followed in which he maintained his name was Erich Weissmann. It became apparent during their interrogation of him that they had questioned Else who, to save herself, had told them his Russian name and that he was a deserter who had forced her to shelter him. She had not told them he was English, perhaps because they never thought to ask and she had only answered questions put to her, or because she did not believe it herself. He was handed over to the Russian authorities.

It was unexpected but fortuitous that they were so inefficient that there appeared to be no record of Alexei Simenov becoming the Englishman Alex Peters. He wondered whether to disclose it himself in the hope they would release him, but decided not to. For one thing, he knew he would be considered a spy and the British authorities would almost certainly deny any knowledge of him. It would cause a diplomatic incident and would not save him. Better to remain Alexei Simenov. He was despatched to Moscow for trial on a charge of desertion and consorting with the enemy, fully expecting to be sentenced to death. He would have been if his bravery at Minsk had not been reported and his sentence was commuted to ten years in Norilsk, one of the many labour camps in Siberia. 'You have been given an opportunity to become rehabilitated,' he was told. 'Do not waste it.'

The journey was even worse than he imagined it might be. The prisoners, many of them sentenced under trumped-up charges, were crowded into trucks like animals; the rations were minimal and toilet facilities disgusting. He lost track of time as day followed day; the weather became colder and only the fact that they were crammed so closely together kept them warm. It came to an end at last when they arrived in the town of Krasnoyarsk, where they boarded a steamboat to continue by river. After another two thousand kilometres, becoming colder and colder, they arrived in the port of Dudinka well inside the Arctic Circle. From here a train took them to the camp. It was snowing hard and they were ill-equipped for the cold. Some had already died on the journey, many more were sick.

Norilsk was a desolate place, built by earlier prisoners using nothing but pickaxes and wheelbarrows in order to exploit the rich mineral deposits in the area. Its nickel was needed for the production of high-grade steel and it had grown into a huge complex. There was no perimeter fence; it wasn't needed. No one could escape from that wilderness, thousands of kilometres from civilisation. They were taken to the administration building for documentation, after which their clothes were taken from them for delousing and they were given a bucket of water and herded to the washrooms to try, as far as they were able, to clean themselves. Their clothes, such as they were, were returned to them and they were taken to the huts which were to become their homes. Alex ducked his head under the lintel of one to follow the man in front of him, in a mood of black despair. The thing he had spent so much time and effort to avoid had come to pass; he was a prisoner of the Soviet system and cut off from all communication with the outside world.

He looked about him. The floor of the hut was simply hardened earth. There was a broken stove in the middle whose chimney leant drunkenly before disappearing out through the roof. Beside it were a few sticks and a pile of coal. Bunks had been constructed around the walls and each man put his meagre belongings onto one of them while one of their number set about lighting the fire. The room was soon filled with black smoke, making them cough and their eyes water, but the fire took the edge off the bitter cold.

It was the cold and the barren landscape which was their greatest enemy. Trying to keep warm, fed and well enough to do the work required of them was the be-all and end-all of their days and nights. The camp was huge; there were copper and nickel mines, coal mines, smelting works, factories for making bricks and another for processing fish, garages for the repair of vehicles, as well as offices, a post office, a theatre and a sports stadium, though Alex suspected the last three were intended for the guards and the growing number of free workers, specialist engineers and technicians, who were needed to run the mines and factories and who, unlike the convicts, were paid.

Alex was put to work in the repair shop, which was supposed to keep the machinery in working order. This was almost impossible, due not only to his lack of experience in that kind of work, but to a chronic shortage of spare parts and the intense cold. When his expertise in languages became known, he found himself in the administrative office, translating the petitions of the non-Russian prisoners and drafting the replies, most of which comprised a firm *nyet*. It meant a slightly enhanced standard of living, if you could call constant hunger and never feeling warm living.

The efforts to separate the male and female prisoners were not always successful and there were many ragged unshod children running about the camp. They reminded him how he had failed to find Yuri and that reminded him of Lydia. It was seven years since he had said goodbye to her in Moscow and he wondered what she was doing. What was England like in the post-war years? Was it returning to normality? Had she remarried? He could hardly blame her if she had. He had not asked her to wait for him; it was too much to ask, given the situation at the time when the prospect of him ever returning to England was so remote as to be discounted. But oh, how he longed for the pleasant green fields, the winding tarmac roads, the old churches and Upstone Hall.

The pleasant green fields of England had disappeared under layers of snow. Drifts up to fourteen feet deep obscured the roads and buried cars over their roofs. Trains could not run. Remote villages and even some towns were cut off. The sea froze at its edge and there were icebergs floating in the sea off the Norfolk coast. To add to everyone's misery, there was a shortage of coal, not only for domestic use but for industry. The mines had recently been nationalised and the stocks, already low, were frozen solid and could not be moved to the power stations. Factories were closed and schools were shut. Peace had certainly not brought an end to the country's problems. Rationing was as severe as it had ever been, money was short and so was housing, even though there was a huge programme to replace buildings which had been bombed. Discontent was rife and there were frequent strikes.

Robert, on leave, struggled up the drive of Upstone Hall dragging a huge branch which had fallen from one of the trees in the park. Bobby, not yet four, was with him, well clad against the cold with woolly hat and gloves. Bobby was a real daddy's boy and, whenever Robert was at home, would follow him about, trying to imitate his ways. Seeing them from the window, Lydia handed Tatiana over to Claudia, donned wellington boots, scarf and gloves, and ran to help.

'It'll keep the stove going a little longer,' Robert said,

stopping to catch his breath. Keeping the stove going was their main occupation. They had turned off all but the essential radiators and had been living in the kitchen where the stove which heated the boiler was situated. It had also been used for cooking until Edward had had an electric cooker installed just before the war. The cooker was next to useless now because there were daily power cuts between nine a.m. and noon and for two hours again in the afternoon. The old boiler was their lifeline.

They dragged the branch round to the stable yard and Robert set about chopping it up. Lydia took Bobby indoors to keep him away from flying splinters. Edward had come to the kitchen to keep warm and was sitting in the housekeeper's old rocking chair, toasting his toes on the fender and nursing Tatiana. He was wearing a dressing gown and scarf on top of all his clothes. He had never been the same man after Margaret's death, but the arrival of Tatiana, which had coincided with the end of hostilities in Europe in May 1945, had given him a renewed vigour. He adored her. She was dark-haired and blue-eyed, a placid child, unlike Bobby, who had learnt to walk when he was little over a year old, and was like a whirlwind and into every mischief he could think of. Seeing his grandfather, he endeavoured to clamber on to his lap beside his sister.

'You cannot both sit on Grandpa's lap,' Lydia said, removing him and divesting him of his outdoor clothes. 'Come and look at your picture book with Claudia while I cook lunch.'

'I hope it's not that dreadful whale meat,' Edward said. 'It's enough to make a body turn vegetarian.' Whale meat had been heralded as a good alternative to beef, but it had not proved popular with the public.

'No, it's chicken. They've stopped laying, so we may as well eat them.' To augment their rations, they had turned over a portion of their large garden to vegetables, half a dozen chickens and a cockerel who scratched in the dirt and ruined the flowerbeds, and a nanny goat which they kept for her milk. Claudia had even managed to make goat's cheese.

'Then what do we do for eggs?'

'Rely on the ration and dried egg,' Lydia said.

'We were better off during the war,' he said, echoing a favourite cry of much of the population. 'What we need is Winnie back at the helm.'

Winston Churchill's Conservatives had lost the 1945 election and Labour under Clement Attlee had come to power. One of their first enactments was to nationalise the coal mines and bring them under the control of a Minister of Fuel and Power in the shape of Emanuel Shinwell. The weather and his apparent lack of forethought over coal stocks, together with strikes and absenteeism, meant he was decidedly unpopular.

It wasn't only the weather that had made everyone gloomy, but the austerity of the aftermath of the war, the strikes and shortages. Factories closed for lack of power. Meat, eggs, cheese, bacon, sugar and sweets were still rationed and so were bread and potatoes, something that had never happened during hostilities. The newspapers were cut back to their wartime size of four pages and holidays abroad were banned. There were those who said Britain had won the war but lost the peace.

The troubles at home were reflected abroad with the need to rebuild Europe. This was not helped by the attitude of the Soviet Union and those eastern countries it controlled. Winston Churchill, in a speech in America the year before, had said: 'From Stettin in the Baltic, to Trieste in the Adriatic, an iron curtain has descended across the Continent.' Neither Lydia nor Edward were surprised by this. It seemed to symbolise the way she had been cut off from Yuri. She would never cease to feel guilty about what had happened, telling herself she should have realised what Kolya and Olga were planning and taken steps to prevent it. But she had been so overcome by misery over her husband's betrayal, she had not been thinking properly. Papa had told her not to blame herself, but she still did. Perhaps one day, when life returned to normal, she might try and find him. But what was normal? Was it never being afraid? Never being hungry? Was it never being short of anything? Was it having time to enjoy life? Being free to travel?

Robert came in carrying a basket full of logs which he put down beside the stove. 'I'll go out after lunch and see if I can find some more,' he said. 'The weight of snow on the branches is bringing some of them down.' He walked into the hall, picked up the telephone and listened for a few seconds. 'Dead as a dodo,' he said, returning to fiddle with the knobs on the wireless. During the war the wireless had been the main means of communication between the government and the people, but even that service had been curtailed to save power.

The news was all about the arctic weather. The temperature in London had not risen above forty degrees Fahrenheit all month and on one night went down to sixteen. Listeners were urged to conserve fuel supplies and find other methods to keep warm. More snow was forecast for the whole country.

'It's as bad as Russia,' Lydia said, peeling potatoes which

had been grown in their own kitchen garden and stored in clamps since the previous autumn. Percy Wadham, their gardener, who should have retired years before, had managed to shift enough snow to unearth some of them, though sadly they were frostbitten. 'Worse really because they are used to it and know how to cope, while we flounder. I wonder what it's like there now.'

'Cold,' Robert said and looked at Edward, who had glanced up from the newspaper he had been reading.

She saw the look that passed between them. 'I'm sorry,' she said. 'I didn't mean . . .' She stopped, unsure what she had meant. Not criticism of Robert, who was the best of husbands and fathers; it was simply something inside her which, even after seven years, stopped her letting go of that part of her life, to put it behind her.

Edward, who understood her better than most, wished she would count her blessings, as he did. All in all, life had been good to him. He had been fortunate to have Margaret's love and devotion and a fulfilling job, a job that had brought Lydia into his life. That had been fate, he supposed, a benign fate. He remembered the traumatised child she had been and the woman she had become – a good wife and mother, but one deeply scarred. He was well aware of how things stood between her and Robert. He could see the bleakness in Robert's eyes whenever Lydia mentioned Russia. The poor man obviously adored her, and though she was always affectionate and loving and, apart from an occasional tiff that was soon over, he had never heard them quarrel, there was something missing, something vital: the beating heart of a marriage. She did not seem to understand Robert's needs, nor he hers. Robert would have to come out of the navy at some point, and then what? They ought to have a home of their own, not live with a decrepit old man. Supposing he made the house over to her and moved out himself, would that answer? On reflection, he didn't think it would because Robert needed to be the provider. He sighed and returned to his newspaper.

Chapter Ten

1953

'I can't think why you want to,' Robert said in answer to Sir Edward's suggestion.

'I just thought we could make a few enquiries,' Sir Edward explained. 'The war's been over nearly eight years, things have settled down a bit and I've still got a few useful contacts.'

The two men were sitting in the library, having a general discussion about Edward's plans for the future. Gradually the country had pulled itself out of the post-war blues. The National Health Service had come into being and London hosted the Olympic Games. Clothes rationing came to an end and the couturiers took full advantage of it and produced the New Look. Full skirts worn well below the knee became the fashion. Lydia loved it.

New houses were being built everywhere, including Upstone, which was growing from a village into a small town, and Edward was considering selling some land on the fringes of the estate for much-needed housing. It was not a subject Robert was particularly interested in; he had no stake in the property. It was after that, apropos of nothing, Edward had brought up the subject of Yuri. 'There must be records somewhere. At least, we could try.'

'Why are you so keen for him to be traced? You're as bad as Lydia. She's too firmly wedded to the past.'

'I'd like to make her happy.'

'She is happy, or so she assures me.'

'Well, she would say that, wouldn't she? That doesn't mean that there isn't a great hole in her life. Knowing where Yuri is and that he understands she had no choice but to leave him in Russia would be the best thing for her. Make her more content.'

'You haven't told her this, have you?' Robert asked.

'No, I wouldn't want to get her hopes up for nothing.'

'And it would be for nothing. Even if you find him, what good would it do? They can't be reunited, that's just not possible. It's past, Sir Edward, past and gone. We all have to move on. She's got Bobby and Tatty and that should be enough.'

Edward had not realised how strongly Robert felt over Lydia's past, but he supposed it was understandable; it was a past he could not share. And now, instead of improving matters, he had made them worse.

'Who's Yuri?' Bobby appeared suddenly, sitting on the floor almost at their feet, startling them both. Neither had noticed him sprawled on the carpet playing with the cat.

His father seemed reluctant to answer him, so Sir Edward did. 'Your mother had a baby in Russia at the beginning of the Second World War and she had to leave him behind.'

'A baby!' he exclaimed. 'How did that come about?'

'It's a long story and best forgotten,' Robert said.

238

'But why did she leave him behind? Did she have a love affair?' Bobby's curiosity had been roused and he wasn't going to let the subject drop.

Edward smiled; where had the boy learnt such terms? 'No, she was married to a Russian. He was killed early in the war.'

'I never knew that.'

'No reason why you should,' his father said. 'Now, run along and play.'

'But I want to know more.'

'Then I suggest you go and ask your mother.'

Which is exactly what he did, when he found her making an apple pie in the kitchen. He loved his mother's pastry, especially when she had a little left over, sprinkled it with sugar and dried fruit before rolling it up and cutting it into slices before baking. He could never wait for the slices to grow cold before he wolfed them. 'Mum, I want to ask you something.'

'Ask away.'

'I heard Dad and Grandpa talking about someone called Yuri. Dad said if I wanted to know about him, I was to ask you.'

She was taken by surprise. 'Why were they talking about Yuri?'

'They were talking about trying to find him; Grandad was telling Dad they ought to make enquiries, but Dad said it was useless. When I asked who Yuri was, Grandpa said he was your son and Dad said if I wanted to know about him to ask you. I never knew you had another son, Mum.'

Lydia looked at Claudia who was busy peeling potatoes. The older woman put down the knife, dried her hands and left the room.

Lydia sat at the kitchen table and pulled Bobby down on the chair next to her. He knew she had been born in Russia, she had told him in his first term at the infant school, when he complained about taunts of being a poor little rich boy. Wealth or its lack had never entered his head. He had all he needed and he supposed he was lucky to have all that garden to play in but it didn't make him different. He rebelled when the bigger boys had demanded money off him and wouldn't believe that his pocket money was even less than theirs. Lydia had advised him not to give in to them, that if he did, they would only ask for more. She had told him about when she first went to school at Upstone and how frightened she had been, especially when she hadn't been able to speak English properly.

'Not speak English!' he had exclaimed. 'What language did you speak, then?'

It was then she had told him about being born in Russia and how Grandpa Stoneleigh had saved her and adopted her. He was not her real father and therefore not their real grandfather. She had not said anything about her return in 1938 and the birth of Yuri. She had known one day she would have to tell her children they had a half-brother, but had put it off until they could understand why there had ever been anyone in her life besides their father. Now it seemed the time had come.

She smiled. 'And you are curious?'

'Of course I am. Why was I never told? You think you know all about someone and then you discover you don't know anything at all. And why should Dad and Grandad argue over him?'

'Were they arguing?'

'No, not exactly, but Dad got a bit hot under the collar.'

240

'I'm sorry for that. It's nothing they should be arguing about. It was all so long ago.'

'What were you doing in Russia and why didn't you bring the baby back with you? And what happened to your Russian husband?'

'Were you eavesdropping?'

'Not on purpose. I was playing on the floor. They didn't know I was there.'

She and Andrei had played on the floor at Kirilhor, she remembered, and had heard things they shouldn't which had only become clear years later. Believing, as she always had, that if children asked questions, they deserved honest answers, she told him a watered-down version of what had happened

'Wow!' he said when she finished. 'That's like a fairy story. Can't you find him again?'

'I don't think so. Russia is nothing like England, you can't move about freely and if you are a foreigner you can only go where the Russians choose to take you. And it all happened too long ago.'

'But you must think about him.'

'Sometimes I do. It's only natural, I suppose.'

After he had gone, Lydia returned to her pastry, musing as she rolled it out. Her son had set her thinking about the past again. Fancy Papa thinking they ought to try and find Yuri. Of course, it was impossible. She didn't like them arguing over it and she must warn Papa not to mention it again. And she must make a point of taking Tatty on one side and telling her the story before she heard a garbled version from Bobby.

How swiftly the years had flown by, Lydia mused. The children were no longer babies, they were little people with personalities and temperaments all their own. Nine-year-old Bobby was like Robert, though not so patient and tolerant. He might learn those virtues as he grew older. He was certainly brainy. Tatty, two years younger, was intelligent but could never sit still long enough to learn her lessons; she would rather be active, skipping and running, climbing trees, taking part in sport. But she was also tender-hearted and would weep buckets over a wounded bird. How she would react, Lydia did not know.

Getting the children ready for school next morning, after an unusually stormy night, she was only half listening to the breakfast news on the wireless; she was still musing on Tatty's reaction to her tale. Her daughter had gazed at her in wonder and asked all sorts of questions Bobby would never have thought of: What colour was Yuri's hair? His eyes? Was he fat like her friend Chloe's baby brother was? Did he cry much? When was he coming home? All of which she had endeavoured to answer. Tatty must have been satisfied because she had gone to bed and straight to sleep, and hadn't mentioned it since waking up.

Struggling with Tatty's wellington boots, she heard the newsreader speak of extra high tides which, combining with wind and rain, had caused widespread floods down the east coast, from Lincolnshire to Kent. It was feared there was some loss of life and many injuries as people tried to escape the water. Some were trapped in the upper storeys of their houses, some had gone out onto the roofs of their bungalows and sat there awaiting rescue. Thousands had lost their homes, especially those close to the low-lying coast.

'It reminds me of 1947,' Edward said from the rocking chair by the kitchen hearth. He was still a handsome man, white-haired, a little bent, but still active, refusing to give way to old age. 'Do you remember? Robert took a rowing boat out and helped rescue people and brought them here, and you and Claudia wrapped them in blankets and gave them tea and soup.'

'I remember. It was a terrible time.' Valleys all over the country had become lakes; the Fens, so close to Upstone Hall, had become a vast inland sea. Field after field had become inundated, the farmers lost their crops, cows had to be rescued using boats. But it was not only the floods, the shortages and the strikes which made it terrible, but the fact that Robert had not been able to settle down in civilian life and gone back into the navy. She sometimes wondered if he needed to get away from Upstone and her memories. However careful she was not to mention Alex or Yuri, he knew she could never completely let go. It filled her with guilt because her husband deserved to be more than second best.

He had left very early that morning to return to duty. The war in Korea between the Communist North and the non-Communist South had been going on for three years. South Korea was being backed by troops from America and Britain and it involved the Royal Navy.

'When Robert comes home again, I think you should think about taking a holiday,' Edward said, almost as if he had read her mind. 'He needs you to himself sometimes, you know. Claudia will look after the children.' Claudia was still with them, but for how much longer, Lydia did not know. The fifty-year-old was courting a bus driver who drove the bus that passed their gate and took passengers into Upstone. Apart from two women who came in daily, she was the only live-in servant left, though no one thought of her in those terms. She was a friend and helpmate to everyone, especially the children, whom she adored. She had told Lydia she was torn in two when Reggie had proposed, not wanting to leave Upstone Hall, but Lydia had told her not to be so silly and to go ahead.

'I know. We'll talk about it when the time comes.' She finished putting Tatty's coat on and buttoning it up, then turned to Bobby. 'Are you ready? Have you got your lunch and your football boots?'

'Yes, Mum.' He picked up his satchel and all three said cheerio to Edward and left by the kitchen door. The wind was still howling round the house and it was raining hard. Water was streaming down the drive like a small river.

The school was within easy walking distance and usually she encouraged the children to walk there and back, but today even she was struggling to stand upright. 'I think I'd better take you in the car today,' she said. In 1950 when petrol rationing was abolished, Robert had bought Lydia a new Morris Minor.

The storms abated at last. Over three hundred people had lost their lives, twenty-four thousand houses had been damaged, some beyond repair. In the countryside thousands of animals drowned and fields inundated by salt water could not grow crops. Winston Churchill, who had been returned as prime minister after the general election of 1951, declared it a national disaster.

Stalin died in March and Lydia wondered if it would make any difference to East-West relations. The entente of the war years had soon disappeared and the Soviet Union and its satellites were as cut off from the Western world as they had been when Churchill spoke of an iron curtain.

Any news from Russia set Lydia thinking of Alex and Yuri; she supposed she would never stop thinking of them, but the pain had dulled, leaving a quiet nostalgia that she deliberately kept at bay. To let it come to the forefront of her mind would be a catastrophe and unfair to Bob and her children. They deserved the very best she could do for them.

One happy event was the coronation of Queen Elizabeth on the second of June, which was televised almost in its entirety. It was a day of great pageantry, which the country loved. They turned out in their thousands to watch the procession as Elizabeth travelled to Westminster Abbey in the golden State Coach.

The Korean War ended and Robert came home in time to take them all on holiday in Scotland during the school holiday. The weather was kind to them, and they had a lovely time, walking in the Highlands and sailing on the lochs. They returned sunburnt and happy, and then Robert and Lydia left the children at Upstone and went to Balfour Place for a long weekend. They wandered about doing nothing in particular, seeing the sights, shopping, going to the theatre and making love. 'We'll do more of this when I leave the service,' Robert said.

'Are you thinking of leaving?'

He laughed. 'They'll kick me out when my time's up.'

'What do you want to do? Afterwards, I mean.'

'I don't know. I'll have to think about it.' He paused, then went on in a rush. 'Lydia, don't you think it's time we bought our own home? We can't live with Sir Edward for ever.'

She was startled. It was the last thing she had expected. 'Why not? It's plenty big enough for all of us. And you

245

know Papa loves having the children round him.'

'It's too big,' he said. 'An anachronism. It costs the earth to keep up, even though we only use half of it. If we bought a nice house, near the sea, he could have a small bungalow nearby.'

'He'd hate that. And it isn't as if he's poor.'

'No, he isn't, but that's half my point. We rely on him too much. It makes me feel less of a man.'

'Robert, I never heard such nonsense. You're all man.' She gave a cracked laugh. 'I can testify to that.'

He managed a half-grin, though he was too concerned with making his point to laugh at her joke. 'I want us to have a home of our own, you, me and the children. Can't you understand that?'

'In a way I can, but it's just masculine pride. I can't imagine what life would be like living anywhere but Upstone Hall. It's my home, Robert, the only one I've ever known. Even when I was in Russia with Kolya, all I wanted to do was get back to it.'

'Will you at least think about what I've said?'

'Yes, I'll think about it.'

She did, but it always came back to one thing: she could not bear to leave Upstone and her father. 'It would seem like ingratitude,' she told Robert when he brought the subject up again. And because he loved her, he gave up.

In September Bobby went to Gresham's boarding school, Sir Edward's old school, and Holt was near enough for him to be fetched home for weekends, though Papa didn't think that was a good idea. 'He should stay and take part in the weekend activities,' he told Lydia. 'There's always something going on: sport, drama, music, cadets.'

Lydia missed him dreadfully but he settled down well

and wrote frequently about new friends he had made, what he had done and the things he intended to do. Left behind, Tatty informed her one day that she wanted to learn to ride. 'My friend Chloe has a pony,' she announced. 'He's called Tubby, 'cos he's a roly-poly. I asked Grandpa and he says he doesn't see why not.'

Lydia smiled at the way her daughter unashamedly used her grandfather to get her own way. 'Did he? I rode a lot when I was young.'

'So I can, can't I?'

'If you are good.'

'I am good.' It was said loudly and vehemently. So Tatty got her pony, took to riding like a duck to water and started competing in local gymkhanas. She always took the rosettes she won to show Grandpa before hanging them on her bedroom wall. The child idolised him, which was another reason in Lydia's mind for not moving.

Another year passed, a year in which rationing finally ended after fourteen years; children were able to buy their lollipops, gobstoppers and chocolate without having to produce coupons; Roger Bannister became the first man to run a mile in under four minutes; rock and roll came to Britain from America with Bill Haley singing 'Rock Around the Clock', something the youth of the country took to their hearts, but which the older generation deplored.

Lydia fetched Bobby home from school for the following Christmas holidays in thick freezing fog. 'We've been talking in class about what we want to do when we leave,' he told her as she drove very slowly along the country roads. The windscreen wipers were sticking to the ice on the glass and she had to stop every now and again to get out and scrape it off.

'Goodness, that's a long way off.'

'I know, but we've been told to think about it because it's important to know where you're going in life and we have to decide what exams we want to take.' At eleven years old he was tall for his age, a well-built lad with fair hair and blue eyes like his father. He had other traits of Robert's too: thoughtfulness and consideration and a way of looking at her which made her want to hug him, but hugging was definitely out; he considered himself too old for that. 'I think I'd like to be a diplomat like Grandpa.'

'He'd like that,' she said.

'Perhaps they'll send me to Russia.'

'Would you like to go?'

'I wouldn't mind. After all, I've got roots there, haven't I?'

'Yes, but I doubt you'll be able to find any connections now,' she said, as she drew up outside the house. 'It's been too long and Russia has changed.'

Christmas Day was dull but overcast, but it did not dampen their spirits. They all went to church, including Claudia who was still with them, but would be going to spend the afternoon and evening with her fiancé after Christmas dinner. Poor Claudia, she was as undecided as ever.

'Time for presents,' Tatty said as soon as the meal came to an end and they all left the table and trooped into the drawing room, where a large tree stood in the corner glittering with lights and tinsel. Beneath it was a heap of colourfully wrapped parcels. Tatty acted as postman and soon everyone was unwrapping presents, exclaiming and thanking the givers.

Lydia watched them all: her father, husband – home on Christmas leave – children and best friend and sent up a little prayer of thanks for her good fortune. Somewhere, thousands of miles away, she prayed another child, fourteen years old now, was also enjoying his Christmas, even if it wasn't called Christmas anymore.

The fog lifted, but at the beginning of January it snowed and it continued to snow for a week, made worse by blizzards which piled it up against walls and hedges, and covered cars. More than seventy roads were blocked and hundreds of vehicles abandoned in drifts. Trains couldn't run and everyone was struggling to get to work; schools were shut and livestock was dying and old people suffering. Lydia did what she could to help those old people in the village, trudging out in wellington boots, taking soup in thermos flasks and making sure they had heating.

Ice grew thicker and thicker on ponds and rivers, much to Tatty's delight, who informed them that the ice on the lake was several inches thick.

'You are not to go on it,' Lydia said. 'The water is deep, and if you go through, you'll never get out. You heard the news, children drowning all over the place falling through the ice. I don't want you to be one of them.'

'No, but Mum, they've flooded the fen at Earith and that's only a few inches deep. They're going to hold the speed skating championships there. The snowploughs have cleared the roads; my friend, Chloe, told me so.'

And so they all went in Edward's Bentley: Edward, Robert, Lydia, Bobby and Tatty. The large expanse of ice was crowded as everyone for miles around came to take advantage of the rare chance to skate and watch the speed trials. Those without skates walked on the ice, slid and fell over laughing. Tatty was soon whizzing about, followed by a less-sure Bob. Lydia and Robert went hand in hand more sedately, while Edward watched from the warmth of the car.

'It's like a Russian winter,' Lydia said, cheeks glowing.

She was, Robert decided, looking especially beautiful. 'You don't remember Russian winters, do you?'

'Not as a child, except that dreadful day when Andrei was killed, but it was pretty cold that first year of the war. You remember, you were there.'

'So I was, but I didn't have much time to notice the weather.'

'No, you were too busy looking after me. You saved my life – not only my life, but my sanity, and I never thanked you enough, did I?'

'Just being you, and loving me as you do, is all the thanks I need and want, sweetheart.'

It was an ambiguous statement which made her realise how he must feel about a marriage that was perfect except for one missing ingredient. His stoic acceptance of that made her feel guilty. She made a resolution to try even harder to love him as she ought.

He went back to duty at the end of the week, but the big freeze continued until March, when Tatty's school reopened and Lydia took Bobby back to Gresham's. The snow was still piled up on the sides of the roads, some of it higher than the car, making her nervous. Driving along between the walls of snow, with black overhanging trees making it dark, she was suddenly back in Russia in the droshky

250

with Ivan whipping up that great carthorse and Andrei laughing. He had not laughed for long and she shuddered at what had become a rare recollection. It was the snow, she supposed, and its menace.

Mentally trying to shake off the image, she drove faster than she ought to have done. As she turned into the drive, the car skidded when it encountered the ungritted surface and slid off the gravel into the shrubbery where it stalled in a heap of snow. Shaken, she leant forward over the steering wheel, thankful she was not hurt. 'Damn! Damn! Damn!' she said aloud. Then she picked up her bag, left the car where it was and trudged up the drive.

'I'm back,' she called to Edward, as she took off her coat and went into the drawing room.

He looked up from the newspaper he was reading. 'I didn't hear the car.'

She laughed. 'No, I skidded turning into the drive and ran it into the bushes. It's in a snowdrift. I'll ring Andy at the garage to come and drag it out.'

'Are you hurt?'

'No, just feeling foolish. I should have known it was icy just inside the gate.'

'I thought Percy had gritted the drive.'

'So he did, but he ran out of grit before he got to the gate and the store didn't have any more.' She went back into the hall and telephoned the local garage.

'Andy's out with his recovery truck,' she said when she returned. 'There's been a nasty accident on the Norwich road. Sue doesn't know when he'll be back.'

He stood up. 'I'll go and have a look at it. I might be able to back it out.'

'No, leave it, Papa. It's not doing any harm.'

'If it's in the way someone else might run into it and be injured.' He went into the kitchen, donned coat and boots, picked up the car keys from the table where she had dropped them, and left the house. He fetched a shovel which was leaning against the stable wall where Percy had left it after clearing the paths after the last lot of snow, and went off down the drive. Lydia put her coat back on, found a spade in the shed and followed.

When she joined him, Edward was already tackling the snow behind the car, shovelling it to one side. She bent to do the same and by the time they had freed the car they were both exhausted. Edward, particularly, was finding it hard to breathe. 'Get in the car, Papa,' she said, putting the shovel and spade in the boot.

He did so and she drove carefully the four hundred yards to the house, when he got out, leaving her to take the car round to the garage. When she returned to the house, she found him collapsed in the rocking chair beside the kitchen hearth, one boot off and one on. His arms hung limply over the sides of the chair, his eyes were shut and his face all lopsided.

'Papa!' She flung herself on her knees beside him, and though she had no reply, she felt a flicker of a pulse when she picked up his hand. Thank God, he was alive. She rang for an ambulance and in no time he was on his way to hospital with her following in the Morris, praying with every breath she took that he would recover.

The doctors brought him round briefly and she was able to talk to him. She sat at his bedside holding his hand and told him how much she loved him, that she needed him to get well again, that the children needed him. He was not to give in, he had always been a fighter; now he had the biggest battle of his life. Understanding, he smiled with one side of his mouth, but did not speak. If she could have given him some of her strength and vitality, she would willingly have done it.

At three o'clock he drifted off again and she became alarmed. The ward sister came quickly when summoned, but said he had simply gone to sleep. Relieved, Lydia stayed a little longer watching him, then left to be at home when Tatiana came home from school.

She broke the news to her daughter and saw the usual happy face crease in a worried frown. 'But he will be all right, won't he? He isn't going to die, is he?' She had been quite little when her mother had explained her true relationship to Sir Edward. She had been shocked at first, but then accepted it. He was still Grandpa Stoneleigh, white-haired, a little crotchety, but always loving and generous.

'I don't think so. I pray not.'

'So do I. I can't imagine this house without Grandpa. Have you told Bobby?'

'I rang the headmaster and he is going to tell him, but I don't think he need come home. He's only just gone back.'

The next few days were critical and Lydia's time was taken up with visiting the hospital and trying to keep Tatty and herself cheerful. Robert was informed but whether he could get home she did not know. In any case, there wasn't much he could do. It was a question of waiting and hoping and praying.

Her prayers were answered in that Edward rallied, but he was left severely disabled. She brought him home and employed Jenny Graham, a qualified nurse who had experience with stroke victims, to help her look after him. Coming home seemed to revive him. He managed a crooked smile for Tatty and Bobby, whom she had fetched home for the weekend, though his efforts to talk to them resulted in their confusion. 'I can't understand what he's saying,' Bobby said to his mother, after spending a few minutes at his grandfather's bedside.

'I know,' she told him. 'It's his illness, but we will become used to his little ways and then it will be easier.'

She wondered if it would. It broke her heart to see the strong upright man he had been reduced to such helplessness, especially when it had been so unnecessary. The car would have been perfectly all right until Andy could come and deal with it. It did not help to be told the stroke could have happened at any time and she should not blame herself. Robert came home and was, as ever, a great comfort to her. She knew she could lean on him when she was overwhelmed with sadness and sheer tiredness. He seemed able to understand the invalid better than most and spent hours talking to him, stimulating him into a response. When he returned to duty, he left them all more cheerful and optimistic.

With the help of a physiotherapist and a speech therapist, Edward's condition improved, though he was never the robust man he had been. He wandered about the house using a couple of elbow sticks, and he liked to watch the television, particularly the news and politics shows. Churchill stepped down as prime minister in April after fifty years in politics. He had inspired the nation with his stirring speeches during the war and his retirement was marked by radio, television and film producers with recollections of the dark days of the war. A film about Churchill's life was the last thing Edward saw. He died in the early hours of the next morning after another stroke.

Lydia, who found him, was so shocked she could not take it in for several seconds, then she threw herself across him and sobbed her heart out. Her beloved papa, who had taken her in as a waif and loved her as well as any natural father, who had fed her and clothed her and educated her, put up with her naughtiness, her wicked betrayal of him and still loved her, had gone from her. It was too much to bear.

It was Jenny Graham who came and gently lifted her from the body and closed the dead man's eyes. Lydia was angry and turned on her. 'You should have been here, you should have seen it coming. Where were you?'

'Mrs Conway, it is six o'clock in the morning,' she said patiently. 'He was all right when I went to bed. I could not have foreseen it, and even if I had, there was nothing either you or I could have done.'

Lydia gulped and pulled herself together. 'I know. I woke early, and something, I don't know what it was, told me to come and look at him. I'm sorry. I shouldn't have spoken to you like that. Will you ring for the doctor? I'll stay here a few minutes. No need to wake Tatty yet.'

Jenny left her and she sat beside the bed and took her father's hand. It was already drained of blood, the white bone of his knuckles showing through the thin skin. 'Papa, I shall miss you dreadfully,' she murmured. 'You have been the backbone of my life and now I have to stand on my own.' Even as she spoke, she thought of Robert. She was not alone; she had a husband who was an unfailing support and children who needed her. And they must be told. Tatty would wake soon and want her breakfast, happily eager for life and the day ahead. She was going to have to shatter that happiness. Should she defer it, send her to school and tell her later? That would be a cowardly thing to do and she would hate her for it later. And she must ring Bobby's school and get in touch with Robert. He had been on his way to Gibraltar when she last spoke to him by phone.

'The doctor is on his way.' Jenny had returned; Lydia in her grief had not heard her. 'I'll stay with him, if you like. I thought I heard Tatty about.'

Lydia stumbled to her feet and went in search of Tatiana who was singing 'The Yellow Rose of Texas' in the bathroom as she showered. Lydia waited for her to come out, wrapped in a bath towel and rubbing her hair. 'Tatty, sit down, I have something to tell you.' She sat on the edge of the bed and pulled her daughter down beside her. 'You have to be very brave.' She found herself overwhelmed with tears again and for a few moments could not go on.

Tatty looked at her in bewilderment. 'Mummy, what's wrong? Why are you crying? Have you hurt yourself?'

'No, I am not hurt.' She managed a weak smile. 'At least, not outside. Inside I am hurting a lot. You see, it's Grandpa. He's . . . He fell asleep in the night and . . . and I'm afraid he isn't going to wake up again.'

Tatty stared at her. 'You mean he's dead?'

'Yes, darling. But it was a peaceful end.' Oh, how she hoped and prayed that was true, that he hadn't been calling out for help and none came.

'I don't believe it. He was all right yesterday, shaking his stick at the television – you know, how he does when he's agitated.'

'I know. But he was an old man and he had been ill a long time.'

'I don't want him to go,' Tatty said, her lip trembling. 'I want him to stay here with us. It's not fair.'

'I know, I'd like it too,' Lydia said, then as Tatty began to sob in earnest, she gathered her into her arms and put aside her own grief to comfort her.

Jenny returned to tell them the doctor had arrived and Lydia gently disengaged herself and went to her father's room to meet the doctor.

The nurse had laid Edward out straight, washed his face, combed his white hair and crossed his hands on his chest. Lydia almost gave way again at the sight of him, but remembering her children, she straightened herself up and prepared to deal with practicalities, after which she decided to go and fetch Bobby home. She shouldn't leave it to the headmaster to break the news.

The funeral took place in a crowded Upstone church a week later. Sir Edward's work colleagues were there in force and so were the villagers. A handful of Russian émigrés whom Edward had helped came to pay their respects, as did some of Lydia's friends and colleagues who had also known Sir Edward. The local vicar, the Reverend Mr Harrington, took the service and Lydia was asked to say a few words. How she got through it without breaking down she never knew and she didn't have Robert to support her. He was on his way back but had not arrived in time. She ended with the hope and belief her father had joined his beloved wife and invited everyone back to Upstone Hall for refreshments.

They left the church behind the pall-bearers for a short committal service at the graveside. As they stood about the newly opened grave, with heads bowed, Lydia caught a glimpse of someone standing in the shadows of the great yew tree which stood close to the lychgate. Her heart did a crazy somersault and then began to beat so quickly she could not breathe. She took a half step towards him, her legs buckled under her and she fell to the ground.

She came to her senses lying on the grass beside the grave with her head in Claudia's lap. Her eyes took in Bobby's legs clad in his dark-grey school trousers and she raised her head to find him looking down at her, his face screwed up with worry. Tatty was kneeling beside her, clinging to her hand. She scrambled into a sitting position and stared towards the yew, but there was no one there. Had she seen a ghost? She must have. He was dead, had been dead fourteen years. And yet he had seemed so real, albeit older, grey-haired and very thin.

'It's all been too much for you,' Claudia said. 'Shall I tell everyone to go away?'

Lydia shook her head, as much to deny the apparition as to answer Claudia. 'I'll be all right. Help me up.'

Claudia helped her to her feet and she took the children's hands in each of hers and led the way to the funeral car which took them back to the Hall. By the time she arrived, she decided she had been seeing things. Alex was dead. She must remember that and not be so foolish.

She supervised the refreshments, talked to everyone, thanking them for coming, joining in as people told their own stories about the Sir Edward they knew, some of which raised a laugh. Afterwards there was the reading of the will, though Lydia already knew its contents. Sir Edward had been very generous to long-serving servants, to Claudia, the church and his favourite charities, and he had set up a trust fund for Bobby and Tatty. He had no male heir and the baronetcy had died out with him, and so the residue of the estate, Upstone Hall and the flat in Balfour Place had been left to Lydia. It was enough to keep her in comfort for the rest of her life and to enable Robert to leave the sea and take up whatever occupation he chose. And he could buy that yacht he had been talking about for ages.

He arrived home just as everyone was leaving. 'I'm sorry I couldn't get here in time,' he said, hugging her and then holding her at arm's length to look into her face. 'Are you all right?'

'Yes. Oh, you don't know how glad I am to see you.' And she flung herself back into his arms.

He held her a few moments, then gently put her aside to look to his children, taking Tatty to sit beside him on the sofa. Bobby remained standing, looking down at them.

'I don't like the house without Grandpa,' Tatty said. 'It seems all wrong.'

'His spirit is still with us,' Robert told her. 'If you love someone, they can never really die.' A statement that made Lydia, remembering the vision in the churchyard, gulp.

'The funeral was awful,' Bobby told him. 'Everybody was so miserable, though some of them were only pretending; they were laughing afterwards and guzzling sherry and cakes like it was a party. I don't think Grandpa would have liked that. And Mum fainted. In the churchyard with everyone watching.'

Robert looked up at Lydia, his eyebrow raised in a query.

'It was nothing,' she said. 'My legs just buckled under me. It only lasted a second or so. Nothing to worry about.'

She did not tell him she thought she had seen Alex. It had been an apparition, born of her distress; he had not been real, and telling Robert would only upset him to think that after all their years together a ghost still haunted them.

* * *

259

Alex had wanted to pay his last respects to the man who had been a second father to him. It had not been his intention to reveal himself. He had watched from the shadow of the tree, knowing there was no place for him in the group around the open grave. When Lydia had fainted, he had longed to go to her, but seeing her rise and take her children away, he had left. But he had come back later when all the cars had gone and the gravediggers had filled in the grave. He stood over it, reading the cards on the flowers and musing on a life that had brought him so much love and then snatched it away again.

Since returning to England he had discovered Sir Edward still lived at Upstone Hall and Lydia had married Robert Conway and had two children. He had known, when he had sent her away from him in Moscow, he was shutting the door on his own happiness. Someone like Lydia needed a man in her life, to love and be loved, needed children to mother. He ought not to mind. She would not wish to have the past dragged up again and in any case it would only hurt everyone: Lydia, Robert and their children, not to mention his own battened-down feelings.

He stooped to read the inscription on the largest of the wreaths laid at the head of the grave. It was made up of white and yellow roses. 'In love and gratitude to the best of fathers and grandfathers who gave freely and asked nothing in return. May you rest in peace. Robert, Lydia, Bobby and Tatiana.' Fighting back tears, he put his hand under the wreath and plucked a tiny yellow rosebud from where it would not be missed and slipped it into the top pocket of his suit behind the triangle of white handkerchief that peeped from it. Then he went back to his car and drove out of the village and along the road past the gates of Upstone Hall, continued on, and took the main road to Norwich.

Chapter Eleven

It was the death of Stalin in March 1953 which had started the process to set Alex free. As soon as the news reached Norilsk, the prisoners rejoiced, thinking they would soon be sent home. Lavrenty Beria, Stalin's successor, was known to want to dismantle the Gulag system and as a first step he transferred the administration of the complex from the gulag to the Ministry for Heavy Industry. It paved the way for the prisoners to apply to the Soviet Procuracy for a review of their sentences. Those whose sentences were shorter than five years, who consisted mainly of the criminal element, women and the elderly, were granted an amnesty, but the so-called politicals and enemies of the people, which included Alex, were left behind, and conditions, already harsh, became worse.

The guards were afraid that if the prisoners were released they would lose their jobs and were anxious to prove that to grant an amnesty to such prisoners would endanger the security of the country, and so their cruelty increased. They did not seem to understand that, if everyone was suddenly declared innocent, it would make the state legal system look inept, if not worse. When the guards shot at a convoy of prisoners on their way to work it triggered a whole wave of protests which were brutally put down.

Alex was kept so busy processing the prisoners' applications for a review of their sentences he did not have time to see to his own. It was a miracle that his years in the camp had not degraded him as it had many another. Thin and in rags he might be, but his mind still worked, perhaps because of the translation work he was given which kept his brain cells from going rusty.

It was this office work which had brought him into contact with one of the engineers in charge of the steel works. Leonid Pavlovich Orlov and his wife, Katya, lived in comparative luxury in a larger-than-usual house on a part of the compound reserved for paid workers. Alex didn't know Madame Orlova, but he had seen Leonid about, directing workers and prisoners, treating both with humanity, something almost unknown in the camp. Sometimes he would come into the office and talk to Alex. He had, he told Alex, worked his way up in his career by diligence, ambition and not a little risk. 'I seized my chances,' he had said on one occasion. It was well below freezing, both outside and in, and he was warmly clad in a padded coat and fur hat, which was more than Alex had. 'During the war Russia needed engineers, people who could design and make weapons, tanks, transports, things like that and I took full advantage. Not everyone in Russia is poor, you know; a man can get on if he's determined enough. I own my engineering business.'

'Then what are you doing here?'

'Advancement,' he had said, laughing. 'Here I have been allowed to grow even stronger, to make even more money. Mining and engineering together make a lucrative partnership . . .'

'Should you be saying this to me?'

Leonid had laughed and looked about him at the empty office. Alex felt he had deliberately chosen that moment to speak to him when everyone else had gone for their midday meal. 'Why not? There's no one to hear and no one to care if they did. The guards can do nothing to me, I am not one of their prisoners. Besides, I want to ask you something.'

Alex was immediately wary. 'What might that be?'

'You speak English and German?'

'Yes.'

'Then will you teach me?'

Suspicion had become part of Alex's nature and this sounded very suspicious. 'Why?'

'Why?' Leonid repeated. 'Because I want to learn. One day Russia will be doing business with other countries. It's inevitable, and it might come sooner than you think. I want to be prepared.'

'I meant, why me?'

'Why not you? And who else is there who is so fluent and whom I can trust?'

'You trust me?'

'Yes. I have watched you at work. You are scrupulously honest, when anyone else in your shoes would be fiddling the books, hiving off goods and supplies and selling them. Selling the secrets entrusted to you by prisoners too. There are any number of ways in which you could have used your position to better yourself. And yet you haven't. So, what do you say? I'll pay you.'

'Apart from buying extra food and clothes, money's not much good here. And it would only be stolen if I had it.'

'Very well, then – apart from a little tea money, I shall keep it until you get out. You haven't got long to go, have you?'

'Who knows? People are always having their sentences increased, sometimes even doubled on the flimsiest excuse. How do I know it won't happen to me?'

'The sentences are increased because the government needs the labour and prisoners don't have to be paid.' He paused. 'I could make sure you left on time.'

'In exchange for lessons?'

'Yes.'

And so he had agreed, and Alex went to their house on three evenings a week and taught Leonid and his wife English and German. And he was rewarded with supper. It didn't help his popularity with his fellow prisoners and he received more than one beating, not only because they considered him a traitor, but because they thought he might have been given money and they meant to take it off him. Only when they had been convinced he was not being paid more than a pittance and a meal, and he managed to smuggle food out for them, did they leave him alone. He fancied Leonid, who was nobody's fool, knew about this but turned a blind eye.

The comparatively soft life came to an end after two years when Leonid told him he was going back to Moscow. 'My wife has had enough of living out here and she's homesick for the sun,' he said.

'I shall miss you,' Alex said. They had established a

rapport which, in other circumstances, might have been called friendship and he meant what he said. Besides, he'd miss his free suppers.

'And I you, my friend. I shan't forget you. If you need help when you get out, come to me. I will have your fee waiting for you.'

Alex was not such a fool as to believe it – neither the fact that he would get out at the end of his original sentence, nor that Leonid would remember and pay him if he ever did. But then Stalin had died and that had put a whole new complexion on things. To his surprise his application for review of his sentence was granted the following year, probably because he had been a model prisoner and worked efficiently.

In the autumn of 1954, he had found himself, skeletally thin, in a train being conveyed back to Moscow and civilisation. His Certificate of Release had specified he was forbidden to live within a hundred kilometres of Moscow or any other major city and he was given twenty-four hours to make himself scarce or be rearrested. He was given to understand he was expected to make for Potsdam, though no one thought to give him the wherewithal to get there. He had no money, no clothes, no job and nowhere to live, but he was free. He was tempted to go straight to the British Embassy and throw himself on their mercy; he was, after all, a British citizen, but he was plagued by his conscience. He had never forgotten that promise to Lydia. He knew it was an almost impossible task, but he had to try and find Yuri before he could even think of going home. Where was home anyway?

It was then he thought of Leonid Orlov. Would he remember him? Would he honour his debt? He knew the name of the man's business and, by asking the way, found himself outside a huge factory making engineering tools. He had washed and shaved in the communal baths, but there was nothing he could do about his clothes except brush them down.

'You want work?' the man on the gate asked him, looking him up and down in contempt. 'There's no vacancy.'

'No, I want to speak to Comrade Leonid Orlov.'

The man laughed. 'You haven't a hope. He won't see you.'

'I think he will. Tell him it's Alexei Simenov. We knew each other years ago.'

'He's always being plagued by people who knew him years ago. The whole population of Russia seems to think he owes them a favour.'

Alex straightened his back and lifted his head. 'I am not the whole population of Russia. I am Alexei Petrovich Simenov.' It was said with all the authority he could muster, and it worked. The man sighed heavily and picked up the telephone.

'Wait here,' he said when he put it down.

It seemed he had been standing in the street for ages and was beginning to think he might as well walk away, when Leo himself came hurrying out to meet him. 'My dear man, how good it is to see you again,' he said, giving Alex a great bear hug, much to the astonishment of the gatekeeper. 'Come along, you look as though you could do with a good meal.' Leo himself obviously never went short of a meal. He had been plump before, now he was rotund. 'And you need some clothes. You can't go about looking like that.'

Alex breathed a huge sigh of relief. 'I can't stay in Moscow long. I'm supposed to leave within twenty-four hours, and I was wondering how I was going to manage it when I thought of you.'

'Glad you did, Alexei, my friend, glad you did.' He took Alex's arm in a firm grip and led him inside the gate where a monster limousine stood with a chauffeur beside it, who sprang to open the rear door. Leo ushered Alex in and climbed in beside him. 'GUM,' he ordered the driver.

They went to the department store where a whole wardrobe of clothes was bought for Alex. 'A suit and a shirt would have been enough,' Alex protested.

'Nonsense. Three lessons a week for two people for two years, at so much an hour, must come to a tidy sum.'

They left the store with Alex looking and feeling smarter than he had in years. 'Now for something to eat,' Leo said. 'Then you can tell me everything.'

'Everything?' Alex queried.

'Yes, you didn't come to me to beg, I know you better than that.'

'I thought you might remember the lessons.'

'So I did, but there's more to be told. We'll go home, you'd like to see Katya again, wouldn't you? And we won't be overheard.'

In Alex's experience, if there was one place in Moscow to be overheard it was at home where living quarters were shared and everyone lived cheek by jowl in rooms divided by paper-thin walls, so that it was impossible to have any privacy. But Leonid Orlov's home was not like that. He had a privileged apartment in a block of flats in Granovski Street where he and his wife had six rooms all to themselves. It was here Alex had a warm bath, the first since that time with Lydia in that dreadful *kommunalka* with its filthy bath along the corridor. Even that room had been spacious and the bath a luxury compared with how he had lived afterwards. Not that he had cared at the time where he lived when he had Lydia with him, loving him, relying on him. Those times could never come again, neither the worst of them, nor the best of them.

'Now, tell what's been happening to you,' Leonid said, after they had finished an excellent meal cooked by Katya. 'I assume you have been set free?'

'Yes, pardoned after review.'

'Good. I am not going to have the police knocking on my door in the middle of the night, then.' It was said with a chuckle.

'Don't joke about it, Leo,' his wife said.

'You can never tell,' Alex said. 'I can't quite believe I'm free and they won't find some other charge they'd forgotten.'

'You are safe here for the moment,' Leo said, making himself serious again. 'Tell me what your plans are.'

'It is a long story and I'm sure you don't want to hear it.'

'Oh, but I do. I might be able to help. That's why you looked me up, isn't it?'

Alex smiled. 'I suppose it is.'

'Were you hoping to go back to England? I can't help you do that.'

'No. I wouldn't allow you to risk it anyway. It's something else.'

'Fire away, then.' He opened another bottle of wine and refilled their glasses. 'You are not in a hurry, are you?'

'No.' He paused, wondering where to begin. 'Nearly fifteen years ago, I made a promise to someone I love very dearly, a promise to search for someone.'

'In Russia?'

'Yes. Her father was Count Kirilov. She left Russia in 1920, the only survivor of her family. Her father, mother and brother were all killed during the Civil War. She was taken to England and adopted by Sir Edward Stoneleigh. All she had of her old life was a piece of jewellery sewn into her petticoat.'

'Oh, the poor thing!' Katya exclaimed. She was even rounder than her husband.

'She was luckier than some. Sir Edward is a great man. She adores him.' This didn't seem real, this warm room, his stomach replete, his head a little fuzzy with excellent wine and this charming man, who seemed to be listening attentively. He took a deep breath and confided the whole story.

Leo got up suddenly and left the room. When he came back he was carrying a large book. He sat down beside Alex and opened it. It appeared to be about the tsar's court. 'Here,' he said, turning it to show him a photograph. It depicted an autocratic lady in a long straight evening dress, dripping with jewels, including a tiara. Standing on one side of her was a young man, still in his teens, in a white uniform, and on the other the tsar and tsarina.

'Good heavens,' he said, reading the Russian inscription aloud. 'The Tsar and Tsarina with the dowager Countess Irina Kirillova and Count Mikhail Mikhailovich Kirilov at the ball at the Winter Palace, St Petersburg, to celebrate the New Year 1900.'

Alex pointed to the young man. 'That must be Lydia's father and that her grandmother. And that's the Kirilov Star.'

Leo turned the page. 'There is a little more here about the tiara. According to legend the centre stone was cut from a huge diamond found on the banks of the Ob River by a peasant who was fishing and had no idea of its worth. He could not afterwards remember exactly where he found it. In that region, there are no easy landmarks. He took it to the village priest, who thought it might be worth money and made the long journey to Tobolsk where he sold it to a silversmith who in turn sold it to a travelling merchant. It eventually ended up in Novgorod where Count Kirilov owned an estate. It is not known how much he paid for it, but it would not mean anything in today's money, considering we are talking about the eighteenth century. He had it made into a tiara for his wife.'

'And Sir Edward had it made into a pendant for Lydia. Oh, how she would love to see this book.'

'I'll have the page copied for you.'

Alex thanked him, but at that moment the likelihood of him ever seeing Lydia again seemed remote. Yet his efforts to find Yuri were based on that assumption. 'How did the book survive the Bolsheviks?'

'Heaven knows. By all the rules it should have been burnt but I found it years ago in an old bookstore that was closing down and selling off the stock. I bought it because I collect old books that depict precious stones.'

'The Star is famous, then?'

'It was, in the days before the Revolution. Like so much of Russia's history it was repressed by the Bolsheviks. Your Lydia is lucky to have it still. It is as well Yuri knew nothing about it. He would have found it difficult growing up with a background like that.'

'Do you think there's any chance of finding him?'

'She cannot possibly expect you to keep such a promise,' Katya said, referring to Lydia.

'I don't know what she expects, but I will not rest until I've done all I can, though I have no idea how to go about it. Any contacts I might have had have long gone.'

'How old would the boy be?' Leonid asked.

'He was born in April 1939.'

'He'll soon be sixteen then. Is he smart enough to go to university, do you think?'

'I have no idea. His mother certainly was. Why do you ask?'

'I sometimes lecture on engineering at the university and some of the cleverer students manage to get there as young as that, though I must say it is rare, especially if he's had no one to give him a helping hand.'

'As far as I know there is only Olga and she wouldn't have influence, unless she married well. That's a possibility, of course,' Alex said thoughtfully. 'On the other hand she may not have survived the war, and if she did, may not have been able to trace Yuri.'

'It's like looking for a needle in a haystack,' Leo said. 'Isn't that one of the English sayings you taught me?'

'Yes, along with "fire away".' Alex laughed. 'Fancy you remembering.'

'I remember it all, my friend. You make a good teacher. Do you think that's what you'll do when you go home?'

'I don't know. I haven't thought that far. If I cannot find Yuri I am not sure I'll go home, not to England anyway. Getting out of Russia won't be easy. I have a feeling I will embarrass the British Embassy if I turn up there.'

'First things first, then.' Leo spoke cheerfully to dispel

the gloom that had come over Alex. 'I'll try the education authorities.'

'But there are thousands of schools and hundreds of colleges and universities in Russia, we can't ask them all.'

'There's always the Moscow Central Archive,' Katya put in.

'Good thinking.' her husband said. 'Olga's death or remarriage might be recorded there.'

'Or if she had a criminal record,' Katya said. 'It wouldn't surprise me.' Without ever having met Olga, she was prepared to dislike her.

'Is that open to the public?' Alex asked in surprise.

Leo smiled knowingly and tapped his nose. 'There are ways if you know the right people and have deep enough pockets.'

'Oh, I see.'

'It's the way business is done,' he went on. 'You, of all people, should know that the wheels of officialdom turn at the pace of a snail and the only way to speed them up and get the information you need is to take an envelope full of banknotes with you whenever you make any sort of application. It you don't, someone else will and you lose the deal you're going after. It is the same for everything, not just business.'

'I do know that. I meant I have no money.'

'That isn't a problem, Alexei. I owe you.'

'But you've already paid for my clothes.'

'Pshaw! A flea bite.'

'And you are prepared to do this for me?'

'Would you do it for me if the shoe were on the other foot?'

'Yes, I expect I would.'

'There you are, then.'

'But I've got to get out of Moscow tomorrow, if I'm not to be arrested.'

'You could stay here, as long as you didn't venture out,' Katya offered doubtfully.

'No, certainly not.' Alex was adamant. 'I am not putting either of you at risk.'

'Have you anywhere to go?' Leo asked.

'Yes,' he said suddenly thinking of Kirilhor. 'Petrovsk, in Ukraine. Lydia's family had a *dacha* there. There's a man there, Ivan Ivanovich, he'll take me in.'

'That's nice and close,' Leonid said with heavy irony. 'Don't you know anywhere nearer than that?'

'No. Not as safe. You can send me word if you discover anything, and I'll come back, or meet you somewhere.'

'And if I can't?'

'Then I'll have to make up my mind what I'm going to do.'

He stayed with them that night at their insistence, and early next morning, Leo took him to the railway station and bought his ticket, before seeing him to his carriage and bidding him goodbye. Alex had given him the address of the telegraph office at Petrovsk railway station. 'I'll be in touch,' he said, as the carriage doors were slammed and the guard blew the whistle. 'Don't despair.'

It was all very well to tell him not to despair, Alex thought, sinking back into his seat. How could he not? He was probably on a wild goose chase, and how could he be sure Lydia would want the information even if he found Yuri? But deep inside him he did know she would never give up on her son, dead or alive. And dead could be a possibility. So many lives were lost in the war, why should

Yuri have survived? Was he simply using the search as a distraction because he was too cowardly to go home and face whatever had to be faced? The journey was a very long one and he had plenty of time to think about that question, to remember going in the opposite direction with a distraught Lydia. Oh, how he had loved her, still loved her! But he was not the man he had been then, young, strong, confident. He had aged beyond his years, his hair was grey and he limped. What had happened to Lydia? Would there be any grey in her hair?

He arrived in Kiev late at night. Even so the air was several degrees warmer than in Moscow. After living in the Arctic Circle for so long, it hit him like a warm bath. Picking up his case, provided by Leo to contain his new clothes, he made his way to a cheap hotel. Leo had given him money, more than he deserved, but he wasn't sure how long he would have to make it last and so was careful with it. Next morning he continued his journey and by evening found himself once more looking down the Petrovsk main street. The view had not changed, except for being more run-down than ever. He booked into the dilapidated hotel, ate a lonely meal and went to bed early. He tired easily these days and the journey had taken it out of him, which was surprising since it was nothing like as long as the journey from the gulag to Moscow, but put the two together, one after the other, and he seemed to have been travelling half his life. In a way, he supposed he had, and he wasn't at the end yet.

The next morning he set off on foot for the woodman's hut, telling himself the man had been getting on in 1939 and people died young if they never had enough to eat and not to be surprised if he had gone. But Ivan was there, chopping wood as if he had been doing it non-stop ever since Alex had last seen him. His white hair had thinned to almost nothing and his beard, left untrimmed, came well down on his chest. His cheeks had fallen in and his bony hands were covered in dark-red veins. He wore an old leather jerkin, a fur hat with ear flaps and long felt boots. He put down his axe and stared at the newcomer. 'Major Alexei Simenov,' he said, sinking onto a tree stump, shaking his white head in disbelief. 'Surely not?'

Alex laughed. 'So you remember me?'

'I remember you. Did you find my little Lidushka?'

'Yes.'

'Is she well? What are you doing back here?'

'I found her and I'm here because we never found the baby.'

'Ahhh.' It was a long drawn-out sigh. 'You had better come in.' He indicated the door of the hovel. 'I'll make tea.'

Alex preceded him into the only room. The thatch on the roof was wearing thin and he could see the sky through one spot. 'You sound as if you know something. Do you know where he is?'

'He's at Kirilhor. They came back here in 1947.'

'My God! I never thought to find him here.' And then another thought struck him, making his heart race. 'They? Surely not Lydia?'

'No, I never saw her again.' He busied himself over the stove. 'I mean Olga Denisovna. She brought the boy up.'

'She's here too?'

'Yes, though not quite right in the head, if you understand me – violent sometimes, though not with Yuri, never with

Yuri. But, excuse me – if you did not expect to find the boy here, why have you come?'

For the second time in three days Alex found himself telling the story, while they sipped tea from cracked glasses and he ate a little bread dipped in salt. At the end of the tale, the old man grunted. 'You should have stayed away. You won't be welcome and Olga Denisovna has wits enough to denounce you.'

'I've served my time and been given a pardon, she has no grounds for denouncing me.'

'No?' The old man gave another of his grunts. 'What about attempting to lure a Soviet citizen out of the country to be indoctrinated by the West?'

'I never said I intended to do that.'

'She will make it sound as though you did.'

Alex sipped tea. There was a lot of sugar in it. 'What about the boy?'

'He's a good little Pioneer, a real Soviet citizen. He believes everything they tell him. He was even seen to weep when Stalin died. And he loves Olga, looks after her all the time, even when she's at her worst.'

'That's hardly surprising if she brought him up.'

'He doesn't know she's not his real mother.'

'Why didn't you tell him as soon as he was old enough to understand?'

'What would that have achieved?' Ivan answered one question with another. Olga Denisovna had told him, when they first arrived, that if he said one word to the boy or anyone else about who Yuri really was, she would denounce him. 'You'll be sent to a labour camp, and how long do you think you'll survive there?' she had said belligerently. 'Keep your mouth shut.' And so he had. There was no point in stirring up trouble either for himself or Yuri, and there was no one left in the village who remembered Olga before the war or Yuri being born. Besides, if he kept quiet he could keep his eye on the boy and see he came to no harm. It was strange when he thought about it: Yuri was the grandson of Count Kirilov and by rights the heir to Kirilhor. Not that there was anything worth inheriting. It was a ruin. He had once asked Olga, when she was in one of her more sensible moods, why she had come back. 'It's where the boy was born,' she said. 'I thought Svetlana might still be here and help us, but she wasn't. I have no one but Yuri. He's a good boy. And clever too. I am going to be proud of him.'

'I should like to see him,' Alex said. 'At least then I can tell Lydia I have seen him and he is well. Perhaps if I spoke to Olga Nahmova first . . .'

Ivan shrugged. 'You must do what you think is right, but don't blame me if you get less than a welcome.'

Alex thanked him and went back to the hotel.

Yuri Nahmov was chopping down a fir tree in the forest. They needed more logs for the stove. Ever since he had been considered old enough to wield an axe, he had been responsible for seeing the stove was never without fuel. His mother couldn't do it. Half the time she didn't know what she was doing. She often burnt the soup and she went for any visitors to Kirilhor like a wildcat, as if they had evil intent. 'Hide!' she would cry whenever a stranger arrived in the village. 'Hide in the cupboard.' Yuri hated being shut in a cupboard; that was how you were punished at the orphanage and it always brought back unpleasant memories. It made him want to scream and beat his fists against the door, but nothing would satisfy Mama until

277

they had hidden and waited for whoever it was to go away again. She was afraid, always afraid. Did she suppose the authorities would come and take him back to the orphanage?

How he had hated that place! They were half starved and brutally treated, especially those whose parents had been arrested and sent to Siberia. He had had no idea who his parents were and it had been assumed he was either one of those or one of the thousands of *besprizomiki*, street children without family and means of support, who had been rounded up to be made into useful Soviet citizens. He was full of jealousy when someone came to claim a child and take him away amid tears of joy, which didn't happen very often. He would hide his misery in a show of indifference, until in the end his pretence became real and he *was* indifferent.

He was a son of the Soviet system. Stalin was his father and every morning when the children were required to chant 'Thank you, Comrade Stalin, for a happy childhood' he sang out, unaware that there was, or could be, anything different, until one day, when he was about six or seven, a strange woman had turned up and claimed she was his mother. She said his name was Yuri Nahmov and not Ilya Minsky which was the name they called him in the orphanage. Worried and frightened, he had been handed over to a complete stranger and begun a very different life.

'It's not the best tree for making firewood,' Ivan told him, watching him from his seat on a tree trunk. He was fidgety, unable to make up his mind whether to say anything about yesterday's visitor. Perhaps he should, perhaps he shouldn't. 'It's too green. It will spit.'

'It's easier than cutting down one of those big deciduous

trees.' Yuri had long ago decided that Ivan was the nearest thing to a father he would ever have and treated him with gentle tolerance. 'And it won't matter about the spitting if we close the doors of the stove. It's too hot to have them open anyway.'

The tree toppled with a creak and a groan and a satisfying thump. Yuri set about stripping it of its smaller branches, ready to saw the trunk into logs. Ivan got up to help him with the two-handed saw.

When they had filled the basket, Yuri picked it up and hefted it onto his shoulder. He had grown into a big strong lad, uncannily like his grandfather, the count, and the weight of it meant nothing to him. 'Are you coming back to the house?'

'Not yet. Later perhaps. I'll clear up these bits first, maybe make a bonfire. The ash will be good for the garden.'

'It'll spit!' Yuri said, laughing. 'I'll see you later, then.'

Back at Kirilhor, he put the logs down by the hearth in the kitchen and took off his outdoor clothes before joining his mother in the living room. She was cowed on the floor in a corner of the large room, her shoulders hunched into a ragged shawl, her eyes flashing hate at a man who stood watching her as if unsure what to do, a man in a business suit and a clean shirt. 'Yurochka, thank goodness you are here,' she said. 'I don't know what this man wants, but he won't go away. Tell him to go away, tell him we don't want whatever it is he's selling.'

Alex held his hand out to the boy. 'I am Alexei Petrovich Simenov. I am sorry if I have disturbed your mother. I assume the lady is your mother?'

'Of course she is,' Yuri said, shaking the hand. His grip was firm. 'What do you want with her?'

'Nothing,' Alex assured him. 'And I'm not selling anything.' He noticed Olga's eyes flashing dangerously and thought quickly. 'I am sightseeing.'

'In Petrovsk?' Yuri laughed. 'What is there to see in a dump like this?'

'Kirilhor,' Alex answered. 'It has an interesting history. Did you know that?'

'I know it once belonged to a count, but he's long dead, and all his kind. And good riddance too. If he were alive now, I would spit on him. You aren't anything to do with him, are you? You haven't come to claim your inheritance?' And he laughed again.

'No, I have no claim on Kirilhor.' Alex wondered if they paid rent for living there, and if so, to whom. Perhaps they were simply squatting. 'But I know someone who lived here as a child before the Revolution. Her father was Count Kirilov. He died during the Civil War, along with his wife and son. Lydia was the only one who survived and went to England. She returned in 1938 with her husband, Nikolay Nikolayevich Andropov. She remembers it with fondness. I wanted to see the place and perhaps take a photograph to show her.'

Olga was undoubtedly disturbed and the mention of Kolya's name roused her to a furious response. 'Get out!' she yelled, scrambling to her feet. Grabbing a knife from the table she came at Alex brandishing it. 'Get out and leave us alone. We don't care that . . .' she clicked bony fingers at him '. . . for a stiff-necked aristocrat, do we, Yurochka?'

Yuri shrugged his shoulders. 'I'm sorry,' he said to Alex, taking Olga's hand and gently removing the knife from her fingers. 'My mother is not well. She was wounded in the head at the beginning of the war and has never fully recovered. It is best you leave us. I shall have to calm her down. You understand?'

'Yes, I understand,' Alex said, and took his leave.

He made his way along the forest track until he came to where Ivan was tending a bonfire; he was almost obscured by thick smoke. The whole forest smelt of pine resin. Seeing Alex he threw the branch he had in his hand on the fire and came towards him. 'You went to Kirilhor, my friend?'

'Yes,' he said turning away because the smoke was making his eyes water. 'The woman's mad.'

'I told you that, didn't I? What did you say? What did she say?'

Alex recounted their conversation word for word. 'Now I'm in a quandary,' he finished. 'What shall I do?'

'I should go away and forget you ever came here. The boy will be all right. He's clever; he'll grow into a fine man and make his mother proud of him.'

Alex gave a humourless grunt of laughter. 'Which mother?'

Ivan chuckled. 'Both of them.'

'Should I tell her? Lydia, I mean.'

'You must make up your own mind about that, young man, but if I were you I'd say nothing. It will break her heart.'

Alex left him and made his way back to the hotel, booked out and took the train back to Moscow. He knew he ought not to go back there but he needed to tell Leo what had happened and ask his advice.

Leo's advice was the same as Ivan's, even though he had never known Lydia. 'In any case,' he added, 'how were you going to tell her? You are here, in Moscow, where you have no business to be, and the lady is in England. A letter? Not advisable, everything is censored. You are banned from the cities, but that doesn't mean you can go where you like. I stayed around to make sure no one followed you onto the train to Kirilhor, but you can be sure someone will pick up your trail before long.'

'I know.' Alex was drowning in despondency. He had not felt so down since he had been taken prisoner outside Minsk. All his longing centred on Upstone Hall and Lydia, even though he realised, deep inside him, that returning there was an unrealistic dream. Too many years had passed since that tearful parting in Moscow, even though it was the memory of that which had kept him alive when he could so easily have succumbed to cold and hunger and cruelty, as many another had done. And with no good news to take back to her . . .

'Cheer up, my friend,' Leo said. 'You were taken at Potsdam, weren't you?'

'Yes.'

'It's in the Russian zone; the authorities won't stop you going back to where you came from and you never know, you might be welcomed with open arms. Even if you're not, you'll be nearer the West. More chance of hopping over the border.'

This was subversive advice from someone who lived in the Soviet Union, but it sounded like sense and Alex was too tired to argue. 'I don't like abandoning the boy,' he said.

'I'll keep an eye on his progress. If he shows promise, I'll see he gets to university or technical college.'

'Why should you do that?' Alex asked in surprise. 'You don't even know him.'

'For our friendship's sake and because Russia needs

educated men. Too many were lost in Stalin's purges.'

Alex couldn't stay in Moscow a moment longer. He took his friend's advice, bidding him and his wife goodbye, choking back tears.

Potsdam was not where he wanted to be. Leo had been right; even as a free man, he could not return to England. Freedom was relative and he would still be inside the Russian zone, stuck until he could think of a way to cross to the West. And it soon became obvious to him that the nearer he came to the border, the more roadblocks and checks there were. Every time the train rushed over a crossing, he could see them from the window. And there were wide swathes of a kind of ploughed-up no-man's-land between one side and the other, designed to allow no cover for anyone trying to cross.

Arriving in Potsdam he discovered Else had married in his absence and had two children. She was not pleased to see him and anxious enough to be rid of him to persuade her husband to show him where there was a weakness in the rows and rows of barbed wire that separated East from West. He was guided to the spot at the dead of night and quietly abandoned.

He took a deep breath and dashed across, ready to start dodging if the bullets came, but strangely no one saw him. Once on the other side, he trudged westwards, his senses keyed to every rustle in the undergrowth at the side of the road, every drip-drip of water from hedges, every barking dog, ready to dive into a ditch if anyone came along the road. In a mile or so he came to a crossroads and another of the ubiquitous border posts, but this time it was manned by American soldiers. They stopped him, guns at the ready.

'Take me to the British,' he said.

'You're a Limey?' one asked in surprise.

'Yes.'

The sergeant detailed one of his men to take him to their CO, where he explained who he was and how he came to be in the East. 'Well, I'll be damned!' the man said. 'That's some story.'

Here he was entertained royally with the best meal he had had in years, a couple of glasses of lager and a fat cigar. Later, in their officers' mess, he had been quizzed again, this time out of curiosity. Most wanted to know what life was like in the Communist East and how he had endured the concentration camp and the gulag. It was dawn when they found him a bed and he collapsed exhausted into it.

Later that day, a gum-chewing driver and a lieutenant with a pistol in a holster took him by jeep to Bonn, the capital of West Germany, where he was left with an aide to the British ambassador. Here he was debriefed thoroughly and given accommodation, while they verified his identity. Two days later he was on a plane heading for London.

The interrogation and the debriefings at the Foreign Office went on for several days, even though they must have been sent the notes of his interrogation in Bonn. When they were satisfied he was who he said he was, he was asked what he intended to do. It was a question he could not readily answer. A quick look at the telephone book had confirmed that Sir Edward Stoneleigh still lived at Upstone Hall and he had been tempted to ring him but decided not to; if he went there he would have to see Lydia, and how could he go there and not tell her he had seen Yuri?

'I need work,' he said. 'And somewhere to live.'

'You have a job here and all your back pay – years of it.'

'Thank you, but I've had enough of the diplomatic corps. I need to be out of doors, leading the simple life.'

He recognised he was not the man he had been, nor ever would be again. What he had been through would colour the rest of his days. The man of decisive action had been too long inured to obeying orders instantly, to half expecting the blows raining on his shoulders for no reason except the guard was in a bad mood, or one of his fellow prisoners suspected him of stealing his food. After years and years of communal living, of not being able to call his soul his own, he needed solitude. He bought a smallholding in Northacre Green, a small village near East Dereham in Norfolk, where he grew vegetables and reared a few pigs and chickens and kept himself to himself.

Sir Edward Stoneleigh's obituary in *The Daily Telegraph* had caught his attention and dragged him, unwillingly, back into the real world.

Robert was working on the deck of the *Merry Maid*, lovingly polishing the brass work, when Alex found him. 'Hallo, Rob,' he said quietly.

Robert whipped round. 'God God, Alex Peters! It is you, isn't it? You're as thin as a rake.'

'Yes, it's me.'

'We thought you were dead. Sir Edward heard it through the embassy. Where the devil have you been?'

'Here and there. In a German POW camp and then Siberia. It's a very long story.'

'Come aboard and tell me about it.'

Alex walked up the gangplank and jumped on deck. After shaking hands, Robert led the way down to the cabin. It was clean but untidy. 'Don't mind the mess. I've been too busy on deck to clean up.' He filled a kettle and lit the gas ring. 'When did you get back?'

'About six months ago.'

Robert whistled. 'Why have you waited so long to contact us? Why didn't you come to the house? Sir Edward died, you know, two months ago now. Poor Lydia was devastated. You did know we had married?'

'Yes. It's why I didn't go. Thought it best.'

'Appreciate that, old man.'

Alex smiled. They seemed to be talking in a kind of shorthand but it conveyed their meaning perfectly. He watched Robert put a tea bag in each of two mugs and pour the boiling water on them. He stirred them thoughtfully. Alex could almost hear his brain ticking over.

'We have two children: Bobby, who's twelve, and Tatyana, who's ten.' He sniffed at the bottle of milk, decided it hadn't gone off and added some to the mugs. Alex could not get used to drinking tea with milk in it. He watched Rob dip a teaspoon into an open bag of sugar and put some in his tea. He followed suit.

'I know that too. I congratulate you.'

'Thank you.' He looked at Alex over the rim of his mug. 'Come on, out with the story.'

So Alex told it yet again, while the other drank his tea and listened in silence, until he came to his return to Moscow, a free man. 'If you can call it freedom,' he added.

'How did you get out of Russia and back here?' Robert asked. 'It could not have been easy.'

'That's another story and, in a way, is why I'm here. I went to Balfour Place, thinking that perhaps you stayed there without Lydia sometimes. The janitor told me where to find you.'

'Wondering when you were coming to that.'

'I need your advice.'

'Go on.'

Alex told him about finding Yuri and both his and Olga's reaction. 'I'd like your advice on what to do about it,' he said. 'Should Lydia be told or not?'

'That's a tough one,' Robert said, looking thoughtful, while Alex waited, understanding the man's hesitation. 'If the boy is so anti the West and Olga hasn't told him about Lydia, should we upset her all over again? Is that what you're asking me?'

'I suppose it is.'

'Then I would say, no, don't tell her. Sir Edward tried to locate Yuri soon after the war ended, but failed. She has accepted the boy is lost. Think of the emotional upheaval for everyone, not least Bobby and Tatty. And all for what? It won't reunite Lydia with Yuri, will it?'

'No. You're right.' He drained his mug. 'Does Lydia come on the boat with you?'

'No, she looked it over when I first bought it, but she hates the sea. We had a rough crossing coming back from Russia and she's never forgotten it. This is my private passion.'

'Doesn't she mind?'

'Not at all. She knows how much I miss the sea since I came out of the service.'

Alex stood up to leave. 'Good luck with it.'

'Thank you.'

'I shan't trouble you again. If, at any time in the future, you want to tell Lydia what I have told you, then that's up to you.'

They shook hands and Alex went up on deck and

jumped down onto the towpath. He took a huge breath of air before striding off towards the city and the railway station. He was exhausted. The encounter had taken more out of him than he would have believed possible. What was more, he had condemned himself never to see Lydia again. He knew Robert would not breathe a word.

BETRAYAL

1961 – 1964

Chapter Twelve

July 1961

'Mum, stop fussing. You look gorgeous.' Tatty was sitting on her mother's bed watching her dress.

Lydia stopped twisting herself in front of the full-length mirror in her bedroom and smiled at her daughter in its reflection. If anyone looked gorgeous it was Tatty in a lilac print frock patterned all over with tiny white flowers. She had skilfully used a little make-up, blusher and eyebrow pencil and a pale-pink lipstick. Long-legged, enviably slim, full of vitality and so popular there was always a crowd of friends of both sexes visiting Upstone Hall during school holidays. Lydia supposed that one day there would be a special young man and a wedding and she didn't know how she would feel about that. Tatty always laughed at that idea. 'I'm not going to get married, Mum, I'll be too busy enjoying myself.'

Lydia made no comment; she had heard it all before. 'I can't believe Bobby is old enough to leave school,' she said. 'Where have the years gone? It only seems five minutes since he was a baby.'

'All mothers say that,' Tatty said, standing up. 'Just don't say it in his hearing, that's all. Are you ready?'

They were going to Bobby's last end-of-year prize-giving. He was to receive two prizes and his A-level results from Mr Lockhart, the headmaster, though he already knew what they were. Three straight As in English, European history and politics. How proud she and Robert were of him! And of Tatty too. She had done well in her O levels, which just went to show, Lydia mused, what her daughter was capable of if only she would put her mind to it.

'As ready as I'll ever be.' She slipped into her high-heeled sandals, picked up her clutch bag and took a last look in the mirror. What faced her was a middle-aged woman, whose waist was beginning ever so slightly to thicken and whose hair was growing grey, but she flattered herself she had kept the wrinkles at bay and her skin was still smooth. In the navy linen suit and ruffled white blouse she had chosen to wear she didn't look half bad.

They found Robert in the drawing room. 'Smashing,' Robert said, looking Lydia up and down. He turned to Tatty. 'As for you, young lady, you will have every young buck falling at your feet.'

'Young buck!' Tatty laughed. 'No one uses words like that nowadays.'

'Why not, if it expresses what I mean?' He was grinning with paternal pride. 'We ought to go, we mustn't be late.'

They accomplished the journey in less than an hour in what had been Sir Edward's Bentley. It was getting on in years but it still went well, kept in good repair by Andy at the garage. Lydia rarely drove it, preferring her own little car, but Robert used it to get backwards and forwards to the *Merry Maid*, which was moored at Ipswich.

He had a nine-to-five desk job at the Admiralty which kept him in London during the week, but he came home to Upstone Hall every Friday night. Sometimes he stayed with her until Monday morning, but sometimes he went sailing. Lydia, who had never forgotten that dreadful wartime voyage from Russia to Scotland, did not share his enthusiasm and did not go with him. Bobby and Tatty had been once or twice but they were so busy with their own friends and social engagements it did not happen often. When she asked him who was crewing for him, he said, 'A friend I met at the Admiralty, you wouldn't know them.'

If she wondered why she had never met this crewman, she did not voice it. And if he chose to spend his time away from her, who could blame him? It was her fault, she knew that. She had not loved him as she ought, certainly not as well as he deserved. She hadn't exactly kept him at arm's length, but neither had she cleaved to him, sharing his highs and lows as, in the beginning, he had tried to share hers. She was carrying too much emotional baggage and didn't seem able to let go of it.

The school assembly hall was packed with parents and siblings come to watch their sons and brothers line up to receive their accolades, smart in their school uniforms, their hair slicked down and their ties straight. Cameras were flashing everywhere and Tatty took a picture when it was Bobby's turn. Afterwards there was tea in the marquee put up on the green in front of the school, a word with the head and then home again.

'Phew! I'm glad that's over,' Bobby said as he climbed into the back seat beside Tatty.

'I thought it was a lovely afternoon,' Lydia said. 'And

the head was very complimentary about your results.'

'I worked damned hard for them,' he said, over her shoulder. ' I didn't want to let Grandpa down.'

'Grandpa', Lydia noted, not 'Father', and looked sharply at Robert, but he was looking straight ahead, watching the road. Bobby could not have failed to notice that his father had rarely been at home during his childhood and even now, when he could have been at home more, he was more often sailing his yacht. Grandpa was the male adult to whom he had always turned.

As soon as they arrived home, Bobby changed out of his school uniform and into jeans and T-shirt. 'You can send this lot to the charity shop,' he said, bringing his flannels, blazer and white shirt down to the kitchen and dumping them on the table. 'I shan't need them again.'

'There's plenty of time for that. Take them off the table, I want to prepare dinner.'

He scooped the clothes up, took them into the laundry room next to the kitchen and dropped them on the brick floor. Lydia sighed in exasperation. 'What are you going to do now?'

'I think I'll have a wander outside, see if anything's changed while I've been gone. What time's dinner?'

Lydia laughed. 'Nothing's changed. And dinner is at seven.'

'OK. I'll be back. I might even bring you a nice fat trout.' And he was gone out of the back door, whistling tunelessly.

Her son loved Upstone Hall and its surrounds as much as she did. As soon as he arrived home at the end of every term, he would go out and walk round the grounds. It was a sort of proprietorial beating of the bounds. One day, she supposed, it would be his and Balfour Place would be

Tatty's. She put a chicken into the oven to roast, prepared the vegetables and then went out to find him. He was in a rowing boat on the lake. Seeing his mother, he wound in his line and rowed back to shore.

'Have you caught anything?' she asked.

'Not a thing.' He shipped the oars, jumped out of the boat and tied it up. 'I wasn't really paying attention.'

'Oh,' she said. 'Something on your mind? You're not worrying about going to university, are you?'

He picked up his rod and line and walked beside her. 'No, of course not. I was just wondering if I could have a party, you know, to celebrate the end of school. Most of my friends will be scattered all over the place next year and I thought it would make a good send-off. You'll let me, won't you?'

'How many?' she asked warily.

'Oh, about fifty, perhaps a few more,' he said airily. 'There's plenty of room, isn't there? And we won't make a mess.'

She laughed. 'Fifty young men not make a mess! Impossible.'

'Oh, go on, say yes.'

'I'll have to ask your father.'

'He won't care. He's never here anyway.'

'Bobby, don't speak about him like that.'

'It's true. He's obsessed with that boat.'

'He loves the sea, Bobby, and there isn't any sea about here, is there? I don't begrudge him.'

'So what about the party?'

'We'll see.'

'You always used to say that when we were little, as if that would be enough to shut us up.'

She laughed, taking his arm. 'It didn't work, did it?'

'No.'

'Do you want me to mention it?'

'Yes, please. It'll be better coming from you.'

'Bobby wants a party for his friends from school,' Lydia said to Robert next morning at breakfast. Tatty and Bobby were still in bed.

Robert looked up from the newspaper he was reading. 'Why not? That's the usual thing, isn't it? Do you mind?'

'No. We used to have lovely parties here when I was young. I remember my twenty-first. Everyone came, old and young, all dressed up to the nines. It was when Papa had the Kirilov Star made into a pendant for me. We danced the night away.'

'I am sure it was a glittering occasion,' he said, laconically. 'But young people nowadays don't want that kind of do. They want music by the Beatles and dancing the rock and roll and the twist.'

She should not have said that about her party; it was before she met Robert, before she met Kolya even, but Alex had been there. And as usual Robert had detected the note of wistfulness in her voice. 'We can manage that, can't we?' she said brightly. 'He says they won't make a mess.'

He gave a grunt of a laugh. 'Believe that if you like.'

'I was thinking we should leave them to it,' she began tentatively. 'That's what most parents do nowadays. Bobby's very responsible and we'll only be in the way if we stay around. We could go to a show and stay the night at Balfour Place.'

'No,' he said, somewhat sharply, then moderated his tone. 'I mean, it's no change for me, is it? I'm there all week.'

'Yes, silly of me. What about a run up to the Dales? We could tour around, have bed and breakfast, walk a bit.'

'OK, you see to it.' He folded the paper, laid it beside his plate and stood up. 'I'll be off now. There's a spare part I need to get for the *Merry Maid* and then I've got to fix it. I'll probably stay on the boat tonight.' He had told her of that the day before, and though she had been disappointed, it came as no surprise. Their relationship was one born of mutual respect, parenthood, habit, a kind of fond contentment with no great highs and lows. It was not enough to keep him at home. He bent to kiss her. 'See you Friday.'

She went to the door to see him drive away as she always did, then turned back indoors. Bobby was just coming downstairs wearing jeans and a sloppy jumper. 'Dad just gone?'

'Yes. Why?'

'Did you ask him about the party?'

'Yes. He said you could organise it yourself.'

'Great.'

'But I want to know who's coming, how many, and I want it all over by two a.m.'

'Yes, Mum.' He was grinning from ear to ear.

'Your father and I are going to have a weekend away and leave you to it, so no funny business.'

'Funny business, Mum?' he queried, adopting an air of innocence. 'I don't know what you mean.'

'Oh, yes you do.' She turned from him and went into the kitchen, feeling somehow unsettled. It was as if this milestone in her son's life was a turning point in her own and yet she could not see how that could be. Tatty came down in her dressing gown, rubbing sleep from her eyes, and Lydia left them helping themselves to breakfast and went up to her room, where she sat on the edge of her unmade bed and contemplated her reflection in the mirror on her wardrobe door. She was forty-five years old, there was grey in her hair, and yet inside she felt no older than the twenty-one-year-old who had danced with Alex, ignorant of what lay ahead. How happy she had been. And how foolish.

Suddenly making up her mind, she made the bed, put a light jacket over her cotton dress and left the house. She picked up some stale bread from the kitchen and walked down to the lake, where she stood breaking it up and throwing it to the mallards. In her mind she was the four-year-old refugee again – lost, bewildered, afraid. As clearly as if it had been yesterday, she heard Alex speaking in his half-broken voice. *'Try not to be sad.'*

'I cannot help it.'

'No, I suppose not. But you are a great deal better off than a lot of Russian émigrés. They are finding life in England hard, not speaking English and needing to work. Be thankful.'

Be thankful. Yes, she had a lot to be thankful for. She threw the last of the crumbs and turned back to the house. There it was, four-square and solid, her home, and though the grounds were only half the size they had once been, it was still surrounded by a small park and manicured lawns. It was hers. Thanks to Sir Edward she was wealthy and need never feel cold or hunger or cruelty, though she was well aware they existed. She had always done her best to mitigate some of that, giving generously to charity, helping in more practical ways when she could, especially those refugees from the other side of the Iron Curtain who needed something to get them started in Britain and help with learning the language. Alex's words, uttered to a traumatised four-year-old had sunk deep. Everything he had ever said to her was etched in her memory. '*You are not alone,*' whispered while she queued at Kiev station. '*Sweetheart, you need me, and while you need me, I shall be at your disposal.*' That in Minsk. And at that heartbreaking parting in Moscow. '*I will come back to you, you see, and I might even have Yuri with me.*'

Other memories crowded in on her, more bitter-sweet: a feeling of loneliness – no, not so much loneliness as isolation; her adopted parents, one of whom had loved her more than the other; her first day at school and at college; Kolya, whom she did not want to remember, and Bob, who had been her prop when she needed one most; Yuri lying content in her arms, a chubby, dark-haired baby with surprisingly blue eyes, who had been learning to recognise her and smile a toothless smile. She had never seen his first tooth, never watched his first tottering steps, never sent him off to school with a satchel over his shoulder. He would have finished his education by now, a young man, making his way in the world. She refused to believe he had not survived the war.

And then there was Alex in white tie and tails dancing a waltz with her at the ball to celebrate her twenty-first birthday, even then binding her to him with silken threads which neither time, nor distance, nor death itself could ever sever; Alex in that dreadful uniform, grim with responsibility, torn between love and duty; Alex the lover. That most of all. Oh, how she still missed him!

What had happened to him after she left him in Moscow? What was he doing going back to Minsk when it was being attacked by the Germans? Had he wanted to die? Where had they buried him? Who was the man she had seen standing by the yew tree in the churchyard the day of her father's funeral? She was still plagued by questions, none of which could be answered.

She went back to the house to hear Bobby and Tatty arguing hotly because Tatty wanted to invite some of her friends to his party and he was against it. 'You'll have your own party when the time comes; do you think I'll want to muscle my friends in on that?'

Lydia acted as mediator, as she always did, telling Bobby he should invite some of Tatty's friends so that she did not feel out of it, then decided to go and look round the shops in Norwich. Doing that might banish the nostalgia.

She was halfway there when she ran out of petrol. 'Of all the stupid things to do,' she muttered, switching off the engine and getting out of the car to find herself in a country lane which did not even have road markings. When and why she had turned off the main road she could not remember. Neither could she remember when she had last seen a signpost.

She began to walk. It started to rain, big drops that soon soaked her light summer jacket and dress and plastered her hair to her face. 'Serve you right,' she muttered, stopping to look over a five-bar gate. There was a yard and a cottage and a dog that barked ferociously, but she could also see a telephone line. Taking a deep breath, she opened the gate and made her way towards the cottage, thankful, when she approached, to see the dog was chained. She had almost reached the door when it was opened and he stood in its frame.

'So you found me,' he said.

She could not move, could not speak. Her heart was pounding and her legs felt like rubber. All she could do was stare at him.

He reached out, took her arm and gently pulled her inside. 'Come in, Lidushka, you look like a drowned rat.'

His use of the diminutive of her name sent her flying back to Moscow and yet it served to wake her out of the strange dream she seemed to be having. 'But you're supposed to be dead.' It came out as a croak.

'Am I? Now, I never knew that. I don't feel a bit dead. Feel me.' He took her hands in both his and put them either side of his face. 'Is that substantial enough for you?'

'Alex! Oh my God, Alex.' And she burst into tears.

He took her in his arms to comfort her. 'My poor darling,' he murmured into her hair. 'It was a shock, wasn't it?'

She leant back and looked up into his face. It was his face, no doubt about that, but it was thinner, the cheeks sunken, the eyes somehow darker as if they could not quite shake off the terrors he had seen. His hair was streaked with white and hadn't been cut for some time. 'But what happened? How did you come to be living here? Why didn't you tell me you were alive? And so close.'

He sat her down beside the kitchen fire and, taking a towel from a clothes horse, stood over her and began rubbing her hair dry. It was an intimate thing to do, but so natural she didn't question it. 'Would it have helped to know?' he asked. 'You had made a new life for yourself. You had a new family. I was history.'

'Alex, you were never history, you could not be.' She pulled away to look up at him. 'You are part of me, of what I was, of the woman I am, and, as far as I was concerned,

301

that part died on the day Papa told me you had been killed. I mourned for you, Alex.'

'It is gratifying to know that,' he said wryly.

'How can you be so calm about it?'

'You think I am calm? How little you know.'

'Then tell me. Tell me how you feel, tell me everything.'

He put down the towel. 'Later perhaps. First things first. How did you come to be standing on my doorstep in the pouring rain?'

'I ran out of petrol down the road. I was on my way to Norwich. I must have been daydreaming. I can't remember turning off the main Norwich road, nor even why I should. It was as if fate was taking a hand.'

'It often does. Is your car locked?'

'Yes, I pushed it off the road and started to walk, looking for a phone box. I saw your phone line and came to ask if someone would ring a garage for me. I didn't know I'd be confronted by a ghost.'

'Petrol's no problem. I've got a can of it in the shed. I think you'd better take those wet clothes off. I can find you something to wear while they dry. And while you're doing that, I'll fetch your car and rustle up some lunch.'

'But . . .'

'But what? You think you shouldn't be here? You think you should be on your way, soaking wet? How foolish is that?' He turned to face her. 'And you do want to know what happened to me, don't you?'

'Yes, I do.' She was shivering but whether it was from shock or her wetting she couldn't be sure.

'Then give me your car keys and then come with me.'

He put the keys on the table, led the way upstairs, went into his bedroom, and came out again carrying a pair of trousers, a belt and a shirt which he put into her arms, then opened another door. 'Here's the bathroom. There's plenty of hot water. Take your time. Come down when you're ready.'

She ran a bath, stripped off and lay in the warm water, unable to believe what was happening to her. Alex was alive. Alex was here. Alex, whom she had never ceased to love and never would no matter how many years passed, had held her in his arms again. Oh, the joy of it! Husband, children, home all faded into insignificance beside that stupendous fact.

She dried herself and dressed. In spite of Alex's thinness the trousers were far too big. She pulled them into her waist with the belt and rolled the legs up above her ankles. The shirt hung loosely, its sleeves also rolled up. She smiled at her reflection and went down to join him in the kitchen.

Hearing her come in, he turned from stirring something on the stove and laughed. 'You look very sexy like that.'

'Do I?'

'Not that you weren't always sexy. The years have dealt kindly with you.' He had laid the kitchen table with cutlery and a bowl of salad and beckoned her to take her place.

'Thank you. I've been lucky.'

He put a dish of spaghetti bolognese on the table and stuck two serving spoons in it, then sat down opposite her. 'Help yourself.'

'This is unreal,' she said. She had no appetite, but as he had taken the trouble to cook for her, she put a small helping on her plate. 'I can't believe it. There was I seeing Robert off, thinking about the party my son wants to have and wondering whether letting him organise it himself might end in disaster, forgetting to fill the car with petrol

303

before setting off, forgetting it was Sunday and half the shops would be shut, and then taking a wrong turn on a road I know like the back of my hand and here you are. It's as if you were waiting for me.'

'Perhaps I was,' he said softly.

'Tell me what happened to you,' she said. 'Everything. What were you doing in Minsk? Why did everyone say you were dead?'

'I was looking for Yuri, among other things.'

'Oh. Papa tried to find out where he was as soon as the war ended, but it had been too long. He said orphanages often changed children's names when they took them in, always supposing they knew Yuri's name in the first place. He couldn't tell them, could he?'

'No.' He paused. Should he or shouldn't he tell her? He had given no undertaking to Robert not to tell her himself. 'I'm truly sorry.'

'Not your fault. Go on. You were in Minsk. Then what?'

He told her while the food grew cold on their plates. He told her about the heroism of the ordinary Russian soldier in spite of the incompetence of most of their superiors; he told her of the German advance and being a prisoner in a concentration camp, of his life with Else in Germany and the betrayal that led to his years in Siberia. He spared her the more gruesome details, but what he did tell her was horrific enough to shock her, and he left out his visit to Kirilhor and ended with his escape from Germany and eventual return to England.

'All that time,' she said. 'All that suffering and here was I safe in my own little corner of England. The war we experienced here was nothing compared to that, nor the austerity that followed. The only thing I had to be sad about was leaving you and Yuri in Russia, and that broke my heart, and then the loss of my mother and then my father.' She paused. 'It was you in the churchyard, wasn't it? On the day of Papa's funeral.'

'Yes, I saw the notice of his death in the newspaper and wanted to pay my respects.'

'I thought I'd seen a ghost.'

'I'm sorry if I upset you, especially at that sad time. I didn't mean you to see me.'

'Why not? Why didn't you join us? Why just creep away?'

'I would have been out of place. And turning up suddenly would have distracted everyone from the purpose of the day, to mourn a truly good man.'

'You could have written.'

'I did consider it, but as I said, I had – have – no place in your life, not anymore.'

'Alex, how can you say that? We have found each other again . . .'

'Does that make a difference?'

'You know it does.'

'No, I don't know. You tell me.'

She watched him filling a percolator, spooning coffee into the top if it and putting it on the stove. Then he took two mugs from a shelf, sugar from a cupboard and milk from the fridge. His movements were deliberate, controlled. He did not seem to be nearly as churned up as she was. 'I thought you were dead and I learnt to live with that. I had to. I married Robert . . .'

'Are you saying you would not have done that if you had known I was alive?'

'I don't know. I thought I loved him. I *did* love him.' She told him about that journey from Murmansk and how good Robert had been to her, about Bobby and Tatty and how happy she had always been at Upstone Hall, though he knew that already. She told him about Margaret's dreadful death and Sir Edward's stroke and how Robert had supported her through it all.

'Nothing has changed, Lidushka,' he said gently.

She looked into his eyes, trying to read what was in them. There was evidence of deep suffering, of a stoicism she could never emulate. 'Do you mean you are going to see me off and retreat into your own little world again, while I go to mine, and that's the end of it?'

He poured out two mugs of coffee, added a little milk to each and put one in front of her, pushing the sugar bowl towards her. 'It's what ought to happen.'

She shook her head, not only to indicate she didn't want the sugar, but in an effort to clear her brain, to think straight. 'I can't, Alex, nor can I believe that's what you want. Have your experiences made you so cold you are unable to feel anymore? Is that what you're telling me?'

'No, it is not what I'm telling you.' He took her hand and hauled her to her feet so that she was facing him, standing so close his warmth surrounded her like a comforting blanket. He put her hand over his heart and held it there. She felt it beating, a little erratically but nonetheless strongly. 'Do you think that belongs to a man unable to feel?'

'No.'

'It was thinking of you that kept it going when other men succumbed to the conditions. When I was cold and hungry and exhausted, reduced to little more than a skeleton, that heart beat for you. It still does . . .'

'Oh, Alex!' She flung herself into his arms. 'Tell me I'm not dreaming and I won't wake up any moment and find myself in bed in Upstone Hall.'

'If you are dreaming, then so am I,' he said and kissed her gently on her closed lips. 'And a pleasant dream it is, one I've had many and many a time.'

'Then you won't send me away, will you? Not yet.'

'I won't send you away.' He kissed her forehead, then her cheeks one by one and then her lips. The pressure of his mouth on hers was exquisite torture and she clung to him, kissing him back all over his face. He could not stand against that onslaught.

He took her hand and almost ran with her up the stairs to his bed, where they made love in a frenzy of reawakened passion. It was glorious and frightening in its strength. Nothing could have stopped it. And when it was over, she slept the sleep of the utterly exhausted.

He lay beside her, his head propped on one arm and looked down at her. Their meeting and its likely consequence had an inevitability about it, for which fate, chance, destiny, call it what you will, had been responsible, not he. He had been living and working, going about his daily life half-alive, knowing there was something missing but unable to do anything about it. And when she turned up on his doorstep, he had not even been surprised. In spite of the years, she was still beautiful, still the lovely girl of twenty-one he had fallen in love with, but more than that, her maturity had brought out more of the woman. Her figure was slightly thicker, her hair was less luxuriant; there was even a grey hair or two, but she could still make love with the unbridled passion of youth. He would not have given back a moment of that for a king's ransom.

She stirred, opened her eyes sleepily and reached out for him again. This time their lovemaking was slower, more relaxed, tender and yet still passionate. Guilt did not come into it, nor thoughts of the future. This was here and now and they were as much in love as ever they had been. His eyes had come alive again in the last few hours. He was more like the Alex she had known. But it had to end, if only because they were hungry and thirsty and it was growing dusk. He padded, naked, to the bathroom. She watched him go. How thin he was; there was hardly enough flesh on him to cover his ribs. But the muscles of his arms and thighs were strong; a man used to hard, physical work. Oh, how she loved him!

She did not think of Robert and home until they were once more in the kitchen and she was wearing her own clothes again and he had dressed in jeans and jumper. He had made fresh coffee and they sat opposite each other to drink it.

'What now?' she asked, holding her mug in both hands.

'It's up to you. Will you tell Robert?'

'Do you think I should?'

'That's for you to decide, but I'd say no, not unless you intend to leave him.'

'Oh, no, I couldn't do that. It would break his heart. And there's the children . . .'

'Then you know the answer.'

'I suppose so.' There was hopelessness in her voice. 'I hate secrets and I can't bear the thought of deceiving him, but neither can I bear saying goodbye to you again . . .'

'Then we won't say goodbye. You know where I am

now. If you need me, I am here. I'll give you my phone number, but you don't need to ring. Just turn up.'

They both stood up, facing each other. She looked up into his face, wondering if he might persuade her to stay, but he said nothing. 'Too late to go to Norwich now,' she said in an effort to bring herself back to the real world. 'I'll have to go another day.'

'You know the way back?'

She didn't think he was asking if she knew the way home, but if she could find her way to the cottage again. 'Yes.'

He accompanied her out to her car which stood in the yard. The gate was open ready for her to drive straight out. 'Safe journey,' he said, as she settled in her seat and switched on the engine. It sprang into life, almost drowning his softly spoken words. 'I love you.'

She could hardly see to drive for the tears that filled her eyes. Impatiently she rubbed them away and resolutely set course for home. In the rear-view mirror she saw him watching her go, a lonely, rather gaunt figure with one hand raised in farewell. Alex.

In the event, she and Robert did not go walking in the Dales the weekend of Bobby's party. Robert rang on the Thursday evening to tell her something had come up at work and he had to remain in London over the weekend. She commiserated with his disappointment. 'Another time,' she said.

'What will you do? Will you stay and endure the party?'

'No, I don't think so. I'll stay with an old wartime friend in East Dereham. She's always asking me when I'm going over to see her.' It was the first time she had lied to him and she hated herself for it. And as often happens, one lie led to another.

'I never heard you mention a friend in East Dereham.'

'She's only just moved there and got in touch again. She lived abroad until recently which is why we never visited.'

'Have a nice time, then.'

'I will. Don't work too hard.'

'I won't. I'll be home next Friday as usual.'

'There, that wasn't that difficult, was it?' Pamela asked when Robert rang off. For months she had been trying to persuade him to take her to France on the *Merry Maid*. 'We hardly ever go sailing these days,' she grumbled.

'I have to go home sometimes. I can't stay away every weekend. Lydia needs me.'

'No, she doesn't. She doesn't want you.'

'I didn't say that – not exactly.'

'That's the way I read it.'

Pamela Osborne was several years younger than Lydia. During the day, she wore her long blonde hair up in a French pleat. She had blue eyes and full red lips, an enviable figure and long slim legs, made to seem longer by the excessively high heels she always wore, except when she was on the boat. Then she wore canvas deck shoes, baggy trousers and overlarge jumpers, and she tied her hair back in a youthful ponytail. He found her exciting, the more so because of the secrecy involved. Having two women loving him flattered his ego, though he was not sure, had never been sure, of Lydia's love. The guilt came because he could not find fault with her as wife and mother, and it was her money that allowed him to lead the comfortable life he had and to buy the yacht and indulge his passion for sailing and for Pamela.

He had met her at a party given by one of his friends at the Admiralty. It was a spur-of-the-moment invitation, too late for Lydia to make arrangements to come up to London and go with him, and he had gone alone, not expecting to enjoy it. Pamela was alone too, and they began a polite conversation, each balancing a glass of gin and tonic in one hand and a plate of canapés in the other. They had discovered a mutual enthusiasm for sailing and they discussed the merits of different craft and one thing led to another, and before the evening was out, he had invited her to come sailing with him and she had accepted. It was easily arranged; Lydia would not have wanted to come even if he had asked her.

They had sailed from Ipswich, where the yacht was moored, round the coast to Mersea Island, where they had stopped for a pub meal before returning. He told himself it was all very innocent, but underneath he was aware of currents of sexual attraction and on the second occasion he had made some excuse about storms brewing and they had stayed at the pub all night. A year later, she was as good as living at Balfour Place. He felt guilty about it but he assuaged it by telling himself, and Pamela, that he was not Lydia's first love and that she still hankered for the old one. It had been nearly six years since his meeting with Alex, and as Lydia had long since ceased to talk about Yuri, there had been no occasion when he could have said anything. Or so he told himself. And the longer he delayed the more impossible it became.

Sometimes he wondered if Lydia had guessed about Pamela. Just lately she had been acting a little strangely – subdued, almost in a dream some of the time, at other times overanimated, as if she had a lot of excess energy she needed to expend. And their lovemaking, never very passionate or frequent, had become almost non-existent. It could, of course, be her time of life. He began to wonder what would happen if his affair came out into the open. It was a question he did not like to ask himself and he pushed it out of his mind in the hope it would never happen. He did not want to give Pamela up; she fulfilled a need in him that he had not even been aware existed before he met her. Neither did he want his marriage to break up; that was like a comfortable pair of slippers, worn but still too good to throw away. And at the moment he was enjoying the best of both worlds.

Lydia found Alex feeding the pigs, who snorted and squealed and nudged each other out of the way to get at the trough. He was wearing an old pullover, with holes in the elbows and grubby jeans tucked into wellington boots. She stood a little way off, not wanting to go any closer for fear of dirtying her shoes, but drinking in the sight of him, feeding her hunger for him just by watching him doing the mundane tasks he did every day.

He emptied the bucket and turned, seeing her for the first time. 'Lydia, I didn't hear you arrive.'

'You did say "just turn up". You meant it, didn't you?'

'Of course I did.' He put the bucket down and came towards her. 'I'm filthy.'

'I don't care.' She reached up and pulled his head down to kiss him.

He stood with his arms held out sideways so he didn't dirty her jacket. 'Go indoors,' he said when she stopped to draw breath. 'I'll finish up out here and then I'll be with you.'

She went back to the car, fetched her overnight bag and went in by the kitchen door. The dog left his basket by the hearth and came towards her, wagging his tail. She stooped to fondle it. 'You might look ferocious, but you're not much good as a guard dog, are you?' she said.

The remains of Alex's breakfast stood on the table: a box of cornflakes, a pot of cold coffee, a mug, a plate and a bowl, milk in a bottle, a packet of sugar, a toast rack with one cold piece of toast in it. She took off her jacket, cleared it away and washed up. He came in just as she finished. 'You didn't have to do that.'

'I wanted to.'

'I'll go and clean up and then I'll be with you. Put the percolator on again, we'll have fresh coffee.' It was then he noticed her bag on a chair. 'You've come to stay?'

'Just for tonight. If you'll have me.'

'Have you? My God, do you need to ask?' He left the room and she heard him galloping up the stairs and moving about above her. She picked up her bag and followed him. He was crossing the landing to the bathroom, wearing only his underpants. She dropped her bag and stopped him. 'Since you seem stripped for action . . .' she murmured, pressing herself close to him and nuzzling her lips along his collar bone to his throat.

'Lidushka, have you no shame?' he asked, laughing.

'None at all where you are concerned.'

He walked backwards into his bedroom, taking her with him, and fell back on the bed with her on top of him.

'Now,' he said some time later, as they lay naked side by side. 'Tell me what brought you here today. I didn't expect to see you again so soon. Has something happened?'

'You happened. Oh, Alex, I don't know how I've endured the last three weeks, thinking about you all the time, unable to sleep and then dreaming in the daytime, trying to act normally and not being able to . . .'

'Has Robert guessed?'

'I don't think so, but I can't be sure. We were supposed to be going away for the weekend to keep out of the way of Bobby's party, but Robert said he had to work. He's never done that on a weekend before. He has a nine-to-five desk job which I know he hates, so it surprised me. I said I was going to stay with an old friend from wartime who has recently moved to East Dereham from abroad.'

'Why East Dereham? It's only half a dozen miles from here.'

'I know, but I'm not a very good liar, so I thought it best to stick to the truth as far as I could. You are a wartime friend and you have moved here from abroad, and if anyone who knows me saw and recognised my car, it wouldn't cause comment.'

He laughed. 'You devious little minx!'

'You don't mind, do you?'

'Mind? How could I mind when you are all I want, all I've ever wanted. I wish I had you all the time.'

'Don't let's think of that,' she said, stirring in his arms to take his hand and kiss the palm. 'Let's just enjoy the weekend. I'll help you feed the animals and we can go for long walks and eat and sleep and wake up in the morning side by side.'

'The last time we did that was in Moscow,' he said. 'So much water under the bridge since then, so much to regret, so many memories . . .'

She put her fingers over his lips. 'No, no more of that. I

don't want to be sad. Let's get up and have that coffee and decide what we're going to do.'

They bathed and dressed and drank coffee, sitting over it talking, remembering times in the past they had been together, relating events that had happened when they were apart. He told her about how he had set up the smallholding with his back pay. Then he showed her round. She inspected the pigsties, the chicken runs, the vegetables growing in long straight rows, all neatly hoed free of weeds. 'You are tidier outdoors than in,' she said as they returned to the kitchen.

'I suppose I am, but this brings in money and the house doesn't. And there's only me.'

'It's very different from being a diplomat.'

'That's why I did it. I needed peace and quiet to recoup.'

'You are still too thin.'

He laughed. 'You should have seen me when I first came out of the gulag – skin and bone I was. Now, at least I'm strong and healthy.'

'And as handsome as ever,' she said, smiling.

He ignored that. 'What would you like to do now?'

'Let's go for a walk.'

He stood up. 'A walk it is. Old Patch could do with a run and I know a good pub where we can eat.'

The heath was covered with heather and bracken and scrubby little trees. A kestrel hovered overhead and then swooped on its prey, a rabbit bobbed up out of a hole and seeing them disappeared down it again. A handful of people walked in the opposite direction and they said good morning and went on, coming out onto another country lane which led to a village and a pub. It was crowded with people out enjoying a Saturday evening meal. They found seats in the corner and ordered fish and chips and peas. The food, if a little uninspiring, was substantial and well cooked. Returning to the cottage, tired and content, they made cocoa and went to bed, though it was still only just dusk.

But the next day had to be faced, and after a morning in which he did the chores outdoors and she tidied the house and made soup for lunch, they sat silently contemplating their imminent parting. 'I wish I didn't have to go,' she said, when it could not be put off any longer.

'I wish it too. Having you here has made it into a home. It was never that before, simply somewhere to eat and sleep.'

'Alex, you know I can't leave Robert, don't you?' The words were torn out of her.

'Yes.'

'If you can't accept that, I mustn't come again.' As she said it, she knew how hard it would be to keep away, but she would have to try for Robert's sake, for the children's sake and for her own peace of mind. And for Alex too. Because she wasn't being fair to him.

He understood her so well, could read her mind and knew exactly the torment she was going through. 'You must do what you think is right,' he said. 'But never doubt, I will always be here, to come to the rescue if you need me . . .'

'Like a knight in shining armour,' she added with a cracked laugh.

'The armour is a little tarnished now,' he said. 'But it is still available.' There was silence for a moment, then he said, 'Lydia, you know I said I had been looking for Yuri in Minsk?'

'Yes.'

'I didn't find him there.'

'I realised that. You would have told me if you had.'

'Oh, Lydia, I am so sorry. I should have, I really should. You have every right to know.'

'Know what? Tell me, tell me at once. He's not . . . not dead, is he?'

'No, far from it. After I came back from the gulag, I went to Kirilhor. I was simply looking for somewhere to lie low until I could get home and I thought of Ivan Ivanovich. I had no idea Yuri would be there.'

'He's back at Kirilhor?' That was the last place she expected him to be.

'He was six years ago. He would have finished his education and found a job by now, though I doubt he'd move far from Olga Denisovna.'

'Olga!'

'Yes.' He took a deep breath. 'She didn't die. She was still in hospital in Minsk when the Germans invaded Russia. She was evacuated to Moscow with all the other patients and recovered, though badly knocked about. She spent the rest of the war years keeping her head down, working as a cleaner at the hospital. After the war she went looking for Yuri. She was luckier than you. She found him in an orphanage and claimed him as her son. He has grown up believing himself to be Yuri Nahmov.'

Her heart sank. 'So he doesn't know about me?'

'No. He thinks Olga Nahmova is his mother.'

'How could she do that – how *could* she?'

'She sustained head injuries in the explosion and it may be she actually thinks he is her son.'

'But you told him differently.'

'No, I didn't.'

'Why not?'

'He was in no mood to hear it. He's been brought up to be a good Communist, Lidushka. He hates the Capitalist West and when I mentioned your father, the count – without telling him about the relationship – he was vitriolic in his hate and Olga came at me with a knife. I decided, reluctantly, to leave well alone.'

Tears were raining down her face. 'Oh, Alex. If you kept quiet all this time, why tell me now?'

He wiped the tears away with his handkerchief. 'You wish I hadn't?'

'No. And it's done now, isn't it?' She attempted a smile.

'Yes. I debated long and hard about whether to say anything when you were here before, wondering if you had really given him up . . .'

'No, I hadn't, not altogether. I couldn't.'

'I realise that now.'

'I can't go to him, can I?'

'No, sweetheart, you can't go to him. But take comfort from the fact that he is a big strong lad and very intelligent. You can be proud of him.'

She was silent for a long time. He reached out and put his work-worn hand over her soft one. 'Perhaps I should not have told you.'

'Yes, you should. I needed to know. Now I shall be able to imagine him growing up and making his way in the world, Communist or no Communist.'

'Communism won't last,' he said. 'Not like it was in Stalin's day. Already there are signs of change. The uprisings in Hungary prove that. It will happen again elsewhere and the Russians won't be able to keep putting them down.'

'I hope you are right.' She paused. 'I must go home.'

'I know.'

'I shan't say anything of this to Robert. He doesn't like me talking about Russia and always cuts me off when I start on what he calls "one of my nostalgic trips". I suppose it's because it's part of my life he can't share.' She smiled suddenly. 'In any case, he'd want to know how I found out and I can't tell him that, can I?'

'I suppose not.'

And so she left him, left him to his pigs and his chickens and his untidy kitchen and went back to Upstone Hall, large, comfortable, well kept, even though it took her a week to tidy up after Bobby's party.

Chapter Thirteen

September 1963

Lydia was back in Kirilhor, silently and desperately struggling with Olga for possession of Yuri. The woman would not let her have him. In the tussle the baby fell to the floor with a sickening crump. Horrified, Lydia looked down through her empty arms and realised he was dead. His head was at an unnatural angle, his limbs all floppy and yet his blue eyes were open and reproached her. The shock of it woke her and for a moment she thought she was still in Russia.

She felt the dried-on tears she had shed in her sleep and looked about her at the familiar room with its warm carpet and pretty curtains. Her sheets were white, not the dirty grey of those at Kirilhor, and instead of scratchy blankets, those on her bed were soft. She was safe at Upstone Hall. Yuri wasn't dead; he was alive, Alex had told her so.

She passed the back of her hand across her eyes in an effort to bring herself back to the present. Yuri wasn't dead; her nightmare was false. He was alive and well and for that she should be thankful. She had written to him at Kirilhor soon after her last visit to Alex, explaining why and how she had left him in Russia and how she loved him and thought of him constantly, but her letters had come back unopened and covered in official stamps. It had been a terrible disappointment that wracked her with misery for days. It was not fair on her family to be constantly brooding and wishing, and so she had pulled herself together and hidden the letters away, hidden her pain along with them. But it didn't stop the nightmares.

She had forgotten what had woken her and was startled by a knock on the door and Tatty poking her head round it. Seeing her mother still in bed, she came into the room. 'Mum, are you all right? It's gone eight o'clock.' She was tall and slim, dressed in tailored black slacks and a pink cashmere jumper. Her dark hair was cut in a fashionable bob, with the nape of the neck shaped and the front hair flicked forward.

'Is it? Good heavens, I must have overslept. I'll be properly awake in a minute.'

Tatty looked closely at her mother's face. 'You've been crying.'

'No, dreaming.'

'More like a nightmare, by the look of you.'

'Perhaps. It's gone now.' She attempted a laugh, which was difficult since her dream still haunted her.

'I'm at a loose end and thought we could go shopping in Norwich. I need some things to take to Girton and I want to buy Claudia and Reggie a wedding present.' Now the children were grown up and no longer needed her, Claudia had at last agreed to marry her bus driver. 'What do you say?' Tatty went on. 'You haven't got anything else arranged, have you?'

Tatty was always going off here, there and everywhere with her friends, but they were close, mother and daughter, and they enjoyed going shopping together. 'Give me a minute and I'll be ready.'

She struggled off the bed and went to have a shower. When she returned, Tatty was sitting on her bed, waiting for her. 'What were you dreaming about, Mum? It wasn't Dad, was it?'

'Why do you say that?' she asked sharply.

'He's away an awful lot. He went off again early this morning, didn't he?'

'Yes, but he loves sailing and I don't. He'll be home next weekend for the wedding.' In the absence of any close family, Robert had agreed to give the bride away. Tatty was to be bridesmaid.

'I'm not a child, you know. I've got eyes and ears.'

Lydia smiled. No, her daughter was a beautiful young woman, far too observant sometimes. She was off to Girton in October and then both her children would have left the nest. She sat down beside her on the bed. 'Tatty, I'm not worried about your father, I promise you.'

'Then what?'

'It was something on the news last night,' she said, prevaricating. 'Some poor young man has been killed trying to get over the Berlin Wall. To me, that dreadful wall symbolises the great chasm between East and West, a gulf of hate and misunderstanding nothing can bridge, and it set me thinking about my time in Russia just before the war and I suppose that's what triggered the dream.'

'Tell me about it.'

Perhaps if she talked about it, she could dispel the feeling of guilt, because it was guilt which gave her the nightmares. 'It was a terrible time. No one knew what was going to happen and when the Germans invaded there was panic everywhere. The Russians had been relying on their non-aggression pact with Germany and were taken by surprise. Alex saw it coming and so did most of the Brits in Russia at the time, but of course, no one listened to them. People disappeared, simply disappeared into thin air, and there was no way of tracing them . . .' She stopped. 'I shouldn't be remembering that, should I? I can't seem to stop myself and I feel so guilty . . .'

'Whatever for?'

'I left Yuri behind. I abandoned him.'

'From what you've told me, Mum, you had no choice.'

'Sometimes I ask myself if I should have been stronger and not let Alex persuade me to leave.'

Tatty knew about Alex; he had figured in her tale of leaving Russia at the beginning of the war, before she met Robert, but she had called him a family friend, which indeed he was. He had been frequently at Upstone Hall as a young man and several photographs in the family album featured him but, like everyone else, Tatty believed he had been killed at the beginning of the war. 'Then your life would have been very different. You would not have married Dad and Bobby and I would not have been born. You don't regret that, do you?'

'No, of course not. Not for a minute. Don't ever think it. It's simply that I would like Yuri to know how it was and to understand . . .'

'Perhaps he does.'

'It's not only that I left him, it's that I didn't want him.

When I realised I was pregnant I hated the thought of having a child, especially Kolya's. It seemed to be the end of everything. I couldn't come home and I was so unhappy. The bigger I got the more I hated that lump in my body. I wanted him to be born dead . . .'

'Mum!' Tatty was shocked. 'You never said that before.'

'You were too young to be told and, in any case, the minute he was born and I held him in my arms, I loved him. I loved him all the more for not wanting him in the first place. When Kolya and Olga Nahmova took him I was out of my mind. And then Alex turned up, sent by Grandpa to find me. We searched for Yuri together until he made me give up and come home. I always hoped we would find him, but even when he was traced, he didn't want to know. It was my punishment, I suppose.'

'I didn't know he had been traced.'

She had almost given herself away. 'It was Olga Nahmova found him. They told me she was dying of her wounds, but she didn't die. She recovered and went looking for him. She was his mother. Why should he want anything to do with me?'

'Mum, you mustn't think like that. I'm sure if he understood what happened, he'd want to be in touch.'

'Perhaps, but it wouldn't be easy, you know. There are so many restrictions.' She paused, unsure where the conversation was leading her. 'Come on, I'm longing for a cup of tea, then we'll be off to Norwich.'

To Lydia's relief Tatty did not ask how she knew Olga had found him; she could not divulge that without betraying her visits to Alex and she could not do that. They went downstairs together and Lydia managed to put it from her mind until they were driving past the turn for Northacre Green when she nearly gave way again. Keeping away from Alex was the hardest thing she had done since leaving Yuri in Russia and it was no easier after two years, but she had to do it. She could never have gone on seeing him, returning home so elated or so dejected that someone was sure to notice. It was not in her nature to dissemble, to add more untruths to those already told. She would not have been able to function as a wife and mother if her heart and soul and every thought was geared towards the next trip to Northacre Green and how she was going to manage it. She hoped – no, she knew – Alex understood that.

It didn't mean he was not constantly in her thoughts. She would imagine him in his scruffy pullover, feeding pigs and chickens, hoeing between the rows of vegetables, striding across the heath to the pub, cooking for himself and eating at the kitchen table. And she would re-enact in her head every detail of their lovemaking, his hands caressing her, his lips all over her body, his murmured words of love. It was erotic and dangerous for her peace of mind. Pulling herself together, she drove on.

In Norwich, she drew into the car park behind the castle and they made their way to Bonds, where Tatty bought clothes and new toiletries to take to college, after which they spent some time wandering about the different departments, discussing what gift Tatty should buy for Claudia and Reggie. 'It will be strange in the house without Claudia,' Tatty said. 'She's been there my whole life. I can't imagine her married.'

'I can't either, but Reggie is a nice man and he's been patient a long time. What were you thinking of buying them?' Robert and Lydia had promised, as their gift, to pay for the reception at Upstone Hall. Claudia had a host of friends in the village and there would be about a hundred guests.

'I don't know. Not crockery or cutlery or a toast rack.' She pulled a face. 'Horribly unoriginal. I thought something for their garden. Reggie was telling me he was looking forward to making something of that.'

'What about a garden bench?'

'Good idea. Let's have a cup of tea and a cream cake and then go to the garden centre and order it.'

Lydia was tired but content when they returned to Upstone Hall about six o'clock. Her bad dream, though not forgotten, had been pushed to the back of her mind.

The church was packed for the wedding when Lydia and Tatty arrived, Tatty in lilac silk and a tiara of real rosebuds, Lydia in a petrol-blue dress with full sleeves and a floating panel. A picture hat with a white full-blown rose on the front of the brim served to shade eyes which sometimes betrayed too much of what she was thinking and feeling. Bobby was already there, acting as usher and showing people to their places. Lydia made her way into the church, leaving Tatty to wait in the porch for Robert and Claudia in the bridal car. Outside the bells rang joyfully and inside the organist played softly.

The congregation turned as the bride entered and came slowly down the aisle on Robert's arm. Age meant nothing; she was radiant and the smile her bridegroom gave her was evidence of his devotion. They joined hands and turned to face the Reverend Mr Harrington.

'Dearly beloved . . .' he began.

Lydia, listening to the moving ceremony, prayed that Claudia would be happy married to her Reginald, that whatever highs and lows they had would be minor ones, easily overcome.

It was a wish echoed by Robert in his speech at the reception. Reggie's reply had been carefully prepared and, though he made one or two attempts at a joke, it was on the whole a serious speech in keeping with his character. 'He's too stiff,' Robert whispered to Lydia. 'You'd think all that wine would have relaxed him.'

'He's nervous,' she whispered back. 'And at least he's sincere.'

Everyone was clapping and they joined in. After the last of the speeches, there was dancing for everyone. When the bride and groom set off on their honeymoon in Scotland, the older guests said their goodbyes and left the younger generation to go on celebrating in their own noisy fashion.

'Not like our wedding, was it?' Robert said, when they were alone once more, surrounded by the debris. It was gone midnight.

'It was wartime.'

'Yes, but I meant we didn't have a bean, or at least, I didn't . . .'

'Neither did I. I had a job, same as you. And it wasn't our fault if the war kept us apart.'

'It wasn't only the war that did that,' he said quietly. 'There was never just the two of us, was there? There was always a third person standing between us.'

She was shocked and turned to face him. 'Oh, Robert, I'm so sorry. I tried, I really tried.'

'I know you did and that made it even harder to bear.'

'Is that why you re-enlisted?'

'One of the reasons. The other was that the sea is in my

blood and Upstone is landlocked. I couldn't bear not to be able to see it. And you wouldn't leave Sir Edward and move to the coast. And now the place is yours.'

'We've messed up really badly, haven't we?' she said after several moments of silent contemplation.

'No, not really badly. We've been content in our way and we've got two wonderful children.'

'But it's not enough. Is that what you're saying?'

'It always has been.'

'What an indictment of a marriage! What do you want to do about it?' Her breathing was ragged as she waited for his answer.

'Nothing. Anything else would break the children's hearts and I couldn't do that.'

'Nor I.'

They were silent. Lydia's head was spinning. Why had he brought the subject of their marriage up like that, especially as he seemed not to want to do anything about it? Was he telling her he knew about Alex being alive and living not twenty miles away? Or was he preparing her for his own announcement?

'I'll leave the clearing up until the morning,' Lydia said. 'I'm too tired to tackle it tonight.'

She was in their bedroom in the middle of taking off her finery when he joined her. 'Let's forget I spoke,' he said, hanging his grey silk tie over the mirror and unbuttoning his shirt. 'It was out of order. Seeing Claudia married and too much champagne made me maudlin.'

She did not answer.

Tatty was in the loft, searching for a suitcase to convey her belongings to Girton. It was a nostalgic trip. Toys, tennis rackets, dolls with arms and eyes missing, a doll's house, an inflatable boat they had used on the lake until it sprung a leak. She remembered how she and Bob had been tipped into the water, but it was summer and they were wearing bathing costumes and could swim like fish, so they had towed it back to the shore. Fancy her mother keeping that! It was cracked and rotten. There were a couple of tents too, some old armchairs and a large cracked mirror. She went and stood in front of it and smiled at her distorted reflection. Was that how the past appeared to her mother: cracked and distorted? How many of her mother's memories were clear? Had age distorted them as the mirror distorted all it reflected?

She bent down and lifted the lid of a tin trunk and then she was in another world. It was filled with things her mother had saved from their childhood. Baby clothes, some blue, some pink, some pale lemon and cream. Tiny little four-inch shoes with soft soles, mittens for tiny hands, little embroidered pillowcases, exquisite shawls, carefully knitted and crocheted, all lovingly wrapped in tissue and cotton. She took them out gently and held them up one at a time. Had Mum meant to pass them on? For a moment, she held one of the shawls against her cheek and felt its softness and felt her mother's love for her and her brother which, in all the years, had never wavered.

Slowly she wrapped everything up again and laid it lovingly back in the trunk. As she began to close the lid she saw the lining was bulging and pulled it down. Out fell a large brown envelope. She sat on the floor and emptied it into her lap. It was a treasure trove. A pile of unopened letters fell out, all addressed in her mother's neat handwriting to Yuri Nikolayevich Nahmov at an address she could not read. The envelopes were covered in Russian scrawl which she assumed said something like 'return to sender'. The Russian date stamp on them covered a period from April to August 1961, only two years before. Yuri would have been twenty-two, she calculated, just coming into his stride as an adult. Had he sent them back himself or some unknown official?

'Oh, Mum, how that must have broken your heart,' she murmured, as tears filled her eyes. She could imagine her mother's misery and disappointment at getting the letters back and her reluctance to destroy them, but at the same time she had not wanted to upset anyone else in the family and had hidden them away.

She set the letters aside, unwilling to open any of them, and turned to the rest of the contents, a few badly focused snapshots and some scraps of paper, one a certificate of Yuri's birth and the other a certificate recording the union of Nikolay Nikolayevich Andropov and Lydia Stoneleigh, stamped by someone in Moscow. There was also an official-looking letter in Russian on which her mother had written: 'Notification that Kolya is dead and I am a widow.'

She picked up the first of the snapshots. Her mother, looking incredibly young, was hanging on the arm of a young man, smiling into the camera. So this was Kolya. She studied his features. He was young too, not tall, but slightly taller than his bride and round-faced, looking very pleased with himself. How had he died? Had her mother mourned his death? There was so much she did not know. Another picture was of three adults, Kolya, Lydia and another woman, curvaceous and slightly older than Lydia. Kolya had an arm about each of them. There was another of her mother nursing a baby, wrapped in a shawl. This, she had no doubt, was her half-brother. It was difficult to tell his colouring in a black and white photograph, but he appeared dark-haired. He was asleep so she couldn't see his eyes. The next was an old sepia picture of an aristocratic lady in a long evening dress. She was wearing a heavy necklace and long earrings and on her head a tiara on the front of which sparkled the Kirilov Star. And another of her mother with a handsome young man. Her mother was wearing a lovely evening dress and looking young and starry-eyed and she was wearing the Star as a necklace. Judging by other photographs she had seen, the man was Alex Peters. It must have been taken before her parents met and married. Why had this one been hidden away? Had her mother loved Alex? How had she felt when he died? What had Dad made of it? How much of it did he know? How much did anyone really know about other people? All had their secrets, even her most open and above-board mother.

It was a revelation; first her mother's confidences about how she had felt about her baby, the full extent of which Tatty had never realised, and then to find these letters and pictures. Poor Mum! She could imagine her return to Upstone after that trip to Russia, the tears, the guilt and sorrow, the settling down again to life in England, knowing her baby was in Russia at a time when the Germans were sweeping all before them. She must have suffered unbelievable anguish. Carefully, she returned everything to the trunk and found another case for her purpose.

Bobby, in his second year at Peterhouse, drove himself back to Cambridge, his little sports car so loaded with clothes, books and sports equipment there was no room for Tatty. Robert and Lydia took her in the Bentley, settled her in her room and made a long list of things she was going to need which she had forgotten, and then drove home to an empty house: no Claudia, no Bobby, no Tatty. It was eerie and unsettling.

In the next couple of days, Lydia did her best to act normally, but she was beginning to wonder what normal was. Her conversations with Robert were stilted and confined to practicalities. He spent a lot of time in the garden, talking to Percy, and doing odd jobs about the house, his demeanour one of forced cheerfulness. Lydia wanted to talk to him about what he had said, but every time the opportunity arose, she simply could not find the right words. And so nothing was said which might have eased the tension.

In the middle of the week, as if he could stand it no more, he told her he was going to sail round to Plymouth. After he had gone she went into the kitchen to make lunch for herself. The house was empty and silent: no voices, no laughter, no clatter, no overloud pop music which Robert deplored. Nothing. For the first time in her life, she felt alone. She kept herself busy for the rest of the day, slept badly that night and rose next morning to more of the same. She had hoped Robert would ring her the next day and be his usual cheerful self but the telephone remained silent. By lunchtime the following day, she realised he must be well on his way and would not ring until he returned to Ipswich. Unable to stay in the house, she picked up her bag and car keys and left, not knowing where she was going. She drove to Swaffham and went to the cinema. Driving home afterwards, she was sorely tempted to drive straight to Northacre Green, and might have done if she had not seen Claudia in the village and stopped to talk to her.

'You must feel a bit flat now the fledglings have flown the nest,' Claudia said, after they exchanged greetings.

'Yes. I've just been to the pictures and was hating the idea of returning to an empty house.'

'Isn't Captain Conway at home?'

'No, he's gone to Ipswich.'

'Oh, sailing.'

'Yes. You know how he loves anything to do with the sea, and he was feeling at a low ebb after the children left.'

'Come and have tea with me. We can have a good old chinwag. You can tell Claudia all your troubles. Reggie has gone to a meeting of the Upstone Horticultural Society.'

Lydia laughed. 'I haven't got any troubles.'

'Then you must be the only one who hasn't. Come anyway.' She took Lydia's arm and guided her along the street to one of the houses on the new housing estate.

Lydia could always talk to Claudia, who had been her comfort from the very beginning and had remained her comfort through thick and thin. But even she did not know Alex was alive and that she had seen him. Nor would she tell her, even though she knew she could trust her. The secret was a burden she did not want to put upon her friend who would be aghast that she had betrayed Robert. Nor could she tell her what Robert had said about their marriage. Instead they chatted about the wedding and taking Tatty to Girton, and the changes Reggie was making to their garden. 'He's digging a fish pond,' Claudia said. 'It's going to have a fountain and a waterfall and a little stream.' She laughed. 'Just like Upstone Hall's, only in miniature.'

It was late when Lydia finally went home and let herself in the house. Even though the building was two hundred years old, she had never thought of it as spooky before, but tonight it seemed as though there were ghosts in every corner. She switched on all the lights and was in the kitchen putting the percolator on to make a cup of coffee when the telephone rang. Wondering who could be ringing at that time of night, she went to answer it.

'Mrs Conway?'

'Yes.'

'This is Upstone Constabulary.'

Lydia's thoughts jumped to Bobby and that sports car of his which he drove too fast. Had he had an accident? Or Tatty. Her daughter had never been away from home for any length of time before. 'What's happened?' she asked, unable to keep the panic from her voice.

'I'm afraid your husband has been in an accident. Is it convenient to call on you?'

Robert, not the children, but that was still bad. 'Of course, but can't you tell me about it on the phone?'

'Better not. We'll be with you in ten minutes.'

Lydia put the phone down, shaking so much she couldn't get it on the cradle at the first attempt. She sat on the bottom step of the stairs and waited. It seemed like the longest ten minutes of her life while her thoughts went incoherently round and round. The ringing of the doorbell startled her. She rose to answer it.

A uniformed policeman and a policewoman stood on the step. 'Mrs Conway?'

She nodded without speaking and opened the door wider to admit them.

'I'm Constable David Jackson, this is WPC Penny Brown,' the young man said, as she led the way into the drawing room. 'Earlier this evening we had a call from the Devon police. Your husband's yacht has foundered

335

off the South Devon coast and he is missing.'

'Missing?' she repeated in a voice that didn't sound like her own. 'What happened?'

The policewoman, who looked no older than Tatty, took her arm and led her to the sofa. 'Sit down, Mrs Conway.'

Lydia dropped down onto the sofa with the young woman beside her. 'We don't know the details,' she said. 'The yacht has been found badly damaged on the rocks at Prawle Point. Your husband was not on board.'

'He may yet be found safe and well,' PC Jackson added.

'But how can it have happened?' Lydia asked. 'He is an experienced seaman and knows that coast like the back of his hand. However rough the sea, he knows what to do and it wasn't rough today, was it?' She was talking for the sake of talking, but her mind was only half on what she was saying.

'We don't know what happened, Mrs Conway. We were given no details, simply told to come and inform you. It was better than learning it from a telephone call. We were asked to emphasise that it is early days and there is no reason at this time to surmise that your husband has perished.'

'Thank you.'

'What can we do for you?' Penny asked. 'Shall I make you a cup of tea?'

Lydia jumped up. 'Goodness, the coffee percolator! I put it on before you rang.' She dashed into the kitchen to rescue it, followed by Penny.

The pot had almost boiled dry and the coffee was undrinkable. Lydia put the kettle on to make a pot of tea. 'I must go down there,' she said. 'I can't sit around here waiting.'

'How will you go?'

'I'll drive.'

'It's a long way. Have you got someone to go with you?'

'Yes,' she said, thinking of Claudia. 'I must get in touch with my son and daughter. But not tonight. Tomorrow, when I know more. Robert may have turned up by then. They are both up at Cambridge.'

'I should not delay telling them any longer than that,' Penny said. 'It might be on the TV news and they might see it or be told of it.'

'Oh, I hadn't thought of that. I'll do it before I leave.'

The tea was made and the mugs carried into the drawing room, where they sat drinking in awkward silence. Lydia tried hard to concentrate on what she needed to do: ring Tatty and Bob, and that was going to be difficult. Should she tell them to come home or stay where they were? But she wouldn't be at home herself, better tell them to wait until she had more positive news. Then she must ring Claudia, probably get her out of bed, and ask her to keep her company, pack a bag, cancel the milk, leave a note for Percy about the hanging baskets and tell Mrs Harrington she wouldn't be able to do the church flowers. From practicalities, her mind inevitably strayed to that last strange conversation she had had with Robert. Did that have any bearing on what had happened? 'Forget it,' he had said, but she couldn't, could she?

Had he been hinting that their marriage was at an end? Surely nothing more sinister? Why had the boat foundered? Had he left it before that, or had he been injured and washed overboard by the impact? Had he been sailing alone? Where was he?

The two constables left at last, after she had assured them she was all right and not about to collapse or throw a fit. And then she rang her children. She tried to sound calm and optimistic, telling them not to worry, their father was bound to turn up. She promised to ring from Devon and tell them the latest news and where she could be contacted.

She repeated her questions to Detective Inspector Travis at Salcombe Police Station the following morning. She and Claudia had taken it in turns to drive and had arrived in the Devon seaside town at nine, hot, tired and hungry. They booked into a hotel and ordered breakfast, but Lydia found she could not eat. Her insides were stirred into a froth, wondering what she might learn, and she could not wait to find out. At the police station, she was told there was no news of Captain Conway. The *Merry Maid* had been recovered and would be examined.

'Can I see it?'

'There's nothing to see, Mrs Conway, except a boat with a big hole in its hull and you would not be allowed on board until the forensic team have completed their examination. The young lady's body has been taken to the mortuary.'

'Young lady's body?' she echoed.

'Yes. She was found in the cabin with a head wound. There will have to be a post-mortem naturally, and we cannot rule out foul play at this stage.'

'Are you suggesting my husband might have . . .'

'That's impossible,' Claudia put in indignantly. 'The captain was the mildest of men. He wouldn't hurt a fly.'

'Do you know who she is?' Lydia asked, ignoring her friend's outburst.

'No, we hoped you would know.'

'Unless I see her I can't say, can I? My husband had lots of different people to crew for him.'

'Lydia, you can't,' Claudia protested. 'Don't put yourself through it. It doesn't matter, does it?'

'Of course it matters. I want to know who she is.'

The inspector agreed to take her to the mortuary to see if she could identify the unknown woman. 'She was in shorts and T-shirt, with no means of identification on her,' he said. 'We would have expected her to have a bag with a purse, cards and keys, things like that, but nothing was found on the initial search. It might have been washed overboard. We are searching the coastline for that and . . .' He stopped to open the door and usher Lydia in, followed by Claudia, who had no intention of being left outside.

The young woman was not known to Lydia. She shook her head and they went back to the police station. 'Where was the boat found?' she asked as she prepared to leave, having told the inspector where she was staying.

'Just off Prawle Point. You might learn a little more at the coastguard station there.'

Lydia was functioning on adrenalin and would not listen to Claudia's suggestion she ought to go back to the hotel and catch up on lost sleep. 'I'll go when I know,' she said, irritable with tiredness. Claudia gave in and followed her back to the car. They drove to the car park, as close to the point as they could, and scrambled over the rocks to the lookout station, on the cliffs high above the beach. They were met by one of the officers. Lydia identified herself and subjected him to the same barrage of questions.

'They have hauled the boat out of the water for examination,' he said. 'There's a huge hole in its side where it hit the rocks.' He pointed at the jagged coastline as he spoke.

'I can't understand my husband letting that happen,' Lydia said. From that vantage point they could see the *Merry Maid*, on its side on the beach, swarming with men in protective gear and life jackets. 'My husband was in the navy all through the war and he's been sailing ever since. He knows this coastline as well as anyone and he certainly knows how to read a chart. It doesn't make sense.'

'Perhaps our examination will reveal the answer,' he soothed.

'And why wasn't he on board? Knowing him, I am sure he would have stayed to try and avoid the rocks.'

'It is possible he had already gone overboard before the boat hit the rocks,' he said. 'Are you familiar with the boat, Mrs Conway?'

'I've been on board a few times but I've never sailed in her. I'm a dreadful sailor. It's why my husband had to find others to crew for him. Sometimes our son or daughter would go with him, but since they have grown up and found their own interests . . .' Her voice tailed off.

'Why don't you and your friend go and find something to eat?' he suggested. 'We can find you if we have any news. The Pigs Nose serves reasonable pub grub.'

They went to the strangely named public house and sat over a ploughman's lunch for which neither had any appetite and then returned. There was no news. If Robert had been able to swim ashore, he would have done it long before now, she thought. The alternative was too dreadful to contemplate.

'If . . .' Lydia gulped. 'If it's a body you are looking for, how long will it be before it's washed up?'

'It depends on wind and tide. We have people watching the most likely places.' He didn't say that it might never resurface, but she knew it. People did disappear without trace. Had it been intentional? A way of escape from a situation which had become unbearable? But surely he was too honourable to do that to her and the children.

There was nothing they could do and they returned to the hotel where Lydia telephoned Tatty. 'I'll get leave and come down,' Tatty said.

'No, darling, there's nothing you can do and I don't know where I'll be. I'll ring you again later.' She did not want her daughter to join her, didn't want her knowing about that unknown woman, though she supposed it would come out eventually. It could, of course, be an entirely innocent relationship, captain and crew, nothing more. Why did she find it so difficult to believe that?

Bob was easier to persuade. He was completely confident of his father's skill and knowledge of the coast. 'If he was washed overboard, he would swim away from the rocks,' he said. 'He's probably landed in some cove further up the coast, miles from a telephone. Ring me back as soon as you know something. If you need me to come home, of course I'll come at once and bring Tatty with me.'

She rang off and went up to her room where she fell onto the bed. She did not expect to sleep, but sheer exhaustion saw to it that she did, but even that was disturbed by a nightmare. She was in the sea and so were Robert and their children, all struggling to keep afloat. She could see the yacht bobbing up and down on the waves on its side and Robert was trying to herd them all towards it. But though they swam as hard as they could, the vessel seemed as far away as ever. It was the children she was worried about. They were only small and flagging badly. Robert left her to save them. She felt the water closing over her and woke up with a start, gasping for breath. She had become tangled up in the bedclothes.

Sitting up, she switched on the bedside light. It was five o'clock in the morning. There was no sense in trying to go back to sleep. Every time she shut her eyes, she could see and feel the oily waves closing over her. She put the light out and went to sit by the open window. Dawn was breaking. Everywhere was bathed in a pink light. Not a breath of wind stirred the tree in the hotel garden with its picnic tables and benches, looking forlorn now that summer was gone.

'Robert,' she murmured, watching the sun come up over the rooftops. 'Where are you? I want to say I'm truly sorry I couldn't be the wife you wanted. But did you have to take such a nubile, young crew member on board?' She got up stiffly from the hard chair, showered and dressed, then went along the corridor to knock on Claudia's door. 'Are you awake?'

They stayed in the area three days and still there was no sign of Robert. One question was answered. She was told the steering gear had broken on the *Merry Maid* and that was probably why Robert had not been able to steer away from the rocks with a strong wind and current carrying the yacht towards them. He might even have slipped into the water to try and see if he could mend it, leaving his crewmate on board. He could have been swept away and there was nothing the young lady could do to save the vessel. She had died from a blow to the head when the boat struck and knocked her against the bulwark. Traces of blood on the woodwork seemed to bear this out. Foul play had been discounted.

'Have you found out who she was?'

'Yes, we found her bag in one of the lockers under a sleeping bag. It was sodden, of course. Her name is Pamela Osborne. We have contacted her parents and there will be an inquest. I have no doubt the verdict will be accidental death. We cannot, of course, assume the captain's demise.'

'I understand.'

And so they waited. Mr and Mrs Osborne were coming down for the inquest of their daughter and Lydia did not want to meet them. 'I'm going back to London,' she told Claudia. 'There may be some clues in the flat.'

The clues were everywhere: toiletries in the bathroom, clothes in the wardrobes, a copy of *Vogue* on the occasional table, high-heeled shoes kicked off under the kitchen table. Whoever she was, Pamela Osborne had been perfectly at home. Lydia felt sick. And Claudia was indignant.

'The bugger!' she said. 'Who'd have believed it?'

Lydia refrained from saying 'I would'.

'Let's go home,' she said, resisting the temptation to sweep it all away, and leaving everything as it was. If Robert came back safe and well, she did not want him to think she had been snooping. But how to deal with it if he did?

Robert's body was washed up two days later, found by early-morning swimmers in a sandy cove a few miles along the coast. Lydia made the long trip back to Devon to identify it. By now the media had hold of the story and there was no hushing up the fact that he had not been alone on the boat and they were making the most of it. 'What happened on the *Merry Maid*?' one headline asked. This was followed by a salacious story about Pamela Osborne, who had often been seen in Robert's company, both in London and in Ipswich where the boat was usually moored. She was a model who had had several other alliances. Robert's naval career, his marriage to Lydia and the fact that she was a considerable heiress were all picked over and analysed. They asked Lydia for interviews, which she declined. Even so, there were pictures of her going into the inquest in Salcombe's coroner's court accompanied by her son and daughter. It was a dreadful time. In the glare of the spotlight, they could not even grieve properly.

The inquest did not last long. Boating experts testified that the steering gear had been faulty before the impact and that the injuries to Robert's head were commensurate with his having been hit by the rudder as the boat veered in the current. It was assumed he had entered the water to try and mend the steering. A doctor testified that he thought the deceased had been knocked unconscious by the blow but not killed. His lungs were full of water and death was due to drowning. A verdict of accidental death was recorded.

It was over. Lydia felt numb, though she managed a smile of reassurance for Bob and Tatty when they asked anxiously if she were all right. They left the courtroom to be faced with a barrage of cameras and reporters. Questions were fired at them from all directions. Lydia had asked their solicitor to be present and he made a statement saying the family were relieved by the verdict and hoped they would now be allowed some privacy to grieve. Then they hurried to their car and Bob drove them home in the Bentley to arrange the funeral. Robert's body would be conveyed home later in the day.

No one had much to say on the journey. Bob exchanged a few low words now and again with Claudia who had insisted on coming and was sitting beside him. Tatty, in the back, was valiantly trying to hold back her tears. Lydia, holding her hand, sat immersed in tumbled thoughts; past, present and future all competed for her attention. It seemed an age since she had first gone to Devon, an age in which she had waited, throwing questions, demanding answers from the police and coastguard while she waited for news, not knowing when it would come or even if it would come at all. Everything went through her tortured mind: the manner of their first meeting, their marriage, having the children, through all of which Robert had supported her. It hadn't all been bad, most of it had been good. It really hadn't started to go wrong until after her father's death. Had he been the one holding it together? Or was it when she realised Alex was alive? Had Robert known that? Or was it when Robert met Pamela? How long ago was that? How serious was their relationship? She would never know now.

After the watershed of the funeral what would she do with her life? She would have probate and the will to sort out and she would have to go to the flat and send Pamela's things to Mr and Mrs Osborne. And then what? Go on doing what she had been doing for years: look after the house and garden, go to Women's Institute meetings, serve on the committee for Upstone's annual fete, continue as a governor of the infant school, support her favourite charities with coffee mornings, and work one day a week in the Oxfam shop. All that had once been fulfilling and had rarely involved Robert, so what was different?

Inevitably her thoughts turned to Alex. She had received a very short letter of condolence from him after he had read the news in the papers. It was formally worded, as if he were afraid it would be read by others. She longed for him, longed for him in a way a child turns to a parent for comfort when hurt, knowing it would never be refused. But she could not go to him. She had not been able to go to him again while Robert was alive, still less could she go now he was dead. It made her betrayal seem infinitely worse.

The funeral at Upstone church was well attended. Most of the congregation were Upstone people and naval and yachting friends who had known Robert, but there was a scattering of people who had read about the death and inquest in the papers and were curious to see how the widow handled herself.

Lydia conducted herself with quiet dignity. She was calm, almost numb, as she went through the ritual of the service and the interment. The last time something like it had happened was for her father's funeral and there had been a ghost present. She glanced towards the yew. There was no one there. Turning back to the grave, she laid a single white rose from the Upstone Hall gardens on the coffin as it was lowered. 'Goodbye, Robert,' she murmured. 'You were the best of husbands. Rest in peace and love.' It was what she had written on the card on her wreath.

She stood as others filed past, several of them stooping to pick up a handful of soil and sprinkle it on the coffin, and then, half supporting, half being supported by Tatty, she walked back to the car.

Alex had decided it was best to stay away, although, as a friend of Robert's, it would not have been out of place for him to go. He feared upsetting Lydia even more than she must be upset already. He had read the gossip and his heart went out to her. He would have liked nothing better than to go and help her endure it, but knew it would be inappropriate and the media would have a field day. He threw himself into a frenzy of work, cleaning out the pig pens until they were almost as pristine as the bathroom in the house. He built two new hen coops and hoed the rows between the vegetables. The Brussels sprouts were ready for picking and he would have to get in some casual labour to help with that.

When he could not find anything more to do, he set off across the heath with his dog at his heels and sat for an hour or two in the pub. He had brought Lydia here on that last weekend. They had been happy in their way, though speaking of the future had been taboo. How long before he saw her again? Could he go to her at some time when everything had settled down, or must he wait until she came to him? Waiting would be almost unbearable, but going to Upstone only to be turned away would be worse.

The landlord called time. He got up and went home, followed by the faithful Patch.

Chapter Fourteen

Lydia was helping the staff at Upstone Infant School to decorate the Christmas tree. Missing her children more than she could say, she had volunteered to help in any capacity the headmaster might choose to use her. With children around her, she always felt more cheerful. Life did go on, after all.

The tree had been donated by the local nursery and it had taken two strong men to bring it in and erect it in the corner of the assembly hall. It almost reached the ceiling and there was only enough space for the traditional fairy on the top. A box of coloured baubles and a string of lights had been brought out of their hiding place from last year. 'We'll have to buy new ones soon,' the headmaster said. 'These are beginning to look rather shabby. Still, with the lights shining on them they won't look too bad.'

Rosie Jarvis, who was a dinner lady and whose main job was serving meals and washing up, was hauling a bundle of tangled red, green and gold streamers out of another box. 'Shall I put these up, Mr Groves?'

'Yes, if you like, but you'll need the steps and Mrs Conway is using them. Wait until she's finished.'

It was raining, cold sleety rain, and there was no playtime outside today, so they were working surrounded by children, some of whom were offering gratuitous advice, others dancing round in excitement. When the tree had been decorated to everyone's satisfaction, including fake parcels about its base, the lights were switched on amid cheers. Mr Groves blew his whistle and the children, ranging in age from five to eleven, were immediately silent. He ordered them to set out the chairs for the parents who would be coming for the carol concert and then find their places. For a few minutes it seemed chaotic, but chairs miraculously appeared in neat rows facing the stage. A little more scrambling and all the children were up on the stage, standing in three rows, tallest at the back, the little ones at the front.

Lydia took her seat on the side of the first row as the parents filed in and the concert began. Even the boys looked angelic, though one of them had his socks about his ankles and his school tie awry. He was about eight, she supposed, blond and rosy-cheeked. Seeing her watching him, he gave her a cheeky grin. She smiled back and from then it seemed he was singing *Away in a Manger* especially for her.

The carol telling of the baby born in a cattle shed reminded her of Yuri, though it had not been a cattle shed but a room in an attic. Had he been born in England, he would have had a proper crib and everything an infant might need: the finest baby clothes, pram, toys, medical attention whenever it became necessary. And she would have been well-nourished enough to feed him properly. He had had nothing like that at Kirilhor, where hunger and the search for food had dominated their lives to the exclusion of almost everything else.

When the singing was over, the children helped to serve their mothers with tea and cakes which the mothers themselves had contributed. They had also been instructed to smile and answer the grown-ups' questions politely. The little boy came to Lydia holding out a plate of cakes which looked as if they might slide off onto the floor at any minute. Lydia straightened it up for him and helped herself to a pink-iced fairy cake. 'Thank you, young man. I enjoyed the singing.'

'We've been practising for ages and ages.'

'And you would rather have been out playing, I've no doubt.'

'Yes. I'm going to be a famous footballer when I grow up.'

'I hope you are.' She smiled. 'You are quite a big boy already. How old are you?'

'Eight and three-quarters.'

'We mustn't forget the quarters,' she said. 'What do you want for Christmas?'

'A new bike. And some football boots.'

'You'll have to be good to get those.'

'I know.' It was said with a heavy sigh. 'I've got to go now.' He moved off to offer the cakes to someone else.

Lydia watched him go. Another Christmas, another year passing, and she still longed for the child she had lost. She had Tatty and Bob, and she loved them dearly, but that did not stop her wondering what had become of her firstborn. Twenty-four years it had been, and the only memory she had of him was of a toothless baby who was not as heavy as he should have been.

This would be the first Christmas without Robert, and Lydia didn't know how she was going to cope. Bobby and Tatty would be home and she had to make it good for them. And she had to stop thinking about Alex. It was easier decided than done. She imagined him at his smallholding, going about his daily tasks, taking the dog across the heath. Did he still think of her, or had he given her up as a lost cause? She couldn't go to him. It was too soon, much too soon. How could she tell Bobby and Tatty there was another man in her life, a man who had been there from the beginning and had never truly gone away? She had stayed away from Northacre Green, though the temptation to go to him was at times so overpowering she had to find something to do to keep her away: a meeting to attend, or someone ill in the village who needed a visit, a carol concert in the village school.

In all the noise and jollity going on around her, she felt her misery again and tears pricking her eyelids. Was anywhere proof against her melancholy?

Making her excuses, she left the school to walk home. She would make a cup of tea and do the jigsaw she had started on the day before. It was a big one, a thousand pieces it said on the box. It depicted a farmyard with a tractor, chickens and a dog lying outside its kennel. There were trees in the background and cobbles in the foreground and the sun was casting a dappled shade over all. It was going to be difficult, but that was the whole point of it. It would keep her occupied and keep her mind off Alex. Perhaps she should do as Tatty had often suggested and write her life story, not for publication, but simply to channel her thoughts into a more positive direction. But doing that involved Alex. Everything involved Alex.

The rain had stopped, though the wind was icy cold, coming as it was straight off the North Sea. She had known cold far worse in Russia and she did not mind it. She considered herself completely British, had done so almost all her life, and yet the pull of her roots was strong. She could not quite forget the land of her birth, perhaps because Yuri was there. She imagined him growing up, leaving school, finding himself a job. Why, he might even be married!

'Lydia, where are you off to in such a hurry?' Claudia's voice brought her to a standstill. 'Running to catch a train, are you?'

Lydia laughed. 'No, trying to keep out the cold. How are you? How's Reggie?'

'We're fine. I've just got off the bus. Christmas shopping.' She held up two loaded carrier bags. 'How about you?'

'OK. I've just been to the carol concert at the school. I went every year when the children were there.'

'I know.' She looked closely into Lydia's face. The wind had whipped the colour into her cheeks but, as usual, her eyes gave her away. 'Come home with me. Warm yourself up and let's have a chat.'

'Chat? What about?'

'This and that.' She took Lydia's arm and Lydia went without protest.

'Now,' Claudia said, when they were in her small sitting room nursing cups of tea. 'Tell me how you've really been getting on. And remember it's me, Claudia, you're talking to.'

Lydia laughed. 'I hate the empty nest, especially now Robert's gone.'

'Bobby and Tatty will be back for the holiday, won't they?'

'Of course. And I mean to make it as happy a time as I can under the circumstances.'

'You will. You always have. But there's more, isn't there?'

'I don't know what you mean.'

'You're not brooding over that girl, are you? What's her name? Pamela Osborne.'

'No. I don't think about her at all. And it was no more than I deserved.'

'Whatever nonsense is that?'

Lydia gulped a mouthful of hot tea. It would be so good to tell someone. 'You remember Alex?'

'Of course I remember Alex. You're going to tell me he's alive, aren't you?'

Lydia stared at her in astonishment. 'How did you know?'

'I saw him. On the day of your father's funeral. That's why you fainted, wasn't it?'

Lydia nodded. 'I didn't know you'd seen him too. I thought he was a ghost.'

'I take it you've seen him again.'

'Yes. Twice.' She went on to explain the circumstances. 'I kept away,' she finished. 'I had to. It wasn't fair on Robert.'

'Robert's gone, Lydia. And you are being foolish. I know how you feel about Alex. I've always known.'

'How many other people knew?'

'Sir Edward, I should think, perhaps Robert, but that's about it. Why would anyone else know? It makes no difference. What is important is what do you intend to do about it?'

'Nothing. What can I do? The children—'

'They are not children anymore, Lydia, and they are busy leading their own lives. Given the chance I bet they'd understand.'

'It's too soon.'

'For goodness' sake, go to him,' Claudia said. 'You are free, Robert's gone and he had been playing you false, so you go to Alex. You deserve some happiness after all you've been through.'

'I'll think about it.'

'No. You'll get in your car and go now.' She stood up and took the cup and saucer from her. 'You don't have to tell Bobby and Tatty yet.'

What Claudia was advising was so close to her own desires, she wavered. It wouldn't hurt anyone, would it? Just to go to him, see how he was, let him know that if he still wanted her, she might, sometime in the future . . . Somehow she found herself out on the pavement and Claudia was waving her goodbye from the door. She dithered more than once on the way home, but her car was standing in the drive and it was full of petrol. She got in and drove to Northacre Green, eager and yet half-afraid.

Twice on the way she pulled into a lay-by and sat undecided whether to go on. It was not her feelings she doubted, but her sense of right and wrong, her scruples. She had betrayed Robert; would going on betray Bobby and Tatty? How could she do this to them so soon after their father's tragic death? Going on would be making a commitment. It would change everything; she would not, could not keep it a secret. Where would it lead? To strife with her children? Was she ready for that? She almost turned back, but then she remembered what it was like to be in Alex's arms and the enticement of that was too much to resist. She drove on.

The gate to the smallholding was wide open. She turned in, stopped the engine and sat a minute to still her fast-beating heart. Supposing he was out, should she wait or go home? Supposing he no longer cared. It had been so long . . . The door of the cottage opened and he stood on the threshold, waiting for her, as he had always waited for her, and simply opened his arms. She scrambled from the car and ran into them and was enfolded.

The sheer ecstasy of their reunion told her all she wanted to know. The years rolled away and they were young again, making love, talking non-stop, laughing at each other's jokes, drinking wine and tea and making love all over again. Only later, when they had both calmed down and they were sitting at the kitchen table over a cup of coffee, did he tell her about the letter. 'Do you believe in fate, Lidushka?' he asked.

She laughed. 'You mean, "There's a divinity that shapes our ends, rough-hew them how we will"?' She paused to consider. 'Yes, I suppose I must, after all that's happened to us. Why do you ask?'

'Because when you arrived, I was debating whether to write to you or come over and see you, and here you are, saving me from having to make the decision.'

'Why were you thinking it today especially?'

'Oh, don't think I haven't had that same debate every day since I learnt of Robert's death. But today there was a special reason. Do you remember me speaking of my friend, Leonid Orlov?'

'Yes, he helped you when you came out of Siberia.'

'I received a letter from him today. Goodness' knows

how he managed it but it came via the diplomatic bag. It's amazing the number of pies he's got his fingers in. It enclosed a letter for you from Yuri.'

'Yuri!'

'Yes. It's sitting up there.' He nodded towards the mantelpiece where an envelope was propped against the clock.

She jumped to her feet and snatched it up. He watched as she slit it open and read it, quickly the first time, then more slowly. 'Olga's dead,' she said. 'She confessed the truth before she died. He says he found it hard to believe, but he wants me to write to him. He wants the story from me. Oh, Alex!' Tears blinded her and she could not read anymore. She groped for his hand and he took it and squeezed it.

He remained silent while she recovered herself and read the letter again. 'Why did it come through your friend?'

'Leo has kept an eye on Yuri, watched over his development and made sure he fulfilled his potential. It was to Leo Yuri turned after Olga made her revelation, and I suppose he confirmed the truth of what she had said. I imagine he was one angry young man.'

'I would be angry too, except that I'm too happy. Oh, Alex, I must write to him at once.'

'Wouldn't you rather go and see him?'

She stared at him. 'Alex, you can't mean it.'

'Leo thinks it's possible. You have to be invited through official channels but Leo says he can manage that. Things are a lot easier since Stalin's death. Relations with the West are thawing, thanks to Khrushchev, who has opened up international trade and cultural contacts never allowed before. There is to be a trade conference at the beginning of February in Kiev and Leo says he can invite me onto that as an agriculturist, with Foreign Office approval at this end. I think I can wangle that. Leo suggests I put you down as my personal assistant.'

'But I know nothing about being a PA.'

'Doesn't matter. I don't know much about agriculture. Are you on?'

'But won't you be arrested?'

'I don't see why I should be. I'm Alex Peters, it says so on my British passport. And you are Lydia Conway, also a British subject. Of course, we shall be given a minder, set to watch what we are up to, but we should be able to give him or her the slip with Leo's help, so what do you say?'

'Oh, Alex, need you ask? But Bobby and Tatty . . .'

'They'll be back at college by then.'

'I know, but I'd have to tell them why I'm going and that means . . .'

'Telling them about me,' he finished for her.

'Yes.'

'Can't you?' He was searching her face and she feared to hurt him.

'They know about you because your pictures are in the family album. They were told you were a family friend who had died in the war. I wish I had realised then how much I really loved you, I would never have married Kolya.'

'Then your life would have been very different. You would not have had Yuri.'

'That's what Tatty said once, when I said I should not have let you persuade me to leave Russia; she said then I would not have married her father and she and Bobby would never have been born. I cannot regret that, Alex.'

'Of course not.' He paused. 'We were talking about introducing me to your children.'

It was what had been worrying her all along. Could she? How would they react? 'They loved their father . . .'

'Of course they did, but they are grown-up now and making their own way. I doubt if they'll live at home again and you are entitled to make a new life for yourself.'

He was right, but it still felt like a betrayal. But if she and Alex were to have a future together without secrecy, then it had to be done. 'Would you like to spend Christmas with us?' she said. 'As a family friend who was thought to be dead but has suddenly turned up again, I mean.'

He grinned. 'Family friend is a start, I suppose.' He knew Lydia would not marry him in anything like a hurry. He would have to court her slowly, taking her out, joining in family occasions as she thought fit, getting to know Bobby and Tatty, treading on eggshells. But he would wear her down in the end.

'You know I can't tell them anything else. Not yet. Come in time to go to church with us on Christmas morning at ten-thirty. I'll prepare the ground.' She laughed suddenly. 'I can't believe I'm saying this.'

He stood up and took the coffee cups to the sink and ran water into them. 'Shall we go for a walk?'

They walked and ate and then she said she ought to go home. He helped her on with her coat, wrapping it about her from behind so that she was almost in his arms. 'Don't go.' His voice murmuring in her ear was so close his warm breath made her shiver and sent seductive messages to the very core of her, demanding to be answered. 'You haven't got anything to go home for, have you?'

She squirmed round to face him. 'There's all sorts of things . . .'

'But none that can't wait, surely?'

So she stayed, and the next morning she drove back to Upstone Hall, a very different woman from the one who had left it. She was rejuvenated, gloriously and ecstatically happy, except for one thing. Telling Bobby and Tatty there would be a guest for Christmas, unsure how they would react.

And then, when it came to it, she found it easier than she expected. Both Bobby and Tatty wanted to invite a friend and there would be six of them. Bobby had a girlfriend called Eva and Tatty's boyfriend was Andrew. Lydia could not help it, she laughed until the tears ran down her face.

'Mum, what's the matter?' Tatty asked.

'Nothing. It's strange the way things happen. I wasn't sure how you would feel about adding to our threesome . . .'

'And we were thinking the same,' Bobby said. 'We knew Christmas wouldn't be the same without Dad and so we thought it ought to be totally different.'

'How clever and thoughtful of you both.'

'How did you find out that Alex hadn't died?' Tatty asked.

'He was your father's friend as well as mine and Grandpa's, you know. He saw the announcement of his funeral and wrote to offer condolences. I answered and that was it. He had a terrible time during the war and afterwards, but no doubt he'll tell you that himself. But the amazing thing is that he's found Yuri for me. I've had a letter from him.'

'Oh, Mum!' Tatty said, remembering the pile of letters and pictures in the attic which she had never divulged seeing. Some things were becoming clearer. 'How fantastic!'

In the event, there were eight people gathered for Christmas dinner, which was eaten at one o'clock after everyone had been to church: Lydia, Alex, Bob and Eva, Tatty and Andrew, Claudia and Reggie. It was noisy and argumentative in a cheerful way. Lydia, listening to them, smiled to herself. They hadn't done too badly, this little family of hers. Bob and Eva were so obviously in love, she didn't think it would be long before they became engaged. She didn't think Tatty's heart was engaged but that was a good thing; she was still very young. She liked Andrew, though. He was a little older than Bobby, self-assured and undoubtedly well off, not to mention good-looking. As for Alex, dearest Alex, he was putting on a tremendous act, making her feel guilty that she asked it of him. But Bobby and Tatty liked him, she could tell, and from that fragile beginning, she hoped they might come to accept him as their mother's lover.

After Christmas dinner, they all took their drinks into the drawing room where the tree stood glittering with lights and baubles, as it had done every year throughout Lydia's childhood and her children's too. 'I'll be Father Christmas,' Tatty said.

There were presents for everyone. Books seemed to be favourite, chosen with care to match the interests of the receiver. There were silly puzzles, gloves, scarves, liqueur chocolates, ornaments and pictures. Tatty had bought her mother an evening shawl. It was gossamer-fine in a multitude of colours merging one into the other like a rainbow. 'Oh, darling, how pretty this is. Thank you.'

'You can wear it when you go dancing with Alex.'

Lydia glanced at Alex and met his answering smile. Tatty, the sensitive one, had already guessed and she didn't mind. 'How do you know I'm going dancing with Alex?' she asked.

'Well, you always used to, didn't you?'

'Well, yes, but that was when I was very young.'

'You're never too old to dance, Mum.'

'No.' Alex laughed. 'It's a date, Lydia. We go dancing.'

He fetched another parcel from the back of the tree and put it into Lydia's lap before returning to his seat beside her.

She undid the ribbon and unwrapped it. It contained a framed copy of the entry in Leonid's book: the picture of her father and grandmother posing with the tsar and tsarina and the notes about the Kirilov Star. She stared at it, lost in wonder. 'Alex, where did you find this?'

'It was in a book Leo had. He had it copied for me and included it with the letter from Yuri. I had it framed.'

'Wow!' Bobby said, from over her shoulder. 'What does it mean?'

'Translate,' Tatty demanded.

'You do it,' Lydia said to Alex.

He did it easily when she might have stumbled, not only because her Russian was rusty but because she was so choked with emotion. When he finished he put it back into her hands.

'Oh, Alex, how thoughtful of you.' She reached up and kissed his cheek. Christmas had turned out to be better than ever she could have hoped.

In the first week of February, they flew to Moscow, touching down at Vnukovo Airport late in the evening, and queued up in the vast marble terminus to have their passports and entry documents checked. That done, they were met by their host, who had been standing on the other side of the hall waiting for them to be released into his care. Leonid Pavlovich Orlov was a thickset man wearing a thick tweed coat, a fur hat and knee-length boots. He greeted Alex effusively, hugging him and kissing him on both cheeks. 'Alexei, my friend, you are welcome once again,' he said in English, then turned to Lydia. 'And this must be Lydia. Welcome to Russia, Lydia.'

'Thank you.' Lydia held out her right hand. He grasped it, but instead of shaking it, used it to pull her to him in a bear hug which took her by surprise.

'Welcome! Welcome!' he said again, releasing her. 'Now, come. Katya is preparing a feast for us.' He picked up her case and led the way to a huge limousine which was parked at the kerb. Its driver got out and took their cases to stow them in the boot, while Leonid opened the door for Lydia. She climbed in, followed by Alex. Leo got in beside the driver and the big car drew slowly away from the kerb.

Once away from the airport they were soon driving at what Lydia considered a breakneck speed through a dark landscape covered in snow.

Moscow, when they reached it half an hour later, was ill-lit and she was able to see little more than the road ahead, which was clogged with traffic, and the footpaths either side, flanked by shops and buildings, some old, many new. The pools of light from the street lamps illuminated pedestrians: men in thick padded coats, felt boots and astrakhan hats with ear flaps. Some women were in fur coats and matching hats, others were less ostentatiously clad, some distinctly ragged. A beggar sat against a doorway, a placard round his neck; a young woman hurried along carrying a baby on her back wrapped in a shawl; soldiers in grey uniforms and jackboots stood on corners. Young and old, they barely afforded the big car a glance. Nothing had changed and yet everything had.

'Here we are,' Leonid said, as they drew to a stop outside a tall ornate building.

Leonid occupied an apartment on the top floor. It was luxurious by Russian standards, though Lydia deplored the decor. It was noisy with clashing colour; there were ornaments all over the place, thick cloths covered the tables on which stood vases of artificial flowers. That was understandable, she decided, it was the middle of winter, after all. It was also overheated and she was glad to be relieved of her fur coat and hat.

Katya Orlova was a rotund woman with a small round head and hardly any neck. Her cheeks were rosy, perhaps from bending over the stove, and her hair was dyed very black. She obviously had a soft spot for Alex because she pulled him to her plump bosom and kissed him effusively, followed by rapid speech in Russian which Alex answered, laughing and disengaging himself to bring Lydia forward. 'This is Lydia Conway. Lydia, Katya Orlova.'

Katya shook hands with Lydia, bidding her welcome and hoping she would enjoy her stay and take a good report back to England.

'Thank you.'

'Speak English,' Leo commanded his wife. Then to Lydia, 'Katya speaks good English. We both do. Alexei taught us when we were in Siberia.'

'Yes, he told me. You speak it very well.'

'Thank you. Now, I will show you round the apartment and where you will sleep, while Katya finishes the cooking.'

The apartment took up the whole floor of the building. As she followed him round, Lydia found herself wondering about the sleeping arrangements. Had their host assumed she and Alex were living together? Was that accepted in Russia?

She was answered when Leo threw open a door. 'Lydia, you will sleep here,' he said. 'My friend, Alexei, will have the room next to this.' He laughed and thumped Alex on the back. 'You will be close, eh? The bathroom is at the end of the corridor. You will wish to wash and change. Your cases are in your rooms. Come back to us when you are ready.' And with that he turned and left them.

They stood facing each other. Alex laughed. 'He is not the soul of tact, is he? But he means well.' He stepped into her room, pulled her in and shut the door. 'Alone at last.'

Lydia laughed. 'Alex, don't be silly.'

'I'm not. We've been together all day and I haven't kissed you once.' And he proceeded to make up for lost time.

She squirmed away from him, somehow uncomfortable making love under someone else's roof. 'I must wash and change. I feel grubby and unkempt, and we mustn't keep our hosts waiting for their supper.'

He sighed. 'OK. I'll leave you. Don't take too long in the bathroom or I'll come and join you.' He blew her a kiss and departed.

She had brought only two dresses suitable for evening wear: a soft dove-grey crêpe and a blue silk. Less than an hour later, refreshed and dressed in the blue silk and with her hair neatly rolled into a pleat, she rejoined her host. Alex was already with him. He stopped speaking in mid-sentence to turn towards her and whistle appreciatively, raising his glass of vodka to her in salute before taking a mouthful. The men in Russia drank vodka whatever time of day it was and seemed to be able to put away vast quantities of it with little effect.

The thick cloth on the table had been covered with white damask and laid with cutlery and soup bowls for four. Katya came in carrying a huge pan of steaming soup and set it on the table. Leonid beckoned Lydia to take her place. The soup was delicious. Lydia asked what was in it. 'It is *solyanka*,' Katya said. 'It is made from chicken and ham with potatoes, pickled cucumber, onions and tomato, olives, lemon and soured cream. You like it?'

'Very much.' It would have made a meal in itself, but that was followed by a gargantuan main course of meatballs in a rich sauce with heaps of vegetables, all washed down with an oversweet wine. She was not allowed to stop there. Katya disappeared and returned with a plate of pancakes and insisted Lydia had at least one. It was filled with berries and honey and topped with soured cream. Having eaten it, she put her cutlery down feeling ready to burst.

There had been little conversation over the meal, as if eating was more important than talk and they could not do both at once, but as they sat over the remains, finishing off the wine, reticence was overcome. Lydia thanked them for the meal and laughingly said she would become very fat if she stayed with them very long, which they took as a compliment. 'I am grateful to you for being such generous hosts,' she added. 'You know why I have come to Russia again?'

'Yes, Alexei has told us. He told us all about you. We feel we know you already.'

'And I you, and I must thank you for the copy of the picture and article you sent to England. It meant a lot to me.'

'You are welcome.'

'But I am anxious to know about Yuri.'

'Of course you are. He had a poor childhood, but he did well on his own merit. He attended Moscow State Technical University and was an outstanding student. After graduating he went to work in my electronics factory in Kiev.'

'That was good of you.'

'Not at all. I promised Alexei when we parted that I would do what I could for him, in the name of friendship, you understand, but also because Russia needs brilliant engineers. He has done very well. His mother can be proud of him.'

'Oh, I am. When shall I see him?'

'I have arranged for him to be given some leave. You are to meet him at Kirilhor the day after tomorrow.'

'Kirilhor!'

He grinned. 'I thought you might like to see it again.'

'Oh, I shall, but how . . . ?'

'We fly to Kiev tomorrow and must attend the first session of the conference for appearance's sake,' he explained. 'Then I will keep your minder busy so you can slip away and catch the train to Petrovsk. I have some Russian clothes for you. You will be less conspicuous in those.' It was said with an appreciative look at her evening dress.

'You seem to have thought of everything and I am truly grateful,' Lydia said. She rose to her feet. 'Now, if you will excuse me, I think I shall go to bed.'

Both men rose and kissed her cheek. She hugged Katya and was gone, to lay in bed too excited to sleep. She was going to see Yuri and it was Alex who had brought it about. Dearest, devoted Alex . . .

* * *

367

Petrovsk had changed little since Lydia had last been there. The paint on the wooden houses was still flaking, the windows were still cracked, the hotel even more sleazy. The church and the school had not changed, not even their paint by the look of it. The tarmac on the roads was cracked and broken and full of potholes.

It did not fill Lydia with confidence and she expected Kirilhor to be even more of a ruin than it had been when she last saw it; instead she found a substantial house, its roof the dark green of the forest, its wooden walls painted white, its many windows reflecting the low sun of a winter morning. Its garden was well kept, its gravel drive free of weeds. 'It's been restored,' she murmured in surprise. 'Are you sure Yuri is here?'

He smiled. 'We might find out if we knock on the door.' He took her arm because she seemed to be holding back. 'Come on, sweetheart, what is there to be afraid of?'

The door was opened by Yuri himself, who had been warned by Leo to expect them. Lydia stood and drank in the sight of him. If she felt like throwing herself into his arms, she was constrained, not only by shyness but by his expression. It was wooden. 'Do you know who I am?' she asked.

'My mother.' It was said without inflexion, a mere statement of fact engendering no emotion.

This was not what Lydia had expected. But what had she expected? Hugs and kisses? Wasn't that asking too much? She looked despairingly at Alex, who reached out and took her hand, squeezing it gently.

'You had better come in.' Yuri led the way into the drawing room. The dilapidated room she remembered had been nothing like this. It was well furnished with two huge well-padded sofas – not like the one she remembered whose stuffing had been coming out – bookcases and ornaments. Here they were introduced to Sophie, whom Yuri had recently married. Sophie shyly bade them welcome and then left them to prepare a meal.

There was an uncomfortable silence after she had left. 'Why didn't you answer my letters?' Lydia asked, because that question was in the forefront of her mind. 'I only wanted to know you were safe and happy.'

'I had no letters. And I did not know you existed until last year. My mother – I mean Olga Nahmova naturally – told me when she was dying.'

'That must have been a shock.'

'It was. I wished she had not told me. It was her conscience troubling her and she wanted to confess before she died. I don't know who I hated most at that time: Olga for not being my mother and keeping it from me, or you, Lydia Andropova, for abandoning me and condemning me to the orphanage.'

'I didn't abandon you. You were taken from me. I searched for you, Alex will bear me out, but we could not find you and then the war came to Russia and everything was chaotic.'

'I made her leave,' Alex said. 'It was too dangerous for her to stay. Believe me, it wasn't easy. She was heartbroken about it. Surely you want to know this or why did you change your mind about seeing her?'

'Curiosity.'

'Is that all?'

'Comrade Orlov persuaded me it could do no harm.'

Lydia fumbled in her handbag and produced the brown envelope which she emptied onto the table. 'These are my letters, all returned to me.'

He sat and looked at them as if mesmerised, making no move to pick them up. 'Shall we leave you to read them?' she asked. 'You will want to do that in private.'

'Yes, yes; have a walk round the grounds. Sophie will call you when the meal is ready.'

They left the house by the front door and walked round to the back, past a fir tree which had recently been cut down. The garden was not extensive, being close to the forest, and there was little to see – everything was covered in snow, except the paths, which had been cleared.

'I can't believe I've actually seen him and spoken to him,' Lydia said as they walked hand in hand. 'If he didn't know about his connection with the Kirilov family, how does he come to be living in the family home? Does he know he was born here? There are so many questions I want to ask.'

'I've no doubt he'll have questions for you too.' He paused. 'Now he's found, what do you expect to happen? What do you want to happen?'

'I don't know. I'm still too confused. It would be wonderful if he could come to England, but I don't suppose that's feasible, although we could still write to each other, keep in touch. Perhaps, one day, things will improve between East and West and travelling will be easier.'

They stopped when they were confronted by what Lydia afterwards described as Father Time, a bent old man with a long white beard and a weather-beaten face. He lifted a gnarled hand. 'Lydia Kirillova,' he said in a quaking voice. 'Is it you?'

'Yes. It's me.' She took his hand and kissed his cheek. 'I am so glad to see you, Ivan Ivanovich. I never thought to find you still here.'

'Where else would I be? I've served this estate all my

life. I shall be here the day I die. The Reds, the Whites, Bolsheviks, war and famine have come and gone and still I survive. Yuri Nahmov is good to me.'

'Do you know who he is?'

'Of course I know who he is. He is your son, grandson of Count Kirilov, though that counts for nothing these days.'

'He says he didn't know himself. Why didn't you tell him?'

'Some things are dangerous to know. Better to be ignorant. But I watched over him. When Olga Nahmova brought him back here after the war ended, I watched him growing up. Now he watches over me. He's a good boy.'

'No longer a boy,' Alex said. 'He's matured since I last spoke to him, mellowed, you might say.'

'He's had a lot to contend with. Olga Denisovna wasn't easy to deal with. Her brain had been affected.'

'The *dacha* looks lovely,' Lydia said. 'Who owns it now?'

'Leonid Orlov. He lets Yuri stay here when he wants.'

Lydia turned to Alex in surprise. 'Did you know this?'

'No, I didn't, but it's typical of Leo.'

Lydia was blinking back tears as they bade the old man *dosvidaniya* and returned to the house.

Yuri had carefully arranged the opened letters in chronological order and had just finished reading the last one. He looked up as they entered. 'I never knew,' he said, his voice rough with emotion. 'I never knew.'

It was not until after they had eaten the meal Sophie had prepared that he felt ready to talk to Lydia about his life.

'My earliest memory is of being in an orphanage in Solikamsk when I was about three or four. There were thousands of children there, all with shaved heads. We had

371

a hard time of it. I remember always feeling hungry, but if we stole food we were severely punished. I still have the scars on my back.'

'I am so sorry,' Lydia murmured, which to her was inadequate.

He went on as if she had not spoken. 'Hunger, or rather fear of hunger, is something that never really leaves you. Even toddlers learnt to hoard food. When the war ended and the Germans left Ukraine, I was sent to another orphanage in Verkhnedneprovsk. It was a little better than before, but not much, and I was given a rudimentary education, aimed at making me a good Soviet citizen. I had been there two years when Olga Nahmova came to claim me.

'I had to take her word for it that she was my mother. She told me we had been separated when a bomb went off at a railway station on the way to Minsk. My father was killed and she was badly injured and not expected to live. But she survived and was in Minsk when the Germans invaded Russia. She was evacuated to the east along with the other patients and recovered, if you can call it a recovery. She was deeply scarred by it.

'She brought me to Petrovsk, expecting to find friends here, but the war had scattered them. I don't know how we lived. We had nothing – no money, no clothes. The land wasn't being farmed and the tractor factory was ruined by bombs. We squatted here and my mother did whatever work she could find to keep us from starving and to send me to school. All we had to eat was bread, soup and potatoes, and little enough of that. She would clean lavatories, carry bricks, hoe the fields when the kolkhoz started up again, anything to keep us from starving. She cultivated the bit of land around the house and grew vegetables and flowers which she sold in Petrovsk. She would buy things off the peasants who needed money to buy food, and sell them for a profit.

'I had to help her. She was as hard a taskmaster as the orphanage had been and she was excessively possessive. I could not go out and play with my friends, I had to stay by her side, and if I was even a few minutes late home from school, she would be out searching for me. I supposed it was because she had lost me once and was afraid it might happen again. After she told me who I really was, I wondered if it was because she worried that someone might tell me the truth.'

'Who could have done?' Sophie asked.

'Ivan Ivanovich, for one. He befriended me.'

'He knew me and my parents and brother.'

'I didn't know that. He never said.' He paused to drain the vodka in his glass and open another bottle. He filled Alex's glass and offered some to Lydia but she shook her head, more interested in his story than in drinking. The more he talked, the more she could see a family resemblance, a fleeting gesture, a slight movement of the head; the way he used his hands.

'But you must have done well at school,' she said. 'You went to university.'

'Yes. Stalin wanted engineers and technicians and we were encouraged to study and apply for a place. I got on by working hard and keeping out of trouble. If the authorities had known who my true mother was, I would never have got in, so I owe my adoptive mother that debt. After I graduated as an engineer and mathematician, I was given a job in Leonid Orlov's factory. I married Sophie a year ago. Most of the time we live in our apartment in Kiev, but

Leonid Orlov allows us to use the *dacha* for vacations. He is a very influential man and I owe him a lot.'

'So do I,' Lydia said, with feeling. 'And Alex.' She turned to smile at him as she spoke. He was not saying anything, simply letting them talk.

'He came here,' Yuri went on. 'Years ago. My mother was terrified of him. She was worse for weeks after he came, jumping at every sudden sound and running to hide. She wasn't quite right in the head, you understand. It was the result of her injuries in the explosion.'

'Did you know Kirilhor once belonged to our family?' Lydia asked him.

'No. My mother told me I had been born here and she often spoke of her time here before my father died as very happy. I had no idea of the truth. Even last year, when she was dying and told me she was not my real mother, she said my real mother had given me away so that she could go back to England. The authorities would not have allowed her to take a Russian child out of the country. These letters . . .' he tapped the pile which he had put on the arm of his chair '. . . tell a very different story. It is very confusing. I ask myself which is the truth.'

'What I wrote is the truth,' Lydia said. 'I grieved for you all the years I have been parted from you and could not find you. It is because of Alex's promise to me we are reunited now. You have a half-brother and sister. Perhaps, one day, when travel between our countries becomes easier, you will meet them.'

'Tell me about your life, how it is in England.'

It was so late when Lydia finished talking they were invited to stay the night. Yuri seemed to have accepted the truth at last, and as the evening wore on and the vodka relaxed him, they were able to talk more easily. Lydia showed him her photographs, all the ones that had been tucked away in the brown envelope and others of Bobby and Tatty and Upstone Hall. Sophie was excited to think that her husband's grandfather had been a count, known to the tsar. The years of Communism had not extinguished a curiosity about that ill-fated man.

'Satisfied?' Alex asked her, as they boarded the plane back to Moscow the next day.

'Yes, oh, yes, my darling. Thank you. Thank you.'

'And now that's all out of the way and you have your son back where he belongs as part of your family, what about me?'

'You?'

'Yes, you know what I mean. I want to be part of the family too. Bobby and Tatty have met me, they're not blind, they can see how we feel for each other and we've wasted too much of our lives already . . .'

'We couldn't help that.'

'No, but we can make up for it now. So how about naming the day?'

'When we get home. I promise.'

'I'll hold you to that.'

Bobby and Tatty were at home when they returned, anxious to hear their adventures, and it took ages to tell everything and look at the pictures they had taken, which she had put into an album. Here she was with Leo and Katya sitting round their dining table. Here was Alex, walking beside her in the forest at Kirilhor, which was taken by Yuri just before they left. Here she was talking to Ivan Ivanovich,

Yuri and Sophie. Yuri cutting logs with Ivan. Here was the son she had lost who was lost no longer, and the best of it was he now knew and acknowledged she was his mother. Now she could forgive Olga and be grateful to her for bringing him up and keeping him out of the orphanage. Tatty and Bobby crowded round to look over her shoulder while she explained each one.

'I knew about the envelope in the trunk,' Tatty told her mother. 'I found it by accident.'

'Why didn't you say?'

'It seemed too private. But I was curious about the young man in the white tie and tails.'

'Alex.'

'Yes, so I realised.' She laughed and looked at Alex.

Alex took the album from Lydia and set it aside. Taking a small box from his pocket he opened it. 'Lydia Conway, I love you,' he said. 'And I cannot see any reason why we cannot spend the rest of our lives together. Please say you will marry me.'

Seeing the diamond and ruby ring he was holding and which he had every intention of slipping onto her finger, she looked from him to her children who were grinning broadly. 'You knew about this?'

'Of course.'

'And you approve?'

'Oh, Mum, you don't have to ask us,' Tatty said. 'But yes, we approve.'

'So?' Alex said to her, looking anxious in spite of their assurances. 'What do you say?'

She laughed through a veil of tears. 'Yes, Alex, yes.'

He kissed her, long and hard, and then pandemonium broke out as Bobby and Tatty vied with each other to congratulate them. The excitement was almost too much to bear and Lydia was exhausted long before anyone else and she needed a moment of quiet contemplation. 'I think I'll go up to bed, if you don't mind.'

She kissed all three goodnight and made her way to her room. It was the room she had occupied as a child. Here she had always felt safe and happy, and she felt safe and happy now. She smiled as she took off the pendant and ran her fingers over the Kirilov Star. It was a link to past and present, to history and to the future, infinitely precious, not because if its worth, but because of what it meant. Picking up the album, she sat looking at the pictures, touching Yuri's face with her forefinger, as if she could feel the flesh. 'Yurochka,' she murmured. She let the album drop and looked across at the framed picture of her father and grandmother with the tsar which stood on her bedside table, next to the one of her and Alex at her twenty-first birthday ball. Even on a black and white photograph, the Star seemed to sparkle at her throat.

She put it on her bedside table, while she prepared for bed, then she climbed between the sheets and wriggled down on the pillows. Alex wouldn't come to her tonight but it didn't matter. There were lots more nights to come. The rest of their lives.

Acknowledgement

I would like to acknowledge the invaluable help given to me by Sir Rodric Braithwaite, British ambassador in Moscow 1988–1992, author of several books, articles and reviews on Russia and the international scene, who kindly agreed to read the manuscript and set me right on Russian spelling and points of fact. Any errors that remain are mine.

BIBLIOGRAPHY

I read many, many books in researching *The Kirilov Star*. Here are some of them:

NON-FICTION

Beevor, Antony, *Stalingrad* (Viking, 1998)
— *The Mystery of Olga Chekhova* (Penguin Books, 2005)
Braithwaite, Rodric, *Moscow: 1941, A City and Its People at War* (Alfred A. Knopf, 2006)
— *Across the Moscow River: The World Turned Upside Down* (Yale University Press, 2002)
Buber-Neumann, Margarete, *Under Two Dictators: Prisoner of Stalin and Hitler* (Pimlico, 2008)
Dimbleby, Jonathan, *Russia: A Journey to the Heart of a Land and Its People* (BBC Books, 2008)
Erickson, Ljubica and Erickson, Mark (eds.), *Russia: War, Peace and Diplomacy – Essays in Honour of John Erickson* (Weidenfeld & Nicolson, 2005)
Figes, Orlando, *Peasant Russia, Civil War: The Volga*

Countryside in Revolution 1917–1921 (Phoenix Press, 2001)
— *The Whisperers: Private Life in Stalin's Russia* (Allen Lane, 2007)

Hughes, Michael, *Inside the Enigma – British Officials in Russia 1900–1939* (Hambledon Press, 1997)

Klier, John and Mingay, Helen, *The Quest for Anastasia: Solving the Mystery of the Lost Romanovs* (Smith Gryphon, 1995)

Matthews, Owen, *Stalin's Children: Three Generations of Love and War* (Bloomsbury, 2008)

Pares, Bernard, *The Fall of the Russian Monarchy* (Phoenix Press, 2001)

Thomas, D.M. *Alexander Solzhenitsyn: A Century in His Life* (St Martin's Press, 1998)

Steinberg, Mark D., *Voices of Revolution, 1917* (Yale University Press, 2002)

Zinovieff, Sofka, *Red Princess: A Revolutionary Life* (Granta Books, 2007)

FICTION

Helen Dunmore, *The Siege* (Penguin, 2002)
— *The Betrayal* (Penguin, 2010)

Alexander Mollin, *Lara's Child* (Doubleday, 1994)

Boris Pasternak, *Doctor Zhivago*, trans. Max Hayward and Manya Harari (Collins & Harvill, 1958)